Praise for Kelly Rimmer

"Get ready for fireworks in your book club when you read *Before I Let You Go*! One of the best books for discussion that I've read in years."
  —Diane Chamberlain, *New York Times* bestselling author
of *The Stolen Marriage*

"Thought provoking and deeply affecting, I couldn't put this one down until it was finished."
  —Karma Brown, bestselling author of *In This Moment*,
on *Before I Let You Go*

"*Before I Let You Go* is an unforgettable novel that will amaze and startle you with its impact and insight."
  —Patti Callahan Henry, *New York Times* bestselling author
of *The Bookshop at Water's End*

"Kelly Rimmer has raised the already high bar with this unforgettable novel."
  —Bestselling author Sally Hepworth
on *The Things We Cannot Say*

**Also available from
Kelly Rimmer**

*The Things We Cannot Say
Before I Let You Go*

Unexpected

KELLY
RIMMER

HQN™

ISBN-13: 978-1-335-50495-1

Unexpected

Recycling programs
for this product may
not exist in your area.

This edition published by arrangement with Harlequin Books S.A.

For questions and comments about the quality of this book, please contact us at CustomerService@Harlequin.com.

www.HQNBooks.com

Printed in U.S.A.

For Jodie

Unexpected

CHAPTER ONE

Marcus

"So, I WANTED to talk to you about something tonight…"

There's a strange edge to my best friend and room-mate's voice tonight, but I've just walked in the door after a thirteen-hour day at the office and I'm so hungry I can barely think straight. As curious as I am about whatever's going on with Abby, I need to get organized before we talk.

It's Monday night. That means we eat dinner early because Abby meets her gaming friends online at 8:00 p.m., and it also means that it's my turn to cook. Tonight, I'll be "cooking" Thai, courtesy of Seamless.

"Just let me quickly get this order in, then I'll be all ears, I promise. Do you want the chicken laksa? Or do you feel like seafood tonight?" I double-check the detail, because while I know her orders by heart, the chicken versus seafood in her curry-soup debate has been going on for a while and still seems far from settled.

"Chicken, please. And listen, I've thought about this a lot, and I have my reasons—this isn't a whim."

"Sure…spring rolls?"

"Most definitely. Actually, can you get me a double serving?"

"Of course."

"No, wait…"

"Let's get a double and if you don't finish them, I will."

"Okay."

I finish the order, then set the iPad back down onto the coffee table and turn to face Abby. We're sitting on the couch in our usual places, our postures mirrored. I'm on the right, next to the armrest where the remote controls live, because according to Abby I'm a control freak and I need to drive the TV. Abby is on the left, because it's closest to her bedroom and thus her bathroom, and she seems to pee every five minutes.

"Now, what were you saying?" I prompt her gently. Abby's gaze is distant as she absentmindedly runs the pad of her finger around the rim of the half-full wineglass she's nursing. Before she can speak, the iPad makes an odd sound—a notification I don't immediately recognize. Abby raises her eyebrows and points to the device.

"Check it," she says pointedly. "It might be a problem with the dinner order and I *cannot* deal with Hangry Marcus tonight."

I flash her an apologetic smile and reach for the iPad, but the notification isn't some obscure Seamless error—the only thing on the screen is a Facebook message. When I recognize the icon, I almost put the iPad right back down…but then the words on the screen actually register in my brain.

Warwick Chester wants to connect with you.

I turn the iPad to Abby, who squints at the screen, then gasps. For a long minute, we just stare at each other in disbelief. Then I set the iPad firmly on the coffee table, screen down.

"No," I say. My voice is rough, so I clear my throat, then try again. "Just…no." I draw in a sharp breath, then huff it out heavily. "Yeah. Let's just forget that even happened. Now, what did you want to talk about?"

"Are you kidding me?" Abby squeaks. "No, we are *not* talking about my thing right now. Are you going to open the message and see what he has to say for himself?"

"No," I say, but my gaze keeps drifting back to the iPad. "Fuck. I don't know. Do you think I should?"

"Yes!"

I move to reach for the iPad again, but hesitate at the last minute. Whatever this message says, it's too little, too late. Maybe I should just block him.

"Hey," Abby says softly. "Let me?"

I nod.

Warwick Chester is my biological father. He was an excellent parent, right up until a few weeks after my seventh birthday, when he left for work and never came home.

All I remember from the first weeks after he disappeared was feeling impatient. I was so sure that he loved us too much to leave us forever, so I *knew* it was only a matter of time before he came back.

It's been twenty-five years, and the message Abby is reading right now is his first-ever attempt to contact me. Warwick *did* show up at my grandfather Don's funeral last month, but he sat at the back and left as soon as the service ended. He didn't even acknowledge me or my twin brother, Luca. I wouldn't have seen him at all if I hadn't joined Mom onstage to support her as she read the eulogy.

It was a confusing day even before I noticed Warwick. My grandpa Don loved his family fiercely, but he had a mean streak, especially with me and Luca. Mom was devastated to lose her father, but my feelings on his passing were more complicated. I didn't have the brain space to try to figure out how to feel about Warwick's presence that day, so I chose to simply ignore it.

"It's a group message to you and to Luca."

I guess that makes sense, as much as any of this makes sense. "Do you remember when he first left?" I ask her quietly.

"I was, what…five years old? I *do* remember sitting in the tree house with you and Luca while you tried to figure out where he'd gone."

"You cried with us," I say softly. Abby offers a sad smile.

"I remember wishing that I knew where he was. I thought I could go just get him for you guys."

Abby, Luca and I grew up in Syracuse in upstate New York. My mom and stepdad, Jack, still live in the house I was raised in. On the other side of the small park next door, Abby's parents still live in the house *she* was raised in. Abby's two years younger than me and Luca, but for as long as I can remember, she and I have been best friends.

It's fitting that she's helping me navigate this, because she's been there for all the other key moments in my life, too.

"Should I read this to you?" she asks.

"Does he want a kidney?"

"What? No! Why would you even think that?"

"Seems odd that he's suddenly messaging us on Facebook like a long-lost camp buddy," I mutter. "He wants *something*, right?"

Abby extends the iPad toward me, and I take it with a sigh.

Dear Marcus and Luca,

Maybe it's unfair of me to drop into your lives again like this, but Don's passing last month has left me in a difficult position. Now that he's gone, I'm going to lose track of you altogether if I don't speak up and take the chance that one or both of you might be willing to try to rebuild some kind of a relationship with me.

I have no excuses for my absence—only a depth of regret and sadness that is impossible to convey in this message. Will you consider a call with me?

Warwick

I exhale, then set the iPad on the table again. Abby throws her arms around my waist and rests her cheek against my chest with a sigh.

Abby smells like strawberries. I think it's her shampoo, and I really like it. In fact, I like it enough that I'm momentarily distracted by it. We are firmly just friends, although for a brief moment earlier this year, I hoped we might become something more. That's passed now and the only throwback to that phase of my life is that sometimes I notice cute details about her...like the fact that she smells heavenly all the time.

"I'm sorry," she whispers. "I can't even imagine how you're feeling right now."

"I'm fine, Abs," I tell her with a quietly confident laugh. Of *course* I'm fine. I'm thirty-two years old, for God's sake. I have a great apartment and amazing friends and I'm the co-owner of a software startup that's growing so fast my life feels like some delicious dream.

Abby isn't fooled for a second. She sits up to stare at me, and the piercing look in her big brown eyes forces me to interrogate my own reaction.

The pain of it finally hits—and for a second, I don't feel like a successful thirty-two-year-old man at all. Instead, I feel an awful lot like the seven-year-old kid who kept sneaking out of bed to sleep on the rug in the foyer because he needed to keep an eye on the front door in case his dad came home.

"Don't even bother pretending this isn't a huge fucking deal," Abby says flatly. "We've been friends for way too long for that macho bullshit. You know what? You need a drink."

I laugh weakly and rub my chest, trying to push away the awful, uncomfortable emotions bouncing around in there. All at once, I'm confused and resentful and upset and…hopeful. I need to squash that last one *real* quick.

"Yeah. I guess I do."

Abby fetches two glasses of Scotch from the liquor cabinet, and passes me one as she returns to the sofa. We knock our glasses together, down the drink and share a matching grimace at the burn. She sets her empty glass onto the coffee table in front of us…and for maybe the first time since she moved in with me two years ago, she actually uses the coasters.

I know that gesture is just for me, and I laugh softly. Abby smiles reluctantly, too, then murmurs, "That message makes it sound like Warwick has been in contact with Don for all of these years, keeping tabs on you guys. Do you think that's true?"

"No fucking way." I shake my head without hesitation. "Don would have mentioned that at *some* point over the last twenty-five years. It's not like he shied away from talking about Warwick." Sure, pretty much everything Don had to *say* about Warwick was an insult, but he still mentioned him enough that I know it would have come up in conversation if the two men were still in touch.

"What are you going to do?"

"I don't know. Does he deserve a reply? There'd be some kind of poetic justice in me just ignoring him, the way he ignored us for all of these years. Right?"

With anyone else I'd be embarrassed at my bitter tone, but Abby won't judge me. That's not how this friendship works.

"Maybe you just have to do whatever feels right here. If ignoring him feels right, then go right ahead."

"There's no chance I'm going to fucking *call* him." I sigh. I run a hand through my hair, then rub the back of my neck. "I do need to call Luca, though."

A fleeting shadow crosses Abby's face.

"Well…maybe you need time to process this on your own before you talk it through with Luca." Abby gnaws her bottom lip, and there's a crease in the space between her brows—a sure sign she's worrying about something.

My gaze drops to her hands on her lap—she's tapping her fingers against her thigh. I reach for her hand and squeeze it. "Hey. This is annoying, but I'll be fine."

She nods, but she's still unsettled. I'm touched by the depth of her concern, even if I am a little confused by it.

Hmm. Something else is going on here.

"What was it you wanted to talk to me about tonight?"

She shakes her head. "It's nothing. Anyway, we're *not* talking about it tonight. Not now."

I know Abby better than I know myself, so I'm very familiar with that stubborn tone. I'm concerned enough that I want to push her some more, and maybe I will... once I've had a little more time to get my head straight after *that* message from Warwick.

I pick the iPad up again, load the message and stare at it. I click on Warwick's profile picture, and his face fills my screen. He's standing on his own at the front of a bluestone building, his head cocked to the side. He's wearing jeans and a knit jumper. He's smiling, but the smile doesn't quite reach his eyes.

It's eerie staring at a photo of Warwick Chester because it's like getting a glimpse of the future. Warwick would be in his sixties now, and Luca and I are identical twins who share most of Warwick's facial structure and that same dark, curly hair. Warwick's hair is still thick, but sprinkled with silver. Luca wears his hair long now and keeps it perennially pulled back into a man-bun, but Warwick and I have a similar hairstyle—

we both leave our curls longer on top, but the back and sides are a little shorter.

I click on his Facebook profile, hoping to find more photos, but he's locked the profile down...and I'm sure as hell not ready to send him a friend request.

Several minutes pass where we don't speak. The silence is gentle—Abby and I know how to be quiet together. There's freedom in the easy, familiar rhythms of my life with her. This isn't the first tough moment we've navigated together, and it won't be the last.

"I really do need to talk to Luca," I say eventually.

Abby nods, but that odd look passes over her face again. Her fidgeting returns in an instant.

And both times this happened I was talking about my brother.

"Did you have a fight with him?" I ask.

"Me and Luca are always fighting." She laughs weakly. Well, that's certainly true. Abby and Luca are great friends, too, but they bicker like siblings sometimes—the kind of messy bickering most people grow out of by adolescence. Their "arguments" are always good-natured and innocent, though. What's confusing is that there's nothing innocent about the guilty shadow on Abby's face.

"You're clearly anxious whenever I say his name, Abs," I say softly.

"You're hungry, and upset, and imagining things," she says lightly, but she's an infamously bad liar. Something is definitely going on. I know Abby and Luca aren't romantically involved—Luca is happily married, and Abby literally could not be *less* his type. Luca's husband, Austin, is a chef and restaurateur and, undoubtedly, the love of my brother's life.

I reach for my phone, and Abby squeaks, "What are you doing?"

Curiouser and curiouser.

"I'm going to call Luca."

I'm bluffing because Abby tells me everything, and I'm momentarily certain that she's about to blurt out the truth of what's really going on. Instead, she gnaws her lip while I pick up my phone to place the call, and picks at imaginary fluff on her hoodie to avoid looking back toward me. Luca's phone rings and rings, but eventually goes to voice mail. Typical—he never answers his damned phone.

"It's me. Have you seen your Facebook messages? Take a look, then call me back when you can."

Abby is visibly relieved when I hang up, which only makes me more determined to know what's going on.

"Spill your guts, woman. What's he done this time?"

The intercom sounds and I sigh at the relief that crosses Abby's face.

"Don't think I'm dropping this," I warn her. When we settle back on the couch, food in hand, I look at her expectantly. Abby squirms.

"There is something I need to talk to you about," she admits reluctantly. "But I really can't talk about it tonight."

"Don't let that shit with Warwick put you off. I was in shock for a minute there, but I'm good now. Let's talk."

"I know you're okay, but you've had a really full-on night, and I'd rather we just wait and discuss it tomorrow. Can we please just watch some TV and relax for a while?"

My eyebrows rise. "Aren't you going into your cave tonight?"

Abby makes her living creating digital content about video games, and via a series of screen dividers, she's converted part of her bedroom into an office that doubles as a studio for her videos—aka "the cave." Her schedule is set in stone, and Monday night she *always* retreats for a marathon session of gaming-for-fun. She'll periodically, reluctantly, vary her routine on other days, but she *never* misses Monday night's leisure gaming.

"Not tonight," she says quietly.

"Abby, seriously. What the fuck is going on? I'm going to worry until you tell me now."

"It's nothing to worry about, I promise. I just feel like hanging out with you tonight." She gives me a hopeful look. "TV?" I sigh and reach for the remote, then navigate to the media center to load the sci-fi series we've been watching. "No, not sci-fi," she says. "Let's watch the news for a while."

I nearly choke on a spoonful of my curry. I feel like I'm in a real-life Twilight Zone tonight.

"The *news*?"

"Sure. Isn't that what you like to watch when I'm not around?"

"Exactly. 'When you're not around.' You're clearly 'around' right now." She shrugs and reaches for a spring roll, and I narrow my gaze at her. "Abby, I do not need your pity news watching."

"It's not 'pity news watching,' if that's even a thing. I just thought it might be your turn to choose."

"If we're supposed to be taking turns, I think mine is several years overdue," I say, still not convinced.

Abby's laughter fades just a little. Her eyebrows knit. "I'm not that bad."

"You're that *good.*" I'm laughing again, and I click the button to load the sci-fi show, anyway. "You've trained me so well."

"Maybe you've actually started to like sci-fi?" she suggests, and I grimace.

"Or maybe it's Stockholm Syndrome. In any case, let's just see if these mutants can escape the starship tonight."

"They aren't mutants, they're aliens," she says, then she settles right into the couch with a sigh of pleasure as the show begins, but she can't quite help but correct the rest of it even as the theme song starts. "And it's not a starship, it's a time machine. Have we even been watching the same show?"

I chuckle to myself and settle in to watch the awful show Abby inexplicably loves. My workload is insane right now. It's a testimony to just how much I adore my best friend that I sit through this shit several nights a week, just because she likes it.

A few minutes into the episode, Luca texts.

I saw the message. Really need to talk to you, anyway. Drinks tomorrow night?

"Is that Luca?" Abby asks. Her voice is so high I'm sure dogs six blocks away just howled. I raise my eyebrows at her and she flushes.

"Yes, it's Luca," I say. "We're going to catch up tomorrow night."

Abby swallows. I look back to my phone with a frown.

Marcus: What the hell is going on with you and Abby? She's acting really weird tonight.

Luca: It will only make sense if I explain it over beer. Possibly many, many beers. I'll talk to you tomorrow night—usual place, usual time.

I set the phone down, just as Abby slides hers from the pocket of her jeans and starts furiously tapping the screen. The intense concentration on her face morphs into a scowl before she throws the phone onto the carpet near her bedroom door in frustration.

"Yikes." I raise my eyebrows at her.

"I want it on record that I did *not* want to talk to you about this tonight," she says fiercely.

I reach for the remote and pause her show. "Huh. You know, I could almost have guessed that myself."

"It's not fair to dump this on you *tonight* after the Warwick thing," Abby exclaims.

"Dump what on—"

"Luca is *making* me tell you and I want you to know that before I even…you know—" she exhales in frustration "—*tell* you."

"Okay," I say, softening my tone. "This is all Luca's fault, got it. Now what is 'this'?"

Abby squeezes her eyes shut very tight and draws in a deep breath. When she finally speaks, her words tumble out so close to one another it sounds like she's saying one ridiculously long word.

"I've-decided-to-have-a-baby-on-my-own-and-today-I-asked-Luca-if-he-would-be-my-sperm-donor. I know this might seem sudden, but I want you to trust me when I say that this is what I *need* to do. And that's final."

When she opens her eyes again, a moment or two has passed, but I'm still staring at her, slack-jawed at her announcement. I think I'd have been less surprised if she told me she was moving to Antarctica or that she'd decided to shave her head.

Abby as a mom? Yes. I can very easily imagine that. I know that on the bookshelf in her "cave," she already has a binder full of information about parenting, complete with preferred schools for a hypothetical child, and a list of possible baby names. She's made no secret of the fact that she desperately wants kids.

Abby as a single mom? Sure. She's tough, caring and capable.

But Abby *choosing* to be a single mom, at thirty years old? Nothing about that makes sense. Abby has that damned binder on her bookshelf precisely because she is the kind of person who plans her life carefully and she's been thinking about her sickeningly stereotyped nuclear family forever. It's not just potential children she's put an immense amount of thought into—it's also her potential future husband, and the life she wants to build with him.

"But…" Even when my voice decides it's ready to work again, my brain is still catching up. It doesn't matter, because Abby silences me with a fierce wave of her hand.

"And it's not something we're going to discuss tonight because *you've* had a tough day, it's late and *I'm* feeling very emotional about it and I'm not even close to being ready to explain to you why this is happening. We'll talk about it in a few days when Luca has decided if he's going to do it. Okay? And don't you even think about trying to talk him out of it."

"I've never been able to talk Luca *in* to or *out* of anything, not that I'd do that to you, anyway," I say slowly. "I just don't understand. You've always known exactly the life you want for yourself. What happened to the gamer husband you were going to find? What about the house in the suburbs where you're going to settle down? What about the rescue dog named Charlie? How does…" I'm struggling to even say the words. "How does *Luca's* baby fit into that picture?"

"It won't be *Luca's* baby," Abby snaps at me, and leaps to her feet. "This will be *my* baby. Luca will be the baby's annoying uncle, which is exactly what you will be, too. No one will know any different but me and Luca and…Austin and…" She groans in frustration. "Now *you*. End of story."

I'll respect her decision if she goes ahead with this. I'll support her all the way. How could I not? Abby is smart enough to know what she wants, and strong enough to handle all the challenges of parenthood, even on her own.

It's just that the more her announcement sinks in, the less I understand it. Abby is the least impulsive person I know—if she's seriously considering this, there's got to be something more to the story. My suspicion is confirmed by the glint of tears in her eyes. She blinks rapidly, but it's quickly apparent that she's not going to be able to control her emotions. Her face crumples even as she turns away from me.

"I'm sorry to dump this on you tonight," she chokes. "It's not fair that you have to deal with Warwick and now this…"

"Abs," I say, bewildered. "You aren't dumping anything on me. Please sit back down and talk to me, help me understand—"

"I *can't* talk to you about this yet," she whispers. "Please just respect my decision and I'll explain when I… I'll talk to you about it when I'm ready."

"But…"

I rise, too, ready to pull her into my arms, but she shakes her head and jogs quickly to her bedroom. Before I can even take a step, her bedroom door slams shut.

The sound echoes through the apartment—an undeniable full stop on one of the most bewildering nights of my entire life.

CHAPTER TWO

Abby

SOME PEOPLE WORK out just to look good. Other people exercise because if they don't, they build up a mental lather that completely clogs up their entire lives.

I do a class at my gym pretty much every day. Between gaming for fun and gaming for work, I spend most of my life alone at the computer in the corner of my bedroom. A daily visit to my gym gets me around other humans on a regular basis, and moving my body is a key part of my strategy for maintaining my physical and mental health. There's nothing more important, and I've learned that the hard way over the last few years.

On a normal day, I do a class at 6:00 p.m. This morning, for the first time ever, I'm here for my friend Isabel's 6:30 a.m. barre class. Marcus is safely out running or at his own gym, because that's where he always is by 6:30 a.m. By 7:30 a.m., I'm usually crawling out of bed and we often have breakfast together before he leaves for work.

I tell myself this is going to be a fun and relaxing way to start the day, but the truth is, I'm still half-asleep and I hate *everything* about the world right now. I don't want to admit to avoiding Marcus, but the only thing

that would motivate me to leave the house at this ungodly hour is the knowledge that there's something
even worse to face at home.

If I were in the apartment when he returned from
his workout, he'd try to make me talk about the Luca-
sperm-baby situation. Marcus has my back—I don't
question that, because he *always* has my back. There's
no doubt in my mind that eventually he'll understand
why I need to do this. But before he can understand,
we need to have a conversation I'm dreading, and I'll
be avoiding that for as long as humanly possible, thank
you very much. At least until much later in the day,
when my brain is actually functioning.

Isabel is standing at the front of the room stretching,
but does a double take when I walk in, then immediately jogs over and pretends to take my temperature
with the back of her hand.

"Are you sick?" she gasps. "Is your apartment on
fire? I didn't even know you were physically capable
of getting out of bed this early."

I roll my eyes and grunt something about insomnia, and that makes two new records for me: out of
bed before 7:00 a.m., and outright lying to a friend
before 6:15 a.m.

After an hour of torturing my muscles, Isabel wraps
up the class, and I have to find another excuse to avoid
going home. Marcus is always at the office by 8:30 a.m.,
so if I can stay out of the apartment till then, there is
zero chance I'll have to face him this morning.

"Right," Isabel says after she's said goodbye to the
other participants. "What's going on with you?"

"Nothing," I say with what I hope is a reassuring smile.

"Something is wrong. You wouldn't be here this early if something wasn't seriously wrong."

"Just a nasty case of insomnia!" I dismiss her concern with a laugh, but then glance at her hopefully. "Got time for breakfast before you go to work?"

Isabel raises an eyebrow and peers at me for a long moment, then she shrugs.

"Okay. But while we eat, you can tell me what's really going on."

I'D LOVE TO vent to Isabel as we walk to the café. She's one of those gentle, earthy types—all calmness and compassion, and that makes her a great listener. If I told her what's going on in my life, she'd be sympathetic and supportive and encouraging. The reason I *won't* tell her the truth is that our complicated, interconnected social group has recently seen enough drama. Marcus has two business partners at his software startup, Brainway Technologies—Jess Cohen and Paul Winton. Paul happens to be Isabel's soon-to-be ex-husband.

Until a few months back, we were a merry group most Saturday nights—me and Marcus and anyone either one of us happened to be dating, Paul and Isabel, and then Jess and the *ever*-revolving door of guys she met on Tinder. Until Paul's brother, Jake, moved to California a few years back, he often hung out with us, too. Our social circle and the Brainway business life had always been closely connected, but that had never been a problem.

Then Izzy left Paul, and everything went to shit. Isabel, Jess and I are still close, and Marcus and Paul still spend a lot of time together…but we *never* hang out as a whole group anymore. Izzy and Paul have been locked in mediation for months trying to finalize their property settlement. Things are so bitter between them now. I can't imagine us all hanging out as a group ever again.

Navigating the waters of their separation has been intensely complex for all of us and I've adopted a carefully adhered to and currently frustrating rule: I don't dump my shit on Isabel because she has enough of her own. I still have Marcus to vent to, and Jess at a pinch...although *she's* not exactly a gentle shoulder to cry on. Marcus is sensitive. Isabel is supportive. Jess is brutally honest at best. I love her like a sister, but I only vent to Jess when even *I* know I need a reality check.

Speaking of which, she skipped our regular dinner last Wednesday and I haven't heard from her since. I glance at Isabel.

"Did you see Jess over the weekend?"

"No, pretty sure she's still been busy with that guy."

"The accountant?"

"No, the accountant was last week. This guy's a screenwriter, I think."

"I wish I could find potential boyfriends as easily as Jess does." I sigh.

Isabel laughs softly. "Maybe if you went out every now and again *without* Marcus, you would."

I glance at her, surprised. "You think Marcus is the reason I'm going to die old and alone?"

"I don't think it," she says, opening the door to the café. "I *know* it."

I frown. "You actually think I'm going to die old and alone?"

Isabel ponders this for a moment. "No, so let me correct that. You *are* going to die old and single, but you won't die alone, because Marcus will be right there beside you. You two are practically joined at the hip since you moved in with him. You may as well just hook up with him and be done with it."

I can't help the too-loud peal of laughter that bursts from my mouth. Several sets of curious eyes turn our way, and I press my hand over my mouth to try to contain the giggles.

"That is the most ridiculous thing I've ever heard," I assure her, still chuckling. Isabel's gaze grows skeptical.

"Is it, though?"

"Yes, it really is."

"Sometimes he looks at you with this affection…"

"Oh, he's *fond* of me," I agree. I know exactly the look she's talking about. Sometimes I can see warmth burning in his eyes, too. It's understandable how someone might misinterpret that. "We're emotionally intimate, but honestly, that's all there is to it. And people have been trying to pair us up since we were kids. They see what they want to see." I raise my eyebrows at her. "That's what you're doing."

"Are you sure that's not what *you're* doing?" she asks me, and I frown. "I mean…if he *was* into you, would you go there?"

I *have* thought about Marcus Ross in a romantic fashion, but only once. It was an apparition—a fleeting moment of complete impulsivity and one of the worst mistakes I've ever made. I like to think of it as The Kiss Which Shall Not Be Named. The Voldemort reference fits, because speaking of it aloud would unleash all manner of evil, and the truth is, I'm not so great at facing the dark arts. I don't even let myself think about that night anymore.

"Unless I had some nasty zombie virus and his semen was the cure, I'd probably try to avoid it."

"But *why*? He's so great."

"He has two main flaws. One, he doesn't like gaming." I shrug. "Between work and fun, I spend most of my life playing games, so I've decided I'm only going to date men who like online games, too. I think that's where I went wrong with Roger. He was forever complaining that I wasn't spending enough time with him."

"Where you went wrong with Roger was that he was a fucking idiot."

"That, too." I smile sadly. "Anyway, the number one problem with Marcus is an absolute deal-breaker. You said the word *date*. And what's dating, Isabel?"

"Well, I'm a little rusty on the concept," she says wryly. "But I'm pretty sure it still means spending time with someone with a shared goal to forming some kind of romantic relationship with them."

"Exactly. So, by that definition, Marcus doesn't date. He has periodic flings with women who are happy with a no-strings arrangement, but he always maintains a very careful distance. If he thinks they're catching feelings for him, he gently calls things off."

Isabel shakes her head. "Lots of people think they don't want long-term commitment until they fall in love. Take Luca, for example."

"Luca is a different kettle of fish altogether. Sure, he used to say he wouldn't settle down, but *I* always

knew he would—he wasn't nearly as cynical about relationships as Marcus is. Marcus just isn't the kind of
guy who falls in love. I've seen him flirt plenty, but
I've never seen him *giddy* over a woman. Ever since
we were old enough to understand what marriage even
is, Marcus has been sure that's not what he wants for
life. He's not going to settle down."

*If we're still single when we get to forty should we
just get married? To each other, I mean.*

I was joking when I said that to Marcus last year, at
Jess's legendary New Year's Eve party on her building's rooftop courtyard. We were both more than a
little tipsy, and we somehow ended up cuddled under
a blanket together. It was completely innocent at first.
Romance was the farthest thing from my mind—in
fact, we got to talking about how messed up I was after
I broke up with Roger, and I half joked that I was giving up on men altogether.

I was actually hinting for him to say something
more typical of Marcus…something reassuring like,
Oh, Abs, you're so great—you'll find someone! I wasn't
at all serious—at least in part because I know Marcus
has zero interest in a wife, even a pretend one. But his
reaction really caught me off guard; he scowled, and
then snapped, *You know I'm never going to get married. And anyway, I could never think of you that way.*

If I hadn't guzzled some unknown quantity of pricey
champagne that night, I'd probably have told him where
to go and we'd have laughed about it and carried on as
we were. But between the bubbles and his apparent re-
fusal to see me as a woman even just for *one damned*

hypothetical moment...well, frankly, I was more than a little pissed *and* pissed off.

So I kissed him, and nearly ruined everything.

Just the memory is enough to *still* make me feel heavy with regret and confusion. For that and a million other reasons, I have no desire to repeat the experience. I don't want us to *have* kissed, but I can't change the past. The closest I can come is to deny the incident altogether, which is why I never told anyone. Not even Izzy.

It's a strategy that's worked well. It was awkward at first, but everything went back to normal within a few weeks.

"I know it's unusual for two people to be as close as we are and just be friends," I say softly. "But it's also really special, you know? We couldn't be more different but...the tension of those differences is kind of the fun part for us. We balance each other. I mean, we also challenge each other, and we call each other out, but we never try to change one another—not really. And to quote *Grey's Anatomy*...he's my person. It's perfect and amazing as it is. No way am I ever fucking *that* up with—"

"Fucking." Isabel laughs, and I grin at her.

"Exactly."

"So let me get this straight, Abby. You're saying he's the best guy ever. You two are super close. You live together well. Even your differences are somehow compatible. But there's *no chance* you'd ever consider anything more with him, even if he wanted it?"

I sigh and shake my head.

"Izzy, my love life is a disaster zone."

"You've had a run of bad relationships, that's for sure."

"I couldn't inflict my relationship chaos on Marcus." I'm trying to keep my tone light, but it drops as I think about the awful confrontation I had with Roger when I caught him with another woman.

It's not me, it's you! Between gaming and working you're at the fucking computer fourteen hours a day. Even when you do take a break, you'd rather spend time with Marcus than me. A man needs to feel needed. If I ran into her arms, it's only because you drove me there.

Isabel frowns. "Roger cheating on you was *not* your fault."

"It doesn't matter, anyway," I say, then I clear my throat. "Marcus is the only guy I've ever known who *gets* me—*really* gets me. He understands that I need a lot of alone time, but he also understands that I need to be gently nudged out of my shell to socialize, too. He is simply too important for me to take any risks with our relationship. How lucky am I to have someone in my life who knows exactly who I am, and every single one of my secrets? I wouldn't risk that for anything."

Isabel seems momentarily satisfied by this, and she starts to chat about the new seniors' fitness program she's developing at the gym. Meanwhile, I can't help the way my thoughts drift, because I just lied to her. Again. I'm losing count, but I think that's three times now. Before 8:00 a.m.? That's definitely a record and not one I'm proud of.

I told her Marcus knows every single one of my secrets, but he doesn't. He used to—until last month.

My cycle has been a little weird for the past year or so, and I'd been putting off a visit to my gynecologist for a while. But then we went home for Marcus's grandfather's funeral, and my mom was doing what she often does and hinting at me about grandbabies and I guess that kicked my butt into gear, because I finally went in and had some tests.

It was only a few days after my appointment that my doctor called me back into her office, and she stared at me with visible pity as she delivered a blow I was completely unprepared for.

I'm so sorry, Abby. These test results suggest a diminished ovarian reserve.

I've spent the last few weeks alternating between pretending this isn't happening and trying to understand what it all means, but the main implication is that I'm running out of time. If I want to be a mom, I need to get pregnant now, or better still, yesterday.

And I do want to be a mom. I've *always* wanted to be a mom.

I've just always had this picture in my mind about what my adult life would look like. Marcus teases me a bit about it—he calls my dream guy Mr. Perfect. In my mind, Mr. Perfect is someone who likes nerd culture and periodically turning down exciting party invitations only to sit at home and binge-watch entire seasons of our favorite shows on Netflix.

Mr. Perfect and I would fall in love quickly—maybe it would even be love at first sight. Later, we'd get married at the church near Mom and Dad's house, and I'd ask Marcus to be my man of honor. Marcus would grumble, but he'd do it, anyway. My husband and I would move out of the city and into a two-story house just like the one I grew up with—a house with lots of bedrooms and a big yard bordered by a white-picket fence. The yard was important. We'd need it for our rescue pup, Charlie. Eventually, me and Mr. Perfect would have our perfect pair of babies.

I've spent an embarrassing amount of time planning and dreaming about this future over the years, but at the end of the day, it really was just a fantasy, and almost all of the details were negotiable.

I was always pretty sure this last one was not: I'd adore my husband, and he'd adore me, and together, *we* would adore our kids. I think that's what's so confusing about where I am right now. Sure, I can still find Mr. Perfect and achieve the rest of the dream, even if I do have a baby with donor sperm. But now everything *has* to happen out of order, and the fact that I'm even considering this makes me feel…chaotic.

I don't do chaotic.

The very reason I've spent so much time thinking about this over the years is that uncertainty makes me anxious and having a very specific plan in my mind helps me to manage that. It's the same principle that led me to fall into the well-worn schedule I keep each week. If I always know what's coming next, I'm always prepared.

I haven't told anyone about my potential fertility issues. I haven't told Isabel or Jess, or Mom and Dad. I'll tell them all—eventually, I guess—but… I haven't even told Marcus yet, and he's my go-to person for the life-changing stuff. Keeping this discovery to myself is a clumsy way to avoid accepting it. Once I tell *him*, it's real. I didn't even tell Luca the whole truth. I just told him I wanted a baby. I couldn't bear to guilt him into doing it.

I would have lost my shit completely if Marcus had pressed me for details last night. Everything inside me feels fragile, like pieces are shifting and shattering and I'm only just holding it all together while I figure out a way forward. Maybe I'm a coward, but avoiding an open discussion with Marcus about this until I *have* to is a form of self-preservation. Until I say the words aloud—*it might already be too late for me to become a mom*—I can pretend it's not true.

It's not like I haven't tried to find my happily-ever-after. Until these last few years, I dated a lot. I've had a seemingly endless series of boyfriends that I hoped might just be "the one." I just can't seem to make a relationship work.

"Hey." Isabel reaches across the table to wave her hand in front of my face. "Where'd you go? You zoned out on me there."

"Sorry," I mutter.

"I figured I'd ply you with organic apple juice and you'd spill the beans, but I'm starting to think you *really* don't want to talk about whatever is going on," Isabel says gently.

"I don't," I sigh, and grimace at her. "Is that okay? I'm sorry."

"Abby…" She sighs, too. "We've been friends for a while now, so I've learned to deal with the way uncomfortable subjects trigger your avoidance issues."

"I don't know what you're talking about," I mutter, but she grins.

"What's my swine of a soon-to-be ex-husband's name, then?"

I narrow my gaze at her. "You know what it is."

"Sure I do. I say it *all* of the time. *Paul is a swine. Paul is a robot. Paul has binary code where his feelings should be.* But you? You never say it. I haven't heard you say his name since I called you to tell you I'd left him."

"I thought it would make it easier for you if I didn't mention him."

"It hurts that my marriage turned to shit. It *doesn't* hurt that Paul is still in business with Jess and Marcus and you're inevitably going to see him sometimes."

"Sorry," I sigh. "I thought I was helping by not bringing him up."

"Maybe that's a part of it, but an equally big part of it is that you, Abby Herbert, *suck* at confronting things. You suck at confronting painful things, and difficult things, and most definitely awkward things—and watching two of your closest friends get divorced is about as awkward as it gets."

I groan as my head flops forward onto my chest dramatically. "It's too early for you to force me to talk about this."

"I know you are a nocturnal creature and this daylight-hours socializing is probably difficult enough for you." Isabel laughs softly. "So just do one thing for me and I'll wrap this up."

"Anything," I beg her. "Just make it stop, at least until I've had a few dozen coffees."

"Say his name."

"Whose name?" She groans and rolls her eyes. I wince. "Oh. Your swine of a soon-to-be ex-husband."

"That's his title, *not* his name."

"If I say it, can we immediately change the subject back to something that doesn't make me want to squirm my way out of the café?" I check, and her gaze narrows further.

"Say it, Abigail."

I sigh heavily, then mutter, "Paul."

Isabel presses a hand against her mouth and blinks rapidly, as if she's trying to dispel sudden tears. I panic and reach to console her.

"I'm so sorry, Izzy. I just *knew* if I said—"

Her expression clears in an instant as she laughs at me. "Got you."

"That was mean!" I protest.

"No, *that* was revenge for you lying to me when you said nothing was wrong. Eat your breakfast, go home and stop avoiding Marcus."

She's seen right through me. I reach for my apple juice, wishing it was something stronger.

"I'm not exactly avoiding him…"

"You're out of the apartment before noon, Abby," she says wryly. "We both know you're avoiding *something*."

THE TEXT ARRIVES from Luca just after lunch.

It's a no from me on the sperm thing.

It's a pretty typical Luca-text. Blunt, to the point, not quite enough detail—and unapologetic. I picture him at work on a jobsite. He's probably standing on a ladder with a paintbrush in one hand and his phone in the other, bashing out the text to me, then getting right back to it without another thought.

Marcus is charming, the quintessential "people person." His twin, on the other hand, was born without a filter. I took a leaf out of Luca's book yesterday when I took him out for lunch. I don't think I even said hello— I just opened with *Luca, would you consider donating sperm so I can have a baby?*

I really thought he was a good candidate for this little project of mine—he's attractive and healthy and smart, and although Luca and I have a thirty-year-long relationship almost entirely based on verbal sparring, he *is* a wonderful guy. Luca has been open about his plans to remain childless, so I thought maybe he'd consider an arrangement where he could make an anonymous donation and have no responsibility for the child. I thought he'd make a few lighthearted, awkward jokes, then shrug and tell me he'd talk to Austin about it.

I didn't realize, though, that Austin desperately wants kids, too. And they've only just started trying to figure this out themselves.

Luca did ask me to tell Marcus and promised he'd talk to Austin about it, so I clung to a shred of hope, even though, on some level, I did realize that his personal circumstances were more complicated than I'd realized, and he was probably going to say no.

I haven't logged into my go-to chat app today—because I know the moment I do, Marcus will try to talk to me. However, talking to Marcus is the only thing that's going to ease the ache now. I log in and, as expected, a message pops up immediately.

Marcus: Have the kidnappers returned you already?

Abby: Kidnappers?

Marcus: Well, you weren't in bed when I got back from the gym, so I assumed someone had taken you against your will. I spent the whole morning figuring out how much ransom money I was willing to part with to get you back.

I laugh softly, wipe my cheeks with the back of my hands, then reply.

Abby: I'm priceless, we both know that. You'd have given them every cent you have and it would still have been a bargain.

There's a pause, then I see the indicator flash up to show that he's typing again, so I beat him to it.

Abby: Still not ready to talk about it. Besides, Luca said no, so it's not happening, anyway, and I'm super pissed at him for making me tell you for nothing. So really. Don't get me started. Not today.

On that note, I scoop up my phone and start to draft a furious text to Luca for making me tell Marcus unnecessarily. The computer sounds before I can send it and I glance back to the screen.

Marcus: I'm really sorry. If you don't want me to push you, I won't—but when you're ready, let's talk about it. Until then, you just tell me what I need to do to support you.

There's a flush of something warm inside my chest—relief? Gratitude? Affection? Marcus is the most important person in my world, but at times like this, I can't help but think back to The Kiss and I kick myself all over again. That was the only time in my entire life I've taken a risk with this relationship and I still can't believe my stupidity. I *need* Marcus. He's the yang to my yin, the icing on the cake of my life, my moral support, my sounding board and my living, breathing motivational poster. I draw in a deep breath, thank him and then delete the angry text to Luca— instead, I reply with something a little more mature.

Thanks for letting me know, Luca. Of course I'm disappointed, but I do understand. And for the record, if you and Austin do decide to have a family one day, you're going to be a great dad.

I send it, but then I read it again, and realize how soppy it is. That's definitely not my style with Luca, so I hastily add:

A super annoying dad, mind you, but a great one.

But then I feel completely shitty, because I suddenly remember what else Luca and Marcus are dealing with right now, and there's a good chance that Marcus wasn't just looking for me this morning because he wanted to hear me talk about *my* problems.

Abby: Marcus, are you doing okay with the Warwick thing? We got so sidetracked last night with my shit, and I feel awful that I wasn't here for you today.

Marcus: I'm just fine, Abs. I'm not even thinking about it. Still don't know if I'll bother to reply.

I'm not really sure about any of that. I can't predict how Marcus is going to deal with Warwick's reemergence—it's too left field. I do have my own stuff to deal with, but I really need to do a better job of supporting him while he figures this out.

I sigh and open my Brainway browser—of course I use the software Marcus's company develops. I stare at the address field for a long moment.

I don't want my baby's father to be a stranger, but I don't have any other way forward. I'll never forgive myself if I don't even *try* to have a baby before it's too late.

My fingers move slowly, but I force myself to type the URL for the fertility clinic I'll be visiting next week. I log in with the account information they sent me, and ignoring the sick feeling in my stomach, I navigate to the sperm donor database.

CHAPTER THREE

Marcus

EVERY FEW WEEKS, Luca and I meet after work at a sports bar just a few blocks from my office. He usually arrives late and offers neither an excuse nor an apology. He's always still dressed in his work coveralls, and right from his shoes all the way up to his messy man-bun and unkempt beard, he's generally covered in paint splatters.

I love my brother, but there's no way around it—the man is a slob.

"You need a haircut. And a shave. And to shower as soon as you finish work," I greet him, and he grins at me as if I've just said something cute. We shake hands, then he slides onto the bar stool beside me.

"Great to see you, too, little bro."

I'm three minutes younger than Luca. He calls me "little bro" to irritate me, but I'm far too focused on my mission today to bite.

We *will* get to Warwick—but before my brain explodes, I need some more information about this whole Abby/baby/sperm donation. Even after turning this over and over in my head half the fucking night, I still can't understand why on earth she'd want anyone to donate sperm right now, let alone *Luca*.

"So…she said you're not doing it," I blurt.

"We're talking about Abby?" Luca says mildly. "And me knocking her up, right?"

I glare at him.

"You know that's what we're talking about."

Luca ignores me for a moment while he orders himself a beer.

"Another for me, too, please."

We sit in silence until the beers arrive, then just as I raise my glass to my lips, Luca says matter-of-factly, "Look, in an ideal world you'd have figured this out for yourself, but I'm worried that you're running out of time here so I'm just going to come right out and tell you." He pauses, then looks me right in the eye and says, "I'm pretty sure you're in love with Abby, Marcus."

I squint at him, then laugh.

"Luca, you've lost your fucking mind."

"Have I?"

"Yes!"

"Things have changed between you two this year," Luca says quietly. "I'm not the only one who's noticed. Austin and Mom have both mentioned it, too. Hell, even *Jack* asked me if you guys were a thing now."

We sit in silence for a moment. I'm surprised anyone noticed at all, mostly because my infatuation with Abby only lasted a few weeks.

"Okay, I see where you're mixed up. We kissed, but it's not as serious as…" I clear my throat. It's hard for me to even repeat the accusation he's just made. "It's not as serious as all *that*. It was just a drunken, one-time thing."

"And?" he prompts impatiently.

In the weeks after New Year's, all I could think about was that kiss. Life went on, but some part of my brain was stuck in that moment in time. I fixated on how perfectly in sync we were, and how inevitable it felt—even though I'd never considered kissing Abby Herbert to be an option until the moment our lips actually connected.

"It was incredible," I admit.

"Well, why was it just the one time, then?"

"Abby..." I clear my throat. "She wasn't interested."

Luca barks a laugh. "Presumably not incredible for *her*, then."

"Thanks, Luca."

"Ah, shit—Marcus, you know I'm not good at this touchy-feeling stuff. I just meant if she...you know. If she liked it, she'd have kissed you more. That's generally how it works."

"Well, she seemed to like it well enough at the time," I mutter. "She just freaked out afterward. I think she was worried it would change our friendship."

"And did it?"

"For a little while." I shrug. "It was last New Year's Eve. We were talking about what happened with Fucking Roger..."

Abby tends to move *really* slowly, so when she moved right in with Roger only a month or two after she met him at the comic book store he worked at, I wasn't sure what to make of it. When I checked in with her, she said she'd finally found her Mr. Perfect and that she was in love. What could I do? Roger was at least an improvement on her previous boyfriends, mostly because he had his own apartment and a job. I've never liked *any* of the guys she's dated, and believe me, I've tried.

I didn't like Roger, either, although at first I wasn't sure why because on paper he seemed fine. The pattern gradually emerged—Abby was running herself ragged trying to make that asshole happy. She paid more than her share of the bills, she handled all the domestic work around the house and she was *forever* excusing his rudeness when we were out in a group.

He was threatened by how much time she spent gaming and threatened by how much time she spent working. He was threatened by her friends, especially Jess, who seemed to scare him half to death. Roger was so threatened by how close Abs and I were that he'd always come up with lame excuses to join her if she and I were due to catch up.

It turned out Roger was an irresponsible man-child like the rest of them, and a particularly insecure one at that.

She'd been with him for less than a year when I got home from work one night and found her in a ball on my sofa. When she tried to tell me what had happened, all I could make out was the sound of her heartbroken sobs and the look of sheer humiliation on her face. At first, I thought she'd just had enough of playing mommy to a grown man, but it turns out, he wasn't just a lazy idiot, he was an unfaithful bastard, too, and she'd walked in on him in their bed with one of his colleagues.

I've been Abby's friend for a long time—through plenty of ups and plenty of downs. I'd seen her hurt and I'd seen her disappointed. I'd seen her happy and, looking back, I'd probably seen her depressed a few times, too.

I'd *never* seen her broken before, but that's exactly what happened after Roger.

I hastily set her up in my spare room. For weeks, she lived under a cloud. Left to her own devices, Abby was spending most of the day in bed. She wasn't gaming for fun anymore, and she wasn't even trying to keep up with her work—and Abby *loves* her job. She's worked so hard to build her business that her sudden disinterest in it scared the shit out of me.

I was sure I could fix things for her. I took her to the theater and dragged her to the gym and helped Jess and Isabel convince her to leave the apartment every now and again. I didn't understand just how dark her mood had become. I also didn't understand that all Abby needed from me was support—I couldn't rescue her or fix the situation for her. After a few weeks, I finally did what I probably should have done in the first place, and asked what I could do to help. She admitted she was in trouble, and asked me to come with her to the GP. So that's exactly what I did.

Later, she told me that she'd suffered from anxiety and periods of depression for years, but she'd always tried to keep the struggle to herself. The breakup with Roger just exposed issues that she'd been trying to ignore for a very long time.

When Fucking Roger called me a few weeks after Abby left, I assumed he was calling to check on her welfare. It turned out he had packed up her things into trash bags, and he wanted them gone before the end of the day because his new girlfriend was moving in.

Hence his nickname, *Fucking Roger*, now uttered as a curse word by our friends and family alike—except Abby's mom, Eden. She never swears so she calls him *Fishing Roger*, but we all know what she really means.

The last time I saw Roger was the day Paul, Luca and I went around to pick up the last of Abby's things. I'm not a violent guy and I like to think I have an excellent handle on my temper. But Roger was so smug, and he patted me on the back and tried to lay the blame on Abby for the end of their relationship. In my blind rage, I didn't pay attention to most of his vile nonsense, but I do remember him calling her "a moody loner" just before I lost my shit. If Paul and Luca hadn't pulled me back, I'd have torn that bastard to pieces.

I've always thought a lot of Abby, but having watched how hard she fought to get her life back during those months, I am now convinced that my best friend is the strongest woman in the world.

"*Fucking* Roger," Luca echoes right on cue now, and his nostrils flare.

"Exactly," I say as my hands clench into fists automatically. "We were talking about just how bad things got for her, and how hard it was for her to claw her way back. Then Abby said she was done with men and she made a joke about me being her backup spouse. Then she just…kind of threw herself at me. She climbed onto my lap, and next thing I knew, we were—"

"You can spare me the details, Marcus," Luca interrupts me. "Just skip to the part where you two talked this through."

"I tried. You know her—do you think she wanted to sit down and have an awkward heart-to-heart about that kiss? The harder I tried to force the issue, the more she avoided me, until the day I came home from the gym and caught her sitting on the couch looking at Craigslist room-for-rent postings."

Luca winces. "Ouch."

"She made sure I got the hint—pretty much rubbed the laptop screen on my face."

"You should have called her bluff."

"That's the thing, Luca, it wasn't a bluff. She *would* have moved out. And I knew if she did, she'd stop avoiding the subject of the kiss and start avoiding me. I figured I'd wait and raise it again once she'd cooled down, but whenever I tried, she found some convenient excuse to end the discussion. It's obvious that if Abby *did* notice the chemistry that night, she's decided it's just not something she wants to pursue." I shrugged. "So… I locked that shit down, too, and life went on."

Luca frowns at me.

"Abby kissed *you*, right?"

"Yeah. At first."

"So, what makes you so sure it was just an impulse? Maybe she was… I don't know. Maybe she's been into you for a while, too."

I pause for a minute, trying to figure out how to answer without sounding like a conceited ass.

"Just because there *could* be something more between us doesn't mean we have to give in to it. I'm pretty sure I'm too important for Abby to let herself want me like that. I'm the constant in her life. Things change, and change can be hard for her, but when life feels unstable, she's always had me. At a guess, I'd say the idea of rolling the dice on our friendship scared the pants off her."

"Actually, it sounds to me like the problem isn't scaring the pants *off* her at all." Luca smirks, and I roll my eyes. "So, you're saying things never went any further because Abby was scared? Not *you*?"

There's another pause; this one feels slightly uncomfortable. I clear my throat and admit carefully, "Abby is important to me, too, but we're on really different pages when it comes to the future. So yeah, maybe I didn't push as hard as I might have if I wasn't so worried that it would all end in tears, anyway."

"She wants the whole package. Marriage…kids…" Luca surmises. I nod, and he tilts his head at me. "And you still don't."

I've never understood why people think of marriage as an achievement. To me, it seems like an empty promise—how can you *ever* promise a person that you'll want to be with them forever?

The annoying thing about this is that once upon a time, Luca would have agreed with me about how hollow wedding vows are and how much smarter it is to keep relationships casual. Since he met Austin, though, he's like some kind of happily-ever-after evangelist. I love Austin and I love how happy my brother is these days, but I'm still completely bewildered by the abrupt about-face.

It's time to change the subject before he starts trying to sign me up for Bachelors' Anonymous, so I motion toward my phone on the bar and ask, "So, what do you think about that Facebook message…?"

"I have no idea what to make of it." Luca runs his hand over his hair and then vaguely motions toward my phone, mirroring my gesture. "I was thinking maybe we should at least write back."

I look at Luca in surprise. "And say *what* exactly?"

My tone is too sharp, and Luca raises an eyebrow. "It sounds like Grandpa Don had been keeping him in the loop about us."

"That's bullshit."

"Are you so sure of that?"

"Actually, I am."

"Why?"

"Don't you think Don would have *mentioned* that at some point?"

Luca shakes his head. "Not necessarily. I mean, he was a miserable fucker, wasn't he?"

"That's one way of putting it."

"And pretty much everything we know about Warwick…"

Luca trails off, and contrary to our lifelong insistence that we are *not* the kind of twins who do this very thing, I finish the sentence. "We learned from Don."

I can't ever remember Mom talking about Warwick without being prompted to, and even then, she changed the subject quickly. She's moved on and she's so happy with Jack, but over the years, it's been obvious that she was deeply wounded by the breakdown of her first marriage.

"But *none* of what Don told us was ever positive, was it? He was hardly a reliable narrator, Marcus. Think about Don's snide fucking comments over the years. Even his compliments to *us* were usually backhanded digs at Warwick…" Luca looks at me and says quietly, "Especially with you. Do you remember? That was some messed-up, manipulative bullshit he put on you when we were kids. And he *knew* it was wrong. He never said those things when Mom was around."

School comes so naturally to you—what a clever kid. Just like your sneaky dad—he was clever, too, did you know that?

Marcus is so good at sports. You know, your dad's favorite sport was running…running around on your mom, that is.

You're just like your father, Marcus. Such a ladies' man. What goddamned charmers you pair turned out to be.

They aren't pleasant memories, but Don was bitter—who wouldn't be? Warwick walked out on the man's only daughter, leaving her to raise two boisterous sons on her own.

Two boisterous sons who looked *exactly* like the man who hurt her…and one who acted like that man, too, apparently.

"Be that as it may," I say stiffly, "Warwick still left. He still abandoned his family. I don't even give a shit if he really was covertly checking in with Don all this time, although I still find it hard to believe that's true. When we needed Warwick, he wasn't there, and that's all that fucking matters."

"Yeah," Luca sighs.

"Should we tell him we're not interested in calling him, then?"

"You're *sure* that's what you want to do?"

"I don't know." I stare down into my beer. It's the

hopeful tone of Warwick's message that's messing with my head. It brings back memories of the happy, early days of our childhood—the memories I have that don't quite gel with the version of my biological father I've come to know through Don. There were plenty of happy days *after* Warwick left, too—especially when Mom remarried our stepdad, Jack, and Jack became New Improved Dad 2.0: now with staying power.

But it's kind of funny and bewildering how a part of me has always missed the first version of our family, at least the way I saw it at the time.

"It took twenty-five fucking years for him to get in touch with us," I say suddenly. "Surely we have the right to take a few days or a week or two before we decide whether or not we actually want to reply to him."

Luca nods, and his gaze lands on the TV over the bar. I stare at the TV for a while, too, and we finish our beers in silence.

"You're definitely not going to do it?" I ask Luca after a while. I've changed the subject again, but he knows exactly what I'm talking about.

"Look, it's Abby, so…if she'd asked me a few years ago, I probably *would* have done it. Let's face it, I was jacking off, anyway, right?" He gives me a crooked grin that quickly fades. "But now…how can I help Abby to have a family when my husband and I aren't even sure what we're going to do about our own? Plus…I knew you'd kill me."

It's curious that he's right about that, because I *know* he's wrong about my feelings for Abby. My infatuation with her was intense, but it was also brief. I know I'm over her, so I'm not exactly sure why the idea of her having a kid with my brother makes me feel so uncomfortable. It's like my suit is suddenly six sizes too small.

"Marcus, I know you think I'm an insensitive prick, and I can be sometimes, but…I do care about Abby. A lot. I've never seen her so desperate." He hesitates, then admits quietly, "I don't know what's going on with her, but something is up here."

"I don't get what the fucking rush is on all of this. She's only thirty."

"Well, whatever's going on, bro, she's in a real hurry. She's going to get pregnant no matter what. I really think she needs you, Marcus."

"I'll support her no matter what she does." I frown. "I always have. I always will."

"I didn't doubt that for a second," Luca says softly. "It's just that sometimes life throws a curveball, and instead of ducking to get out of the way of it, you can lift your hands up and catch it, you know?"

I blink at him.

"That is the worst analogy I've ever heard. You don't dodge or catch curveballs, you *hit* them with a fucking bat. And since when are you into baseball?"

"I'm not, but Austin is, although he hasn't quite explained the finer points of the game to me yet." Luca grins, then nods toward my empty glass. "Stay for one more beer?"

"Do you promise to stop playing Dr. Phil?"

"Deal."

CHAPTER FOUR

Abby

IT'S 2:00 P.M. and I'm sitting at my computer playing my favorite video game, scribbling notes so I can plan out the walk-through I'll be doing live tomorrow. I write for a few digital magazines, too, but most of my income these days is from my video content. I livestream twice a week, although my content isn't usually as exciting as *this* sneak peak will be.

This video will be huge—it will give my 1.5 million subscribers a glimpse into forthcoming expansions to the online game *World of Warcraft*. Views of my videos equals money for me through sponsorship and ad revenue, and the secret to my success is knowing my audience and giving them exactly what they want.

The first bit is easy—I know what my audience wants because I *am* my audience. Gaming is my hobby and my passion; that's exactly why I love what I do for work. Quality delivery is where it gets tricky. I'm competing with a lot of other gaming commentators online these days, but much of the other content out there is sloppy.

My content is *never* sloppy. I plan my videos down to the second. I've invested in equipment to make sure that my video and audio quality is top-notch, and I have a team of freelancers on standby—they make sure that the editing and graphics on my videos are world-class.

I also use freelancers to handle the only downside to my job: the inevitable harassment and trolling. That kind of thing was bad enough when I was just a random female gamer, but now that I'm a female gamer with a high profile, it's a daily reality. Fortunately, I fiercely protect my privacy, and have a brilliant social media freelancer who filters out most of the negative stuff before I have the chance see it.

A familiar notification echoes from my speakers and I pause the game-play and check my instant-message client to find it's a message from Marcus. I love how he and I chat during our workdays. It's the ultimate reinforcement that our friendship goes both ways. He's so busy, and he has so many staff members now to talk to in person. It makes me feel special that he also makes space in his day to connect with me.

Marcus: About this baby thing.

Abby: What a subtle way to raise the subject. Have you been taking lessons from your brother?

Marcus: No point beating about the bush on this. I hope you know I'll support you whatever you decide, and I'll be here for you whatever happens.

I *do* know that, but it never hurts to be reminded. I smile softly.

Abby: Thank you, Marcus.

Marcus: You're better off without Luca's stupid sperm, anyway. Sure, he's good-looking, but he can be kind of a jerk.

Abby: You literally share his DNA.

Marcus: Exactly, so I would know.

There's a pause, and I see him typing, but it takes a while for the next message to come through.

Marcus: What's the rush? I know the last few years have been tough, but you're just too young to give up on Mr. Perfect.

Tears fill my eyes, and I blink them away before I reply.

Abby: I'm starting to think maybe you're on to something with this lifelong commitment to staying single.

Marcus: And maybe I'd buy that bullshit if I hadn't spent the last twenty-odd years listening to you wax lyrical about your house in the suburbs and Charlie the puppy chewing up your laundry while you and your handsome husband play Warcraft late into the night.

The tears spill over. I brush them away with the backs of my hands.

Marcus: Tell me to butt out if I'm way out of line here, Abs, but I'm worried about you. Is there a reason you need to do this now?

There's a lump in my throat I can't quite swallow. I should have known he'd figure it out.

Abby: Yeah. Health stuff.

Marcus: I'm so sorry, Abby.

Abby: I'll be okay.

Marcus: Do you have a backup plan in mind now that Luca can't do this?

I open my browser, navigate to bookmarks and screenshot my favorite of the sperm bank listings I've shortlisted.

I still don't love the idea of having a baby this way, but Candidate 1986 is slowly growing on me. He's a software developer and amateur photographer who runs ultramarathons in his spare time. I like that he has an interest in technology, like I do. I like that he's creative. I like that he looks after his health.

I hate that he's a stranger. I hate that he'll always be a stranger, to me *and* to my baby. But these are things I'll have to deal with—compromises I have to make to reach for my dream.

I survey the screenshot for a moment, then send it on to Marcus. I think he'll approve of this guy—they have a lot in common. The more I think about that, the more I like Candidate 1986 myself. But then several long minutes pass before Marcus replies with:

Marcus: Sorry, Abs, have to run.

I sit back in my chair and look at the screen in surprise. Is that a curt response, or am I reading too much into plain text?

Surely it's the latter. Marcus is a very busy man. Something must have come up at his office.

CHAPTER FIVE

Marcus

I MEANT WHAT I said: I'll support Abby regardless of whatever choices she makes here. It's her life, and I know she'll make decisions that are right for *her*. Sooner or later she'll explain more to me about this "health stuff," but I don't need to know the details to know it's serious.

If it wasn't serious, Abby wouldn't be considering selecting her baby's father based on a four-line description in an internet database. When the screenshot of her potential donor's details appeared on my screen, I was actually winded for a second. I really didn't like the idea of Luca being Abby's baby-daddy, but turns out, I fucking *hate* the idea of some anonymous stranger doing the job.

I exhale and push my chair away from the desk. I have a meeting in ten minutes, but I need some fresh air to clear my head first. It feels like someone has put my fucking brain in a blender this week.

"Hey, Isaac?"

My assistant looks up from his screen and gives me an expectant, eager look. "Yes?"

"Can you push back the digital campaign review? I need to take a lunch break."

"How long do you need?"

"Give me an hour."

Isaac's eyebrows shoot upward, as if I've said something shocking, and I guess I have. Lunch breaks are not exactly a regular fixture on my schedule these days. "I'll move that meeting to tomorrow since you have an opening at ten."

I nod but as I walk past his desk, he calls after me. "You *do* have that workshop with Jess and Paul at four to run through the schedule for the company meeting next week."

I wave over my shoulder to let him know I'll be back in time, and then switch out of work mode as I head toward the elevator bank.

I was in my second year of college when Paul Winton told me he had an idea for a new kind of internet browser. We'd taken a freshman coding class together and had been partners for a group project, so I already knew that Paul was a prodigy. It seemed inevitable that one day he'd be talked about in the same awed tones our peers reserved for Zuckerberg and Jobs.

Everyone I knew respected his intellect, but even so, they generally thought Paul was an asshole—his social skills were woefully lacking. He was two years younger than the rest of our cohort because he'd skipped a few grades at school, and he was so focused on programming that he had little time for networking or even making friends.

But social skills are *my* superpower, and during that group project, I'd already figured out how to work with Paul. He couldn't read subtext so I had to be direct. He didn't tolerate stupidity so I either had to catch up quick or focus all of my efforts on clearing the way for *him* to do the work. He generally couldn't tell when he offended people, but I had a pretty tough skin, and over the course of the project, I actually grew to like Paul's no-nonsense style. When he asked me to help him develop his concept browser, I couldn't say yes fast enough.

The first few years, we just toyed around with his ideas in our spare time, and an unlikely friendship formed. I helped with basic coding when I could, but mostly, I worked with him to refine the interface, adopting better design principles so the app was easy to use and pleasant to look at. By our senior year, we had something that kinda-sorta worked, but we had no idea how to take it to the next level. That's when I suggested we bring Jess Cohen in. She was a business major, but in the classes we'd shared, Jess had equal parts terrified and impressed me with her cutthroat attitude and her skill.

Terrified and impressed is exactly how I feel about Jess twelve years later, by the way. She's a force to be reckoned with, and every day I'm glad I'm working *with* her, and not against her.

Right after graduation, the three of us decided to go all in. We borrowed money from our families, locked ourselves away in the cheapest apartment we could find and set up our own "incubator" to develop our business plan. Paul and I slept in bunk beds in the only bedroom and Jess slept on the sofa…not that anyone did much sleeping in those days. Abby was still at college then. She used to bring us coffee and ramen, and she called us vampires because we didn't see sunlight for months at a time.

It was two long years before we launched with more of a whimper than a bang, and then still more years where we only just made ends meet. But we held on and we kept the faith in the dream, and a few years ago, all of the hard work began to pay off.

Everyone said we couldn't build a profitable business with a browser alone, but we did. Everyone said corporate clients wouldn't pay to use a browser when their operating systems provided one for free, but they do. The Brainway browser provides a different kind of value—innovative security features, integrated social media and, if I do say so myself, a vastly superior interface.

Jess, Paul and I have hundreds of staff members to help us now, and we're actually making real money. A few years ago, I repaid Mom and Jack the seed money they lent me, and because they refused to take interest, I paid off their mortgage and bought them a new car. Jess and her team are working toward an initial public offering on the stock market, and when that happens, we will have turned all those years of work into more money than we'll know what to do with.

We've moved offices several times as the team grew, and now we lease a floor in a high-rise in the Financial District. We've also leased a small building in Silicon Valley and there's a growing team there, too, although that office isn't without its challenges. It's hard to instill company culture remotely, and every now and again, Jess hints that I should head over to California to oversee west coast operations for a year or two. There's far too much keeping me in New York for me to seriously consider her suggestion. Aside from my apartment and Abby and my *life*, most of my team is here.

My life looks exactly the way I always wanted it to, and it's pretty fucking great. I have plenty going for me, and exactly zero nonwork commitments tying me down.

That's exactly what I wanted.

Exactly what I *want*, I mean. It's exactly what I *want*. That hasn't changed.

Has it?

I step out into the street and walk down the block to a coffee shop. I order a coffee and a sandwich and take a seat in the corner. I tell myself I'll work on my perpetually out-of-control email, so I pull out my phone, but instead I find myself navigating to the Favorites folder in my camera roll. Inside, there are just four photos.

There's one of me, Luca and Austin at their wedding in Hawaii last year. There's a second shot from the wedding, this one of Mom and Jack. There's a shot of me, Paul and Jess on a working weekend away together at Paul's vacation home at Greenport. Finally, there's a casual photo I took of Abby last year.

She had done a livestream for her European timezone subscribers earlier that day, so she's wearing a full face of stage makeup and her chocolate-brown hair is carefully done. She's wearing an Adventure Time T-shirt, and she's holding a coffee mug, laughing at something I said.

She had just received a royalty payment but it had been much larger than she'd anticipated. Abby was so proud, and I was struck by the contrast in her from those awful months where I was genuinely afraid she'd never be happy again. Her happiness made *me* happy, and the glow in her face really was a sight to behold, so almost unthinkingly I picked up my phone and captured the moment. It's a candid photo. It's a work of art not because of my photography skills, but because of the radiant happiness on her face.

When Abby heard the sound of my camera shutter, she rolled her eyes and called me a weirdo. I sent the image to her mom, Eden, who accidentally replied with an eggplant emoji, followed that up with a GIF of a kitten saying "sorry" and then finally called me to thank me and tell me how beautiful Abby looked, how amazing it was that Abby had built such a successful business out of her hobby and how glad she was that Abby has me to look after her. I told her Abby didn't need looking after, but that I agreed with everything else she'd said.

Staring at that image now, I'm surprised to feel a confused mix of emotions rising. I'm worried about Abby. I'm nervous about her health situation—what's wrong? I'm also scared not just for her health, but because of the sheer compromise she's making in pursuing a pregnancy this way. She's clung to an oddly specific dream for her life for so long, and I *know* how she operates. Abby doesn't change easily—planning out her life provides comfort and peace.

Abby as a mom, though…that's an exciting prospect. I love kids, and the only real downside to my decision to stay single long-term is that I wasn't sure I'd ever become a dad. Fatherhood itself doesn't scare me—it's the lifelong tie to a baby's mother that makes me queasy. But if Abby has a baby, I'm going to be a big part of this kid's life, and maybe that's a reasonable second best to becoming a dad myself.

I can easily imagine myself getting up in the middle of the night to care for the baby so Abby can catch up on sleep; I'll rock that tiny little person in my arms as I pace the hallway near my bedroom. Then it occurs to me that Abby's bedroom/office is just one big space. Where will this baby sleep? Maybe we should swap rooms. I have a large bedroom, too, but right beside it is my home office. Abby will need all the room she can get once she's juggling her business and the baby.

Although…maybe swapping bedrooms isn't enough. I mean, my apartment is perfect for two adults. It's adequate for two adults and an infant. It's *far* too fucking small for two adults and a toddler. Maybe we should all move, then? I could afford something bigger now… something a little more luxurious for Abby and her baby. Maybe I should talk to her about it when the dust settles.

I guess the first hurdle is Abby getting pregnant. Now *that's* going to be a sight to behold. I'd never paid any attention to Abby's body, not until she was pressed up against me on that rooftop in January and I was suddenly very aware that my best friend was, in fact, a *female* best friend. Abby is magnificently curvy, and when she's pregnant, all of those…assets…are only going to be more prominent.

Will she glow? She'll be so excited. It'll be nine long months of joyous anticipation. I can't wait to share that with her. I can't wait to do the midnight ice-cream runs and to rub her back when it's sore. I can't wait to set up a crib with her and to go shopping for stupid baby things I won't know how to use. In fact, now that I really think about it, I'm kind of envious that I'll just be a casual bystander—

And that's when my brother's stupid pep talk starts to make sense.

She's going to get pregnant no matter what. I really think she needs you, Marcus.

And what was that nonsense fucking sports metaphor?

Sometimes life throws a curveball, and instead of ducking to get out of the way of it, you can lift your hands up and catch it, you know?

I fumble for my phone and send him a text.

Were you seriously trying to suggest I donate sperm to Abby?

I'm feeling odd—slightly flushed with a bizarre mix of panic and excitement that doesn't make any sense. I stare at my phone, but of course Luca doesn't respond immediately. I pick up the sandwich, but I'm no longer hungry. No interest in coffee, either. Maybe I've had too much caffeine already today because the jitters are setting in.

Just as I step off the elevator into the office at 3:58 p.m., my phone sounds.

Luca: Jesus Christ, Marcus. You're supposed to be the smart twin. Did you only just figure this out? You might think you're allergic to commitment, but you've always loved kids. And as for Abby, why do you think she asked me, idiot? Do you think maybe it had something to do with the fact that I'm your identical twin?

I stop walking and stare at the text, because he's making a damned good point. It's the obvious question, sure, but it's one I haven't even thought to consider until right this very minute. Why *didn't* Abby ask me in the first place?

"Good, you're back." I look up in time to see Jess stick her head out of the boardroom and motion for me to hurry up. "Time is money, Marcus!"

"Just…give me a minute…" I say weakly.

I look back down at Luca's message on my phone, and then back up at Jess, who's staring at me now through a narrowed gaze.

I need to really, really think this through, and now just isn't the time. Maybe later, when the office is quiet, I can process these thoughts and figure out if I should talk to Abby. For now, though, my mind is running a million miles an hour.

Just how quickly is she going to go ahead with this sperm bank guy?

Do I even have time to think about this, or do I need to talk to her right fucking now, before it's too late?

Could I really just donate sperm to her, and pretend to her kid that I'm just an uncle? Or is this a chance for me to be a *real* father, on my own terms?

When did Luca get so smart? Is this Austin's influence?

I sigh and slip my phone into my suit jacket, then step into the meeting and pretend to pay attention as my partners plan our yearly strategy workshop.

But as soon as the meeting is over, I go into my office and close the door. Staring out the window at the street below, I start to ask myself hard questions I never thought I'd want to know the answers to.

Because maybe there's a way I can help Abby fulfill *her* dream…and at the same time fulfill a brand new dream of my own.

CHAPTER SIX

Abby

I'M CURLED UP on the sofa when I hear Marcus open the front door. I finished a livestream a few hours ago, then joined in for an online quest with some gamer friends. My hands are tired and my eyes are bleary, but I can't sleep yet, so I've curled up on the sofa to watch some late-night TV.

Something about this entire day has felt off to me. It's not unlike Marcus to work really late or even to head out after work for a drink or dinner, but he always texts me to let me know. Tonight was my turn to cook, and unlike Marcus, I actually *do* cook. Before I went live tonight, I texted him to see where he was, and he didn't even reply. All of this oddness has happened on the back of the abrupt end to our instant-message conversation earlier, so I can't shake the feeling that he's upset with me, even though I don't really understand why that would be the case.

"You're still up." He stops at the door to hang up his coat and to slip off his shoes. "How'd the livestream go?"

"It went great," I say as lightly as I can. "I wasn't sure if you were coming home so I saved you some stir-fry."

"Thanks," he says. I turn back to glance at him, and

that's when I notice that he's still in his suit but not carrying his laptop. When he leaves his computer at the office, he's usually been on a date, and I'm immediately annoyed. I've spent the evening worried that he's angry with me for some reason, and he's been out on a date but couldn't be bothered to let me know? The annoyance ramps up further when Marcus turns toward the hallway that leads to his study and his bedroom, and for a moment, I think he's not even going to say good-night.

I sigh and turn my attention back to the television, but I'm startled when he says softly, "Abs?"

He didn't go into his room at all—in fact, he's now standing right behind me. I'm frowning as I turn back to face him again.

"Yeah?" I say a little defensively, but then I notice the bags under his eyes and the pinched look on his face. He's been working so hard lately, and that stupid message from Warwick must be playing on his mind, too.

"Are you okay?" I ask, just as he blurts, "Why didn't you ask me?"

"Ask you to…"

"Help you have a baby," Marcus says stiffly, then he repeats, "You asked Luca. You're looking at fucking strangers on the internet. I'm right here, Abby. Why didn't you ask me?"

"I… We're…" I clear my throat, then whisper, "We're just too close, Marcus."

"You're close with Luca, too."

"Not like I am with you."

"Did you not want *me* to be…" He breaks off, uncharacteristically struggling to express himself. But he doesn't need to finish the question, because I know what he's asking.

Did I not want him to be the father of my baby?

All of my anger drains away. I climb up onto my knees on the sofa so that I don't have to stare all the way up at him. Our gazes lock.

"Of course that's not it. It just didn't seem fair to ask you, and I was pretty sure you'd say no, anyway." I did consider asking him for about *five frigging seconds,* until I remembered what it was like between us in the weeks after The Kiss, when everything felt stilted and awkward and how utterly miserable I was at the thought that I might have damaged the most important relationship in my life. "I just didn't want to ask too much of you and risk making things awkward between us…" I say. His brow furrows, until I add very carefully, *"Again."*

His expression clears as understanding dawns. Marcus nods curtly, then turns as if he's going back to his room. But he doesn't leave; he just freezes where he is. He's only a foot or two from me but he's facing away, staring at the ground.

"Marcus?" I prompt uncertainly. His shoulders are locked stiff, and he's still staring down at the floor. My heart pounds against the wall of my chest as I stare at his back.

"I'm open to the idea," he murmurs. "I need a little time to think it through. When do you need to decide about the donor?"

"I have an appointment next week. At the fertility clinic," I croak.

"What day?"

"Wednesday."

"Okay. We'll talk more before then."

He disappears from view, and I sink back onto the sofa as I hear his bedroom door quietly close behind him.

IT'S RARE FOR Marcus and I to go more than a day without talking. If I'm not out of bed before he leaves for work, we almost always catch up in the evening. Even if we do miss each other in person, we're forever chatting on IM or text.

Friday blurs past me, and soon it's the weekend, and we've all but disconnected. We smile carefully at each other when we pass in the living areas. He doesn't message me on our IM app. He doesn't text me. He's coming home insanely late every night.

I know he has a company meeting next week, and that means he'll be running sessions and workshops with his entire team—all of the marketing and sales staff from his company will be looking for him to set a vision for the coming year. I know that means a lot of planning for him. Even so, when the weekend comes and he's out all day, too, I know he'd at least be working from home if he wasn't thinking about a decision that might completely change our lives.

I'm quite busy myself. I often do work on weekends, even if it's just reviewing my freelancer's proposed social media schedule or replying to the fan mail she's flagged as positive, but I've never worked as hard as I'm working right now. I'm putting every ounce of energy I have into occupying all of my thoughts. It's the only way I can stop my hopes from soaring too high, because this is pretty much a no-brainer for me. If Marcus does offer to help me have a baby, I know I'll accept. He's everything I could ever have wanted for the father of my child, and with our purely platonic relationship, a donor arrangement with Marcus feels almost as safe as our friendship itself.

MY APPOINTMENT AT the fertility clinic is coming at me like a steam train now. It's Tuesday morning, and Marcus was long gone before I even got out of bed today—I didn't even hear him leave.

He's leaving this decision to the last minute and I'm increasingly convinced that's not a good sign. But when I log into the IM system at lunchtime, he messages me right away.

Marcus: You free tonight?

My mouth is suddenly dry.

Abby: Gym until seven.

Marcus knows my schedule as well as I do, so I'm not even sure why he asked.

Marcus: Okay, let's chat after.

I draw in a sharp breath, hold it, then exhale steadily, trying to slow my suddenly pounding heart rate.

Abby: Are we talking about what I think we're talking about?

Marcus: Yeah, let's talk. It's my turn to cook, right?

Abby: Sure. But promise me you aren't actually going to cook.

Marcus: I was going to make you pasta!

Abby: I'm still trying to recover from the last time you made me pasta. Seriously, who puts mayonnaise in bolognese sauce?

Marcus: I was trying to be creative.

Abby: By all means, Marcus Ross, be creative. Just funnel all of your creativity into ordering up food that someone else has cooked for you.

Marcus: Alfino's, it is. See you tonight.

I sigh and minimize the chat window, but then pause. Alfino's is the Italian restaurant fifteen floors below our apartment that *is far too fancy* to offer takeout dishes for their customers—except for Marcus, who managed to sweet-talk the sixty-four-year-old *nonna* who owns the place. I asked her for takeout, too, once, and despite the fact that he and I eat there regularly and I'm sure she knows we live together, the *nonna* acted like I'd insulted her and reminded me forcibly that they are a "fine dining establishment, not a takeout."

Typical Marcus.

He doesn't abuse the privilege, but there is one occasion when Marcus always uses his take-out superpowers. He hasn't had much time for dating this year, but last year was a whole other story. When he broke up with those women, he always brought Alfino's home.

I was curious, and although I felt pretty bad about it, I did eavesdrop on those conversations a few times.

That's why I know what his script is.

He sits them down at the dining room table and delivers a very gentle *Honestly, it's not you, it's me—I did tell you I wasn't interested in anything serious.* He's charming and gentle about it, and Alfino's is apparently his consolation prize. And good call, too. If someone was going to dump me, I probably wouldn't care if they did it over pasta like that.

But now, my heart sinks, all the way to my toes.

Maybe this conversation isn't going to go the way I hoped it would if Marcus is already planning on consoling me with gourmet food. I glance at the clock on my desk and sigh—2:15 p.m.

It's going to be a long day.

THE APARTMENT I share with Marcus is right on the edge of Tribeca, just a few blocks from his office in the Financial District. I told him he was showing off when he moved into this place three years ago. He told me the second bedroom was mine if I ever needed it. I was completely wrapped up in Roger at the time and I laughed at him. Three months later I moved in "for a few weeks." Two months after that, he asked me to move in permanently.

I love living with Marcus. Despite our differences, we've found such an easy, comfortable rhythm together. Marcus has always understood when I need space and when I need company.

It's also handy that the apartment happens to be located within a short subway ride or even walking distance of just about every place I regularly visit. Even the gym where Jess, Izzy and I work out is a block away.

Unfortunately for me tonight, that one-block walk from the gym after my Pilates class is exactly enough time for me to work myself up into a bundle of nerves, and by the time I walk in the apartment door, I have butterflies in my tummy and my mouth is dry. It doesn't help that as I step into the lobby, I can see Marcus setting up the dining room table.

Fancy wine. Loads of Alfino's…far too much food for us to actually finish. He's even laid out the good dinner set and a formal cutlery arrangement.

"Marcus," I sigh, and toss my coat onto the rack and dump my shoes on the carpet before I walk toward the table. "You didn't have to go to all of this trouble." I scoop up some bruschetta and take a bite, and groan as the taste hits me. "This stuff is so good."

"It's no trouble," he says.

I don't like the tone of his voice—it's too serious, and I can tell by the way he's staring at me that this conversation is going to be every bit as intense as I feared. Marcus clears his throat. "Please sit down?"

He pulls my chair out for me, and I feel a shiver run down my spine.

I inhale slowly, then exhale, calming myself. My therapist would be proud of the way I'm mastering my breathing right now. Diligent practice is making meditation second nature, and within a few seconds I've cleared the swirling thoughts from my mind. Tears prick at my eyes, and I blink them away furiously.

This is shit. All of this is shit and it's so unfair and now Marcus is going to tell me he can't help me, either.

He passes me my wine.

"Abby," he says very gently. His eye contact is steady and generous—the way it always is, but now his focus is entirely on me, as if whatever I'm about to say is the most important sentence in the history of the world. "Tell me about these health issues. I want to understand."

I shiver and pull my hoodie tighter around myself. There's an awful lump in my throat—the shape of the unspoken hopes and dreams that might just choke me. "Do you remember my mom and dad tried to have another kid?"

"A little."

"Mom had fertility issues from a really young age. They were lucky even to have me. And when we went back home for your grandfather's funeral, she was hinting about being a grandmother one day and…well, things haven't seemed normal with my periods for a while, but I'd been putting a checkup off. Anyway, I finally went in and had some tests. The doctor said there's no way to be sure, but most likely, my fertility has already started to decline."

"Oh, Abs," Marcus says. "I'm so sorry. Why didn't you tell me?" The sympathy in his gaze and the gentle tone of his voice bring fresh tears to my eyes.

I reach for the wine and down a whole glass. "Oh, no, you don't. You don't get to do that sad face and make me feel all guilty for keeping a secret from you. I'm allowed some privacy, and it's taken me a few weeks to even get my head around it. I *couldn't* have explained this last week. I couldn't even think about it calmly, let alone talk about it."

Marcus nods, and then it's his turn for a gulp of his wine. He sits stiffly, the muscles in his shoulders and neck locked, and as he lowers the wineglass to the table, I see his hand clench into a fist. Then he clears his throat, and the sound is bizarre. I've never seen him so nervous before, and I feel sick.

"I promise I'll understand if you can't do it," I blurt. "It's a huge thing for me to ask of you."

"You didn't ask it of me," he reminds me, then he clears his throat. "And actually, I really..." He pauses, draws in a sharp breath and then meets my gaze. "Abs, I really like the idea of us doing this. Together."

All day I braced myself for a "no," but now that means I'm completely unprepared for the "yes." Marcus is waiting for my reaction. Without breaking off the eye contact, I reach down for my bruschetta and stuff the whole piece of bread into my mouth. My cheeks puff out from the too-large serving of food and it's all I can do to close my jaw enough to chew.

Marcus's eyebrows shoot up, and he laughs unevenly. "Nervous eating?"

When I finally manage to swallow the mammoth mouthful, I blurt, "You mean it? You'll give me sperm so I can have a baby?"

"Uh...kind of."

My stomach drops to my toes and I scowl at him.

"This isn't something you can *half* do."

He does that oddly anxious throat-clearing thing again and says slowly, "I definitely want to do this, Abby. The thing is, I want to ask something of you, too. Because... I don't want to be 'Uncle Marcus.'"

I frown at him.

"You can be whoever-the-fuck-you-*want*-to-be if you're serious about this," I say blankly, but he shakes his head firmly.

"I want to be *Dad*, Abby." I stare at him and try to make sense of what he's said, but I can't attach meaning to the words. I push my bangs back from my eyes and squint at him as he tries to clarify. "Last week you said this would be *your* baby, not Luca's. But I want this to be *our* baby. I want the kid to know who I am."

"Who you are?" I'm still not getting it. I'm trying to keep up with the conversation, but my brain can't quite wrap itself around the enormity of what he's saying. Instead, I narrow my focus down to what I *can* handle. The best part.

Marcus is willing to help me.

He'll give me a baby.

Everything outside of that beautiful realization fades away and a warm flush of excitement runs over me. I'm focused only on how happy I am, until a rational thought surfaces in my brain.

"But *why*?"

"Well, when I first started thinking about it, I liked the idea because *you* want this, and I want you to be happy. I'd do anything for you."

"And I'd do anything for you."

"I know."

"It's just…" *Shut up, Abby. Don't talk him out of it.* But as desperate as I am, I can't, and I *won't*, risk Marcus doing something he regrets here. I take a deep breath and force myself to be a good friend. "I know you love kids. I've seen you at your mom's family picnics—the way you light up when you play with your bazillions of second cousins and their bazillions of offspring. It's just…you've been pretty clear that you *don't* want children of your own. And now you're…

what? You don't just donate sperm, but you actually help me to raise this baby?"

He sighs and reaches for his own wine.

"I did kind of figure that marriage and kids would go together so I just accepted I probably wouldn't have the chance to be a dad. But the more I've thought about it over the last few days, the more I realized how much I *want* this. I get to have a family with someone I care about, but I don't need to trap myself in a miserable marriage to do it. This just feels…right. Natural, once I really thought about it."

Perhaps the very worst part of my find-a-sperm-donor plan was the inevitable moment when I'd have to move out on my own with the baby. That idea is terrifying on so many levels. I don't even have any siblings, so no nieces or nephews, either. I wasn't the kid that babysat for money in my teens—I was the geeky kid who fixed broken computers and helped set up webpages.

In lieu of actual experience with children, I only have book smarts. I've been doing a lot of reading about pregnancy and parenting over the last few years, but it's hardly the same thing. If I'm lucky enough to have a child, I'm going to face a steep learning curve, no matter how many articles from mommy blogs I print off for myself between now and then.

For the last two months, since Dr. King told me about my ovarian reserve, I thought I'd have to master that learning curve all on my own.

And it's not just my inexperience that frightens me when I think about moving out on my own. The drive within me to have a baby is strong, but that doesn't mean I'm not terrified of the responsibility. I've never even been able to keep a boyfriend happy, how am

I supposed to care for a baby, all on my own? What happens if I have a baby and I get depressed again, to the point where I don't ask for help? What happens if I don't even want to get out of bed and that baby needs me to?

I'm fucking *petrified* when I think about motherhood, but I still want a chance at it. I just thought this was going to be one of those things I'd have to do despite the fear. Like moving into my business full-time, since the doctor gave me the news about my fertility I really thought motherhood was something I'd have to do alone, and something I'd have to do *afraid*. But life is just better when I share it with Marcus, and I feel only *relief* and *joy* when I think about sharing the responsibility and the challenges of parenting with him.

"So I'd live here? After?"

"Of course you'd live here." His eyes widen. "Wait, were you going to move out?"

"I figured I'd have to. I can handle my bedroom being a bedroom-slash-studio, but bedroom-slash-studio-slash-nursery is probably pushing it."

Marcus frowns, but then he tilts his head thoughtfully.

"I was thinking eventually we could look for somewhere a little bigger. Something we could find together so it's your place, too—*really* your place—but if you didn't like that idea…"

I nod hastily, because it sounds amazing, but then it really starts to sink in how complicated it might be and I exhale heavily.

"We share everything already, Abby," Marcus points out, instantly picking up on my tension.

"We don't share everything," I correct him automatically. "We share *almost* everything."

And just like that—the humiliation of that night on the rooftop returns to me. I remember the way he'd stared at me in such horror when I made that "be my backup spouse" joke at New Year's. *I could never think of you like that, Abby.* Now I see him shift awkwardly in his seat and I know exactly what he's thinking. He's wondering how to tell me he wants to do this, but not *directly* with me. And that's fine by me, but this conversation is rapidly getting awkward and I'm not sure how to diffuse it.

This. This is why I didn't ask you, Marcus. Awkwardness between us means distance between us and I need you too much to risk that.

"You said you have a fertility clinic already? And an appointment tomorrow?" Marcus asks suddenly.

Is he changing the subject? Maybe he feels as uncomfortable as I do right now. I answer his question with matching caution.

"Yeah…"

"If Luca had said yes, would you have asked him to that appointment?"

"That's right. That's why I asked him last week."

"Well, I'll just come to that appointment, exactly as Luca would have," Marcus says softly. "You know what I'm saying, right?"

I know exactly what he's saying, and he's giving me the answer I *want*, but I'm stung, anyway. I pause to ponder the odd sense of disappointment that's settled in my chest.

This is exactly the kind of feeling that led to The Kiss Which Shall Not Be Named. I felt rejected and hurt and confused. And drunk. The next thing I knew, I was trying to tear his shirt off. I set my wineglass down *very* carefully and decide that's quite enough alcohol for this discussion.

"Good," I say. "That's perfect."

And it is—much better than the alternative…of more of those sizzling kisses, or more of my body pressed up against his, or more of the butterflies that came out of nowhere—

Shut it down, Abby. Don't fuck this up now. This is exactly why I don't let myself think about that kiss. But it's kind of like the universe wants to mock me, because no matter how hard I've tried, I can't *quite* forget how good it was.

I look back to the bruschetta and help myself to another piece.

"Look, there are so many advantages to what I'm proposing," he says, as if he needs to convince me. "We're already used to living together and it works really well—and while it's obviously not a necessity, surely it's a bonus for a kid to have two parents, and two parents who live in the same home, right?"

"I know *you're* not planning on it, but what if you do find someone you want to settle down with? Or what if I do?"

He gives a lopsided smile.

"I can't see me doing something silly like that any time soon, but if you do, we'll still be no worse off. We could always adjust the plan and coparent like separated couples do, but without the antagonism, I guess."

We're best friends. We're already partners, in a way. And we do care for each other—maybe not *that* way—but it's a pretty special kind of relationship nonetheless. We can work together to raise a baby. We can build a family.

Such a beautiful picture forms in my mind that I'm beaming.

"I just think we're on the same page on so many things," Marcus says, visibly relieved by my smile.

"We are," I agree.

"And the things we disagree on, we're in balance. Like…you'll probably have them reading *Harry Potter* when they're three but you'll also want them to have unlimited screen time…"

"And you'll insist they learn a sport or two." I smile softly.

"And you'll be relaxed when they spill their cereal all over the carpet."

"And you'll make sure they actually know how to make a bed."

We laugh, and just like that, we have a shared vision of our future family. This is the kind of effortless communication that only comes from knowing someone better than you know yourself. It's the kind of partnership I always dreamed of for the father of my child.

I guess I'd anticipated there'd be at least a little *more* sex and romantic love than *none whatsoever*, but I can live with that. I feel light inside—hopeful and excited about the future for the first time in weeks.

"I'd support you even if you decide you don't want to do this with me," Marcus says. "But I'm excited about this. I really *want* to do it. If you want me to, that is."

There are countless facets of complication and joy and fear and potential mess that come from this proposal. I wish I could pause this whole situation to consider all the ways things could go wrong—because if

I've already prepared for the worst, I'm never caught off guard.

The problem here is that invisible deadline my body has set. It hangs over my head like a guillotine and there's no way to know how long I have before it's too late.

"You've definitely thought this through?" My voice breaks, and I reach for his forearm and squeeze it, hard. "You *have* to promise me you've thought this through."

"Yes," he says quietly. "I realized pretty quickly that I'd be happy to make this happen for you, but I needed to be sure what role *I* wanted to play here before I discussed it with you. And I *am* sure, Abby. I really am."

We stare at one another for a moment, and I'm trying desperately to assess him and see how deeply he means what he's just said. He pries my fingertips out of his forearm, but flips our hands, so that his rests over mine.

"Abby," he whispers. "I can't tell you how happy it would make me to have a baby with you. I *want* this."

I blink hard and try to keep a grip on my composure. I'm not a weepy sort of girl, but the tears swell and leak and very quickly turn to sobs. I hold a hand up toward Marcus as I try to compose myself, but he walks around the table and crouches beside me. I give him a helpless look, and he pulls me into his arms.

"Abs," he whispers. "Don't cry. It's going to be okay."

"I know," I weep. "I'm just so…grateful."

"So that's a 'yes'?"

"You have no idea how much of a 'yes' that is. *Thank you.*" I'm blubbering now, and I hold my palms up against his cheeks and I stare right into his beautiful blue eyes as I whisper it again. "Thank you so much."

"Jesus, Abby," he laughs softly, but there is a decidedly rough edge to his own voice until he adds, "Don't thank me yet. You have no idea how difficult I'm going to be. I mean—for a start, I'm going to make you stand guard on the other side of the door while I jerk off just so you can feel as awkward as I do."

I laugh, too, this time, and wipe my eyes with the back of my hand. I'm a little embarrassed about my tears, so I try to lighten the mood with a joke, too.

"Yeah, like that'd be the first time I've been in the same place as you while that's happening. We've lived together for two years, remember?"

Marcus grins right back at me. "Your vibrator sounds like a chain saw."

I gasp. "It does not!"

"So you *do* have one?"

"This baby thing doesn't mean you suddenly get to know all of my secrets, you know." I laugh softly, and Marcus suddenly sobers. Still in a half squat beside me, he brushes my bangs back from my face. His gaze is steady on mine, and there's that look again— the one that even Isabel noticed. The fondness in his eyes is undeniable.

I'm so fucking lucky to have this man in my life.

"I mean it, Abby. I'm excited for this, and I'm ready to do it. Are you?"

"I am."

"It's an unconventional arrangement but—"

"So was what I proposed to Luca."

"Yes. I'm going to be there for you every step of the way."

I draw in a deep breath, then smile.

"Okay." My gaze flicks to the table, and the rapidly cooling gourmet food waiting for my attention.

"Abby," Marcus sighs, getting back to his feet. "We were having a moment there. And all you can think about is the tortellini, right?"

"Heaven help you when I'm actually pregnant."

Marcus sinks back into his chair, a broad grin on his face. "I've been thinking about that all weekend."

"And as baby-daddy, you'll need to do the midnight ice-cream and pickles run."

"I thought about that, too. And we both know I'd have been doing that even if I *wasn't* the baby-daddy," he says wryly. "Speaking of that original scenario, what *was* your plan, before Luca made you tell me? When were you going to clue me in?"

"I was going to tell you when I could talk about it without getting upset."

His gaze drifts downward for just a moment, then he changes the subject. "They didn't have the lobster bisque tonight."

"The bruschetta is even better."

"I got tiramisu *and* gelato for dessert. I was hoping we'd be celebrating."

Double dessert? I smile so hard my cheeks ache. "What on earth did I do to deserve you, Marcus Ross?"

He winks at me and starts serving out the food.

"Just lucky, I guess."

CHAPTER SEVEN

Abby

I SPEND THE next twelve hours doing a mental happy dance at the surprise turn my journey to parenthood has taken. I float through the morning on a tide of pure elation, sitting at my desk as if I'm working, but the only thing I *work* on is my baby binder.

Yes, I have a binder of information about parenting already prepared for a situation like this. In fact, I probably need to split it into two volumes soon. It's already bursting at the seams and I know that's only going to get worse over the next few months.

I started reading about parenthood a few years back, mostly on blogs and parenting sites, saving the URLs into a bookmark folder called One Day. At the time, I was just emerging from the dark period after my breakup with Roger, and having a baby seemed like a distant dream. Collecting those pages started out as a way to focus on a positive future, and I eventually felt comforted by the idea that when I did finally find Mr. Perfect and we were ready to start our family, I'd at least be prepared.

I had fantasies of snuggling up on a couch, holding my iPad. I'd be clicking through the URLs while my husband read over my shoulder as he rubbed my swollen belly and marveled at how lucky he was to have a wife with such forethought.

Alas, the One Day folder soon became a little unruly and I needed a way to manage my lists, too. Lists of names, lists of other things to research, lists of things I might need to buy…stuff like that. I could tell it was going to be difficult to keep track of all of that information in digital form, so I soon decided it would be easier for future husband and me to work from printed pages.

So one rainy Sunday morning, I stayed in my pajamas, sent a crap load of pages to my printer and set up the binder. I carefully decorated tabs for Pregnancy and Childbirth, Handling a Newborn, Terrible Toddlers and The Preschool Years. Marcus knocked on my door and asked if I wanted a coffee, and when he saw the chaos of printed pages and highlighters and Post-its in my room, he came in to help. I'm sure organizing a binder full of information for a purely hypothetical pregnancy didn't entirely make sense to Mr. Wing-His-Way-Through-Life, but that didn't matter one bit. He sat with me for hours, punching holes in printed pages for our two-person production line…all so I could feel more in control of my life.

In the last two months since I found out about my fertility issues, I've added tabs for the practical matters I had never even thought to worry about back when I was just daydreaming about hypothetical babies with rosy cheeks and adorable little wrinkles on their thighs. Now I have tabs for Selecting a Preschool Program, Elementary Schools and Zoning, Surviving Adolescence and, probably the scariest tab of all, Resources for Perinatal or Postpartum Depression.

I prepare for every eventuality because it makes me feel like I'm in control of my life. Sometimes, though, my hyperorganization has the opposite effect. It rubs potential problems right in my face and reminds me that no matter how organized I am, living life means accepting a certain amount of chaos and there's nothing at all I can do about that.

I am capable. I am resilient. I am resourceful. I am not alone. Whatever is coming, I'll find a way to manage it, and anyway, now Marcus will be my partner in this and we'll navigate it together.

It's time to refocus my thoughts on something positive. Half an hour later, I've amassed quite the collection of photos of cute baby clothes. I feel better about my momentary anxiety earlier. I open my chat client and send a picture of a newborn in a jumpsuit styled like a tuxedo.

Abby: For Marcus Junior?

He doesn't respond for almost forty minutes, by which time I've given up on my bookmark hunt and I'm death-glaring at the screen, waiting for his reply.

He never takes this long to write back. He's always in front of his computer or his phone—usually both, given the man can multitask like a work-at-home mother with a dozen young children. I remember watching him in awe one time as we ate breakfast and he was juggling his laptop, iPad and phone—preparing a presentation, handling a staff emergency *and* reading his emails, somehow all at once.

When the indicator that Marcus is typing finally flashes up, panic breaks through and I drop my hands onto the keyboard.

Abby: It's okay if you've changed your mind.

The indicator disappears, then returns. I hold my breath until his reply pops up.

Marcus: Of course I haven't. Marcus Junior is going to rock that suit. But given who his mother is, he'll probably wear it to a kindergarten dress-up party and tell the girls he's Joss Whedon accepting his Oscar.

Abby: Joss Whedon has never won an Oscar. Which tells you everything you need to know about how broken the industry is, but that's beside the point. Why did it take you an hour to reply if you haven't changed your mind? It's okay. Tell me. I can take it.

Marcus: Abby. What the hell?

Abby: You can't even commit to a relationship, Marcus. How are you going to handle becoming a dad?

I hit Send on the message, then freeze. Oh, fuck it, that was so much harsher than I meant it to be. I know I can't delete it, but I frantically mash the delete button, anyway, and then I try to backpedal.

Abby: I'm sorry. I didn't mean it like that sounded.

The pause while I wait for him to reply is agonizing. While he's a pretty resilient sort of guy, I've clearly upset him. He deserves so much better than that, especially from me.

Abby: Marcus. I'm so sorry.

He replies immediately this time.

Marcus: Actually, Abigail, if you really think about it, I think you'll find there's at least one relationship I've been committed to for my entire life.

There's a pause, then:

Marcus: As trying as it may be at times.

Another pause, and he adds:

Marcus: Take THIS very moment, for example.

My face feels hot, and tears prick at my eyes. I blink them away and rest my hands on the keyboard for a moment, forcing myself to cool down before I reply.

Abby: Forgive me? I'm freaked out. I'm scared I'm just asking too much of you.

Marcus: If you're worried I'm not committed, you should have seen the schedule acrobatics I had to do to free myself up for the appointment this afternoon. By the way, what day is it today?

I wipe away a tear and frown at the screen for a moment before replying.

Abby: Wednesday.

Marcus: And…

Ah. That's right…

Abby: Your company meeting is on, isn't it?

Marcus: There it is. I had my phone on silent and my IM was muted because I've been doing a presentation. I'm sure my entire senior staff would have enjoyed the cute baby in the tux, too, if I'd let them see it, but it might have required an explanation I'm not really sure we're ready to give, especially to Paul and Jess, who were sitting on either side of me at the time.

Abby: I thought you were having second thoughts. It feels too good to be true.

Marcus: Well, now you've really offended me. Do you know me at all? Because if you did, you'd know I would never have gotten your hopes up if there was any doubt in my mind about this.

A soft smile creeps over my face. Marcus has his flaws, but when it comes to *me*, he's more than proven the bond between us. He has never, ever let me down, not in any way, big or even small.

Abby: I'm really sorry, Marcus.

Marcus: There's a lot riding on this for you, I get it. But you doubt me again and I'm going to punish you. Maybe I'll pry off the control panel to the heat and take it with me when I leave for work. And winter is coming, Abby.

Abby: That's just cruel!

Marcus: I never make empty promises. Not even about heating control panels.

Abby: I know. I'm sorry.

Marcus: I'll meet you at the clinic this afternoon, okay?

Abby: Okay :)

CHAPTER EIGHT

Marcus

LESS THAN TWENTY-FOUR hours after talking to Abby about a potential baby, I'm sitting beside her in the waiting room of a fertility clinic while she picks at the lime-green polish on her fingernails and makes a supremely irritating clucking noise with her tongue. She's a ball of anxiety, and if she's making any attempt to hide it, she's failing miserably.

"Abs," I murmur, touching her shoulder gently. She looks at me. "Chill out, okay?"

"I'm chill. I'm so chill I'm icy," she assures me, but her eyes are wild. I pull her close and squeeze my arm around her shoulders, then kiss her hair gently.

"Liar," I murmur, and she swallows and goes right back to picking her nails.

This appointment came at the worst possible time for me—falling on the one week of the year when all our senior staff are locked away for our company meeting. Paul and Jess are workshopping plans for next year with their executive teams this afternoon, which is what I'm supposed to be doing, too. Instead, my team is sitting back at the office twiddling their thumbs while I'm here with Abby.

To make up the time we've lost, I had to get the west coast staff to postpone their return by a day, which not only cost the company a fortune in hastily rescheduled flights and hotel bookings, it didn't exactly earn me goodwill with the staff or, apparently, their families.

There's an email in my in-box from Jess which has no body—just the subject line: *What the actual fuck do you think you're doing?* And while we are all partners, she *is* the CEO. I'm accountable to her, particularly for the budget. That conversation is going to be hell.

Pissing off Jess to be here for Abby?

Worth it.

Pissing off my entire staff to be here for Abby?

Definitely worth it.

I'm completely sure about this decision—I agonized about it over the weekend, trying to talk myself *into* being uncomfortable with it, but I couldn't. I just know that Abby is going to make a great mother, and that whatever else happens in our lives over the coming decades, we have enough of a proven track record between us that we will always care for each other and the kid.

Maybe I'm not husband material, but I'll be a good dad—I'll make sure of it. Between Warwick and my stepfather, Jack, I've been on the receiving end of the best and worst parenting has to offer, and I'll use all of those experiences to raise our kid right.

I'm already daydreaming about playing catch with my son or daughter in the park, or leaving work early to pick them up from preschool so we can go to the library for Storytime. I picture a scrappy toddler with Abby's big eyes and my curls, and there's an incredible hopefulness inside me. I'm actually grateful to

Abby, because I just hadn't realized how much I *want* to be a dad.

There is more riding on this for Abby than there is for me, though, so I need to just let this play out so she can see how *excited* I am to be doing this with her. If she needs reassurance, I can give that to her. I take her hand and squeeze it.

"Abby. Seriously. I'm not going anywhere. I won't let you down."

"What if we try this and it doesn't work? Mom and Dad tried for years to have another baby after me and they never even came close. I'm already five years older than Mom was when she had me."

Apparently, Abby's anxiety is not just about my role here. "Anything could happen," I admit reluctantly. "But, Abs—at least we're *going* to try, right?"

"Abigail Herbert?" a voice calls from the other side of the waiting room, and the color drains from Abby's face.

"Come on, Abs," I say gently. I hold her hand as she rises, and we walk toward the doctor. He's younger than I expected, not much older than Abby and me, and the reading glasses he wears perched on the end of his nose look like something he might have borrowed from his grandfather.

"Hello, Abigail. I'm Dr. Vualez—but please call me Manny. It's lovely to meet you."

"Marcus Ross," I say quietly, and I release Abby's hand long enough only to shake the doctor's.

"Welcome, Marcus. Come on through."

"I'VE REVIEWED DR. KING'S NOTES, and I do share her concerns about your testing results, Abby. Unfortunately, fertility isn't always the kind of thing we can predict with certainty. I've had women with worse testing results fall pregnant on the first cycle, but I've seen far less favorable outcomes, as well."

"I know," Abby says quietly. "I've been Googling."

"Google is a useful tool, but also a dangerous one. So go ahead and do your own research as we go through the process, but please remember—I did go to a slightly better medical school than Dr. Google, so if you have questions, always ask me directly." Abby laughs softly and nods. "So, you're here to talk options?"

"Actually." Abby glances at me, and I try to offer her a reassuring smile. "I've already settled on an option. Marcus and I want to have a baby together."

"So, you'll be Abby's sperm donor?"

I shake my head. "No, we're going to parent together. We live together already."

"Ah, sorry—I misunderstood—that wasn't in the referral," Manny says, and he reaches for a pen and scrawls a note on the folder on his desk. "So, how long have you been trying for?"

Abby winces. "Oh, no—it's not like that, either. We're here to talk about artificial insemination. We're just roommates—but we want to have a baby together."

For some reason, that stings and I clarify. "Well, we're *more* than roommates. We've been best friends since we were born."

"But you're not..."

"No," Abby says firmly, and Manny holds his hands up.

"Okay," he says. "Got it now, sorry. Well, let me tell you a bit about AI. If you're both sure this is how you want to proceed, the first step is a round of sexual health checks. Then we strongly suggest our known donors to undergo a series of counseling sessions and complete a donor agreement. That can take a while, so as a first step, you can find a therapist together, but you should each engage your own attorney to set up negotiations."

"Wait, we don't need that," I interrupt. "Seriously, I'm not actually *donating* anything. Abby and I are a couple, just not a romantic one. We need help with the mechanics of the conception, that's all."

The doctor hesitates a moment, then he slides his reading glasses from his nose and drops them onto the desk.

"Look, there are all kinds of variables here that you probably haven't even thought to discuss. I've seen known-donor arrangements fall through in counseling over the smallest things—like whether or not to use a pacifier or how to decorate a nursery. And then there are the big-ticket items you need to negotiate— have you even talked about religion? Whether to breast- feed? How you'll explain the arrangement to a potential child? If this is all discussed in a formal, careful way before conception, everything is easier down the track."

"I can see why that's ideal, but…" Abby frowns. "Isn't time of the essence in my case?"

"Potentially, yes," the doctor concedes. "But you can still be smart about it."

"Well, what if we were a regular couple and I might have limited time and we wanted to get started quick- smart. What would you say to us?"

Manny gives her a wry look. "Go away, have intercourse every second day for the next six months and come back and see me if it didn't work."

Abby grimaces. "Yeah, okay. I see the problem."

"Wait," I interrupt. "Every *second* day? Is that how often you'd do the insemination?" I imagine scheduling a repeating calendar entry for *masturbate for Abby* and wonder if it's time to *unshare* my calendar with Isaac, but then the doctor shakes his head.

"No, I'd monitor Abby's cycle for a month or two, likely use some medication to support ovulation and then we'd do the insemination at the optimal time."

"So what if we decide *not* to have the counseling and we did just skip the lawyer stuff," Abby says cautiously. "How soon could we start?"

The doctor hesitates, then he glances at the paperwork again.

"Well, if we do the sexual health checks today and that's all fine, the next step is to take a sperm sample and we conduct a test freeze. Then, after we've confirmed the sperm is adequate and freezes and thaws well, we take further samples which we do recommend are quarantined for six months before—"

"Six months?" Abby gasps, and Manny nods.

"You can choose to waive that, Abigail. But again, it's strongly recommended that you don't—there are some screening tests which should be repeated after an interval before we utilize any sample of sperm—"

Abby reaches across and grabs my hand. She squeezes it hard.

"I don't want to wait six months," she says fiercely, directing the words not at the doctor but at me. "I *can't* wait six months. I know you're fine. I know *we* are fine."

"Okay, Abs," I say softly. "We'll figure this out."

"If—" Manny sighs "—for argument's sake, you do opt to ignore my advice on both the counseling, the legal agreement *and* the sperm quarantine…then we could likely start within a few cycles."

Abby and I share a glance. We hadn't discussed it, but apparently neither one of us was expecting a significant wait before we could get started. I know we're both thinking exactly the same thing, but it's Abby who voices the unspoken question.

"Can we just do this at home? Ourselves?" she asks.

"Artificial insemination?" Manny hesitates. "Look, you couldn't do any harm trying provided you've both had clear sexual health reviews, but your chances of success would be lower. Even just based on your age, there's only a ten to fifteen percent chance of it working on each cycle here in the clinic, even with our sterile conditions and with sperm-washing and…if I do say so myself, my well-practiced technique with applying the sperm. I know the formalities beforehand seem like a big commitment, but—"

"We could just have sex," Abby blurts. She's staring at the floor as a flush rises in her cheeks. My mouth falls open. Abby flushes harder and continues to avoid my gaze as she mutters, "We could make it work, somehow."

The silence that fills the room is positively stifling. I find myself desperately trying to think of something to say—but the words that leave my mouth only make things worse.

"The old-fashioned way might make things simpler?" I say, but the words come out of my mouth as a high-pitched question, and Abby's flushed face turns a shade much closer to purple. She finally meets my gaze for a split second, then she groans and shakes her head.

"God, I can't believe I just said that. I'm so sorry, Marcus."

I clear my throat...once, twice and then a third time before it finally works.

"Hey," I say softly. "It's not a stupid idea. I was just...shocked for a minute there." I glance toward Manny. "Would, ah, would the odds be better, Doc?"

"It's impossible to say accurately. But *assuming* your sperm is healthy and you time it right, intercourse generally means a fifteen to twenty percent chance of conception per cycle."

"That's *all*?" I frown, and the doctor nods.

"It's quite normal for it to take up to twelve months to achieve a pregnancy even in young, very fertile couples."

Abby exhales heavily, then rubs at her eyes.

"Okay," she says, her voice totally flat. "It was a silly idea, anyway. It wouldn't work."

I honestly don't know how I feel about this, but it's surely worth discussing. "Twenty percent isn't a lot, but it's double the chance. And this could save us months of counseling and freezing and quarantining, not to mention the cost."

We haven't talked money yet, but I'm assuming this is going to be fucking expensive, and I *know* we'll end up squabbling over splitting it. Abby is fiercely, ferociously independent. When she first moved in with me, she had so much going on I didn't want her to even think about contributing anything financially to our living costs. When I refused to take her money, she found out how much my neighbor pays in rent and utilities, and half of that amount started appearing in my account each week.

"It might save us time, but it won't work, anyway, because it's *us*," she hisses through a forced smile, and I survey the crimson flush of her cheeks and the brightness of her eyes. This is uncomfortable for both of us, but now that I'm past the initial shock, I definitely don't *hate* the idea. Looking at Abby, I have a sneaking suspicion that *she* doesn't hate it, either.

"We kissed once," I remind her quietly.

"And we've spent almost a year now trying not to talk about it," Abby mutters.

"Uh, I think you two probably need to discuss this between *yourselves*, then maybe come on back and see me," Manny says, and given he literally spends his days handling infertility and body fluids, he's clearly uncomfortable with the turn our conversation has taken. "Once could be enough, of course, but…whatever route you go down, you'd probably want to cover your bases, so for the week Abby's ovulating, I'd recommend intercourse or insemination every second day. And— Abigail, particularly if you're going to rush this, you really should start a folic acid and vitamin D supplement immediately."

"I've been on one since my appointment with Dr. King."

"Excellent. Well, good luck with your decisions." His tone suggests we're doomed, anyway, and he's ready to wash his hands of us. "Are we still doing the sexual health checkup today?"

Abby and I both nod. We're taken separately into

nurses' cubicles, but we both finish at the exact same time and end up stepping back in the hallway together. We walk out of the clinic in stiff, uncomfortable silence. As soon as we're on the street, she turns to me and thumps me, *hard*, in the arm.

"Ow!" I protest. "What was that for?"

"Simpler?" she says incredulously. "What the fuck about *that* would be simpler?"

"First, it was *your* idea. And second, I'm sure we could make it work." I shrug.

"Even if we *could* 'make it work,'" she snaps, making the air quotes beside her face with a fierce motion, "it would inevitably ruin our friendship. How the fuck could we come back from *that*? It would change everything."

She's freaking out, so I nudge her and tease, "Are you worried if I let my magic penis near you, you'll fall in love with me?"

"Marcus, quit being a dick," Abby snaps, and I'd make a pun about her word choice except that she clenches her hands into fists against her temples. "God, maybe this is all too complicated."

I sigh and pull her into my arms. She's stiff against me for a moment, but as I rub between her shoulder blades, she slumps into me and presses her forehead into my chest.

"It's a bit more involved than we'd expected. It's just a hurdle, right? Since parenting is going to be *full* of complications, we can't let this deter us. It's just practice for the day Abby Junior flounces out from her room and tells us she wants to quit high school and go to LA to audition for a reality TV show."

Abby laughs weakly. "But did you hear what they want us to do? Six *months'* sperm quarantine?"

"It's all of the counseling and legal stuff that got me." I shake my head. "They obviously aren't used to dealing with high-functioning friendships like ours."

"We could just turkey-baster it." Abby pulls away from me, assessing my reaction. I blink.

"Turkey baster?"

"I'm pretty sure I saw someone get inseminated with a turkey baster in a movie once," she says faintly, and I laugh.

"An *actual* turkey baster?"

"I think so. I'm sure Dr. Google could tell us how to get the job done since Dr. Vualez wasn't much help."

"You heard the statistics."

"The statistics weren't good for *any* option." Frustrated, Abby swipes at her eyes. "I've left this too late. I'm never going to be a mom."

"Bullshit," I say firmly, and I catch her shoulders and turn her back toward me. "Abby, we're going to make this happen one way or another. Even if *all else* fails, there are plenty of other options, and we're in this together, okay?" We stand in silence for a moment, then I ask her softly, "How long until you're due to ovulate?"

She groans, and the flush returns.

"I can't believe I have to talk about *this* with you now."

I laugh. "I can tell when your period is coming, so I could probably figure it out myself." She glares at me, and I give an exaggerated wince as I tease, "Soon, then?"

"Haha, smart-ass. I'd be ovulating—" She pauses, then frowns. "I'm not really sure. I'll have to do some research. But…if it's a few weeks into my cycle, it would be soon."

"Soon? Like next week?" I release her shoulders as my palms start to sweat.

"I'm not sure. Maybe."

"Go think about it, Abs. Think it all through, and then we can talk about it for a few weeks. Try whatever we decide *next* cycle. One month isn't going to hurt, surely."

"Yeah. Who knows how long those sexual health checks will take, anyway, right? Be days at least, probably weeks. Maybe months."

I try but fail to suppress my smile. "*Months*, Abs? Really? You think it takes months to do an STI check?"

"I don't know," she mutters, flushing harder now. "Everything else in that clinic seems to take an inordinate amount of time. I waited weeks for an emergency appointment just to be told it will be months of stuffing around before they can even try to help me? That's just cruel."

"It doesn't even *matter* when we get the all clear. Let's not pressure ourselves. We'll take our time and think about it."

Abby will need to work this through in her mind for a while. She'll consider it from every angle, and for something *this* big, that's going to take time.

"We can each do some soul-searching and figure out what the right option is?" Abby says now.

"Exactly," I say quietly. Her gaze flits around, like she can't quite meet my eye again. I know what that means—she's not saying the words, but regardless, I'm hearing loud and clear that she needs space. I step away from her and murmur, "I better get back to the office."

"Okay. Thanks for coming with me."

"You okay?"

"Yeah." She steps toward me and kisses my cheek; then, as she sinks onto her heels, gives me a cheeky grin. "Don't think that was me coming on to you, by the way."

I laugh and try to return the joke.

"Go home and think about having sex with me."

"Ew," she says, and she shudders dramatically. Is she joking? I can't tell. I peer at her.

"You stroke my ego too much sometimes."

"Maybe if I imagine you're Ryan Gosling…" she says, but gags, anyway. "Nope, even that didn't work."

"Just a reminder, I'll be home late tonight. I'm taking the team out for dinner." Isaac is probably on the phone right now, trying to make a booking for us all. And this bill is coming out of my pocket, not the company's. It's a *please don't hate me for being a shitty boss* gesture.

"Okay."

"And I won't be on IM this afternoon, or tomorrow actually. I'm still in workshops."

"Okay."

"But I'll keep my phone on silent, so if you want to text me—"

"Marcus, I'm fine. Go to work."

I take a few steps away, then glance back at her again and catch her frowning after me.

"Abs," I say softly. "Think about it, but don't *over-*think it. Promise me."

She sighs, then gives me a weak little wave as she says, "Okay. Have a good day."

CHAPTER NINE

Abby

I'M IN A blind panic as I catch the train back to our apartment. Google confirms that my likely ovulation date *is* over the weekend.

Shit.

We could wait a month like Marcus suggested, but I don't want to—not now that I finally have an option for falling pregnant. It could be too late already, so it seems foolish not to start trying straightaway. But if we are going to start this month, there really isn't a lot of time to consider our options.

In one sense, that's absolutely fine, because there are only three possibilities.

One, we jump into bed together.

Two, we figure out some clinical way to do it at home, and get it done with as little emotional risk as possible. Assuming it eventually works.

Three, we wait and do it properly through the clinic—counseling and attorneys and waiting periods and all. Although the nurse had passed me the financial information on the way out, and even at a glance, the number of zeroes involved made my eyes water. I *knew* this was going to be expensive—I've been researching this clinic since my doctor referred me here all of those weeks ago. Even so, facing the actual figures is shocking. There's an eighteen-month waiting period with my insurer for fertility treatments, but I only thought to *get* the coverage after I got the test results, so there's still a long wait ahead. I can afford to start the process myself in the meantime—but unless I dip into my 401k, my savings will be history.

My palms start to sweat, and as I wipe them on my jeans, I notice they are trembling. Things are going so well for me with my business at the moment, but it's not like I have a guaranteed income. The industry changes so fast and so often, ever since I left my last job I've always been careful to keep a healthy buffer of savings in case my income drops.

The thought of wiping out that buffer just to *get* pregnant is sickening, because of course pregnancy is the start of an incredibly expensive journey, not the end of it. There's so much I need to plan for—so much I need to consider.

Sometimes, that binder in my room feels like overkill. Other times, like *right now*, the preparation I have done feels laughably inadequate.

This is going to be the scariest thing I have ever done. There's just so much to be afraid of, and there's no way I'm going to be able to mitigate *all of the risk*. If we decide to use the clinic, I *know* Marcus will offer to pay, but that is *not happening*. He's already doing enough—he's not paying my medical bills. Not in a million years.

The problem is that all of my options here seem like terrible ideas. Each one is risky in its own way—even the clinic, which aside from the risk of nearly bank-rupting me, also brings a risk that it will take too long and whatever window I have for a baby might close in the meantime.

On the seat opposite me, a harried woman is wrangling an adorable infant *and* a screaming toddler. Most people in this subway car are probably irritated right now, given the dirty looks a few are casting her way, but all I feel watching that scene play out is a sharp sense of envy. The woman lifts the newborn onto her shoulder and scoops the toddler up with her other arm, cuddling him close, too. The toddler's shrieks gradually fade until he gives his mother a sleepy, grumpy look. She kisses his cheek, then whispers something with a gentle smile. The toddler sighs and nestles against her shoulder. Only a few seconds pass before his eyes drift closed.

That woman's arms are literally full, but judging by the contented smile on her face, so is her heart. I want to know what that feels like, and I want it with a passion so fierce I'd risk anything to achieve it.

I feel my heart rate kick up a notch again, and I struggle to keep a handle on my impatience. I need to think about this rationally. Sure, the option that gives us the best chance of conceiving quickly is the old-fashioned way, but it's also the scariest.

I want a baby, but I also need to protect what I already have. What if we have sex, and Marcus starts to shut me out? He's my safety net. *He is my person.*

And then there's logistics. Specifically, logistics for Marcus.

I could never see you that way, Abby.

What if he couldn't even get aroused? *Argh*. Now that would be *mortifying*. I've had my share of bad, awkward sex. Even if things with Marcus weren't fireworks and butterflies, I'd survive. In fact, that might even be preferable to the alternative. I mean, what if we did have sex, and it was awesome—how on earth would we go back to being *just friends* after *that*? If that kiss last year was an indicator, there could be chemistry between us, at least for me.

Amazing chemistry.

Impossible-to-forget-no-matter-how-hard-I-try chemistry.

Oh God.

There's a very good reason I don't let myself think about that stupid kiss. There is just too much at stake if things go wrong, especially now.

I start to Google fertility statistics to distract myself, but a text from Marcus arrives.

Marcus: Stop it.

Abby: Stop what?

Marcus: Overthinking it. Whatever you decide, it's going to be fine.

Abby: Whatever I decide? You get a say in this, too.

Marcus: Your body, your choice.

Abby: Your body is involved here, too. That's kind of the point.

Marcus: Abs, I'm totally okay with however you want to proceed. Don't twist yourself up in knots about this. Why don't you stop Googling baby stuff and start watching your competitors' game reviews on YouTube?

Abby: Okay. Thanks :)

Marcus: That's what I'm here for.

He is too wonderful to me. Which is exactly why I can never rock the boat of our relationship, not for any reason, no matter how important it might be.

But what if "rocking the boat" of our relationship is the best chance I have of becoming a mom?

I draw in a deep breath, open the YouTube app on my phone and search for a preview of a game I've got waiting at home for a review article. Once the video loads, I take a screenshot of my phone and text it to Marcus.

Marcus: That's more like it. Want to get breakfast before work tomorrow? Would have to be early—7:30 a.m. But you've proven you can manage to get yourself out of bed that early now so…

Abby: That was definitely a one-off and I'm still recovering.

Marcus: We can skip it if you want to. Talk tomorrow night instead?

Abby: If I'm lucky, I'll need to get used to disrupted sleep :) 7:30 a.m., it is.

I switch back to YouTube and force myself to fix my focus on the screen.

I can't afford to let my mind wander…mostly because if I do, I know it will wander all the way back to New Year's Eve, and a kiss so intense the very thought of it can still curl my toes nine months later.

CHAPTER TEN

Marcus and Luca,

It's been over a week since I sent that message and I can see that you've both read it. I understand it must have come as quite a shock. I want you to know that I'm not at all surprised or offended that you haven't replied.

I remember when you two were learning to walk. Your mother and I kept walking back into rooms just in time to see one of you fall to your butt. This went on for days until, one night, I was dressing Luca at the change table. Marcus, you were sitting on the floor playing with a toy when you pulled yourself to your feet and took several completely stable steps. I set Luca down, then I called your mom and we were cheering and clapping, trying to get you to do it again.

But, Luca, you saw the fuss we made over Marcus, and you refused to be outdone. You scrambled up onto your feet and walked across the room, too.

You were both far too stable for these to have been your first steps, and your mom and I were finally sure that you'd both been walking for a while. It just took some time before you were ready to let us know about it.

Anyway, all that's to say I know that you two will decide about getting back in contact with me in your own good time, and I have a feeling you'll make that decision together.

Till then, boys, please know that I always have and always will love you.

Warwick

Marcus

THE SOUND OF Warwick's second message landing on my phone wakes me at 5:00 a.m. Where does he live that he's messaging both in the early morning and late in the evening? It still seems unlikely that he's losing sleep worrying about whether or not we'll reply. I read the message several times, then sigh and climb out of bed.

A few months ago, Paul asked me if I was interested in training with him, and ever since then we've met to work out together five mornings a week. He's infamously a hyperfocused work machine, and while his obsessive nature has been a big part of our success, it's always worried me a little. He hasn't said in as many words, but it's clear that since Izzy left him, Paul is trying to engineer a healthier life for himself.

He jogs down from his apartment in Chelsea on Thursday mornings, starting earlier than I do so he can meet me at six at the corner of Chambers and West Side Highway. We run back toward his apartment together along the river, and I leave him at Chelsea Piers. He cools down as he walks the remaining blocks to his apartment, and I make the return journey back to my place on my own.

This morning, by the time Paul comes into view, I've already done a series of sprints and I've sweat through my clothes despite the cool morning. Paul looks bewildered.

"Am I late?"

"No," I mutter. "I just couldn't sleep."

I don't even know how to explain to him all of the sudden chaos in my life—between the situation with Warwick and the situation with Abby, everything is changing all at once. Maybe Paul would understand, given his life has been upended this year, too. Should I explain the upheaval I'm experiencing?

Maybe Warwick is on to something about the timing of things, because I'm just not ready to talk this through yet. *That* thought triggers a burning anger in my gut, because I hate that Warwick can disappear from our lives for twenty-five years and still predict my behavior with any accuracy.

I take off at a blistering pace, knowing Paul will fall into step beside me…or if heavy foot traffic demands, just behind me. Most days, we take turns at the front, generally trying to outrun each other. Today is not one of those days, and Paul runs just behind me for the entire route.

There's a fair number of other joggers and cyclists, all trying to cram some fitness into hectic schedules, but they blur around me as I run. The breeze off the river is cool against my sweat-slicked skin, but early-morning sunlight is filtering through the New Jersey skyline to the east, and the morning is glorious. I breathe it all in, letting my tension drain away as I slip out of my own head and into the moment.

It's only when Chelsea Piers comes into view that I tune back into the messages my body is now screaming at me. My calves are burning, my lungs are on fire and sweat stings my eyes.

We take this route every Thursday and every Sunday morning. Only this morning instead of our standard steady jog, we've sprinted the whole way.

"Marcus," Paul says between pants. I'm slowing to a jog, too out of breath to speak yet. "If you need to talk, you know where I am, okay?"

It's possibly the least *Paul-like* statement in the history of our friendship, given he's somewhat infamous for his lack of empathy. I stare at him for a moment, trying to understand where *that* came from, and he looks away, almost self-consciously.

That's when I realize what's happening here: out of the chaos of his own life this year, my buddy isn't working out with me just to get fit. He's actually trying to become a better human being.

I thump him on the back, and he returns the default awkward gesture of male bonding.

"Appreciate that," I say gruffly when my breath finally returns. "Same here, Paul. And that offer *always* stands."

"Catch you at the office," he mutters. He turns away from me, and I hesitate, then call after him.

"You're a good friend, Paul."

He glances back just long enough to flash me a wry look. "That statement is historically inaccurate, but I'm working on it."

And then he's gone, and I smile to myself as I turn to make the return trip home alone.

By 7:35 A.M., I've been home long enough to shower and dress for work, but I haven't heard a peep from Abby. I'm not all that surprised. This isn't the first time we've made plans to go out for breakfast and she's slept right past the time we were supposed to meet. I knock on her door, and when there's no answer, I throw it open, expecting to find that she's still in bed.

She's not in bed.

She's wearing her headphones and is twisted in a yoga pose on a mat by the open window. She's bathed in early-morning sunlight, and of course she is, because I'm pretty sure she's never once closed those drapes since the day she moved in. She knows she spends too much time indoors, and says the natural light helps her to stay cheery. Maybe she's on to something, because right now that natural light is making me very cheery indeed. It falls over her, illuminating the perfect, pale curves of her body.

Abby is dressed only in her underwear. That's nothing I haven't seen before, because Abby has no qualms at all about crossing the living areas half-naked if the need arises, but something feels different today. The innocent nature of our relationship has been changed by the mere mention of sex, and there's a sudden danger in the air.

I hastily avert my gaze toward the ceiling and yell, "Abigail Jolie Herbert!"

She squeals as I step out of the room and take some meditative breaths of my own. Through the door, I hear drawers opening and slamming closed, and Abby is cursing to herself. And then she steps into the living area, wearing jeans and a hoodie. Her face is flushed raspberry, and those big brown eyes are downcast. She glances up at me, then looks right at the floor again.

The only thing that's really new about this situation is the possibility that there might be more exposure to Abby's underwear in my future. Maybe that possibility leaves us both raw and a little exposed. She looks vulnerable, and I feel strangely uncertain because I just had to resist some *very* X-rated thoughts and that makes no sense at all because *I am completely over her.*

"It's after seven thirty," I say, just to break the awful silence. It slips out as an accusation, and Abby's eyebrows snap inward.

"Sorry," she says defensively. "I just lost track of time."

"Do you always do yoga in your underwear in the mornings?" I try for a teasing tone, but instead I sound breathless. She gives me a searching look, and I clear my throat yet again as I shrug. "Seems like a strange decision for a person who's supersensitive to the cold." Abby runs the heat so high I swear I nearly melted during that first winter we lived together.

She runs her hand through her hair, detangling it, then smoothing it over one shoulder. But she can't see herself, so she doesn't know that her heavy bangs are messed up, too. I reach down and drag my fingers through the bangs, sweeping it to the side a bit the way she likes. It falls perfectly into place as Abby stares up at me. She keeps right on staring for just a second too long, then her gaze drops to my lips.

I've only seen that look on her face once before, and it was New Year's Eve last year, right before she launched herself at me.

Now, she tilts her chin upward, and licks her parted lips. It's *almost* an invitation, and it's an invitation I discover I desperately want to accept. I never thought I'd get to kiss her again.

Would it be just as good the second time around?

It would. I just *know* it would.

But I force myself to ignore it because I also know that any second now Abby's going to jump away from me like she's been startled. Then she'll say something awkward.

Right on cue, Abby leaps away from me, a beet-red flush stealing over her features.

"I, ah… The… I…"

"Your bangs were messy," I interrupt. "I was just fixing it for you."

"I shouldn't have done that." Our eyes meet again. Her blush intensifies. "The meditation, I mean," she blurts, lying in her usual style—that is, without finesse or conviction. "I mean, I normally don't do that at this ungodly hour. But I do it later in the day. I mean—I wasn't planning on it. I was just getting dressed and I was feeling really anxious—I couldn't sleep last night thinking about…you know…*things*. I was listening to a guided meditation. I wanted to clear my head before we talked but it wasn't working so I turned it up really loud and I didn't hear you come in, so I'm sorry."

I decide to let her babble until she burns off some of that frenetic energy—that's the only chance we have of having anything like a comfortable breakfast together. As she rambles, I flash her half a smile and head toward the door. Abby follows but she keeps just *slightly* more distance between us than usual, and I wind up a few steps in front of her.

She pauses at the coatrack to pull on her beanie, and I remember the drugstore bag I picked up on the way back from my run this morning. I scoop the bag up and pass it to her.

"What's this?" she asks.

"It's a present. I was going to give it to you at breakfast, but you can have it now."

She opens the bag and peers inside, then withdraws one of the thick, needleless syringes the pharmacist recommended when I explained our situation. Abby gives me a wide-eyed look.

"Turkey basters are so 1980. DIY-AI is *all* about syringes these days." I keep my tone light as I open the door for her, and Abby drops the syringe and the bag back down onto the hall table before she steps through. She glances at me again, but doesn't say anything, and so I offer her more of the information I discovered Googling yesterday afternoon during the very important yearly planning workshop that I did a pathetic job of facilitating. This whole baby project will be a moot point if Jess rips off my balls, which is an increasingly likely possibility the way I've been underperforming at the office lately.

"So, the tricky thing is getting the sperm close to the cervix on your own. I could help if you wanted, but given what that entails, surely that's even weirder than…you know. And you're probably flexible enough, so maybe it's just time to put all of that barre to good use—"

Her footsteps stop abruptly, and she laughs. "Marcus."

"Yes?"

"You are hereby forbidden from ever saying the word *cervix* to me in a public place ever again. Do you understand?"

"We're in the hallway. How is this a public place? And since when are you squeamish about female anatomy? There's no shame in cervixes. Or is it cervixi? What *is* the plural of cervix? That seems like something good parents should know."

"Yeah, I'm sure it's one of those questions a toddler always asks. We should be prepared." She hits the elevator call button and frowns.

"Did I do the wrong thing?"

Abby shifts her weight from one foot to the other, then grimaces and shrugs.

"Other than the long discussion about me reaching my own cervix, no. What you did was perfect, like it always is." She clears her throat, and her voice is very small as she adds, "So, does this mean you decided this is the best way for us to proceed?"

"Abby, I told you. I'm fine with whatever you decide—I just wanted to make sure you knew that. Now we're prepared. Whenever it's the right time, we can go ahead however you choose to."

"I think the right time might be soon. I think maybe I'd be ovulating a few days from now," she whispers, and my stomach drops to my toes.

"Oh," I say, and the elevator doors open. We step inside and stand beside one another as it travels to the ground floor. I dare to glance at her in the mirrored doors, and find she's studying her shoes furiously. "We can wait for next month."

"I don't want to wait. I want to start trying as soon as we can." She doesn't look up, even as she adds hesitantly, "Is that okay?"

"Of course it is." The elevator seems to be moving much slower this morning than it usually does. "My results came in on email last night. It's all clear."

"Mine, too."

My stomach is in my throat now. I feel like I'm on a roller coaster.

"Okay."

"I just don't know what to do. I think the ideal time for us to do a first insemination might be today or tomorrow."

"Okay," I say again, because the blood is thundering in my ears and I can't think of anything more helpful to offer her. I'm hyperaware of my body as the elevator crawls downward. My breath is shallow, my palms are sweaty, my face feels hot—but my dick is already hardening. *Shut it down, Ross.* I try to subtly adjust myself before Abby notices, but when I glance at her, I see that she's still staring at the floor. I could probably burst into song right now and she wouldn't so much as react, she's *that* determined not to look at me.

It's a relief when the doors finally swing open and we can step out from the confined space. We cross the lobby and out onto the sidewalk, where we're greeted with a blast of traffic noise from the street. Abby leads the way as we slip into a gap in the foot traffic outside our building, only to find ourselves caught just behind a young family. They are walking along *far* too slowly for the morning sidewalk rush, clogging up the stream of workers racing to their desks. Some step hastily around the family, casting them sharp looks. One particularly sour guy mutters under his breath.

Maybe any other day, I'd be overtaking the family, too, but not today. Abby and I automatically slow our footsteps and fall into a slow rhythm just behind them. By some unspoken agreement we have apparently decided on a spot of people-watching. A woman in a suit is on the right, a man in jeans and a sweater is on the left, and caught between them a toddler in a superhero costume holds one of each parent's hands in hers and walks as if every single step is worth savoring. She's chatting excitedly about the coming day at daycare, and her parents keep exchanging fond glances over her head.

It's all pretty standard for a family with a young kid, I guess. It's also ridiculously adorable, and I feel a sudden and surprising pang of *longing*. Abby stretches up to whisper in my ear.

"That might be us soon."

Judging by the wide set of her eyes and the tension in her shoulders, she's equal parts excited and terrified. I reach for her hand and squeeze it gently, and I can't temper my grin.

"I really can't wait."

We continue our too-slow walk along the sidewalk, crawling along at a snail's pace behind the young family until the toddler decides she's had enough walking and the father stops to pick her up. Abby and I step around them at last, but it's only then that I realize I'm still holding her hand. The gesture was supportive and encouraging a moment ago. Now, I'm not sure *what* it is—all I know is that it takes surprising effort for me to convince my hand to let go of hers.

I open the door for her when we reach the café, and Abby flashes me a quiet smile as she steps inside. I watch her face brighten as she takes in the space—this is one of her favorite places to eat out, and I think part of the appeal is how homey and simple it is. This café is quietly understated, with exposed brick walls and well-worn decor. The food is unpretentious and tasty, and the coffee is consistently fantastic.

Just like Abby herself, this café is real, warm and perfect in an absolutely unique way.

We place our regular order as soon as we're seated, and as the waitress walks away, Abby and I share a moment of sudden, shocking eye contact. Sparks of electricity fire in my gut and I force my gaze to a group of diners behind her, trying to clamp down on the feeling.

I really was over her. I was *so* over her. I *am* so over her. I repeat this again and again in my mind, but the mantra isn't helping at all. My body is having a pretty serious regression back to that momentary infatuation this morning, and I have no idea what to do with how excited I am about the idea of *touching* her. I'm stunningly, shockingly conflicted.

"What are we going to do, Marcus?" she asks, her voice low and unsteady. "What's the best way to proceed here?"

"I honestly don't know," I admit heavily.

"One of us is going to have to make a decision." Abby's nervous laugh gives me an idea.

"Well, maybe we can make it easier."

"Oh?" She sits up a little, encouraged by the idea

of an out. "So, we're going to roll dice or something? I think I have a dice app on my phone—"

"No, Abby…" I laugh softly. "Let's get dinner tonight, have a few drinks and then decide. I don't think either one of us is ready to make a decision on this right now, so let's put it off until we really *have* to figure it out."

"Yeah, okay…" Abby says thoughtfully. "All right. We'll just do whatever seems right when the moment comes."

"Exactly. So you don't need to spend the whole day gagging at the thought of bumping uglies with me." I try to make her laugh, but she doesn't.

Instead, she offers me a weak smile, which quickly becomes an embarrassed grimace as a squeaky teen voice asks, "Excuse me, are you Abby Herbert?"

Abby and I both look up as three teenage boys approach our table. They're about thirteen or fourteen, all limbs and awkwardness, heavy schoolbags hooked over their bony shoulders. The hopeful excitement on their faces is unmistakable.

"Hi!" Abby says, flashing the boys a smile. "I sure am."

For the next few minutes, she chats with them about her gaming videos and an action role-playing game she recently recommended that they are all in love with, and their plans for an "epic sleepover"…just as soon as they can convince their parents to let them play games online for twenty-four hours straight. Abby opens her purse and slips out three glossy stickers with her website and social media details. She even has a Sharpie on hand, so she signs the stickers and then poses with the boys while I take a photo for their Instagram accounts.

When Abby hands me her phone and asks me to take a shot for *her* Instagram, too, I'm genuinely concerned that one or more of the boys is going to injure a cheek muscle. They can't even play it cool anymore, their smiles are *that* wide.

She skillfully wraps up the conversation and says goodbye to her surprise fan club, and I don't think they even realize they've been dismissed. They are so completely under her spell, they're grateful for any attention she was willing to give them.

Abby used to be so shy with everyone but her closest friends. I'm certain she got into online gaming originally because it was a place for her to hide. Even now, she's still introverted as hell, but somehow, gaming has bolstered her confidence to the point that when circumstances demand it, she's also a confident, successful youth celebrity. Grown-up Abby is so many wonderful things all at once.

And I know a thing or two about how those boys feel, caught under Abby's spell. Staring at her now, it's a little too easy to imagine myself slipping all the way back there, just like I was in January.

"It's still weird every time that happens," she mutters, glancing up at me through her lashes.

"You made their day," I say softly. She waves her hand dismissively at me, but I know it's true. "How does it feel to have an army of teen fans at your beck and call?"

"My plans for world domination are coming together nicely."

The waitress approaches with our coffees, but the interruption has stalled the conversation, and the awkwardness quickly descends again. We sit like that until our breakfast arrives, stirring our coffees for far too long, each waiting for the other to speak.

"So...we'll just meet up for dinner?" Abby asks eventually. I do have dinner plans with my team, but I don't want to come home and battle awkwardness if we don't have something to keep us busy until it's Go Time.

"I've got evening meetings again today." Besides, if anyone can handle two dinners, it's me. "But I'll be home by 9:00 p.m. so we could do a late one."

"Okay."

"So we're okay?"

Abby draws in a deep breath, then she nods.

"Yep. We're good."

And I almost believe her, except for the fact that she flashes me a very quick smile and starts picking at her fingernails, which at some point since yesterday morning she's painted bright pink.

I can tell the conversation is going nowhere, so I let it drop and we sit in the slightly strained silence as we eat. Eventually I take out my phone and work on some emails, but every time I raise my gaze to Abby, she's staring at me, and each time she looks away. Even after this happens twice, I still feel her eyes on me, but I pretend I don't notice. I just let her stare. I keep moving my fingers over the screen, but I'm not achieving anything.

How could I possibly focus with the tension crackling in the air between us this morning? I swear the sight of Abby in her underwear under that window has been burned into the backs of my eyelids—every single time I blink I see it again.

Until this morning, I've been pretty calm about the idea of Abby and I actually having sex. I haven't been dwelling on the possibility, nor have I been worried about it. I was confident we could make it work as a means to an end, but I didn't think too much about what it would *mean* if we did.

This morning, that calm has disappeared, and I'm not really sure what to make of that. If we do this, it's just to make a baby. That's got to be it.

If we do this, it's hopefully just a few nights, and then everything has to go right back to normal.

If *Abby* decides to do this, she'll have thought it all through and she'll be certain that she can get the deed done tonight, and still look at me the same way tomorrow.

But what about me? It was surprisingly difficult for me to move on after that kiss on New Year's. When I realized Abby wasn't even willing to discuss the subject with me, it took every bit of my self-discipline to suppress my attraction to her.

What if, this time, I can't put the genie back into the bottle? For the very first time, I'm nervous about this pregnancy project, and the shocking thing is, it isn't even the potential baby that scares me.

CHAPTER ELEVEN

Abby

IT'S ANOTHER DAY of silence on instant messaging, and I force down my paranoia by reminding myself that Marcus is genuinely busy. There's a limited-edition, USB-powered *Dr. Who* clock on my desk beside my monitors. Marcus got it for my birthday four years ago. It's never lost time before, but today it plays tricks on me. I watch the second hand and I swear it ticks backward sometimes, which might explain why the day feels like it takes weeks to end.

But eventually the hands reach 8:50 p.m., and right on time as always, I hear the front door open and Marcus calls out to me.

"Hey, Abs. Give me five minutes. I just need to change."

Knowing Marcus, "changed" will only mean swapping one button-down for another. I, on the other hand, have changed three times this afternoon.

First, I searched through my underwear drawer and selected the sexiest set I own. It's crimson, mostly lace, with a demi-cup bra and a skimpy G-string that *I* think makes my curvy ass look amazing. I peered at myself in the mirror and was quite pleased with the end result. I sat at my computer, and for just a few moments, I let myself imagine us coming home from dinner. I pictured him sitting on the couch—*our* couch—the place we've innocently leaned into each other hundreds of times while we watched TV. Except this time, I stripped slowly, seductively, out of my clothes and I saw desire in his eyes.

There was no denying the buzz of excitement that burned in me while I fantasized about that, which was completely confusing and terrifying. And as soon as I acknowledged it, the fantasy popped, and instead, I saw myself stripping down, but instead of desire in his gaze, I saw mortification. *Uh, Abby. Lingerie? You do realize this isn't actually about seduction, right? This is purely about procreation.* Then I imagined us undressing each other and getting into bed and him admitting he wasn't sure he could make it work. *Shit, Abby. I'm so sorry. I can't get it up. This has never happened to me before with any other woman, but then again, it's not surprising that my penis just doesn't want to come to the party on this particular occasion, is it? Because I could never think of you that way.*

At that thought, I tore the red lace set off and buried it under a pile of dirty laundry as if it represented a physical threat to my safety. Then I went back to the plain white cotton set I had already been wearing. After that strangely uncomfortable yoga incident this morning, he's already seen me in this set today and that's weird enough…but somehow, it feels wrong that I'm not even wearing clean underwear for the occasion of us possibly conceiving a child.

So I changed again. This time I went for a plain cotton black bra and a pair of cartoon character panties. The set doesn't match. Frankly, it's the least sexy underwear I own, and that feels more appropriate.

I put my regular clothes over the top *again* and tried to laugh at myself for overthinking all of this, but the laughter got stuck in my throat, and so I sat at the computer and waited for Marcus to come home.

Another unproductive day.

When this is all over and done with, I'm going to have a huge backlog of work to wade through. I guess that will help distract me while we're waiting to see if I'm pregnant.

"You ready for dinner?" Marcus asks from the door to my room, and I turn to face him, feeling suddenly guilty.

"Yes. Of course I am. But it's so late—didn't you already have dinner with your team?" It sounds like an accusation, and he tilts his head at me.

"I didn't really eat. I wanted to wait for you. Although I can see that my plan didn't work for you, either."

"Plan?"

There's a smile in his eyes. "We were trying to completely postpone the decision until the exact moment when it had to be made."

"I've barely spared it a thought all day," I say, and he laughs at me.

"If you knew how bad you are at lying, you'd never even try."

I poke my tongue out at him and shut off the computer, then rise and take a deep breath.

"Time for wine," I say, and he nods solemnly.

We're seated quickly in our regular booth at Alfino's. Marcus orders wine, but his charm appears to have disappeared—he delivers the request without social niceties.

"And vodka," I blurt as the waitress moves to leave us.

The hostess looks at me, eyebrows high, then checks with Marcus. "Was that a *bottle* of wine?"

"That's right."

"And how many wineglasses?"

"Two," I answer for him, then I add, "Plus the vodka."

"Neat?"

Why is this so hard for her to understand? I give her a pointed look as I nod, and I'm surprised when Marcus mutters, "Make that a bottle of wine and *two* vodkas."

The hostess shrugs, and Marcus and I share a nervous laugh as she walks away. But then we're alone and unfortunately sober. I start to pick at the scant patches of pink polish that remain on my fingernails until Marcus catches my hand. "Abby. Calm down."

I don't know what I'm more nervous about—the risk that this could ruin everything, the fact that we're about to cross a line I never thought we'd cross or the actual goal of all of this—*motherhood*. Even on its own, the thought of *actually falling pregnant* is terrifying. The only thing that's *more* terrifying is the thought that it might never happen.

It's no wonder I'm nauseous about everything that's happening right now. My whole world is about to change.

Am I really up to the challenge of this?

"We *can* wait a month. Until you're sure," Marcus adds now. I glance at him.

"Do you really think *more* time to think this through is going to help us?"

"Well, let's at least talk about it. What are you thinking? What are you feeling?"

Scared. Scared. Scared.

Kind of turned on.

Confused about that.

Excited. Nervous. Anxious.

Scared.

Annoyed.

"Why do you always try to make me talk about things?" I demand, and he raises his eyebrows at me.

"Why do you *always* avoid difficult subjects?"

"Because it's easier. And in this case, it's survival."

"Okay, then. Let's go back to the original plan—the same plan I use with my dates most of the time. We'll have a few drinks and pray for the best."

I laugh weakly, and Marcus slips his fingers through mine to stroke the back of my hand with his thumb. He stares out into the restaurant, and his gaze is distant, like the weight of the world rests on his shoulders. I watch him out of the corner of my eye, and I'm conscious of how seriously he's taking this. He doesn't seem worried, but despite the quips, his brow furrows as if he's concentrating hard. Then I look down at his hand through mine, and for just the briefest of moments, I know *exactly* what I want.

The gentle, innocent movement of his thumb over the back of my hand is giving me butterflies—the good kind, not the sick-with-nerves kind. I pause and focus on that for a moment, and the feeling starts to grow. Soon the butterflies are flapping harder, and I feel the warmth low down in my abdomen.

That's just him holding my hand. So if we were, say, stark naked—

That pleasant train of thought grinds to a screaming halt as all of the disastrous possibilities occur to me again.

Maybe he'd never look at me the same way again.

Maybe I'd never look at *him* the same way again.

Do I really want a baby that much? What if we fall pregnant, but it costs us our friendship?

I snap my hand away, and Marcus clears his throat and is about to say something when the waitress returns with the vodkas. She sits them on the table, and Marcus and I each grab for a glass.

"To risking everything," I say, by way of a toast. I'm trying to make a joke, but Marcus frowns as he knocks his glass against mine, then pauses before it reaches his lips.

"To *gaining* everything," he counters quietly, and I down the entire half glass of vodka in one smooth movement and close my eyes as it burns its way down to my stomach.

"If you need to be drunk to do this, we're *not*. Doing it." The words are stiff and punctuated with awkward pauses. I shake my head stubbornly. "Abby, I know you suck at talking about things that are uncomfortable and I know this situation is the very definition of that, but you just *have* to talk to me."

"It's not me I'm worried about," I blurt, and *argh*—I'm blushing so hard I'm probably luminescent. "I can do this. I mean—all I have to do is lie there, right? But you…" I sink underneath the table a little as I look away. "You *have* to be into it. What if we try and you can't even bring yourself to do it? How on earth are we supposed to come back from *that*?"

He doesn't say a word. I reach for the wine. I'm suddenly wishing we'd opted for a white so it was cold and I could press a chilled glass against my face. Ah—maybe I'm getting the flu? I feel feverish. It's very uncomfortable. Perhaps I should go lie down.

"Abby," Marcus says softly. "It's going to be fine."

Not once in my entire relationship with Marcus have I ever felt awkwardness *this* thick between us, and I hate it. I press forward with my idea, still tracing the tablecloth stitching with my gaze. "We could just make this easy. We each go to our rooms and…prepare. Then I could come to your room and get on my knees. I could wear a skirt that you could just lift up a bit so I'm covered. You can pretend I'm someone else and—"

Marcus winces, and I fall silent. It's pretty obvious that he desperately wants to say something but just can't find the words, so I prompt him. "What? Just say it."

I know what he's going to say, and it already hurts. *I could never think of you that way, Abby.*

The blow doesn't come this time. Instead, he surprises me with a quiet outrage.

"Are you really suggesting that I go jerk off until I'm just about ready to go, and you do—God, I don't even want to *know* what you're proposing at your end—and then I just hammer away at you from behind while you think of England? And *that's* how you want to make a baby together? If that's seriously how you need this to play out, I want no part in it."

"I just want to make this work for you," I whisper, and he sighs. It irritates me. "Stop *doing* that. What do you need to say?"

Marcus swirls the vodka around in his glass for a moment, then he sets the glass down and reaches for my hand. He gazes at it thoughtfully until I see something change in him. There's a tired acceptance in his eyes, and I don't know what it means.

"Trust me?" he asks quietly, and I nod without hesitation. Because I do. I really do.

Now he draws in a deep breath, and then lifts my hand to gently rest it against the bulge at his groin. He isn't hard—but he's well on the way. He stares right at me as my eyes widen in shock, and I'm struck by the way that the gleam in his gaze is at once both alien and familiar.

Fondness, I frantically tell myself. But is it really fondness I see there? Or...

"I'm good with this, Abby," Marcus murmurs, and the rumble of his deep voice sends shivers through me. My hand is still beneath his, against his rapidly hardening dick, as he adds softly, "It's *you* I'm worried about."

Well. That just makes no fucking sense. No sense at all. How often is *that* happening when we hang out? I snatch my hand away and stare at the table, conscious of the heat rising pretty much all through my body. This is a very different kind of flush. I'm hot in the face. Hot in the chest. So hot that fireworks are starting to go off, and shooting stars are lighting up the nerve endings all through my body.

But once the rush of confused arousal fades, all that's left is anger.

"What the *fuck*, Marcus?" I snap, and I clench my hand into a fist, as if that will relieve me of the memory of the feel of him beneath it.

"Uh…"

"You said you could never think of me like *that*." I bite the words out.

"What?" he gasps, and shakes his head slowly. "When did I say *that*?"

"Jess's New Year's party," I hiss, and comprehension dawns in his eyes. For just a moment, his gaze dips to the table, then he raises it again to stare at me.

"Yeah, okay. I did say that. Right before you kissed me and proved me wrong." I wince even at the mention of it—the embarrassment and regret rising with the intensity of the flush on my cheeks. His voice deepens as he mutters, "Jesus, Abby. Surely you noticed that I kissed you back."

"I was drunk," I mutter. "I don't remember."

"Really?" he asks. His tone is almost neutral, but when I flick my gaze to his face, there's a challenge in his eyes.

"Really." A lie. I saw the shock in his eyes that night—and it ran deep. That kiss blew his fucking socks off.

It went both ways. The man should teach classes on kissing. Maybe in the future, I'll make a rule to only kiss guys who have taken and passed those classes because, *hell*—Marcus knew what he was doing. Our kiss went on and on, and every variable was perfect—the pressure, the movement, the pace, *just* the right amount of tongue at just the right moments. I remember how hard his body felt against mine, because he's lean and tall but he's muscled in all the right places, and how I wanted to rip the layers of clothing away so that I could feel the heat of his torso. I remember how he cradled the back of my head in his hands, and my heart raced so fast, and I wanted to melt into him because everything about the moment felt so right.

Everything about *us* felt so right.

That's what freaked me out in the end. Me and Marcus were kissing on a rooftop on New Year's and I wanted him so badly I could feel the *need* in every beat of my heart. I was happy for a moment, because I thought…well, we already live together. We can just go home and see where this leads us.

But *that* thought hit me like a freight train, because I'd been living with him for a year by then, so I'd seen firsthand what happened to Marcus's flings. Hell, just a few weeks earlier he'd broken up with Liesel, and she'd been completely crazy about him—no amount of charm or Alfino's was going to soothe *that* ache. I remember overhearing as she screamed at him and stormed out of the apartment, and when I came out to check on him, he was packing up the dishes as if nothing had happened at all and he gave me a sad smile and shrugged as he said that he'd *warned her he wasn't looking for anything serious*.

As if he'd done everything right, and she was a fool to feel something for him at all.

I really liked Liesel. She was madly in love with her work and kind of quirky.

A bit like me.

Thoughts of poor, heartbroken Liesel were a bucket of cold water over that kiss, and I did the sensible thing. I pulled myself away from him, told him we were going to pretend it never happened, and then I ran home and hid.

"I tried to talk to you about it," Marcus adds now. I remember how desperate I was to stuff all of the chaos back into Pandora's box before it could really hurt us. But he was so stubborn—he just kept trying to raise the subject, and so I did something manipulative.

I sat on the couch with my laptop when I knew he was due home from work, opened, sat there with that stupid Craigslist page maximized on my screen until he came in, and made damn sure he saw what I was looking at.

He didn't try to talk to me about it after that. I was relieved. Ashamed, too, but mostly relieved.

But now? All of these months later? I just feel cornered by this discussion, and when I feel cornered, I get angry and my temper starts to simmer. Doesn't he understand how dangerous all of this is? I *need* his friendship. We can't let that kiss—let alone any potential *future* kisses—get in the way of that.

"Well, thank *fuck* I didn't let you talk to me about it," I growl. I push my bangs back from my face and take a steadying breath. "I should never have kissed you. It was stupid and impulsive and reckless. All of this is—*all of it*—it's just too risky."

"Okay," Marcus says.

He's completely calm. I am the only person here sweating bricks, and that enrages me further, so I say incredulously, "*Okay?* That's all you're going to say?"

"Tonight…*this*…it isn't actually about that kiss. It's about making a baby, and I just wanted to let you know that I'm up for going about that however *you* want to," he says quietly. The rational logic and stark reminder of the ultimate goal of all of this—*a baby*—work to quell my anger, just a little.

I'm being an idiot. He's done nothing wrong.

Marcus wants me.

Okay. Maybe he doesn't *want*-want me. Maybe he's just realized he's able to want me if the circumstances dictate. Surely that's it. It's not an out of control forest fire of need, which is what I seem to be battling inside right now. I glance under the tablecloth again, thinking about the feel of Marcus's cock beneath my hand. I want to reach for it again, to rub a little, to see if I can make him moan.

I have a feeling we'd both like it if I did that right now. And that isn't alcohol talking. That's *me*. It's the undercurrent that I've skirted around, but never dared to acknowledge. That was some Olympic-level denial I've engaged in since New Year's.

Gold star to me for being stubborn.

I glance at him, and the gleam is still there in his eye. Is it fondness, like I've told myself for all of this time? Or is the dark edge to that expression actually latent desire?

Holy shit.

This is all so confusing. Terrifying, messy, awkward…and I hate those things. God, I've planned my entire life to *avoid* those things.

I'd just like to go back to my room and play *Warcraft*

now, please. There in the game, I slip into my character and I'm *free* from chaos like this.

The tension here is suffocating. The only thing I want more than to make that go away is a baby. I focus on that and manage to push down the urge to flee. I take a steadying breath in, and when I exhale, I successfully release the last of the desperation to retreat.

"What if it's weird?" I whisper, staring at the table again.

"Was the kiss weird?"

I raise my eyes to his, and a gently reassuring moment shifts and morphs until it's something altogether different. We're both thinking about the kiss, and his gaze heats and I feel my breathing quicken. I drag my eyes away, but not because things are awkward.

It's because my hands are itching to pull him closer. It's because if I don't, I'm going to throw myself at him again, and there's a good chance my motivation will have less to do with having a baby and more to do with the pull between us that I'm just fucking *tired* of resisting.

Everything about this moment is dangerous and I can't avoid it.

"Let's plan to use the syringe," he says. "Let's have dinner and relax because we know that we're *just going to use the syringe*. Then when we go upstairs, and if you *don't* want to do it the clinical way, then you just let me know. I'm completely fine with either option. I just need for *you* to be okay—nothing else at all matters to me. Not even a little bit."

"Syringe," I agree stiffly, and then the waitress returns with a notepad to take our orders.

Our usual free-flowing chatter never makes an appearance, and neither one of us seems willing to reinitiate it—it's like the tension is too solid to try to breach. We just sit and eat and drink, and the wine disappears, but while I wait for relaxation to hit me, it never comes.

I'm achingly aware of the gravity of the moment. I feel out of my depth, twisted up in my own thoughts, isolated in a prison of my fear. Every now and again, I glance at him.

This is Marcus. He is my best friend, the most important person in my world. He's seen me weep. He's seen me happy. He's held my hair back from my face while I vomited when I was sick, and he's supported my deepest hopes and soothed my deepest fears. He's made me laugh until I cried. He's been *home* to me for my entire life.

Sex would be a new intimacy, but it would come after a lifetime of others. He would never, ever hurt me. If *he* thought this could damage our relationship, he'd never allow it to happen.

"Dessert?" Marcus suggests when we've finally finished our mains. His tone is light-as-air, as if we're about to go back upstairs just to go to sleep on any ordinary night in our life together, and I question everything all over again. *Does he actually want this at all?* His gaze assesses mine, but I can't read him now. He's pulled shutters over his eyes.

"No dessert," I whisper, and he exhales and plays with the stem on his wineglass. Marcus has nice hands—the hands of a man who works with his brain— neat fingernails, strong, thin fingers. In my mind, I am replaying other moments from our shared history—the broad expanse of his naked torso that I've seen and noticed and told myself I wasn't impressed by.

It's been much harder to convince myself this year that I had no interest whatsoever in that torso. But now, just for tonight, I can stop arguing with myself. I can stop pushing down the quiet voice that wonders: *What if?*

I don't need to wonder anymore. I can know for sure.

"Let's go upstairs now," I say, and Marcus glances at me.

"You're okay?" he asks, and I nod. He follows as I slide out of the booth to walk to the counter. Even after all these years he always offers to pay when we go out and even after all these years I always insist we split the bill, but not tonight. I let him swipe his card to cover the whole amount, and as he does, I watch the distracted smile he flashes the concierge. I let my gaze wander over the stubble on his jaw and his chin and I wonder what it would feel like to have that against my cheek as we kiss. It would be rough, I think, but the good kind of rough…a stark reminder of his masculinity and the contrast between our bodies.

As he finishes up with the bill, he turns to me and catches my gaze. The air between us is so thick I have to force myself to breathe.

We walk side by side in silence as we head toward the elevator. Marcus reaches for his security card and calls the elevator, and when it comes, we step inside and turn to face the door.

Side by side.

Still more silence. And we're still not touching.

It's just the two of us in this elevator. Maybe it's just

the two of us in the world, because everything outside of this space has ceased to exist in my mind.

My heart is racing, and my pulse is so loud in my ears that he *must* hear it. I glance at him in the mirrored doors and catch him staring at me. His dark gaze locks with mine, and the tension hums louder between us. Is it there to stay? How am I ever going to wake up tomorrow morning after feeling *this* and see Marcus again as nothing more than a friend? We haven't even *touched* yet, not really.

But it seems I've made my decision, because those concerns are quiet echoes instead of the screaming protests they were earlier. I can ignore them now.

And I will.

For a baby. We're doing this *for a baby.*

Everything else is incidental. It has to be.

We walk from the elevator, down the corridor to the apartment, and he opens the door and waits while I step inside.

"Syringe?" he asks mildly, and I draw in a deep breath and take his hand. He turns and stares down at me, and I stare back. I know my eyes say it all, but he checks verbally. "You're sure?" I nod slowly. Now he says it again, in case I've missed it the first hundred times. "I mean it, Abby. No pressure. Not even a little bit."

I step toward him, until I am right where I would be if he hugged me, but we aren't touching other than at our hands. I breathe in his scent and close my eyes and give myself a final moment to back out.

But suddenly, everything seems simple. I do desperately want a baby, and I want to have that baby with Marcus…but by God, that isn't all I want. I want to touch him, and I want him to touch me. I raise my face to his, and I reach up and touch his cheek. I feel a triumphant thrill as I realize that I was right; his stubble is *just* the right kind of rough against my fingertips.

"I'm sure," I whisper, and then lick my lips.

"Which room?" he whispers back, and *at last*, there's a breathless, rough edge to his voice. That distracts me for a moment, and I miss the question, hearing only the desperation—but he waits for my response. I do a mental rewind and realize what he's asking.

Where will we have sex for the first time? I ponder all the implications of this. My brain is so addled—with lust and excitement and fear—but my mind races forward, to *after*.

I don't want to cuddle him. I mean, maybe I *will* want to, but if we are going to keep this as just sex—and just sex for a brief period of time—then I'm going to have to protect myself. If I do something stupid, like fall in love with him…well, *that* is a surefire way to guarantee things break between us.

We can have sex to make this baby, but it must be something we do separate from our friendship. Cuddling with him afterward is the first step to blurring the lines between the two, so I can't let it happen. Equally, though, I can't exactly kick him out of my bed, so it's infinitely easier if we go to his room, and then I can just leave afterward.

But I miss him already.

Oh, fuck it.

"Yours," I say, and Marcus gently pulls me along behind him to his room. I close the door, as if someone else might walk in on us or we need to hide what we're doing from some mysterious third party in the apartment. Then I turn to face him.

He is breathing hard, and so am I, and the world is quiet except for those ragged, shaky sounds. We're about to take off each other's clothes, but that feels like something I should be doing with a lover, not with Marcus. If he undresses me, then from that moment on, once upon a time he *undressed* me.

I don't know why this realization is so terrifying, but it is. It's not too late for this to feel clinical, is it? I need to take my clothes off myself, as if I'm at a doctor's office. How am I going to explain this to Marcus? I don't know how to start, and after staring at him and panicking for a moment, I blurt, "Just give me a minute," and run into his bathroom.

CHAPTER TWELVE

Marcus

I STRIP AND climb into bed. Maybe Abby won't ever come out of the bathroom. Maybe I'll wait all night and she'll hide in there and talk herself out of this.

She's probably changed her mind, and that's completely okay.

That doesn't mean I'm not staring at the bathroom door willing it to open with all my might. Because I am; I'm staring at the door so hard my eyes are aching. I even try bargaining with the universe.

If she comes back out, I'm going to remember to donate blood every month until I die.

If she comes back out, I'll send all of those thank-you cards my mom always nagged me to write.

If she comes back out, I'll sit her down right now and tell her that I was the good kind of messed up after we kissed, and it was all her—her smile and her laugh and her curves and her wit and her kindness and her quirks. I'll admit to her that getting over my infatuation for her was one of the hardest things I've ever done, and maybe I'll even admit to myself that maybe I didn't make it *all* the way back to "just friends."

Okay. I won't do any of those things. But I *will* be

grateful. I'll be so grateful and excited I'm not even sure how I'll manage to play it cool long enough for her to cross the five feet from the bathroom door to the bed.

The door opens a crack. Abby's arm reaches out and turns the light off. I sit up and reach for the lamp, but she gives a little squeak.

"No, please. Leave it dark?"

"Okay," I croak, but I remain upright, waiting as she inches toward me. My racing heart kicks up a notch further as I realize that she's naked, holding her bundle of clothes in front of her torso like a shield. As she reaches the bed, she drops the clothes to the floor and, in one swift movement, ducks under the sheets. She covers herself, right up to her chin, then exhales. I could reach out and touch her, but she's gripping the sheets, and her hands are trembling.

"It's *still* not too late to back out," I say, but instead of the relief I've seen in her eyes every time I've said this all night, she turns to give me a pointed glare as if I'm issuing her a challenge.

"I'm game if you are."

Holy shit. This is really happening…and now *I'm* shaking like a leaf. That's new, and holy shit, it's embarrassing. *This isn't your first rodeo, Ross. Pull yourself together.* I gather up the charm and bravado I'm pretty sure I normally possess in bed, and I move just a little closer to her.

"I'm game," I murmur. I reach to gently brush her hair back from her face, and she sucks in a sharp breath. Now I run my finger over her shoulder, onto her collarbone. Goose bumps rise on her skin, and her sheet-covered breasts rise and fall faster as I come close. I want to pull the sheet back and expose her, to see her body. I want to pull her into my arms and kiss her with the full force of the passion and urgency I feel. I want to let myself go, and I want to take her with me. *Right fucking now.*

I know we're doing this to make a baby.

I *am* doing this to make a baby.

But even so, this is a chance to *stop* repressing the chemistry between us, and to let myself feel it and explore it with Abby.

"Should we kiss?" she blurts. It's dark in here, but not so dark that I can't see the huge expanse of her pupils as she stares at me. She's nervous, but she's excited. I laugh softly, and trail my finger lazily down toward the sheet, then up to cup her jaw in my palm.

"I think that's a good place to start."

She leans toward me, and I bend in to gently place my lips against hers. We both move too fast, and our noses knock as we awkwardly come together. That does nothing to shatter the tension, but we do break apart again and share a soft, slightly breathless giggle.

But then she brings her mouth right back to mine, and now she meets the movements of my lips with confidence. I bring my other hand up into her hair, so that I've cupped her skull with my palms just like I did on the rooftop. I wonder if she remembers but I only wonder for a second, because I hear the half-muffled groan she gives and she presses her mouth hard against mine. Her tongue darts forward to brush over my lip—hesitantly, testing the waters.

I didn't expect her to take the lead—but I'm delighted that she wants to, so I pause as Abby wraps her arms around my neck and *she* deepens the kiss.

Even if it kills me—and it might, given the urgency I'm feeling already—I'm going to let her set the pace here. I'll let her explore the landscape of the spark between us as fast or as slow as she wants to.

That's why, for a long while, we just sit there and we kiss. It's like we're new to kissing, and neither one of us knows how to move things along, or maybe we're just trying to make up for thousands of missed opportunities to kiss one another over the years. It's almost like a trial run—each movement merely a test to see how the other reacts. We take turns gently dominating— Abby kisses me passionately, then retreats, and then I kiss her back with just as much fire, and every time we cycle around like that, the heat between us seems to intensify, until I hear little catches at the back of her throat when she breathes.

Dear God, I could build my life around those sounds. It's like a gift or a melody—like birdsong at dawn on the first morning of the rest of my life. Then again, that could be my erection talking. He's apparently an overdramatic bastard when he's finally allowed to call the shots.

Eventually, I do need to move things along because there's only so much a guy can take. I lean away from her and check in.

"Abby…still okay?"

She pulls me impatiently back to her mouth, and I laugh softly and run my hands down her shoulders, over her bare upper arms, then gently, hesitantly, across to cup her breasts through the sheet.

I want to worship at the altar of Abby's breasts. They're everything I've tried not to notice from afar— full, heavy, perfectly shaped, luscious—filling my hands like they were built for them. Would she freak out if I told her just how beautiful she is like this?

Maybe. But I can't *not* tell her.

"Abby," I whisper, and I tear my gaze back to her face. Her eyes are heavy-lidded, and she stares at me from the shelter of her eyelashes. "Your body is incredible."

She whimpers. There's no mistaking the sound— this isn't fear or uncertainty, it's pure, unadulterated *need*. Her shoulders shake, and she tilts her head back, exposing her neck to me. Her breathing is ragged, and her death grip on the sheet releases. Something in my brain snaps altogether when I realize that all that's holding that damned sheet up is *my* hands.

I tear the cover away from her body abruptly and ease her back down into the pillows as I kiss her again. This time the kiss is hard and demanding, and she doesn't back away from it. My hands are drawn back to her breasts, and her nipples pull hard and tight against my palms. Everything is moving faster now. I need to kiss her everywhere, and I do; her fingers claw into my neck as I bring my mouth *oh-so-close* to her nipples only to pass them by, teasing a long line from her neck to her navel and back to her mouth. I'm toying with her—refusing to give her what she wants, and soon she's twisting and trying to force me to shift my attention. I laugh a little when I hear the curse she tries to muffle, and then she laughs, too.

"Stop *teasing* me," she whispers, a glint in her gaze.

"No. It's fun," I whisper back, and our eyes lock until we laugh again. I'm surprised by the levity—because inside I feel like I'm on fire, but this is Abby. And we laugh together all the time; apparently even when we're pawing at each other like wild animals. In this particular moment, our laughter is as soft as a whisper, as intimate as the interplay of our bodies.

But Abby has had enough teasing; she's even had enough laughter. Her expression sobers as she slides her hands into my hair and firmly directs my mouth to her breasts, leaving no doubt in my mind that she will no longer tolerate my games.

Who am I to deny her? Her fingers are hard against my scalp as I take a turn at each breast, kissing, licking, nipping… God, I could do this all day. Soon she's moaning softly, and her legs are shifting restlessly against the bed. I raise my gaze back to hers. Even in the darkness of my room I can see the flush on her skin. Her pupils are huge and her eyelids are heavy. Best of all, her gaze is focused and the intent in her eyes is clear. She wants me. She *wants* me.

She wants *me*.

"I'm ready," she breathes.

"Oh, Abby," I say, and I lean back up to brush my lips over hers. She groans softly in complaint when I pull away again. "Sweetheart, you are just getting started."

I shuffle farther down the bed, and Abby squeals and shifts away from me as she realizes my intention.

"You don't have to do that," she whispers stiffly, and I smile at her gently.

"*Have to* has nothing to do with any of this," I say, and she searches my gaze.

"Don't you just want to…"

She trails off, but she doesn't need to finish the sentence. Don't I just want to skip to the main event, and bury myself in her body? Don't I just want to find release; after all, isn't that what the goal is here?

Of course I do.

But miss the chance to taste her?

No fucking way.

"If you don't want me to, of course I won't," I say, and I marvel at the mild and patient tone of my voice. It's all fake. The voice inside my head would have me plead with her: *Please, Abby. Let me put my mouth on you. Let me breathe you in.* I can smell the scent of her arousal in the air as I bend to kiss near her belly button. I just *know* she's going to taste like fucking heaven. *Please, Abby.* I kiss her pale thigh, beside the hands she's entwined to cover herself. "Abs…if you're comfortable with it…I'd love to…"

Abby whimpers and her hands fall away from her body to ball into fists beside her hips. I stare down at her body and feel the full force of the moment. It hits me hard in my chest, and I'm totally out of my depth here.

I just adore her. Abby is everything, and there's no pretending otherwise. Not now, and maybe not ever again.

As my lips touch her body, Abby releases a groan. I glance up to check that it's the *good* kind of groan and find her eyes are squeezed shut again. She's breathing hard, like she's been sprinting.

She's every bit as into this as I am, and that re-alization sends a thrill through me. But my patience and self-control are shot to hell. There's no way I can draw this out as much as I want to, so I focus my attention where it counts, using my hands and my mouth until her hands are in fists against my sheets and she is wound so tight…so wet, well and truly ready for me but… I'm greedy. I want to know all the secrets I've never let myself wonder about. Is she noisy when she comes? Does her face screw up, and then relax? Does she sigh in relief?

"Marcus, I can't take much more," she whispers as she tugs at my hair, trying to break me away, but I'm not moving—not yet. I lift my face from her body to look up at her, but my hands stay busy.

Abby stares down at me, completely caught up in the moment now, bold enough even to hold my gaze right up until she starts to spasm around my fingers. She smiles the whole damned time, even once she's closed her eyes and gone completely limp and she's catching her breath. I'm smiling, too, like a total fucking idiot, so caught up in her climax that I feel ten feet tall just having watched it happen. Have I ever felt so pleased to bring a woman to orgasm before?

No.

It always mattered to me to be a considerate partner, but not like this. Because I'm a selfish bastard when it all boils down and being able to make my lovers come was actually about me—*my* manhood, *my* skill in bed, *my* performance.

This is different.

This is pure, unadulterated selflessness. Her pleasure *is* my pleasure.

The minute Abby's eyes open, she shoots me a still-so-desperate look and then she's reaching for me, pulling me up over her again. Her hand goes right for me and I can't even let her touch me because I just *can't wait another second*. I shake my head and redirect her hand and I'm clumsy with urgency and desperation. I fumble in the drawer beside my bed, automatically reaching for a condom. I tear it open with my teeth and move to slide it down over myself—until Abby gives an out-of-breath laugh.

"Ah, Marcus…did you forget who you're with?"

She sounds so relaxed now compared to that awful, awkward dinner—back to the easy, teasing friend I am used to. I look at her fondly, and then I realize what I am doing—what *we* are doing. I curse and toss the condom over my shoulder.

"No," I mutter as I pull her into a sitting position to kiss her deeply. "I forgot *why* we're doing this." As she kisses me back, I shuffle against the pillows, dragging her with me until I can lift her onto my lap. Abby straddles me automatically, and our gazes lock.

She is perfection—and as Abby sits naked in my arms, I can't help but let myself pretend that, just for a moment, she's *my* perfection.

"I've never done this bare before," I admit.

She cocks an eyebrow at me and says wryly, "I'm not surprised, given that you've never been with anyone long enough."

"That's *not* why." I brush the hair back from her face and kiss her softly. Abby laughs and pulls away just a little to add, "Yeah, I suspect another important factor might just be that you never *wanted* to get someone pregnant before."

I laugh, too, and then the laugh somehow morphs into kissing, and another moment of lightness is lost as the passion resurges. I lean back into the pillow and watch as she gently lowers herself around me. As she takes me within the warmth of her body, a loud groan bursts from my lips, bouncing around the silence of the room.

"Are you okay?" She pauses, her gaze growing alarmed, and I give an uneven laugh as I nod.

"Too good, Abs. This feels too good."

Her eyes fall closed again, and she shifts to take me in deeper. "Does that feel okay?" she asks.

Through clenched teeth I reply, "Don't worry about me. Just do whatever works for you."

"I can't—I don't—I mean, I just won't…not again. Not twice in the one night," she says unsteadily. I catch her hips in my hands to still her.

"Just because you haven't before, doesn't mean you can't," I whisper. I hold her like that for a moment, until the slight tension in her face releases again. I guide her hips, moving her forward so that she can grind herself against my pelvic bone. "Sometimes it's just about patience…different sensations…maybe the second time you need a different kind of pressure. But you're in control here, Abs. Try to adjust how you move, until you feel yourself becoming aroused again. Okay?"

"So not only are you a recently qualified fertility expert, you're also a sex instructor?" she says, and laughs. "Do I know you at all, Marcus Ross?"

I slide my hand along her body, up to cup her cheek and to hold her gaze steady with mine. I sit up a little so I can kiss her, then whisper against her lips, "You know me better than anyone else on this planet, Abby Herbert."

Silence falls as Abby closes her eyes as she moves. I watch, spellbound. I'm gritting my teeth and praying for patience, but I get to see the shift in her breathing and the delicious tension rise back to her features as the pleasure starts to build in her again. She looks at me briefly to check. "Are you sure this is okay for you?"

"Sweetheart…just about anything you want to do to me at this point is going to be okay with me." I groan, and she laughs huskily. I have to close my eyes now as she starts to move faster because the sight of her rocking against me is just too much. I'm frantically trying to think *unsexy* thoughts about budgets or branding or the quarterly marketing plans—anything to calm myself down. I'm not going to last, and I desperately want to—for her. I want to feel her come around me. I want to follow her over into the abyss, especially now that she doubted she could orgasm twice, but by the strained sounds she's making, I suspect she's about to prove herself wrong.

She's rocking faster now, and harder—her movements less controlled. She holds on to my shoulder tight with one hand, and with the other, she clutches at my waist. I run my hands up and down her shape—from her thighs to her hips, then up her back and then all the way down, loving the softness of her skin and the way that she just fits with me.

Soon, no amount of distraction will help me, and

I just can't hold back anymore. I grasp her hips and I flip her, and she squeals and laughs as she rolls onto her back. I brush the hair back from her forehead and rain kisses over her face and her neck.

"Are you close?" I croak against her, and she nods, disbelief registering in her gaze. We kiss, and she's greedy, too, now—meeting the passion in my kisses with demands and promises and heat. "Good," I whisper, but what I'm really thinking is *thank fuck for that.* "Can I go a little harder?"

She moans her assent, and I lean my elbows beside her face so that I can take some of my weight as I give in to the instinct to find my release within her body. She meets my increasingly frantic thrusts with eager, demanding movements of her own, and then I hear her cry out my name. And then she comes, and that's it for me—I'm lost, too. The orgasm is torn from me, its echoes rolling on and on along my abdomen and into my legs.

It's the kind of climax that changes you—a singular, perfect moment of clarity and oneness.

But as I collapse onto Abby, and my thoughts return, I realize that she *was* actually right about one thing. Everything has changed tonight. This isn't the kind of sex you can just forget ever happened. For better or worse, things between us are never going to be the same.

CHAPTER THIRTEEN

Abby

MARCUS RESTS HIS forehead against mine. We're both panting; the heat of our breath mingles in the tiny space between our lips. I want to stay just like this—with the exceedingly pleasant weight of him over me, and the quiet intimacy of his cock still within me, just starting to soften. I want to fall asleep here, and wake up with him spooning me. Maybe he'd be hard again, pressing against my lower back. I want my turn to take him into my mouth. I want to explore his entire body the way he's explored mine.

I thought I knew all of his secrets. And maybe I do know him, but I'm starting to suspect I don't actually know *us* at all.

At this thought, my brain switches back on and I push him gently off me so that I can roll away from him onto my side. I try to remember what the websites said about this moment. *Roll onto your side or on your back with a pillow under your hips to aid gravity.* I'm supposed to stay like that for fifteen to twenty minutes.

I've never read anything about what you should do if your supposedly platonic best friend has just given you not one but *two* unexpected intense orgasms. Nor do have a clue what to do now that I find myself in a postcoital bliss right at the same moment that my inhibitions and self-consciousness have reappeared. The articles I read about conception didn't say anything about how much I want to snuggle into him, and let him hold me while my heart rate slows.

If it ever slows.

Maybe it will never slow again.

If I stay, he'll cuddle me. If I stay, he'll try to talk to me.

Holy shit, what is he going to say about what just happened?

"I have to go," I say, and then I shuffle so that I can slide my legs over the edge of the bed.

"Abby, no," he protests, and his voice is still rough. I feel a delicious shiver down my spine at the sound—this is a tone that I've never heard him use, and I marvel again that there is so much more here for me to discover. It's like we're suddenly in a brand-new world, and I want to breathe it in and gaze around in wonder—but I *can't*.

Adrenaline surges in me and I have to get away before he tries to talk through this, or worse still, before all of these surging hormones drive my thoughts to reveling in the new intimacy between us. I stiffen as Marcus tries to tug me back into an embrace. "Stay. Please. You're supposed to lie for at least twenty minutes. We can just—"

"No, I'll do it in my room. I have to go."

"Abs, *please*—"

"N-no, everything is okay," I lie. I sound so blatantly defensive—I know he'll see right through it. "I just need to go to sleep. See you tomorrow."

I fumble for my clothes and literally jog from his room, crossing the living area stark naked with his semen running down my leg.

Semen.

Sperm.

Baby.

Fuck.

I tell myself it won't make much difference; the websites *also* said most of the stuff that runs out isn't the sperm, anyway, and I promise myself I'll lie on my back for the rest of the night to give his swimmers at least a fighting chance. I shut my door, then pull on my underpants and scoop a shirt off the floor before I crawl onto my bed and prop a pillow under my butt.

The buzz is gone altogether now. I find myself simply scared, and oddly alone. I feel like I should be with him, but *that's* not going to happen. Lying in his arms after what we just shared would be too...

Too what?

Too close? Too intimate?

Too romantic, I realize. It would just be too damned romantic, and this is *not* about romance.

None of this makes any sense. We were supposed to get the job done as quickly and simply as possible. What just happened? And how do we come back from it?

He wasn't supposed to be able to read me like he did—none of my other partners ever had. He wasn't supposed to care so much about me. I could have fallen pregnant without a single orgasm, let alone *two* of the most intense of my life.

I should have known Marcus would be an amazing lover. He is a sensitive guy—sure, hopelessly self-absorbed at times, but he really does know how to read people—that's what makes him so great at his job. Plus, of course, I've seen the revolving door of women that have come through his adult life. He's had a *lot* of practice, and I try to tell myself that's probably the only reason it seemed so good to me. It was probably ordinary to him. Boring. Disappointing.

"Abby?" He is at my door, but waits hesitantly on the other side. The sound of his cautious greeting makes my heart race all over again.

I clear my throat. "I'm fine."

"Are you sure? That was—"

"I'm fine," I say again to cut him off, because I'm not at all sure what he's going to say but I *know* the two logical ends to that sentence are "crazy" or "awkward" and I'm not sure I can handle either. What if it wasn't even good for him? He seemed into it, but when things got *really* intense he screwed his eyes closed and what if he was pretending I was someone else, what if he was just trying to be polite and what if—

I can't stand this—the uncertainty, the sudden awkwardness. This relationship is my safe space, and we've made it all chaotic, and *fucking hell what if we can't fix it?* I squeeze my eyes shut tight and force out, "I'm tired. I'll see you in the morning?"

"You're sure?"

"Yep."

He sighs heavily, then *almost* pleads, "Abs, *please,* can we talk? Just a bit."

"I can't. Can you just let me go to sleep?" I know that makes me a bitch, but I don't care. I feel trapped—

cornered—exposed. Nothing good can come from us talking tonight, not while my emotions are running high like this. I try to breathe…try to clear my mind and center myself. It doesn't work.

Maybe it's whole minutes, or maybe it just feels that long, because I'm tense from my head to my toes. It seems such a long while later that he finally walks away.

And I go right back to wondering if I've just made the biggest mistake of my life, because I have no idea how on earth I am ever going to reconvince my body that Marcus is nothing more than my best friend.

As I WANDER around the silent apartment the next morning, rising long after I hear Marcus go to work, I try to convince myself to focus my energies on business as usual. If I ruminate on the situation too much, he'll read me like a book, just as he always does. I'm not surprised when an IM pops up as soon as I log into my computer.

Marcus: Abby. You okay?

I write back quickly, but I'm blushing even as I do.

Abby: Of course! What's up?

Marcus: You know what's up. That was intense last night. You freaked out on me.

Intense. That's the perfect word for it, and I am almost relieved—at least he felt it, too. I wonder how Marcus is feeling today. Is *he* freaked out like I am?

I'm definitely not going to ask him. Denial is a strategy that's proven effective in the past.

Abby: No! I just was tired. You wore me out. All is well.

Marcus: Bullshit. How is it possible that you can't even lie convincingly over plain text?

Abby: Promise, I'm fine. Lots to do today, catch you tonight?

Marcus: Wait. I need to know you're okay. Are we still doing this?

The sensible thing would be to tell him we should just use the syringe. But if I tell him how shaken I am by the chemistry between us, will he change his mind about the baby? Will it then be his turn to freak out?

He's probably used to mind-blowing sex.

He's probably not at all fazed.

Okay, so *I'm* freaking out, but I can't risk extending that to him, too, like some communicable disease. I usually talk to him about almost everything, but in this case surely it's better to stick with the plan, enjoy a few more outstanding orgasms and hope to high heaven that we fall pregnant this month so we can stop before I get my heart shattered.

Abby: Absolutely. Keep your calendar clear for tomorrow night. Talk to you later.

CHAPTER FOURTEEN

Marcus

"Uh, Marcus?"

Absolutely. Keep your calendar clear for tomorrow night. Talk to you later.

"Marcus."

Maybe I've misread things. Maybe she *didn't* freak out? Maybe she just doesn't like to cuddle after sex?

"Earth to Marcus..."

Hell, no, that's not it. Abby is a cuddler, through and through. She likes to cuddle under just about *any* circumstances.

"What the fuck is going on with you lately?"

I close my laptop and try to refocus on the Brainway weekly partners' meeting. Paul looks concerned, but Jessica is genuinely pissed at me—she has been all week, so that's no surprise. They are sitting opposite me at the board table, and I give myself a shake and fix my attention back on the agenda displayed on the oversize TV on the front wall of the room.

"Sorry," I mutter. I'm conscious now that they have been trying to get my attention, but my mind really has been elsewhere for the last ten minutes, and God only knows what they've discussed while I stared blankly at my laptop. Jess is sharp—she probably took advantage of my lack of focus and snuck through that new sales bonus program we've been squabbling over.

"You should be sorry," she says impatiently. "We have fifteen agenda items to discuss and thirty minutes left to do it and you've been jerking your team around all week because of whatever-the-fuck-couldn't-wait-the-other-day."

I scrub my hand over my cheek.

"I have a lot of things on my plate at the moment, Jess. But seriously—I'm really sorry. I'll do better."

"What things?" Jess asks, her tone softening just a little.

"It's personal stuff. Nothing to worry about."

Jess closes her laptop and stands. Paul and I stare at her, and she gives us an impatient look and points to our laptops.

"Pack it up, boys. We're going out for an early lunch."

"Since when?" Paul sighs, but he knows who's boss here. He's already packing up his laptop.

"Since *that*," Jess says, and she points directly at me. "Look at him. He's been walking around with his head in the clouds all week. It's intervention time."

"Wait, we don't need—" I start to protest, but fire flashes in her eyes, and I'm smart enough to know I've already lost this battle. I sigh as I, too, close my laptop. "Jessica, you can be a real pain in my ass sometimes."

"Is that any way to speak to your CEO? The whole reason we're moving this discussion from the board-room to a friendly lunch is that I want to pry into your personal life and I don't want to mix business and dis-pleasure. If you want to call me a pain in the ass, you'd just better wait until we're out of this building and off the clock."

Seven minutes later, as we step out of the building onto the street, I turn to Jessica and grin.

"Jessica Cohen, you are a pain in the ass."

She throws back her head and laughs as she loops her elbow through mine.

"And because we're off the clock I can speak freely, too. Fuck off, Marcus. I'm only doing this because I care about you."

We walk automatically toward our default lunch place—a low-key burger joint a few blocks away. It's far enough away from the office that we don't often run into our staff here, but close enough that we can walk. But shit, it feels like the whole city is full of kids at the moment, because even on the short walk to the restaurant, every second person I notice on the street is pushing a stroller or walking alongside a kid.

Huh. Where *do* small children go all day? What will Abby and I do with our baby when we're both working? I'll bet she has some ideas already, neatly typed up and filed in that binder of hers. I should probably do some research, too... Maybe ask some of my staff...

"Have we ever looked into on-site child care?" I ask suddenly.

"No..." Jess says, frowning. "Why? Did one of your team request it?"

"Ah, no." Oh, shit. Why did I even bring this up? "But plenty of our staff do have kids. I imagine it would be useful if we can afford it."

"We keep saying we want to attract the best of the

best," Paul says thoughtfully. "I think we should look into it."

"Hmm. Good idea, Marcus. I'll check it out," Jess says, but she peers at me curiously, and I clear my throat and thank the gods of awkward conversation that we're finally at the restaurant.

It turns out there's a private function today, and at first, Melinda the hostess tells us she doesn't have room for us. But I have a good rapport with Melinda, so I chat with her for a bit, and the next thing I know, she's seating us at a table.

"How do you do that?" Paul asks, waving vaguely toward the entrance where Melinda is back at her podium.

"Do what?"

"I don't even know what it's called," he mutters.

"It's called *sweet-talking* people, Paul." Jess snorts. "You should try it once in a while."

He flips her the bird, and we all laugh—but then Jess's gaze sharpens and she turns to me.

"Right. What's going on with you? Are you sick?"

There isn't a lot Paul, Jess and I haven't shared over the years. We've supported one another through virtually every up and down life had to offer in the years since college—both personally, and through the exhausting cycle of business successes and the inevitable tight periods when we attempted ambitious expansions and projects. Jess and Paul are my business partners but they're also my friends. Hell, I lived with them for the two most intense years of my life—they're pretty much family now.

But they're also Abby's friends—especially Jess, so maybe I should ask her if she's okay with me telling them what's going on but…fuck it all if I don't need to get this off my chest at last.

"No, nothing like that." I sigh. "There's just a lot happening. My biological father just randomly started messaging me on Facebook."

"Wow." Jess frowns. "Yeah. That must be messing with your head."

"Actually, I haven't really had the brain space to *think* about that yet," I mutter. "Look, the real reason I'm all over the place at the moment is that Abby and I are trying to have a baby."

Paul silently raises his eyebrows. Jessica tilts her head, staring at me.

For a long, awkward moment, no one says anything.

"See?" I say pointedly. "I *told* you not to ask."

"Fuck," Jess sighs, and she glances at Paul. "I'll settle up with you on the way back."

"And that, my friends, is how you play the long game," Paul says smugly. When I scowl at them, he explains, "We had a bet when Abby moved in with you that you two were going to get together."

"We could all see there was something more there," Jess tells me unhelpfully. "I just figured if you hadn't already made a move on her, you never would."

"Keep your cash, Jess," I mutter. "We're not together."

"Well, I'm not sure how much you know about babies, Marcus," she says with a laugh. "But if you're trying to have a baby and you're *not* together, then you're going to be trying for a really long time."

"It's complicated." I really wish I'd kept my mouth shut. How do I even explain this?

"Wait, I'm confused. *Are* you and Abby together?" Paul prompts, and I shake my head.

"No."

"But that's not because *you* don't want to be," Jess surmises. I clear my throat and pick up my menu to avoid her razor-sharp gaze. What *do* I want? Even I don't know today. Last night I was swept up in a way that I'm just not used to, but in the cold light of day, nothing has really changed. I'm still me, Abby is still Abby. Any potential romantic entanglement between us is a recipe for complete disaster.

Even so, I already know that there's no way I'll suppress my attraction to her again. It was difficult enough after we kissed, but *now*? Knowing how explosive our chemistry really is, I'm pretty much fucked. I really thought I was over her. I was *sure* of it.

Maybe what was really happening this year was that I'd just dammed the feelings up and they were quietly simmering away to a boiling point while I deluded myself that everything had gone back to normal. The dam has burst now, but I can't even begin to make sense of the surge yet. All I really know today is that I've never *felt* like this before. It's scorching sex. It's easy, intense friendship. I feel light inside even now, just thinking about her. *What the fuck is happening to me?*

"I'm still not following your situation," Paul says suddenly. "So you're having a baby together, but you aren't actually together. How does that work?"

"Abby and I are best friends. But yes, we're not getting any younger and we're going to try to have a kid together."

"Not getting any *younger*?" Jess repeats, eyebrows high. "She's thirty, Marcus."

"Yeah, I know," I say, but I've already said enough, and I don't want to betray Abby's personal situation. I hope my tone is convincing enough when I simply add, "It's complicated."

"I'll bet it is," she says slowly, then pins me to my chair with a sharp glance. "You could just tell her you love her. Like, *really* love her. Instead of whatever the hell this baby scheme is supposed to be."

Luca made a similar accusation a few weeks ago and I laughed in his face. Today, it feels bewilderingly too close to home and I can't even dismiss it with a joke. Do I love Abby? Of course I do, she's my best friend. But am I *in* love?

I know what lust feels like. *This* feeling is deeper and wider and more intense than lust has been or will ever be.

"Have *you* ever been in love?" I ask Jess, and she narrows her gaze.

"What does that have to do with anything?"

"I'm genuinely curious. What does it actually feel like?"

"It feels like you want everything they have to give, the bad as well as the good, because to you—the good is just *that* good," Paul answers before Jess can respond. "It feels like the connection you have to that person is so strong that it's changed you—for the better." He laughs a little bitterly. "Don't ask me what it feels like when they walk out on you. That answer would be less poetic and more expletive-laden."

Jess and I exchange a shocked glance. Maybe I'm a typical guy and I don't exactly love talking about feelings, but Paul is on a whole other level. When Isabel first left him, I took him out for a beer and asked him how he was feeling. He answered by pulling out the tablet from his satchel and showing me some programming code with a long explanation about "jenga" code and how removing one line from his batch made the whole thing collapse. It was hours later that I realized what he was getting at. That was the first and last time we directly discussed his feelings about Isabel, until right this minute.

This time last year, Paul would have slipped his phone from his pocket the minute we sat down and worked or read as we talked—today he's left his phone at the office. He's engaged and increasingly willing to be vulnerable with us. I know Paul's been on a journey this year, but the changes he's made are becoming more obvious every day now.

"I have been in love," Jess tells me. "It didn't feel like that for me. It was the scariest fucking thing I've experienced in my life. It felt like stripping myself bare and stepping out onto a battlefield. But it's different for you and Abby."

"And how do you figure that?"

"Because you already know that it works, idiot." Jess sighs impatiently. "The scary part of love is that the other person might discover something about you they don't like and cruelly reject you, leaving you heartbroken and pathetic." She nods her head toward Paul, and he glares at her.

"Thanks, Jess. If this CEO thing doesn't work out for you, you could consider grief counseling with sensitivity like that."

"I'd say Paul's been more 'pissed off' than 'heartbroken and pathetic,'" I say, and it's my turn to be on the receiving end of his glare. I raise my hands in surrender. "Hey, man. I didn't say it wasn't justified."

"Seems to me that things with you and Abby have been changing for a while, and you talking about babies and raising the subject of 'love' tells me this isn't going away any time soon," Jess says quietly. Her gaze sharpens again. "But I'm implementing a new policy—you two are only allowed to date my friends if you promise not to fuck it up. The Paul/Isabel fiasco is complicated enough for me without an Abby/Marcus disaster to deal with, too."

An "Abby/Marcus" disaster is my fear, too. Even if I *am* in love with Abby, that doesn't mean I'll feel this way for the rest of my life. I have no way of knowing how long it will last. People fall in and out of love all the time.

And that's all fine so far—because as far as I know, Abby is only interested in being friends who parent together. But what if *her* desires change, too? What if she's avoiding me today because she's feeling as awed by last night as I am?

I don't think I've ever been as conflicted as I am right now. And the worst thing is, there are no easy answers. Patience has never been my strong suit, but the only thing I can do here is to wait and see what happens next.

ABBY IS NOWHERE to be seen when I get home. Her room is empty, and despite the crisp fall day, the heat is down low—which tells me she's been out for some time and isn't planning on an imminent return. I microwave a frozen dinner and take it into my study. There are emails clamoring for my attention, but I flick through them mindlessly.

I can't stop thinking about last night. Memories played on a loop in my brain all day, stealing my attention every time I tried to focus elsewhere. I haven't seen Abby and we've only had that very brief IM chat, but she's occupied a space in every one of my thoughts.

I just want what's best for her. I just want to do right by her.

I always have, and I always will.

Always?

I stare that thought down, but it doesn't scare me one bit. Romance and sex aside, Abby *has* always had an "always" from me. We've been friends for thirty years, and I know we'll be friends for thirty more.

I push back from my desk and pinch the bridge of my nose, about to give up on the laptop altogether, when another uncomfortable train of thought surfaces. I open my browser to navigate to the Facebook message thread of Warwick, Luca and me. Two messages now, both unanswered, a small block of text on the page that represents nothing more than an unwelcome, uninvited intrusion into my life.

Warwick is nothing to me and Luca—he gave up that right when he walked out. Jack is our dad, and he has been since he and Mom met at one of my football games when I was twelve years old.

Logically, I know the most reasonable thing to do here is to tell Warwick that I'm not interested in connecting with him. Luca will follow my lead, and if I end this once and for all, I can move on and focus on my own life.

Focus on Abby.

Focus on our baby.

I swear under my breath and slam closed the lid of

my laptop. The childish part of me wants to leave the door open. It somehow craves both revenge and closure—I want to torture him with my silence, then learn why he left with a reason so big that it becomes a valid excuse. Maybe then I could understand him.

Maybe then I'd be less scared that I'm just like him.

Just then, the front door to our apartment slowly creeps open. Abby doesn't call out as she usually would—instead, I don't hear anything at all. I have a feeling she's tiptoeing through the living area.

Perfect. A distraction. I keep my footsteps light, too, hoping I'll catch her sneaking past me. As she comes into view, my gaze sweeps from her bare feet all the way up her body. She's wearing her yoga clothes and the leggings cling to the curves of her hips and ass. I want to leap across the couch, push her up against the wall and kiss her until she's jelly-limbed.

Maybe tomorrow night, that's what I'll do. But tonight, I have to reconnect with her in a different way. Our friendship still matters most of all.

"Are you absolutely sure you're not avoiding me?"

She spins toward me and winces.

"I *wasn't* avoiding you. I was out with Isabel. We just decided to get dinner after Pilates."

It's Friday night, which means that Abby would normally turn down all but the most tempting social engagements. Her routine on Friday evenings is a class at 6:00 p.m., followed by dinner and then gaming until late. She's not exactly known for her spontaneous dinner dates, not even with her girlfriends. She has a meal with them every week—but it's always on Wednesday, and occasionally brunch on Sunday.

I let it slide, though, because forcing the issue is going to make her defensive. Instead, I smile and ask, "Sounds like fun. How is she?"

"Well, I wouldn't say she's great," Abby mutters. "These mediation problems are really getting to her."

That's the first time since Isabel walked out on Paul that Abby has actually answered when I asked about her friend's welfare. Every time I tried to check in on Izzy until now, Abby deflected me and insisted that we refrain from discussing it. I kind of understood where she was coming from, given how close Paul and I are. But now that she's opened the door, I try to keep the conversation flowing.

"Yeah, Paul mentioned she was being stubborn," I say.

"Actually, she *just* wanted the house at Greenport, and that's the only thing he won't give her." Abby's gaze becomes a glare. "Why do you have to take his side? From what she said, she was miserable for ages before she left. I like Paul, too, but he has no people skills *whatsoever*."

She's a ball of tension; her hands are in fists by her thighs and her jaw is set hard. I take a step toward her, and she takes a step back—her legs colliding with the couch. She glances behind her, as if she is sizing up the distance to her bedroom.

"I'm not going to fight with you, and I'm sure as shit not going to pounce on you. I just wanted to talk. I missed you today."

"I was busy—" she starts to say, but when I raise my eyebrows pointedly she falls silent, then sighs. "I freaked out, okay? I did."

"No kidding," I say gently, and she sits on the sofa, and I sit beside her. "Talk to me. We can deal with this as long as we keep *talking* to each other."

"I don't think there's anything to talk about," she murmurs. "I wasn't prepared for that…last night."

"What *were* you expecting?"

The flush is light across her cheeks, and she avoids my gaze as she mutters, "You know at the beginning when we crashed our noses and we laughed?"

"Yeah."

"*That*. Lots of that. Lots of 'Ow, move your elbow,' and 'Ew, that's gross,' and 'Can you hurry up so I can go to sleep?'" Abby says, and when I laugh again, she shrugs. "I kind of figured it would be awkward, messy and simple."

"We know each other too well for that, Abs. It was always going to be good."

"Well, you could have told me that so I could have been prepared." She rubs her forehead wearily.

"You're complaining that sex was *too* good. People don't complain about that," I say pointedly. The curve of her neck reminds me of the way that she arched her head last night when she was moaning and writhing around. I want to cross the space between us to kiss her again. I wonder what she'd do if I did.

"I wasn't complaining. I was just explaining to you why today…why last night… I just needed some space."

"Okay. And you've had some space. So how are you doing now?"

"I'm good. Ready for round two tomorrow," she says, forcing an unconvincing smile. "If you're up for it."

"You know I am."

"Right," she says, and claps her hands against her thighs. "Well, I'm going to bed."

"Wait. I need you to do something first."

"What's that?"

"You need to come over here and hug me."

Her gaze narrows.

"Seriously?"

"I want to show you something."

"Oh, you don't need to show me. I saw it plenty last night," she says wryly, and I laugh again as I shake my head.

"I'm serious. Come here."

Abby sits up, but she doesn't move toward me. Instead, she stares. "What are you doing, Marcus?" she says, her voice dropping.

"Come here," I repeat softly. She swallows, then shuffles along until she's right beside me. I turn and wrap my arms around her for a completely innocent hug. "See? I'm still me. You're still you. We're still *us*. Nothing is broken."

"Okay," she whispers, then turns to lean against my chest. "Yeah, okay."

"So tomorrow, don't hide from me."

"Okay."

I swallow the lump in my throat. "Abby, if last night was too intense for you, then we won't do it again—we'll just find a way to use the syringe. The sex was great—amazing. But even if it gets us a baby, it's not worth it if it damages *this*."

I *really* mean it, even though a part of me wants to punch myself in the face for reminding her there's another option here. But then Abby throws her arms around my waist and rests her face against my chest, and I'm glad I remembered to be a good friend.

"That's exactly what I needed to hear," she says, this time on a contented sigh. "Yes. Okay."

"So we're good?"

"We absolutely are." I can't see her face, but I can hear the smile in her voice, and I know she means it at last.

"Fantastic." I kiss her hair, then playfully push her away. "Keep your hands off me. I need to rest my rocking bod so I can be at your service tomorrow."

She laughs freely as she rises to her feet.

"Good night, Marcus."

"Night, Abs."

I relax into the sofa and watch her walk to her bedroom. It strikes me that I've almost been in a holding pattern since she blew my mind with that kiss in late December. In the beginning, I was so scared to push her. I was afraid she'd run away but also... I was scared she *wouldn't*. What if we started something here, and I let her down?

Abby needs a man who understands her, who supports her and who cares deeply for her. But most of all, she needs a man who will always want the best for her and who will stand by her, no matter what.

Can I be that man?

The answer hits me so hard that my breath catches. *I already am that man. I always have been.*

Maybe I'm a selfish asshole sometimes—but when it comes to Abby, I genuinely care about her, especially above the demands of my dick. In January, when I could see that she was freaked out about things changing between us, I *forced* myself to ignore my infatuation with her. Even tonight, when I wanted nothing more than to reach for her again, she wasn't ready, and I didn't think twice.

My highest priority here is to protect our friendship. To protect *her*. And I will. *Always*.

Suddenly it doesn't seem to matter that I don't know what the future holds for us—because I know that I can trust the way I care for her. Maybe I *have* been halfway in love with her all year, or maybe this is just an intense infatuation that's muddled messily with our friendship.

But being sure about all that doesn't even seem to matter, because whatever's going on here, I am absolutely certain of the only things that *do* matter: I'd never hurt her, and that's *never* going to change.

If me and Abby were together, and things got rocky between us, I'd find a way to work it out, and if there wasn't a way to be found, I'd fucking *make* one.

I can't ignore this anymore. I can't pretend I don't want something more from my relationship with Abby. It's time to do what I should have done in the first place.

It's time to back myself. It's time to *trust* myself.

I'll have to proceed carefully, because Abby is skittish, and I can't risk scaring her off. But there's something incredible simmering between us, and if last night proved anything, it's that Abby feels it, too.

I'll let her set the pace for us. I'll let her take her time to explore this new dimension to our relationship.

But I have a second chance with her, and the one mistake I *won't* make is to let her hide.

CHAPTER FIFTEEN

Abby

THE SECOND TIME, I am both sober and prepared.

"Right," I say as soon as Marcus rests his cutlery on his plate. "Let's have sex."

He raises his eyebrows at me.

"Right now?"

The air feels charged to me—atmospheric and heavy, like a storm is brewing. The problem is, Marcus has been so relaxed all day that I'm starting to fear the only place the storm is brewing is in my pants. I shrug, trying to play it cool.

"Sure. If you're ready."

The corner of his mouth twitches.

"You're quite the seductress when you want to be."

"There's a good reason why I'm a thirty-year-old spinster, Marcus."

"I don't think *spinster* is even a word anymore. Even so, I can give you some tips," he says, and he leans back in his chair. "Instead of 'let's have sex,' try climbing on my lap and kissing me."

"I did that once before," I say unthinkingly, and my gaze drops to the table. "You didn't exactly like it the first time."

He draws in a sharp breath, but he waits until I raise my eyes to his before he murmurs, "You know damn well how much I liked it, Abby."

But he doesn't move. His expression is completely impassive, as if he's totally uninvested in the conversation. I scowl at him. What's gotten into him tonight? Does he not want to do it *this* way anymore? The thought is unbearable. If it was only just that *one* time between us, I am going to need to buy shares in a battery company or a superendurance rechargeable vibrator.

"I have to work for it now?" I ask uncertainly.

"Exactly." He shrugs, and then I realize that he's teasing me—trying to taunt me into taking the initiative again, like when we first kissed in his bed. And what would it feel like, to know I'd pushed him to the brink, like he pushed me when he went down on me? What would it be like to see him completely lose control, and to know that I'd done that? Would I feel powerful?

Then I remember—there's no *need* to wonder. I bite my lip as an internal battle plays out. Instinct tells me that all I need to do here is flirt a bit with him, tease him a little as he's hinting toward...but I'm just not sure. This aspect to our relationship is so new I'm not entirely sure where the boundaries are, and isn't this all just about making a baby, anyway? Didn't I *want* to keep this clinical?

Huh. As if *that* plan worked the other night. I draw in a sharp breath as our eyes lock and the want surges all the way through me again.

"So you want me to climb on your lap, huh?" I say softly.

"It was just one idea… It might work," he says with a shrug. I toss my hair.

"But what will I *find* if I climb on your lap?" I murmur, and then I lean my elbow on the table and start to nibble almost absentmindedly on the tip of my forefinger. When his gaze darkens, I draw my finger just a little into my mouth and swirl my tongue around it. Marcus laughs uneasily and stands. I stand, too, but I add wryly, "So much for you criticizing my seduction skills. I'd say that's a new land-speed record."

"I was just playing with you," he says as he extends his hand to take mine and to help me to my feet. I'm about to tease him for being easy, but then he starts toward my room. I plant my feet to tug him back toward his.

"No, your room," I say quietly.

"Not fucking happening, Abby," he says flatly. I hesitate, and he raises his eyebrows at me. "I mean it. This is nonnegotiable for me."

"It wasn't the other night… What's wrong with your room now?"

He gives me an impatient look.

"Abs, I don't actually care which room but…we have to stay together afterward. At least for a while."

"But why?"

"Because…" He hesitates, then mutters, "I can't explain it. It just matters."

"Five minutes."

"Twenty."

"Twelve and a half."

"Seriously?" He stares at me incredulously. "We're now negotiating for *half minutes* of postcoital cuddles? Are you *always* like this with boyfriends?"

"You are *not* my boyfriend," I say a little too abruptly. We stare at each other for a moment, our stubbornness doing battle in the space between us, then I realize I just *have* to be honest with him and I blurt, "It's too intimate."

Confusion flickers across his features, and then he says pointedly, "You let me lick your—"

"Marcus!" I squeal, then turn toward my room. "Fine! You can stay."

"Abs." He catches me at the elbow, and turns me to face him. Then he slides his arm around my waist and pulls me gently against him. He bends his head toward mine, and I'm so relieved that we're ready to get down to business that I melt right on into him.

It *is* a relief that I only had to wait two days for this. How am I going to cope when there is a whole month before I am fertile again? Or if this actually worked this cycle, and this week is all I ever got to have of him? His kiss deepens, and I lift my hands to rest against the hard expanse of his chest. The anticipation of being with him again tonight has had me sitting at a simmer all day and it's only a few moments before I'm pushing at his shirt, impatient to feel his bare skin. Too soon, though, he lifts his head to stare down at me. I reach to pull him back—but he resists.

"Syringe, then?" he whispers. I blink at him, then scowl and step back.

"That is *not* fair."

"No, Abby. *Not fair* is jumping off me the minute

I've come and running away from me like all I am to you is a sperm dispenser."

I swallow, hard, and then look past him to the wall. Marcus catches my chin in his hand and drags my gaze back to his. "I know sex isn't normally a part of how we are together, but that *can't* change the fact that we care about each other."

"Okay," I whisper weakly, and he brushes his lips against mine.

"Now let's go fuck like rabbits."

I giggle as he tugs me toward the bedroom, flicking the light on as he enters the room. I automatically flick it off behind him and he pauses.

"I caved on the cuddle after," I remind him. "The light has to stay off."

"I want to see you, Abby."

"This is *my* nonnegotiable."

He opens his mouth to argue and I decide it is *high time* we stopped talking. I push at his chest, and he stumbles back to sit on my bed. I haven't made it—I never do, unlike Marcus, who learned the habit when he was taught to master hospital corners growing up in Lindy's house. I drop to my knees and tug off his shoes and then socks, and breathe my way all the way up his thighs.

Then I glance up at him, checking his expression in the near-darkness, but his face is set in a mask I can't read. He watches me silently as I undo his buckle and slide it out of the belt loops. My eyes are adjusting enough that I can see his Adam's apple work as I go back for the button and zipper. I tug at his pants, and he lifts his ass from the bed so that I can work them down, then he kicks them away impatiently once they reach his ankles.

He's just wearing boxers, but as I survey the half tent of his erection pushing against them, it suddenly strikes me that whenever I've seen his laundry, he's worn briefs.

"Boxers?" My eyes have adjusted to the darkness, so the self-consciousness in his body language as he shrugs is clear.

"Better for sperm production apparently."

Is there anything in the world hotter than a man who cares? I run my palms up his thighs, then lean forward to kiss his rapidly inflating erection through the boxers. I hear him hiss, and glance up at him again. His hands tremble as they touch my shoulders and then gently brush against the back of my hair, and the intensity in his gaze is breathtaking.

He wants this. Desperately. And there it is—that thrill of power I was wondering about, and even *that* doesn't disappoint. I smile to myself.

"I figured you'd be a blow job guy."

"Aren't all guys blow job guys?"

"Roger wasn't."

"Roger was a fucking idiot in *every* way. And please don't say his name while we're doing this unless you want me to deflate like a popped balloon."

I giggle and run my hands over him, then pull the waistband of the boxers down. When he's naked from the waist down, he pulls my hair back from my face to hold it gently at the nape of my neck. I feel his eyes on me, but when I glance up at him, the intensity in his gaze leaves me unnerved.

"Don't look at me," I say uncertainly, and he reaches down to tilt my chin up. I stare at the wall behind him, anxious at what I might find in his gaze.

"Abby. It would be an unforgivable waste to do anything *but* look at you right now. You're…" He struggles for words, then swallows. "Fuck, Abby. You're just so *beautiful*."

I like the way I look. I think I'm an attractive person, but still…it's difficult for me to believe that *Marcus* thinks I'm beautiful—just because I'm so different from the women he's been attracted to in the past. But he wouldn't lie to me. He might flatter me, he might charm me, but he wouldn't lie. I reluctantly meet his gaze again, and then in an instant, the insecurity vaporizes. There's no way I can deny that look in his eyes. It's affection, yes, but it's laced with a desire so intense it's almost need.

In this moment, I'm not just his friend—I am a woman. A lover. A partner. I am kneeling between his legs, and he is gazing at me like I am the most beautiful woman in the world.

I am suddenly bursting with confidence, and bolstered, I let myself slip fully into the moment. I forget again to think about how weird this should be, and I focus only on *that* look in his eyes. And so I adore him right back—learning the length of him with my lips and tongue, feeling the ridges and veins bulging out along him as his excitement grows. It isn't long before his entire body is shaking with the effort it takes to hold himself back.

He tries to stifle his moans, and it's an intensely erotic soundtrack—each little noise shooting electricity through my body. It's a powerful thrill, how worked up he is, and I'm surprised at how much *I* am into this. I've dished out blow jobs to lovers in the past, but more as a giving gesture—never as something I've particularly enjoyed myself. Now, though, I desperately want to keep going until he comes in my mouth. I want to taste the essence of him and to hear him call out while I am lucid enough to pay attention—and if we get a repeat of last night's fireworks, there's little chance of that happening with him inside me any time soon.

I want to keep going, but I won't. After all, it would rather defeat the purpose of this whole exercise, given swallowing would definitely *not* get me pregnant.

"Okay—I can't take any more," he groans, then he helps me up from the ground. I climb up onto the bed and push him down onto his back. I undo the rest of the buttons on his business shirt to expose his chest, and his hands fumble at my T-shirt. I let him lift it over my head, then he pulls me down against him so that he can kiss me. I straddle him and position myself so his erection is *right* at a sweet spot, but he's not inside of me yet.

It strikes me how the last time we were together we were both hesitant—speaking in rushed whispers, gaining verbal permission from each other. Not this time. Tonight, we are reading each other's reactions, and somehow that is leading to a much more urgent, much brighter explosion.

After two days of thinking about this, it takes exactly the performance of one blow job, a few minutes of kissing and dry humping, and one brush of Marcus's thumbs over my nipples, and I am *just* about done.

I freeze. I'm still wearing my underpants and my skirt is around my hips, but regardless, an orgasm looms. Marcus draws in a deep breath, and I echo it, trying to steady myself.

"Abs?" he whispers, and he stares up at me, his hands gently rubbing against my upper arms. "What is it? Are you okay?"

He's concerned, and the way he cares for me is a thing of beauty. I shake my head and offer him a weak smile.

"I just need a minute."

"What did I do? You're okay?"

"I am."

"Promise?"

I don't think I've ever been with someone who cared about me like this. Even his cautiousness and his determination to pleasure me is somehow intensely erotic.

Fuck taking it slow. I want him inside me, and I want it *now*. I kick my underpants off and come back to him still wearing my skirt up over my hips.

"I can't wait," I groan, and he gives me a cocky grin that fades in an instant when I guide him into my body. Now the hands at my shoulders tighten, and when I look down to check the expression on his face, our gazes lock. He stares up at me, and I can't close my eyes—can't look away—can't even tell myself I'm pretending this is *anyone* else. It is Marcus—*Marcus* inside me, *Marcus's* hands on me, Marcus's scent in the air and Marcus's look of sheer, intense need.

Marcus who sends me over the edge with just a few thrusts.

Marcus who growls at me to keep my eyes open

when I come, and Marcus who comes just a second or two later.

Then it's Marcus who pulls me into his arms and holds me fiercely against him. Marcus who kisses me softly, Marcus who strokes my back, Marcus who brushes away the tears that leak from my eyes even though I try to hide them. This is intimacy of its purest and deepest form—a depth of connection I'd never even known was possible between two people.

And when I drift toward slumber afterward, he is still in my bed and I forget to count the minutes because my entire mind is full of him—full of *us*. Too full to process the danger I am placing my heart in, too full to contemplate all of the ways this can go wrong, too full to even think about the real reason we are doing this—the baby we both want.

And the sensible voice inside me—the one guarding my heart—tries to protest all of this intimacy and this closeness and this intensity, but I drown it out, because they are concerns for the future, and right now, I am concerned only with the beauty of *now*.

CHAPTER SIXTEEN

Marcus

"RAIN, HAIL OR SHINE" seemed like a good idea when Paul and I decided on this workout regime in the summer, but this morning it's sleeting a little, and Abby must be starting to rub off on me because it feels too fucking cold to be outside. I'm not going to be the one to back out from the challenge, though, and when Paul seems unfazed, I fall into step beside him alongside the river.

"This is stupid," he says after about a mile. The ground is icy, and we've both *almost* slipped a few times despite the salt on the pavement. It doesn't help that I'm distracted—I'm thinking about my next move with Abby, since we're supposed to have sex again tomorrow. Paul knocks the pace right back to walking and mutters, "Maybe we should stick to the treadmills when ice is falling from the sky."

"Agreed."

Now that we're not running, we quickly catch our breath, and the silence feels odd. Paul glances at me.

"How's things with Abby?" he asks.

"Going well actually," I say. "Do I ask you how you're doing?"

"We had mediation last week. I think I'm just going to give her the fucking vacation home. It's getting too ugly. I don't understand—she was never *like* this when we were married."

I wince. Paul sounds *utterly* bewildered. It's not a look he wears often.

"Sorry, Paul."

"Yeah," he sighs. "Me, too. So you and Abby—I know there's the baby thing, but do you think you're going to try to make it work? As a couple, I mean."

"Well," I say cautiously. "We're not there yet, but I'm working on it."

"Look at you." Paul laughs. "Never thought I'd see the day."

"Hang on. Didn't you bet money me and Abby *would* get together?"

"Sure." He shrugs. "I thought it was inevitable that at some point you and Abby would date, she'd fall in love and you wouldn't, then you'd smash her heart into teeny, tiny smithereens and your friendship would be shot." I glare at him, and he winces. "Don't take it personally, Marcus, but I've known you for a long time. When you said the *L*-word at lunch last week, I nearly fell off my chair. If Jess had proposed a bet that was about *love*, I'd have bet *way* more money, and I'd have bet against you."

"Thanks, asshole," I mutter.

"So if you've been bitten by the love bug, I guess you've changed your thoughts on marriage, too?"

"Marriage?" I repeat, then I shake my head. "Fuck, Paul, we're not even together yet—not really. That's a bit of a stretch."

"But it is in the cards if you do win her over, right?"

"Can I imagine living with her forever, as friends? Easily. Can I imagine *being* with her together, as a couple? Maybe. Do I think we need to make that formal in any way if we do figure it out and end up together? Definitely not. But if Abby feels the same way I do, we'll figure something out."

"I see," he says thoughtfully. "But…you think you're in love with her, right?"

Argh. The last thing in the world I expected from Paul this morning was for him to make me talk about my *feelings*. I swallow and shrug.

"I don't know. I feel something for her." Something amazing. Something miraculous.

"And this is the same Abby Herbert we've been hanging out with since college, right?"

"I don't like that tone."

"Correct me if I'm wrong, but didn't Abby linger in that job at the online magazine for years after she started making good money off her gaming content?"

"What's that got to do with anything? She plays it safe. I mean—yeah, she probably should have quit a lot sooner, but by that point she had a shitload of cash and a thriving business to fall back on. She's not like us— she couldn't have done what we did with our business."

"Why not?"

"Well, she's just not the kind of woman to throw all of her eggs into a basket unless she knows it's a sure thing." He laughs triumphantly, and I scowl. "Fuck off, Paul."

"So, you're going to tell her you still don't want to

settle down if things start to get serious between you, yeah?"

"I *won't* hurt her, so yes, of course I'll make that clear, too," I mutter.

"Good," he says, and I stop walking. Paul stops, too, and turns back to face me.

"You think she's going to want the tiny handcuffs," I surmise, and he waggles his ring finger at me and nods. My gaze sticks on the solid silver band. He's still wearing his wedding ring, and I don't understand that at all—Isabel left, and she's made it clear that she's never coming back. They can't even have a civil conversation anymore. Why would he *want* to wear that? Surely it's nothing more now than a reminder of the failure of his marriage.

Paul's expression softens, and he says quietly, "They aren't meant to be handcuffs, idiot. They're meant to be an anchor. Storms come in your life together, and the anchor keeps you where you're meant to be. I mean—in my case, Isabel hacked the fucking chain off the anchor and set us both adrift in a hurricane but…the *idea* was that we'd promised each other we'd stick it out together."

"You're not much of a spokesman for wedded bliss, Paul." I sigh, then add, "Are you ever going to take that thing off?"

"One day," he says. He glances down at it, then shrugs. "I still feel married. I made a commitment, and Isabel's commitment might have meant jack shit when the going got tough, but *my* promise to her meant something. I don't know what to make of that myself yet, but I do know…if you and Abby decide to try to be together romantically, sooner or later she's going to be looking for stability. It should tell you something that even I can see that *that* is the kind of woman Abby is. Plus—Marcus, Jesus—I don't get why a fucking *kid* doesn't scare you, but as soon as I say the word *marry*, your balls shrivel up. If you get her pregnant, you're tied to her forever, anyway, so what difference does it make?"

I start to jog again, and he steps around some trash cans and falls in beside me.

"Let's say she feels the same way I do right now, and then we have a baby," I say slowly. "And we're together for a while, and then we don't want to be together anymore. I walk away, she walks away, we still parent the kid together and we don't have to look back at the time we spent together as a couple and see it as a failure. We both go in with our eyes open, and no one is devastated if things need to change. What's so wrong with that? Some people want to get married, some people don't. And some people never wanted to get married in the first place, let alone *after* they heard all about how the happiest married couple they knew split up and now can't even agree on a property settlement."

"Marcus. You're so screwed."

"Well, would *you* get married again? After what you're going through right now?"

He grins at me. "In a heartbeat. If I ever felt the way I felt about Isabel again, I'd want to know that we both intended to be in it forever."

"Even though that meant *nothing* with Isabel. Even though things got rocky and she walked away, and now you're wrangling your way through a messy divorce," I say incredulously. Paul's mouth tightens.

"*Isabel* gave up on us, not me. If I'd known she was unhappy, I'd have gone to the ends of the fucking earth to fix things. The only reason we're in the situation we're in now is that she *didn't* let me know—she just walked away. Even so, there was something great about the years we did have together. There's a kind of safety in a commitment like that."

I shake my head at him.

"I think we're going to have to agree to disagree on this one."

"Or we shelve the conversation and come back to it again in a few months."

"After Izzy fucks you over some more, you might see sense," I mutter, and he laughs bitterly.

"That's a real possibility. But it's far more probable that you'll try this bullshit on Abby and she'll tell you to fuck off."

"She won't," I say confidently. "If we get that far, we'll figure it out together."

"I'd wager another bet right now, but I think you have enough at stake." Paul laughs softly. "Should we call it early and grab some breakfast?"

I sigh and nod. "Yes, but you're pissing me off today, so you're picking up the check."

CHAPTER SEVENTEEN

Abby

THE VERY FIRST thing I'm conscious of when I wake up is that Marcus's scent is on my sheets, tangled up with the musky scent of sex. I lie with my eyes closed and breathe all of this in, letting memories rise. Blood is pounding through my body before I'm even properly awake, and I smile just at the thought of him.

Then I open my eyes and I'm conscious of so many other things—of the silence in the apartment, and the cold expanse of the bed beside me. He's left the apartment, and he didn't sleep in my bed. That is as it should be, and I tell myself I'm not disappointed. I tell myself I don't miss him, and that it would have been strange and awkward to wake up beside him.

I make coffee and curl up on the sofa with my phone to find Marcus has already texted me. It's an image of a tiny cartoon gamer baby, sitting at a little keyboard with a headset on.

And that sound you're hearing, folks, is my heart, melting into a bubbling puddle. I'm smiling to myself as I reply.

Abby: That is adorable. Where are you this morning?

Marcus: Paul and I went for breakfast after our run. I'm in a car on my way back. How are you today?

Abby: I'm good.

Marcus: Really? Not freaking out?

Abby: No, not this time. All is well :)

I'm blissed out today—accepting of my fate. I'll probably freak out tomorrow night, after the last round for this month, but for today—things are as they are, and there's not much I can do to change it now.

Marcus: It was still intense, though.

Abby: I'm glad one of us enjoyed it.

There's a long pause, then he types his reply.

Marcus: Abby. I can't tell if you're kidding.

I giggle as I respond.

Abby: There is a very good chance I am.

Marcus: Don't joke about things like that. I have a very fragile ego.

Abby: There has never been anything fragile about your ego, Marcus Ross. Not for one second of your entire life.

Marcus: I was thinking.

Abby: Uh-oh.

Marcus: Are you sure when you ovulate?

There's a lot of things about this current arrangement I could too easily get used to, but constant menstrual cycle talk with Marcus is not one of them. I grimace as I reply.

Abby: No.

Marcus: Do you have a pretty good idea? Do you get mittelschmerz?

Abby: What the fuck is mittelschmerz?

Marcus: It's the gynecological term for pain or tenderness around the time of ovulation.

Abby: Okay, it was cute before when you knew a few things about this stuff, but now you're freaking me out. How do you know that?

Marcus: Google. And I'm reading a couple of books about conception and pregnancy. Anyway, do you get it? Or any other definitive signs—increased arousal, thicker cervical mucus or fluid retention?

Abby: Marcus. I am not—nor will I ever—discuss my CERVICAL MUCUS with you. Did we not already agree that my CERVIX is off-limits for polite conversation?

Marcus: I'm just trying to help.

Abby: And I appreciate that…but no more cervix talk! And I don't know for sure. I don't get any of that, not that I've noticed.

I pause, then a thought strikes me.

Abby: Does that mean I'm not ovulating?

Marcus: No, not from what I've read—not all women have signs. But if it's not obvious to you and we're not sure of the dates, perhaps we need to rethink our plan.

Oh, shit. What does that mean? I stare at the words for a long moment before I can convince my hands to formulate a reply, and even then, all I can come up with is:

Abby: ?

Marcus: Well, we said every second day this week, but what if it's the wrong week? What if you don't ovulate till next week?

I swallow. Hard. I think I know where he's going with this, and I'm terrified…and delighted. And sick with guilt at how relieved I am that tomorrow night won't be the last time for now.

Abby: Are you saying you want to just keep going?

Marcus: Or you could get some ovulation tests if that's

what you prefer. But they aren't entirely accurate and can be difficult to interpret. Apparently.

Abby: Seriously. Do you have a secret family somewhere I don't know about, and a wife who also happens to have fertility issues? Because you know a bit too much about all of this.

Marcus: I've spent what should have been the busiest week of my working year reading up on this stuff instead of actually doing my job. You might need to help me take a restraining order out on Jess soon.

Abby: All right, Dr. Ross. What were you thinking?

Marcus: Let's forget about every second day. If the mood takes you more frequently, let's just go with it. And let's keep going right through to when your period is due in case you ovulate late.

Now I feel physically sick. I rest the phone down on my thigh and stare at the screen at the confirmation that my fears and hopes have both been confirmed.

Marcus is as into this as I am.

Marcus wants to keep going.

You know when you're riding a roller coaster and you've had a great time riding up to the top of the dip, and then you see the drop, and you're about to crash to the earth far faster than nature ever intended? That's exactly how I feel right now. My palms are even sweaty. The panic swells and overwhelms my excitement at the prospect of *more sex*, and I swipe for the phone again and type quickly.

Abby: Isn't this a little dangerous, Marcus?

Marcus: I guess it is.

My heart is racing now. At least he acknowledges it. So what do we do? Do we stop? The indicator appears, and I can almost imagine the smirk on his face as he adds:

Marcus: I mean…if we keep this up, there's a good chance you'll fall pregnant. Imagine that!

I stare at the screen, and start to laugh. The laughter builds and builds, until I feel a little silly for worrying. Pregnancy *is* the goal of this, isn't it? So what if we up the frequency—surely that's only going to help?

We're just covering our bases, after all. This is a clever idea, given I'm really not sure about the dates and my periods are so unpredictable.

Besides, I can be smart about it. I *can* have sex without falling in love. I've done it before. Granted, those encounters couldn't compare to the intimate connection I feel when I'm with Marcus. In fact, the only experience I've ever had that even came *close* to this was Roger.

But there was a difference with Roger—a critical mistake I made once, and definitely won't make this time. I went into my relationship with Roger with my eyes closed. I was so sure I'd found my happy ending that I let down my guard. I fell into love, let it surge over my head and swamp me. Love swallowed me whole, and then it spat me out.

That will *not* happen this time. I'm going in with my eyes open this time. Marcus and I can just be friends with benefits for a while, and then we can go back to being friends. All I need to do is to protect the friendship, so I'll keep the sex separate from it. No affectionate gestures, no flirting, no reference to it when we're hanging out as friends.

Then, when we go to bed, we can be lovers. And afterward, I can retreat to my room, where I'll be his friend again.

Easy.

We've already survived a lifetime of ups and downs together. It wasn't always easy being best friends. Frankly, it was a miracle we survived adolescence with any closeness left between us, especially after I evolved into a moody, braces-clad geek with a nasty habit of snorting when someone told a joke, and Marcus became captain of the football team and grew into shoulders that went on for days. Our friendship at that stage was unlikely, and it often raised eyebrows with our very separate social groups. And then he went to college two years before me, and physical distance could have changed things, but we simply didn't allow it to.

If we could navigate those challenges together, surely we can cruise through any rough waters when we transition *back* to Just Friends in a few weeks' or months' time. I breathe in, then exhale, and just like that, I've made my decision.

Abby: :) Okay.

Marcus: So, the ball is in your court.

Abby: Don't say that.

Marcus: I just don't want you to feel pressured.

Abby: Well, I don't want to pressure you, either.

Marcus: Abs, I'm up for it. As often as you want. You just seduce me with that "let's have sex" move you pulled on me after dinner and I'm there.

Abby: I don't think it was the dirty talk that seduced you. I think it was what happened after. In my room. With me on my knees.

I type without thinking this time—buoyed by the unexpected development in this new arrangement and the sense of excitement that's building in me *because I don't have to wait until tomorrow night.*

Marcus: So we're adding sexting to our repertoire now?

Wait, what? Ah, shit. No. Text is supposed to be a *friendship* space, not a *sex* space. I'm about to back-pedal, but he beats me to it with a postscript.

Marcus: Not a protest, by the way. I'm up for sexting whenever you want to.

I imagine taunting him. I picture him hard in the car thinking of me, and coming home, bursting through the door and taking me into his arms—
And making a baby. Yes, that's it. *Making a baby.*

Okay, so text can be a sex space, just for a while. After all, how hard could it be to *stop* using innuendo when the time comes?

Abby: Whenever the urge strikes me, you say?

Marcus: Are you comfortable with that?

Abby: How far away are you?

Marcus: Just getting out of the car. See you in two minutes.

Abby: I'll be waiting.

CHAPTER EIGHTEEN

Abby

MY INTENTIONS ARE GOOD. My plan is good.

My execution…is not so good.

At first, I imagine that we will have two distinct modes and I'll *know* when we're being "friends" and when we're enjoying the "benefits." It doesn't work out that way at all, because Marcus and I tumble very quickly into a totally new routine: we're all over each other—all of the time. It's like there's some out-of-control chemical reaction going on in our household and I'm not sure how we can contain it, given that every time our eyes meet now, my thoughts go to how I can touch him. Sometimes, I want to touch him with innocent affection, like to take his hand or brush those curls back from his forehead. I always snap my hand back, because that isn't sex and it definitely isn't friendship, and those gestures are off-limits.

Every time I want to touch him, I just make the contact about sex. This means we end up fucking on Sunday morning as soon as Marcus walks in the door, but then I make myself leave the apartment for a while, so we have some space. I come home in the evening and we have a normal dinner and watch some TV, and then he makes me a hot cocoa and I have this odd desire to kiss him in gratitude…and then next thing I know, I'm taking off his shirt.

Monday isn't much better. I'm in my room when I hear him come home and I make an excuse to get up from the computer just to see him. We chat for a few minutes and I get the urge to hug him, so instead, we just have sex before I meet my online friends for a few hours of *very* distracted gaming.

And the next night, I'm actually quite tired and I yawn and say I might have an early night, and he agrees, and somehow that ends with us going at it on the floor between the coffee table and the TV.

And that's how it goes all week, and all weekend, and into the next week.

I decide I need to refocus our energies, so I've come up with what I *hope* is a genius plan to remind us both what all of this sex is actually about.

"Time for sci-fi?" Marcus prompts as he packs up our plates and returns to sit on the sofa in front of the TV. I shake my head, and he grins and waggles his eyebrows at me. I laugh in spite of myself.

"You have a one-track mind, Ross. No, I was hoping we could talk about some practical matters."

"This sounds serious," he says, his cheeky smile fading instantly. "Is everything okay?"

"Wait here," I say, and I walk quickly to my room and retrieve the binder. When I return to the living area with it, he laughs softly.

"I *knew* it was only a matter of time before the binder made an appearance."

"I've added to it since you last saw it," I tell him gleefully.

"I can see that," Marcus says wryly, and he lifts the

binder carefully from my hands to set it on the arm-rest, then pulls me gently so that I'm sitting close to him. Once I'm in place, he wraps one arm around my shoulders and opens the binder across both of our laps.

We spend the next few hours flicking through the pages, skimming my lists of questions and "to dos," and discussing interesting articles I've found. The binder actually becomes a prompt for us to discuss a whole lot of things I'm sure Dr. Vualez would be reassured to know we've discussed.

We're on the same page about most of the big-ticket items—I already suspected we would be. I'd never have agreed to coparent with Marcus if I *didn't* know he had the same values as me. But it's actually fun looking through my binder with Marcus. He takes my preparation seriously, because he takes *me* seriously.

It's not all smooth sailing. Marcus doesn't love the rough budget I've drawn up for myself for setting up for a baby and covering likely health care costs, but only because he's determined that we'll split those expenses.

"I don't want to argue about this tonight," I say when it becomes apparent that this is definitely going to become part of a much broader discussion.

"I agree," Marcus says quietly. "But we will come back to it, right? If we're doing this as a team, we're doing *everything* as a team, and that matters to me every bit as much as your independence matters to you." The very thought of taking his money is uncomfortable for me. Marcus presses a gentle kiss against my hair. "There are going to be some things I just can't do for this baby, Abby. Gestating it, for one. Giving birth, for another. You're going to have to let me contribute where I can, and part of that means letting me carry some of the load with finances."

"Yeah," I say, then clear my throat. "Yeah, I see your point."

"But we don't have to decide on *any* of that now. We have a lot of time to thrash it out."

"Agreed. Let's talk about something less contentious." I flip the binder open to the baby names tab. "Here are some name ideas I had…"

That discussion derails almost immediately, too, but only because Marcus knows I'm serious about my suggestions of *Anakin* or *Rey* and I know he's serious with his suggestions of *Vernon* or *Edith*.

"Anakin Vernon Herbert-Ross?" Marcus suggests, and we both burst out laughing.

But much like that financial discussion, we can shelve the subject of baby names for later, because we do know we'll find a compromise when the time comes. We haven't actually encountered an issue yet in our lives that we couldn't find common ground on eventually, so I comfort myself that for something we want as much as this baby we're planning, we *can* figure out some of the details later.

After that, we begin to read more closely through some of the articles I've printed out. It's getting late, and my eyelids are heavy, but I'm enjoying this night far too much to let it end, so I try to stay awake to prolong it.

Sleep steals over me, anyway, and soon I slip into a very pleasant slumber in his arms. It feels *really* late when I wake, but I'm still on the couch. The binder is still stretched across our laps, only now, the arm Marcus had wrapped around my shoulders has dropped to my waist and is resting squarely on my belly.

This is exactly *the* moment I pictured when I first made this binder, only I never imagined it would be Marcus holding me like this. He's actually cuddled up even closer toward me since I fell asleep, and his head now rests against mine as he concentrates carefully on the pages across our laps. I glance to see what he's reading, and I'm startled to find he's more than half-way through the section about postnatal depression.

I can't believe I actually forgot all about that tab. I've been so happy over the last few weeks, focusing on hope and a positive future. I must tense up, because Marcus suddenly realizes I'm awake.

"Hey," he murmurs. "You ready for bed?"

I sit up a little and take the binder from him, closing it carefully as I lean forward to set it down on the couch beyond our legs.

"It might happen again, you know," I say. "I might get depressed again when I'm pregnant. Or after the baby comes."

I hope he assumes the rough edge to my voice is from sleep and not the real cause—the fist of anxiety that's immediately squeezing my chest.

"It might," Marcus murmurs, reaching to rub my back gently. "And it might not. We can cross that bridge if we come to it." When I hesitate, his voice drops a little. "Whatever the future holds for us, we'll get through it *together*. Okay? You're not going to be alone."

That reminder doesn't remove the tension inside me, but it does ease it a little. I turn back to face him and our gazes lock. Something swells inside me—some kind of affection and gratitude so big and so powerful it could be all-encompassing if I let it.

I mean, I *won't* let that emotion swamp me, but I *do* have to do something with the pull I'm feeling toward him. A sudden, desperate urge overtakes me—I *need* to feel his skin against mine. I straddle his legs and I twist his shirt in my hands, taken by an urgency of affection that I'm not at all used to feeling. Marcus's eyebrows rise, but he quickly catches on, and by the time I'm lowering my lips to his, he's raising his face to mine. He cups my face tenderly in his palms and he kisses me back with a passion so fierce it almost takes my breath away.

And that's the story of how Marcus and I end up having sofa-sex so vigorous and impulsive that I kick my binder away at some point, and it breaks and scatters pages all over our living room.

It's also the story of the night I go to bed in my room alone after vigorous, binder-breaking sofa-sex, and by the time I wake late the next morning, Marcus has already been to the stationery store and purchased me a new *jumbo-size* binder…because that's just the kind of guy he is.

WE'RE SEVERAL WEEKS into this arrangement now, and I'm spending most of my time either naked with Marcus, or congratulating myself about how clever I'm being by restricting all physical contact with him to sex. It's like the most intense phase of a new relationship where the sex is about getting to know each other and strengthening a fragile bond—except this relationship is nothing like new, and the sex is *just* about getting me pregnant. But this self-lecturing is starting to feel hollow, so I decide to get some outside perspective. I'm nervous about their reaction, but I make myself tell Jess and Isabel what's going on.

"I'm sleeping with Marcus and hopefully we're going to have a baby," I blurt into the middle of an unrelated conversation during our regular dinner after Pilates on Wednesday night. God, I really have been spending too much time with Luca. Isabel's eyes nearly fall out of her head, but Jess is, as usual, scrolling through her phone while we talk and she simply rolls her eyes.

"Oh, what a huge shock. I am so surprised. Look at how surprised I am," she says without so much as an attempt at feigning that surprise she refers to. Then she yawns, and I'm pretty sure she's not even faking it. I'm equal parts confused and insulted.

"There's *no way* you could have guessed this was happening." I frown at her.

"Marcus may have mentioned something about needing to keep his testicles when I threatened to castrate him a few weeks ago. Plus, Abby, the only miracle here is that you've managed to make it *this* long without getting naked together. He worships you, and you clearly think the sun shines out of his nether regions, too. With you two playing house, it was only a matter of time."

She puts the phone down, just for a second, but then at the last minute apparently changes her mind because she immediately scoops it right back up and gets back to work.

"I *told* you Marcus was into you," Isabel says, but she still looks kind of shell-shocked. "Was this happening a few weeks ago when you tried so hard to convince me that wasn't the case?"

"No, it really wasn't." I frown, but I flick another glance at Jess. "Just rewind a bit. He actually *told* you? When?"

Marcus blabbing immediately after we slept together that first time means one of two things: he was either as freaked out by it as I was and he needed to vent, or he was as excited by it as I was and he couldn't help himself.

Neither option seems realistic. Now, I'm just confused.

"I don't see what the problem is, Abby." Jess is typing madly on her phone again as she talks, intermittently raising her eyes. "Did you *ask* him not to tell anyone?"

"I thought it was obvious that we wouldn't be broadcasting our temporary sex life to our *colleagues*," I mutter, and she snorts.

"There's two things about that sentence that make me laugh," Jess says without any humor at all. "First, you think I'm just his colleague. I'm more than a colleague, Abigail. I'm an integral part of his existence, both professionally and socially. *Of course* he would tell me. Plus, he probably thought I needed to know—since I'm also *your* second-best friend after Marcus himself, slightly higher in the hierarchy than Isabel here, who comes in at a commendable number three."

"Hey! At best, you'd be tied with me for second place, surely," Isabel protests, but Jess pats her arm condescendingly.

"Sure, sweetie, whatever you say," Jess says, then she shoots an exaggerated eye roll in my direction before she adds, "The second ridiculous thing you just said was that you think this is *temporary*. You don't start fucking someone you've known your whole life and then stop and carry on as if it never happened."

Her phone makes a *whooshing* sound. She's emailing as we talk. Great. We're out at dinner, dissecting my sex life and my *third*-best friend is working as we do. This is not atypical behavior for Jessica Cohen. She has her charms, but right at this minute I'm struggling to remember what they are.

"That's where you're wrong," I assure her, frowning. "You of all people should know, Jess, sometimes two people just have sex and that's all there is to it. It doesn't mean we're going to fall for each other."

"I of all people should know?" Jess repeats, but she's laughing now. "I'll have *you* know, young lady, I'm in a dry spell."

"Since when?" Isabel says incredulously.

"Almost two weeks now." Jess sighs. She hits the screen a few times, then flashes a profile picture at Isabel, then at me. "That was Tyler. He was a screenwriter."

"What was wrong with Tyler?"

"I missed a call from him, then he texted me three times in an hour."

"And?"

"Stalker much? I'm too busy for a clingy guy—he had to go. And I haven't had time to get back out there since. It's tragic."

"Oh, please, Jessica," Isabel mutters. "Talk to me when it's been a year."

"You can rejoin the game any time you want, Izzy."

"Let me just finish getting *divorced* first. Anyway, weren't we talking about Abby?"

"What *exactly* did Marcus tell you?" I frown at Jess, and she groans impatiently.

"It just came up in conversation that you're hoping to have a baby together. He didn't exactly give us a blow-by-blow review of proceedings, if that's what you're worried about, and it *was* just me and Paul at lunch one day. It was all very appropriate."

"Okay," I say. "Good. Well, anyway, it *is* a temporary thing. It's just about making a baby. Then we stop."

"If you say so. But here's a question," Jess says mildly, then she finally lifts her eyes from the phone to mine. Her gaze grows thoughtful. "Why *are* you two crazy kids suddenly trying to start a family? Shouldn't you... I don't know, figure out your relationship with each other first?"

"I..."

I thought I was ready to tell them without getting emotional, which is the only reason I started this conversation in the first place. Turns out I was wrong. Isabel is at my side before the first tear even hits my cheek, wrapping a sympathetic arm around my shoulder. Jess stays in her chair, but she makes her own attempt at being supportive by putting her phone back in her bag to give me her full attention.

"It might be my only chance," I admit, and then as I cry my way through the tissues that Isabel has the waitress fetch for us, I tell them the whole, miserable story. Isabel, typically, sheds a few tears of pure empathy. Jess doesn't look at her phone again, but she doesn't look at me, either. I know she's listening, but her gaze is locked on the table. She's uncomfortable. Maybe because she can't really empathize—I can't see Jess wanting kids. "So you see, guys, this really *is* just about a baby."

"So the sex is *just* about a baby," Jess asks me quietly.

"Yep," I confirm, and she smirks a little.

"How is it, then?" I feel the flush sweep from my chest to my forehead and she cocks an eyebrow at me. "Say no more."

"We're behind you all the way, Abby," Isabel assures me, glaring at Jess. "We'll support you whatever happens next—both with Marcus, and with a baby."

"Do you think this is a terrible idea?" I ask them reluctantly.

"I think you're being naive," Jessica admits easily, but then she soothes the twist in my gut with a brilliant smile. "But…two wonderful people like you and Marcus bringing a child into the world? How could *that* be a terrible idea?"

It's just after midnight when I get home, and I creep in quietly, expecting Marcus to be asleep. I'm hanging up my coat by the door as he calls to me from his study.

"How was your night?" he says, and I skip down the hall toward him. He's at his impeccably neat desk, typing away into a spreadsheet. He's wearing boxer shorts and a tight-fitting black T-shirt; his hair is all mussed up, and when he turns to face me, I see the late-in-the-day shadow of his facial hair. His aftershave hangs lightly in the air, along with the lingering scent of his after-dinner coffee. I can tell he's tired, but there's no mistaking the way he brightens when he turns his attention to me as I lean against the doorway.

My heart skips a beat, then starts to thump as if I've just sprinted home from the restaurant. *I'll let you get away with that tonight, heart, but don't think you're going to make a habit of it.*

"Dinner was good," I tell him softly. "I told the girls. About my situation and about our baby."

"I already kind of told Jess," he says, and he checks hastily, "Is that okay? Sorry, I didn't mention your health stuff, just—"

"She told me," I interrupt him. He winces a little, and I ponder the guilt in his expression. "She said it just came up in conversation. How does *this* come up in conversation?"

"I…" Marcus hesitates, then he sighs. "They're my friends, too, and this is a big deal for *us*, but it's also a big deal for me and I've been kind of scatterbrained the last few weeks. I wanted them to understand why my focus isn't what it normally is. Is that okay?"

"Of course," I say. "I was just surprised, that's all."

"So you told Izzy and Jess the whole story?"

"Yeah."

"And how did it go?"

"They were great, of course. Well, Izzy was great… Jess was Jess. I cried a bit. I hate talking about it. I can kind of pretend it's not happening sometimes until I go to talk about it."

"You might already be pregnant," he reminds me. I flatten my palm against my lower tummy and breathe in deeply.

"Imagine if we were lucky enough for it to happen the first month."

I glance toward Marcus to see how he's reacted to that possibility. He looks exactly as I feel.

Conflicted.

We don't acknowledge it aloud, but now I know for sure. We're both torn by this possibility. If I'm pregnant, we get a baby—but we need to stop sleeping together.

"It's late," I say, and I straighten and take a step into the hall. "I'm surprised you're still awake. I guess you're pretty keen to get to sleep."

"Well… I'm keen to go to bed," he says mildly.

Our eyes lock, and the undertone could not be clearer, but still, I wait for him to invite me to join him. The moment stretches and stretches, and the anticipation is already building in my gut. I can feel my nipples pulling tighter under my bra. He doesn't say a word, and it suddenly strikes me that he hasn't actually *initiated* anything with me since all of this started. When a moment seems to be leading to sex, he always waits for me to make the first move, or maybe I just jump in before he has a chance. Should I wait and let him take the lead this time? I should. That comment was almost an invitation, but…is he just going to sit there and look at me now?

All he has to do is say…something.

Anything.

I try to wait. I give it another few seconds. The silence is killing me, because if I wasn't already excited about the possibility of joining him in his bed, the ever-darkening look in his eyes would have been enough to get me there.

The silence stretches too long. Now, we're clearly in some kind of "no, *you* speak first" competition, and I have no idea why. I'm also too impatient to let it play out, so I let him win.

"Want me to join you?" I blurt, and he smirks and nods. I pause, then frown at him. "That's what you meant, right?"

"That's what I meant," he says, and he closes his laptop and stands. I'm about to ask him why he always waits for me to make the first move, but I can see the shadow of his erection against the boxer shorts, and instead of leading the way back toward his bedroom I'm drawn toward him. He takes me into his arms and then we're kissing, and I forget why I needed to ask the question. I mean…hell…when he kisses me like that, it's all I can do to remember to breathe.

The observation niggles at me, though, and as he scoops me up into his arms and lifts me up onto his desk, I blurt breathlessly, "This is still okay, isn't it?"

"This?"

"Yes. *This.*"

He leans into me so that I can feel the length of his erection against my belly, and he offers me a wicked grin.

"Does that answer your question?"

"I'm serious." I frown, then I meet his gaze hesitantly. "Why *do* you always wait for me to make the first move? That's on purpose, isn't it?"

He hesitates for just a moment, then he smiles softly and says, "Yeah. I want you to set the pace here. This is different for us and… I just didn't want to overstep."

"Am *I* overstepping?"

"No," he says vehemently.

"Marcus, we've been fucking at least daily. Sometimes twice a day. If you're worried about overstepping, and that's not it, just how much sex *would* be overstepping?" I frown, and he shakes his head.

"It's not about frequency, Abby."

"Then... I don't understand."

"I just felt like this was more of a big deal for you than it was for me. So I wanted to make sure *you* were totally comfortable with how this was between us."

Is he saying I'm taking this physical side to our relationship too seriously? Is he worried that I might be developing romantic feelings for him? Maybe I should reassure him that I know very well where he stands on long-term relationships, and I *know* this is just a temporary arrangement. I glance at him again, trying to assess his expression and whether I should just go ahead and put that out there so he doesn't worry. But... he doesn't seem concerned. He actually seems relaxed and happy. He strokes a finger gently down the side of my face as he stares at me, then he smiles as he leans in to kiss me again.

"I don't get it," I say softly.

"Do you *want* me to initiate sex—is that what you're saying?"

"I'm constantly bugging you for it. I don't want to annoy you."

He laughs softly and tugs at my T-shirt. I let him lift it over my head, and I watch his face as he stares down at my bra-clad breasts. He bends to gently kiss my shoulder, then he unclips the bra, slides it off and throws it all the way out into the hall.

"Abby, you are most definitely not annoying me when you let me touch you like this," he says, coming back to stare into my eyes. The mood is intense again, and just like that, the chat is over.

He kisses me harder now, and when we break for air a moment or two later, I sigh and the sound strikes me. It sounds like longing and pleasure and contentment. It sounds like a woman who has kind of forgotten that this physical relationship is a means to an end, not a new beginning.

I think about that sigh much later, when I've left Marcus and I'm curled up alone in my own bed, cold and lonely and missing him so much it nearly hurts. It's harder to leave him every time. Tonight, it's like he's on the other side of the planet, instead of across the living room.

I wanted to stay with him so much tonight. We fucked *on* his desk, then he carried me to his room and we cuddled on his bed. His body was like my own personal electric blanket and that was nice but…it was so much more than that. I rested my head against his chest and listened as his heartbeat slowed, and I wanted to sleep that way almost as much as I want to see two lines on a pregnancy test.

I just want to be with him. All the damn time.

There's no denying that the borderline I was so determined to maintain between the sex and our friendship is not nearly as well-defined as I planned. It's just that when that spark flares between us now, and that happens so very often, the only thing that soothes the ache within me is to kiss him.

It's not a big enough problem that we need to stop, but I do need to keep an eye on it.

Tomorrow, I decide, just before I fall asleep. Tomorrow I'll keep my hands to myself, just to prove that I can.

CHAPTER NINETEEN

Abby

MY TIMING IS as woeful as my instincts are. Just last night, we talked about Marcus initiating sex sometimes. And now I'm deciding that I want to take a day off, and I'd hate for the first time he approaches me to end in a blunt rejection. I decide early in the day that I need to head him off at the pass, in case he's going to make one.

Then a message pops up at 11:00 a.m.

Marcus: Will you be home at lunchtime?

In the hour after that message arrives, I write and delete four responses.

1: Have to run out for toner, sorry I won't see you.

The toner thing is true; I've been feverishly printing out pages for my binder lately and my printer is running low, so I was planning on going out. *That* plan changed when I heard Marcus was coming home. I opened another window, ordered some for rush delivery and then went back to staring at the chat screen. Then I berated myself for self-sabotaging while I deleted my first attempt at a response. Instead, I thought, I'll just reply and make it clear I'm not up for our how-the-hell-did-this-become-a-regular-thing-so-fast daytime fuck.

2: Yes, but I'm pretty busy.

But that seemed mean, besides which, I'm not really that busy today. I submitted an article this morning for the digital magazine I freelance for, and now I'm just checking out an advance copy of an online game. And I thought it would be awesome and I'd want to play all day, but turns out, it's not that great. I'll see what I need to see and stop playing and then I'll find something else to do. So...

3. Yes, but we can't have sex.

Blunt, to the point—but if I had sent that one, he would have replied with *Is everything okay?* And then I'd have to reply with *Sure, but let's at least take a day off the sex and make sure things aren't weird*, and then we'd have to have a chat about feelings and things would have been either awkward or horrible, depending on how that chat went.

I have an inkling that the minute I say the word *feelings*, he's going to belatedly realize what a terrible idea all of this was. And I don't have feelings for him. I'm just being cautious because things seem a little muddy right now.

4. Yes. I'll be naked and ready, waiting in your bed.

I nearly sent that one, because it was the most natural, honest way to respond. And *that's* the problem, isn't it? Our chats throughout the day are *totally* tangled up in this new physical relationship. And it's not just instant message—it's text, it's email, it's conversations over dinner. We no longer chat as friends, but as lovers, flirting with each other constantly. There's something serious and intimate burgeoning in the way we communicate now, some entirely new connection between us that I can't quite put my finger on.

It's mesmerizing. Hypnotic almost, the way that the rhythm of our day has changed, beating to a different tune altogether in no time at all. Our lives are so perfectly enmeshed already that now that our bodies are in sync, too, I could very easily be lulled into thinking stupid thoughts like *Maybe this is meant to be*.

Luckily, I'm on the lookout for just such stupid thoughts. As soon as I catch even a hint of romanticism about how I'm viewing Marcus, I nip it right there in the bud. I'm doing pretty well with that, but I can't afford to slack off now.

In the end, I'm still procrastinating about how to reply when I hear the front door open, and Marcus is home, and by then I've worked myself up so much that, without a word, I drag him right to my bed.

Later, Marcus kisses me sweetly, takes a lightning-fast shower and returns to work.

Project Keep Your Hands to Yourself for a Day is officially a failure.

MOM CALLS ME later in the afternoon, as I'm tidying up some website stuff and absentmindedly snacking my way through a box of dry Cheerios. I pop my headset on so I can keep typing while we chat.

"How are you, darling?" she asks. "We haven't heard from you for a while, so I just thought I'd check in on you."

"I'm fine, Mom," I say. I smile softly at the concern in her voice. She's an excellent mother. I can only hope I'll be half the woman she is if I'm lucky enough to have a baby of my own.

"What have you been up to?" she asks me, and I feel a little tickle of guilt. I should tell my parents about my test results, but it will worry them. Especially Mom. I know she'll be upset for me, as well as scared that I'll never manage to make her a grandmother. As her only kid, I'm her only shot at grandbabies, and I know how badly she wants them. But suddenly I'm feeling a bit guilty, because it feels almost salacious to be holed up down here going at it with *Marcus* like I have been. I aim for an airy tone and I say, "Nothing."

"*Really?* Nothing at all?" I sit up straight in my chair and swallow. Do I read an accusation in that little word? Holy shit. Did Marcus tell his parents?

No. He wouldn't. Surely.

I didn't think he'd tell Jess and Paul, either, and he did that right away.

Although both sets of parents are now empty-nesters, Marcus's mom and stepdad and my parents are still very close. If Marcus told Lindy and Jack, then my parents, Eden and Peter, will know for sure.

I haven't thought about the potential grandparents in our situation nearly enough. My mom wants me to find someone and settle down. She wants this a lot, but it's not her main priority—most of all she wants me to be happy. She'll understand why Marcus and I decided to do this.

Lindy Ross is a whole other story. She wants Marcus *married* and planted safely in a growing family more than she wants to take her next breath. I was only five when Warwick left Lindy and the boys—so my first memories of her are of the "old Lindy"—the bitter woman she was before she fell in love with Jack. Her happy marriage is Lindy's whole world—and she wants Marcus to experience the same thing.

Sometimes I wonder if his pathological fear of long-term commitment is a not-so-subtle rebellion against her obsession with getting her boys safely married off as soon as possible. As soon as Luca and Marcus were officially men, Lindy was rubbing her hands with glee and demanding to meet her new in-laws.

When Luca met Austin, he didn't even tell Lindy he was in a relationship until *after* they were engaged. She was livid—especially with me and Marcus, because we met Austin months earlier than she did. But we respected Luca's wishes and didn't tell her.

For this reason, I can't imagine Marcus would have told his parents. So surely they don't know, and surely Mom doesn't know. I'm feeling guilty because this is weird and it's making me paranoid. But now, I've paused too long, lost in my train of thought. I hear my mom clear her throat and I frantically try to make up for the pause, but I stumble over my words.

"Just—you know, just busy."

"Abby," Mom says cautiously. "Is everything okay?"

I take a deep breath and force myself to say mildly,

"Of course it is. Everything is fine. How are you and Dad?"

"You're sure?"

"Absolutely. I'm just busy with work."

"You work too hard. You need to settle down with someone." Mom sighs. "Doesn't Marcus have some friends he can set you up with?"

Oh God. There's so much wrong with that sentence I can't even begin to deal with it.

"How's the garden, Mom?"

"Oh, Dad is busy getting ready for the winter—he's out there now actually…"

I listen to her talk for a while, then I wrap up the call and promise to do better with keeping in touch. Later, as I walk to the gym, I'm thinking about Lindy. She'll be delighted to become a grandmother—I have no doubt about that—but I'm equally sure that *if* and *when* we make an announcement about a baby, her first question is going to be about *us*.

And then we're going to have to explain and she won't understand and she'll put *so* much pressure on us. I have no idea how we're going to tell them all that we aren't actually together. *No, no, guys…we aren't in love. We just fucked for a while because the fertility clinic was going to take too long and we got impatient. It didn't mean anything.*

Um, no. I'm already dreading that inevitable challenge, but I have a feeling Marcus is going to find it even more uncomfortable than me. We used to share the laughter when she hinted at us to get together, but he's *never* managed to laugh about the way she's always hounded him to find himself a wife. Having seen him squirm under this kind of pressure from Lindy for years, I can only imagine how much worse it's going to be when she puts him on the spot about me now.

We'll have to lie. We'll have to tell them we used artificial insemination. I just have no idea how the hell I'm supposed to pull off a lie *that* big when I can't even master the art of white lies. It's not even like I have a single "tell" I can hide—I have *all* of the tells. I blush. My voice goes all squeaky. I fidget. I avoid eye contact. I am pretty much the world's worst liar, and everyone who knows me knows it.

I console myself with the thought that by the time we need to announce a pregnancy, we'll have finished this intense phase of our relationship. We won't be sleeping together anymore because there'll be no need. That will help, surely. It might be awkward with our parents, but it won't be awkward *between* us, because we'll both be on the same page and everything will go back to the way it was before.

I just need to make sure they don't find out while we're still sleeping together. Facing that kind of barrage of expectations from Lindy while there's any *hint* of romance between us would be a nightmare. I think I'm still doing okay here—I'm being so careful, and I'm *pretty* sure I don't have any untoward feelings for Marcus.

I daydream as I walk to the gym, but as I step through the front doors, I try to get my head into the zone for my workout. After I've stowed my bag in a locker and used the bathroom, I pause at the sink to stare in the mirror.

It's never been awkward when Lindy hinted that

me and Marcus should get together and settle down, because neither one of us wanted it in the past. Why does the thought of her hints make me so squeamish now? Has something changed for me?

Is there any chance you could be falling in love with him, Abby?

I stare hard into my own eyes, and the answer comes easily.

He's a good friend. The sex is awesome. But that's all there is to it. I am definitely not falling in love with him. A baby with Marcus is my best-case scenario right now and I'm way too smart to fuck it up.

I keep staring, almost willing myself to crumble under the pressure. But the woman who stares back at me looks cool and calm and confident, and suddenly I smile.

I need to stop overthinking this and doubting myself. The idea of Lindy pressuring us makes me feel icky only because this is all unusual and she's going to struggle to get her head around it. I *am* sticking to the plan. I'm a woman who is facing a serious health challenge, but dealing with it via a creative, unique solution. I'm enjoying the best sex of my life without complications. Not *once* have I let myself fantasize about Marcus wanting more from me when this arrangement ends, and if my feelings were getting away from me, that's definitely where my thoughts would be headed by now.

I give myself a mental gold star, and let go of the last of my worries as I head into class.

CHAPTER TWENTY

Hi again, Marcus and Luca,

Perhaps a smart man would have read your silence as an answer in itself, but no one has ever accused me of being smart.

One of the happiest days of my life was of a day in fall, a day not unlike the one we had here in the Catskills yesterday. The air was crisp but the sun was shining. It wasn't a typical red-letter day in the sense that no one was born or died and nothing extraordinary happened. But it was a special day, I just didn't know it at the time.

I picked you up from kindergarten, and when we got home I thought you'd want to watch TV and have milk and cookies and relax. But you didn't, boys. You both begged me to take you outside so we could toss the football around, and so that's what we did. We played until our breath was mist and the sun was setting and your poor mom was exasperated because we didn't want to come inside. We played until our hands were red and sore from the cold. We played until your little stomachs were rumbling with hunger. Even then, the only way I could get you two to go inside was to carry you. I scooped you up first, Marcus, and threw you over my shoulder, then I bent and grabbed Luca.

Luca, I wanted to throw you over my shoulder, too,

but you wouldn't let me. Instead, you clung to my hip so you could wrap your arms around my neck. As I awkwardly kicked open the back door, you whispered into my ear, "Thanks for playing with us, Daddy." I'm sure you've learned your manners by now but you weren't exactly a polite child, so that simple thank-you really meant a lot to me.

Moments like that with you two have become my most precious memories. They were days that seemed ordinary at the time, but in hindsight, I had the world in my hands. You probably don't believe that, and it's probably too late to prove it to you.

Boys, I decided yesterday that I'm going to keep writing to you. You can ignore me or block me or do whatever you need to do, but I'll still be here. I've hidden from the past for too long. If and when you're ready to connect with me, I'll be here waiting.

Love always,
Warwick

Marcus

It's just after 1:00 p.m. I need to be back at work soon, but I'm naked from the waist down and flat on my back in bed when the message pop ups on my smartwatch. I scroll down so I can skim it, but before I can even finish, a separate message arrives—from Luca, just to me.

Luca: Come for dinner. We need to talk.

I groan and drop my hand to the mattress, suddenly feeling heavy. The day was going so well, too. I had a superproductive morning at work and then Abby asked me to come home "for lunch." Pretty much the best day ever until that stupid fucking message landed.

"What's wrong?" Abby asks me. Her voice is deliciously husky from all of those sexy-as-hell noises she was making a few minutes ago. I shiver a little and kiss her temple gently.

"Another message from Warwick. And now Luca wants to 'talk.'"

"What's 'talk' code for with Luca? I can't even imagine."

"He…" I hesitate, then contract my arms around her. "I don't know, Abs. I have this feeling that maybe Luca is ready to talk to him."

"And you aren't?"

"The only thing I actually am ready for right now is to stop fucking thinking about Warwick."

"Hmm," she murmurs thoughtfully, and she rolls over to lie on my chest. She's completely naked and relaxed as we lie together in the afternoon light. It's funny how, at first, Abby didn't even want the light on when we were together. I don't know why I care so much that she's already comfortable being naked with me, but I really do. It's a gift.

I brush her hair off her bare shoulder, then touch her cheek, just because I can. Her gaze is serious, but I can't look away.

"What are you thinking?" I ask her.

"You're the most decisive person I know."

"Is that a compliment?"

"It is. You always know exactly what you want. You

don't need to overthink things like I do. Not usually, anyway."

"You think I'm overthinking Warwick." I frown, but she shakes her head.

"Quite the opposite actually. I think you made up your mind the minute you saw that very first notification on your iPad," she whispers, bringing one arm up so that she can touch her fingers to my lips. "I know a thing or two about avoidance and denial, Marcus."

"I don't know what you mean."

"If you weren't going to respond, you wouldn't have let me read that first message. You'd have declined his request and then you'd have blocked him."

My watch sounds again, and I relish the opportunity to break eye contact with Abby, who apparently can see all the fucking way through me.

Luca: Try to bring Abby if she's not avoiding me. Just tell her that Austin is cooking.

"I *should* have told him to fuck off when he first messaged us," I mutter.

"I don't know about that," Abby says softly.

I glance at her, surprised. "You really think we should get back in touch with him?"

Abby draws in a deep breath. "You know what? I kind of do. I'm starting to think you need to talk to him."

"He abandoned us, Abs. He doesn't deserve—"

"*He* doesn't deserve a damn thing," Abby agrees flatly. "But you do. And so does Luca. I'm sure you're not interested in excuses, but you deserve an explanation." I frown, and Abby runs her hand over my chest, then rests it over my heart as she says softly, "He let you down—so badly. Maybe it's time to confront him, even if it's just to find some kind of closure for yourself."

We fall into silence, and my mind races as I ponder this, then stills when she taps my chest to catch my attention. "But whatever you decide to do, I'm behind you one hundred percent."

The anger drains out of me, because really? I have nothing to lose here. I have everything I need at the moment, regardless of what happens with Warwick. I brush my lips over her forehead.

"I honestly don't know what I'd do without you, Abby Herbert."

"Well, lucky for you," she says with a grin, "I don't intend to let you find out."

"Come for dinner with Luca and Aus tonight," I whisper, glancing back at her hesitantly.

"Is Luca cooking?" she asks suspiciously. My mother ran our house like a military operation—all schedules and boundaries and rules—but cooking was the one skill she never quite managed to transfer to my brother and me.

"Nope."

"In that case, fuck yes, I'll come."

"He thought you might still be mad at him," I tell her.

"Who?"

"Luca."

"What for?"

I clear my throat, and Abby giggles a little self-consciously.

"Oh, yeah. The sperm thing." She shifts farther onto my chest as she adds softly, "I was never mad at him. It was a big ask, and I knew it was a long shot. But he *is* going to tease me."

"Probably," I concede, then add, "I can talk to him if you want…"

"And say what? *Don't give Abby shit about her asking you for your sperm?*"

"Something like that."

"Is that all you'd say to him?"

I realize she's asking if I'm going to tell him about us and our arrangement. I brush her bangs back from her eyes and say softly, "Yes. That's all I'd say."

"You won't tell him?"

"No." And I *won't* tell Luca that in a roundabout way, thanks to him, Abby and I are sleeping together—but I have a feeling I won't need to. "But…seriously. I can tell him you're feeling awkward about it and he should just be a grown-up about it for five minutes."

"You don't need to protect me, Marcus," she says. "He can tease me. I can hack it."

"Okay."

She sighs and sits up, and I pull her back down to wrap my arms around her.

"I should get some things done this afternoon if I'm not working tonight," she protests, and I shake my head and tighten my embrace a little. I always hate letting her go, but I don't usually try to prolong these cuddles. She's always the one to end these moments together, and while I always kiss her goodbye, I don't let myself press for more time.

It doesn't seem fair for me to ask for more from her. Not when I still have no idea where this is going.

"I should get back to work, too," I murmur. "But just stay for a minute longer."

Abby is tense for a moment, but then I feel her relax against me again and she gives a different kind of sigh.

"Okay," she says. "Just a minute longer."

"YOU'RE *DEFINITELY* NOT going to tell him?" Abby asks me, just as I knock on Luca and Austin's door.

"Of course I'm not. But if he guesses…" I let the words hang, and Abby's gaze narrows.

"And how exactly would he *guess*?"

I shrug, thinking of my conversation with Luca at the bar. He's more astute than we give him credit for. I have a feeling he'll notice that I can't wipe the grin off my face these days.

"He knows us pretty well."

"He won't guess," Abby says, then she adds quickly, "And don't tell him."

"Abs, I won't. I promise. Why are you so worried about that?"

"He'd make things awkward," she mutters, and I'm surprised how worried she seems about that possibility given how we're both well versed at dealing with it. Hearing distant footsteps, I reach down and brush a chaste kiss against her lips.

"Don't worry," I whisper. "I won't tell him. And if he says anything awkward, I'll remind him about the time he pooped in the bath when he was four."

"Abby! Please-dear-God-*please* don't ask me for my sperm again tonight," Luca greets us as he pulls open his front door. Abby is carrying a bottle of wine, and she raises it now as if she's going to smash it over his head. He grins and pulls her in for an awkward hug, leaving the wine dangling precariously over his shoulder. I snatch it from her hands and push past them into the apartment.

"Hi, Aus," I call, making a beeline for my brother-in-law in the open-plan kitchen. Austin drops the ladle he's wielding, wipes his hands on his apron, then shakes my hand.

"Marcus," he says. "Great to see you."

"You, too," I say, then I glance at the pots and pans on the stove. "What's for dinner?"

"Leftovers," he tells me, and at my startled look, he grins. "From the restaurant. I precooked at work last night."

"Did you hear that, Abs?" I call, and she squeals and finally escapes Luca's clutches to join us in the kitchen.

"We're having Le Maison food tonight?" she asks, referring to Austin's swanky restaurant.

"We are," he confirms, and Abby hugs him from behind, then reaches around him to jab her finger into the coulis he's been carefully smearing onto a plate. He protests furiously, but she just laughs, then groans as she licks her finger.

"Oh my *God*," she sighs. "Austin, that is amazing."

I'm watching all of this with a half smile frozen on my face, because her sense of mischief may be innocent enough, but the way she is licking that finger is *anything* but. As she goes to town sucking every drop of coulis from her fingertip, the blood drains from my head and pools somewhere south of my belt.

I shake myself and glance at Luca, intending to change the subject, but he's smirking at me, and just like that, I know he's already on to us. I brace myself, ready to deflect the conversation if he says something awkward and Abby gets upset, but Luca surprises me when he silently opens the fridge and passes me a beer.

"Thanks," I say warily. He's still wearing the smirk, but he simply nods and reaches for the wine I've sat on the counter.

"Abby?" he says quietly as he uncaps it and pours a glass.

"No wine for me, thanks," she says, and I wince, waiting for him to say *something* about how she's never refused a glass of wine in her entire life and is there something we need to tell him—but instead, he shrugs, pours her a water and passes the wine to Austin.

"What's new?" is all Luca asks now, directing the question to Abby.

"Not much," she says as she leaps up to sit on the kitchen countertop. Austin elbows her gently.

"I'd have you drawn and quartered for that kind of behavior at the restaurant."

"Ah, so that's why you've never invited me into the kitchen," Abby says wryly.

"Exactly. If you learn some manners, I'll give you a behind-the-scenes tour one day."

"I'd be happy with an open invitation to eat there whenever I want."

"Maybe I'll consider that request when we don't have a three-month waiting list for a table."

They banter on without us, and Luca nods toward the living space. I follow him automatically and take a seat on the upholstered couches.

"Things are obviously going well," he murmurs.

I look over my shoulder, but Abby's been distracted by the fresh sourdough Austin's invited her to taste. She takes a bite of the bread, closes her eyes as she chews it, then begins interrogating him about tonight's menu.

"Yeah," I say softly. "It's going very well."

"So you decided to do the job yourself, after all, huh? The old-fashioned way?"

"I had a feeling you'd notice," I say, then I glance at him. "And people say you're an insensitive asshole."

"How dare you imply I'm *not*." He feigns mock outrage, then murmurs very quietly, "Well, it was hard to miss when you two were eye-fucking each other when I opened the door. Truth be told, I spewed in my mouth a bit." I laugh and take a sip of the beer, and Luca drops his voice even further as he asks, "So—is this, like, *official*?"

"We're not twelve, so no, I haven't asked her to go steady with me."

"No, apparently you're sixteen, so you took advantage of the moment and ripped her clothes off."

"The fertility clinic procedure was more complicated than we expected. They wanted us to go through counseling and waiting periods and…it was just going to take a long time and that's one thing she's short on."

"So *that's* why you ripped her clothes off? How noble of you, little bro."

"*She* suggested it," I say, a little defensively.

"No judgment here. I'm rooting for you."

"She's a little freaked out by how intense things are between us, I think. Please don't draw attention to it tonight. I'm trying to take it slow with her. Let her take some time to adjust to how things are between us now."

"I know things are complicated with Abby. Just… don't be so busy worrying about her needs that you forget about your own, okay?"

"What's that supposed to mean?" I frown.

"It means…shit, Marcus. You basically let her pretend that kiss didn't happen in January, and you have another chance here. Don't blow it. Make sure she knows how you feel."

"*You're* going to give me advice about feelings?"

"I'm a married man now, Marcus," Luca informs me sagely. "Experience and love have left me wise and enlightened."

"If I told her how I'm feeling right now," I mutter, "she'd pack her bags and move to Mars to avoid discussing it."

"Well, at some point you're going to have to tell her you're not just fucking her to make a baby." I cringe, and Luca laughs and thumps me on the back. "Sorry. Not fucking. *Bonking.*"

"What's so funny over there?" Abby calls, and Luca answers her calmly.

"Marcus was just telling me about your last gas bill. You've been abusing the heat again, huh?"

Abby frowns at us, her gaze narrowing as it flicks to me. I smile, and she relaxes a little, then cautiously returns her attention to Austin.

Now, Luca draws in a breath, then releases it slowly.

There's no mistaking the instant tension in him, and I tense, too, because I know what he's about to say.

"I was thinking, bro," he murmurs. "We should reply to him."

I sigh and run my hand through my hair impatiently. "Yeah."

"I know you have a lot going on at the moment but putting this off doesn't feel right anymore."

"I know."

"I can leave you out of it if you want, but I was thinking…maybe I'll just meet with him."

There's a lead stone in my gut at the thought of a meeting like that. My gaze slips past him, to Abby. She's talking about gaming—I can't hear her words because she's speaking quietly, but I know the subject, anyway, because of the animated expression she's wearing and the way her hands are flitting all around her face. She meets my gaze across the room, and her smile changes a little, softening into the gentle, intense one that's reserved only for me.

I drag my gaze back to my brother. He's studying the label on his beer while he waits for my response, and something about my brash, blunt brother looking so unsure twists my gut. The last of my reluctance to deal with this situation disappears completely.

"You don't have to do this on your own," I say. "What are you thinking?"

"That last message says he's at the Catskills. We could drive up there and come back the same day. Austin said he'd take a weekend off, but it's going to take a few weeks for him to organize it."

"Okay." I exhale heavily. "Let's go whenever you

and Austin can manage it. If Warwick has time to see us, I guess."

Luca shrugs. "If he's for real, he'll make time."

DESPITE ABBY'S NERVES about dinner, we manage to make it all the way through the meal without Luca saying anything awkward. Well, he says *a lot* of awkward things—he and Abby spend half the night squabbling over politics, and the other half arguing about whether or not video games are destroying the brains of the next generation—but the evening is lighthearted and fun and *ordinary* for the four of us...

...right up until we get to the door to leave, and Abby is gushing about Austin's amazing cooking and hinting for him to arrange for her to line jump so she can go to the restaurant again. She's animated and magnificent, and she's also completely distracted in the moment when, midfarewell, she reaches down and entwines her hand with mine. Luca's eyes widen, but then he looks right at me and the *you-totally-owe-me-for-not-making-a-big-deal-out-of-this* smirk returns to his face.

"Thanks again," she says. "Austin, that food was—what?"

Austin has noticed our hands, too, and he's gaping at us. Luca slides his arm around his husband's shoulders and reaches to close the door.

"Night, guys," Luca says calmly.

"Good night," I say, and I turn Abby back toward the stairs. She flicks an uncertain glance over her shoulder but falls into step beside me, then she yanks her hand away as she groans.

"I held your hand in front of them."

"Yes."

"Shit!"

"Luca knew the minute he opened the door. Don't sweat it."

"How the hell could he have *known*?"

"He said we were *eye-fucking* each other."

"*Shit*, Marcus. Did you explain?"

"Yes."

"And?"

"And what?"

"What did he *say*?"

"Why do you care?"

"Because I don't want him to think…" She trails off, and I frown as I glance at her.

"Think what?"

"Think that we're *together*."

I don't know what to say to that. I want to say something like "What's so bad about him thinking we're together," or even "Well, we kind of *are*." The silence stretches while I try to figure out how she'd react to such a statement. Is now the moment to say it? I glance at her again, and she groans and mutters, "It's just too complicated to have to explain to everyone, that's all."

"Okay."

We walk in silence for a moment, but as we leave the building, Abby asks, "So does he?"

"Does he what?"

"Think we're together."

"He thinks we're trying to have a baby, because that's what I told him."

"He wasn't weirded out?"

"Since when do you care so much about what Luca thinks?" I ask her.

She looks at me helplessly. "Because no one else is going to understand our arrangement, Marcus."

"So?"

"So!"

"Yeah. So what if they don't understand? It's no one's business but ours." Still she hesitates, so I reach out and take her hand again. "Talk to me."

She shakes her head, then offers me a weak smile.

"Don't worry about it. Let's go."

"Abby…" I sigh. She tugs me toward the road and she's scanning for our ride, and I sigh again as I follow her. Soon we're seated together in the back seat of the car and headed toward our apartment. Abby's staring out the window when it finally hits me. "You're worried about our parents finding out, aren't you?"

"Yeah, a bit."

"They'll be excited, Abs."

"I know. Too excited. That's the problem."

"Too excited about a baby?"

She grunts noncommittally, and I frown.

"Luca never tells our parents *anything*. He didn't even tell them about Austin at first, and that's his own life. If he didn't tell them about his own relationship, what makes you think he'll tell them about us?"

"Don't say it like that."

"Like what?"

"*Us*. We're not an 'us.' We're…" She draws in a sharp breath, then says in a rush, "We're *just* friends who want to have a baby together. That's not an 'us.' Right?"

God, the tension is positively emanating from her.

She sounds panicked, and I don't know what to say to diffuse the situation.

"I don't know why you're so worried about definitions here" is the best I can come up with. "Especially when it comes to our parents. Yours *and* mine are both so desperate for grandchildren they'll be falling over themselves with joy when we tell them."

"Sure. Right up until we explain the part about us not being together and everyone gets confused." I reach over to take her hand, but she's looking away from me and she moves her hand at the last minute. I can't tell if that's because she didn't realize I was reaching for her, or because she *did*.

"We'll just tell them I donated sperm to you, Abby. This isn't a big deal."

"It *is* a big deal," she says impatiently. "You *know* I can't lie for shit."

That's certainly true, but I still don't understand why she's so stressed about this now.

"Okay, so we don't explain anything. We just let them make their own assumptions. Who cares what they think?"

"Marcus! Then they'll think we're an *'us'*!"

"And if they do?"

"We can't let them think that!"

"Do you think it matters to your parents *or* to mine the exact details of the arrangement that leads to their grandchild? Exactly how much detail do you think they're going to want about the conception of our kid, huh?"

She pauses.

"But they'll have expectations…" she says weakly.

"Yeah. They might. Like they could expect that we might give them more than one grandchild one day, and who knows? We *might*."

"I just…" She trails off, then sighs again. "Yeah. Okay."

"You're overthinking this. Can't we worry about this later, *after* you're pregnant?"

Abby sighs again, but this time she lets me take her hand. I entwine it with mine, then rest our hands firmly on my thigh.

"I guess so."

We sit in silence for a few blocks, as Luca's words sound in my brain like a warning siren.

At some point, you're going to have to tell her you're not just fucking her to make a baby.

Every time that thought circles around my mind, it picks up steam, until my heart is racing and I've talked myself into it: I'm going to go for it. Things between us are great right now—in the last few weeks, we've had sex countless times, and we've cuddled and held hands, and Abby has been completely, enthusiastically caught up in us, just as I am. She's probably going to be overjoyed when I tell her I'm *really* into her. I take a deep breath, then say abruptly, "Abby." She turns to me and looks at me questioningly. "I'm starting to think there *is* an 'us.'"

She gives me a haughty look. "There is *not*."

"There *is*," I say gently, and she frowns. Hard.

"This," she says confidently as she waves her hand between us. "This is just about a baby. Nothing more."

Abby is infamously incapable of lying, but she sounds one hundred percent sure about what she just said. "Just about a baby," I repeat carefully, and Abby flashes me an easy smile.

"Two friends. Having a baby together. Nothing more. That's hardly an 'us,' is it?"

Abby calls me egotistical sometimes, and I know she's right—I don't often doubt myself. But I've reached a moment in time where I'm supposed to tell a woman I have feelings for her—*real* feelings…and that's not actually something I've ever done before. I'm just staring at her—waiting for the bravado in her expression to waver, just a little, but she's completely at ease. It's almost like she's proud of her assertion, as if this is an achievement or she's told me something I desperately wanted to hear.

Maybe she's not feeling it.

Maybe it's still too soon. Maybe I need to give her more time.

I can't even imagine how it would feel if I told her that I want more and she has to let me down gently.

I clear my throat.

"Right," I say, then I nod. "Uh-huh. Good. Yeah."

"And I'm sorry about before. I won't hold your hand like that again," she says lightly. "It's confusing if we start doing that around other people. I just wasn't thinking."

Okay, so maybe I can't close this deal tonight, but I don't want to lose ground, either. I fucking *loved* it when she took my hand tonight. It was automatic—totally unthinking—and that showed me that even if she doesn't realize it yet, there's some level of feeling bubbling under the surface for her.

"You don't need to apologize. It's just a sign of affection toward each other," I say carefully. "Maybe it's just a natural evolution of our friendship given everything that's going on between us right now. I like it when you hold my hand, and you like it when I hold yours. We should…you know. Just go with it."

She ponders this for a minute, then nods silently and returns her gaze to the window. I reach across the seat, take her hand again and squeeze it. "We're okay?"

"Yep," she says with a smile. "We're fine."

I lean my head back against the headrest and catch the driver's eye in the rear-vision mirror. He's hiding a smirk, and I glare at him.

This has been an excellent reminder of why I never go to *Luca* for advice.

CHAPTER TWENTY-ONE

Abby

"WANT TO GO on a road trip in a few weeks' time?"

We're sitting at the dining room table eating breakfast together before Marcus leaves for work. He looks so good that I'm struggling to keep my hands to myself. He has some big customer meeting today, and he's in full internet mogul mode—dressed in a charcoal gray suit with a pinstriped white shirt and a tie flecked with the same shade of dazzling blue as his eyes. I want to climb him like a tree.

"Abby, if you keep looking at me like that, I'm going to be late. Did you even hear what I asked?"

"Hear you ask what?" I say blankly, and he laughs again.

"Feel like joining me for a road trip next month?"

"Where to? Are we going home?"

The sparkle in his eyes fades as he shakes his head and slides his phone out of his pocket. He unlocks it and passes it to me so I can read the screen and see the message Luca sent late last night.

Luca: Warwick, me and Marcus would like to meet with you. My husband is a chef and it's hard for him to get weekends off, but we're thinking maybe we could come on a Saturday early next month. Would that work for you?

And then two minutes later, Warwick's reply had arrived.

Warwick: Any time you want to visit, you will always be welcome in my home. I will be honored and grateful to meet with you both.

I glance up at Marcus. He's watching me closely.

"You don't have to come, but—"

"Of course I'll come," I interrupt. "I wouldn't let you do that alone. I *couldn't*."

Marcus smiles at me then—he *really* smiles. He takes our dishes to the sink and rinses them, then stacks them carefully into the dishwasher. I'm still sitting, thinking about this meeting and how it might play out for him. God, I hope I did the right thing encouraging him to do this.

Marcus crouches before me, slides his hands along my neck and into my hair, and presses his lips against mine.

It's a wonderful kiss—affectionate, sweet, tender— but it's not a kiss intended to arouse. It's a kiss that's miles past friendship, but about so much more than sex.

"Thank you," he murmurs. He brushes his thumb over my lip one last time, then smiles as he steps away from me. "I have a meeting in Midtown today around lunchtime. I don't suppose you want to meet me at the vegetarian place you like?"

My head is swimming from the kiss, but not so

much that I'm not excited about that invitation. I love that place.

"Fuck yes."

MARCUS IS WAITING at a little table in the front of the restaurant when I arrive, and I pause in the doorway to survey him. He's staring into space, his expression thoughtful. When he sees me, a smile breaks over his face as he rises. As I near the table, I automatically lean in to kiss his cheek, but at the last minute, he cups my face in his hands and kisses me. The kiss winds me up until I've forgotten we're in *public* and I can barely remember my own name. When we break apart, Marcus is grinning. If I look half as flustered as I feel, I must be a sight.

"Just natural affection," he says, and he flashes me a lopsided smile that makes my heart race all over again. I clear my throat as I take my seat.

"I *knew* there was something more between you two."

Right there beside our table is Liesel, the lawyer Marcus dated for a while around the time I moved into his apartment. And of course she's here—because now, two minutes too late, I remember that she's the person who introduced us to this place, and her office is right across the street…although *that's* not why she's staring at me as if I'm trespassing on her private property.

Shit.

Liesel is still gorgeous—polished in a corporate way I couldn't achieve even if I tried, which, let's be honest, I don't even want to. Her makeup is flawless, her suit is elegant and she's standing confidently on heels that should be impractical. She looks like she just stepped off the pages of a fashion magazine. She looks exactly like the kind of woman Marcus normally has on his arm, and the fierceness in her gaze suggests she thinks she still belongs there. I flush, confused by the guilt I feel.

"Hello," Marcus says, but his voice sounds odd, and although there's recognition in his tone, he's concentrating hard. My eyes widen—he's frantically trying to remember her name. Unfortunately, Liesel picks up on that at the same moment I do.

"You don't remember me, do you?" she says, aghast. Marcus flicks a helpless glance at me, and I hastily mouth *Liesel* to him.

"Of course I do," he says smoothly, then adds too confidently, *"Lisa."*

"Liesel," I hiss, and he has the grace to at least look a little embarrassed. Liesel herself is suitably outraged.

"We dated for over a month, Marcus."

"Well, I wouldn't really call it *dating*..." He tries to clarify, and I kick him under the table. He raises his eyebrows at me, and I try to speak using only my eyes.

Shut up, you handsome dolt! Not even you can talk your way out of this one!

"You really are an asshole, aren't you?" Liesel sighs heavily, then glances at me. "So it's your turn at last? Let's see if he remembers *your* name when he's done with you."

I clear my throat while I try to think of some way to answer *that*, but before I can formulate a sensible response, Marcus stands abruptly.

"It was nice to see you, *Liesel*," he says flatly. "Don't let us keep you from your lunch."

Liesel is apparently unperturbed by his dismissal.

She leaves without a farewell, but I can't help but admire the graceful way she crosses the restaurant in those damned shoes. She takes her seat with a group of people similarly clad in expensive business suits and immediately joins an animated conversation, as if she's completely forgotten the incident at our table in the time it took her to walk from one side of the restaurant to the other. Marcus sits, then reaches for my hand. I let him take it, but my heart is racing.

"Abs? Are you okay?" His focus is entirely on me again, but I feel cheapened by it now.

"You didn't remember her name," I say. "How can you not remember her *name*? You guys spent weeks together, Marcus."

"It was a long time ago…"

"Last year," I remind him uneasily. "It was only last year. I was living with you when you were seeing her."

"We weren't exactly dating." He sighs. "It wasn't serious."

"Well, *you* say so now, but I overheard the conversation when you broke up with her," I say abruptly. "Liesel obviously thought it was serious."

Marcus frowns, then pushes his hand through his hair in exasperation.

"Look. I'm sure I would have explained myself clearly to her—I always do. It can't be my fault that she wanted something more than what I'd offered."

"You're completely sure about that, are you?" I say incredulously, and he raises his eyebrows at me.

"Yes, I *am*. I've always been up front about what I'm looking for. The reason I broke up with her is because I knew she'd get hurt if I *didn't*. I was trying to do the right thing!"

"Forget about it." I'm not even sure why I'm so annoyed with him. I'm just feeling a lot of things right now and none of them make sense, but *all* of them come back to Marcus. The hurt on Liesel's face keeps replaying through my mind like a premonition, and I'm trying to remind myself that I don't have feelings for him, so I'm *not* going to get hurt like that.

But if that's true, why do I feel so scared right now?

Then Marcus leans forward and his gaze is hard on my face as he says, "It could not be more different with you, Abby."

I'm confused even by the way that sentence makes me feel. There's a thrill running through me at the intensity in his voice, but a tightening in my chest at the same time.

"It's the same, except for the baby," I insist as lightly as I can manage. "And it *should* be. I shouldn't have—"

"It was just sex with her," Marcus interrupts me. "Please don't compare *us* to the way things were with me and her. The situations are worlds apart."

"So it's different with me because it's *just sex* with someone who's your *friend* already?" I intend it as a clarification, but somehow, it escapes my mouth with the force of bitterness behind it. Marcus seems surprised, and a sudden nervousness crosses his expression.

"Abby…" He draws in a deep breath. "Actually, I need to—"

I wince and snatch my hand back from his, then hold it up to interrupt him.

"Sorry. Shit. Don't—I didn't mean…" I'm so embarrassed. I try to reassure him, because what I just said sounded *very much* like a demand for him to tell me that *we* mean something more to him, and I know we don't. "I just—that was so awkward with her just now and it flustered me. Everything is fine. I know where we stand, and it's all good."

There's a moment of silence, then Marcus asks quietly, *"Do* you know where we stand?"

"We talked about this last night." I shrug, then offer him a smile. "You know I do."

I feel cornered, and I have no idea why. What the fuck is going on with me today? I see the way his gaze travels over the flush on my face, and then it drifts down to the table. I look down, too, and realize my hands are resting on the tablecloth, clenched into fists so tight my knuckles are white. I release my hands hastily. How do I convince him that *nothing has changed and everything is fine*?

"Tell me again," he murmurs. "I fucked up that conversation completely last night. Let's try it again."

"We're just two friends. Making a baby." I can't look at him right now. I snatch the menu off the table and I scan it with far more attention than the task requires, given I know already that I'm going to order the tomato and basil calzone like I always do.

"And that kiss when you came in?" he says softly. "Do you really think *that* was just about making a baby?"

"Natural affection." I echo his earlier words back to him, and out of the corner of my eye I see him nod.

"That's what we said last night."

"Just two friends making a baby together," I say. There's a wobble in my voice. "That's all."

"Sure. Friends who hold hands these days without even thinking about it, right?"

I don't move my gaze from the menu, but I need to

rest my elbows on the table to hold it steady because my hands are shaking. I know Marcus and I are at some kind of crossroads; I just can't figure out why or what this means. If it was at all possible, I'd stare at the menu forever to avoid his gaze. When I finally do look back to him, he asks me softly, "Is this really still just about making a baby for you?"

"You know the answer to that question." I wanted the words to come out with confidence—strong words, sure words. Instead, they sound uneasy and uneven. I glance at him hesitantly, waiting for him to panic. Instead, he raises his eyebrows.

"Actually," he says, "I'm starting to think I do. But do *you*?"

This has to stop. *Now.* We're in a busy restaurant, for fuck's sake. He can't force this discussion here and I have to stop it. I'm feeling uncomfortable and exposed and on edge and awkward—which is all kinds of familiar, because I was just thinking about this exact combination of feelings yesterday.

This is how I knew I'd feel if I was facing Lindy's usual hints for us to get together.

That's when it hits me.

Self-denial is a bastard of a thing. Sometimes when I do it, it's almost deliberate. That's what it was like when I ran away from our kiss on New Year's—the kiss scared me, and so I stopped thinking about it.

Other times, like now, I just believe my own lies too easily. These last few weeks I've been telling myself that friendship and sex could be kept separate, as if they were like oil and water…things that don't mix. I'm just starting to realize how ridiculous that is. Friendship and sex mix all too well. Agitate those ingredients in the right way and you've got yourself a nasty case of something altogether different.

And that's exactly why I couldn't bear the thought of Luca or Lindy or anyone else knowing about us wanting a baby. Because I knew once they did, they'd be all hopeful that Marcus and I would decide to be together, and I'd find it almost impossible to refute those hopes when deep down inside a part of me was hoping for the same thing.

I need time to process this and privacy to freak out about it, so I can figure out what to say to Marcus. He's obviously picked up on how I'm feeling, and he's probably preparing for his "letting Abby down gently" confrontation.

No fucking way are we doing that here, right now.

I am *not* crying in front of Liesel. Not today. Not ever.

"I'm having the calzone today," I say lightly.

"For God's sake, don't change the subject now." He's hardly ever impatient with me—but those words are so clipped. I wince a little.

"I really don't want to do this *here*," I plead with him, flicking my gaze back to Liesel on the other side of the café. She's leaning on the table, talking intently with the man on her right, but she raises her eyes just as I glance at her and our gazes meet. I look away, and feel the flush returning to my cheeks.

"So what's your plan?" Marcus asks pointedly, then his tone sharpens again. "You're going to do the typical Abby thing and pretend this doesn't need addressing?"

"Typical Abby thing?" I repeat incredulously. He winces, and I toss the menu on the table between us and lean forward to hiss, "Actually, my plan is that we

don't have this awkward conversation while the ex you actually *forgot* existed until five minutes ago sits on the other side of the café shooting daggers at me from her eyes. I just had a very public reminder that you have a history of being completely clueless when it comes to women, so do you really want me to be *honest* with you right now?"

Marcus stares at me for a moment, then it's his turn to reach for a menu to hide behind. We're both taking some very deep breaths, and we accidentally do it in sync, so I shorten mine just *because*. After a while, Marcus drops the menu onto the table and flags down a waiter.

"Tomato and basil calzone and a coffee?" he guesses calmly as the waiter approaches. I nod, and Marcus orders for me and himself, then as the waiter walks away, he says quietly, "I'm sorry. You're right—that was a really bad time for us to have this conversation. I tried last night in the cab, but it was harder than I expected."

I swallow. Hard. Something big is coming when we talk, and I don't know how to prepare myself for it. I glance at him, and he's staring off into space again. There's that same distracted gaze he was wearing when I came in.

"I'm sorry, too," I whisper. "I didn't mean to snap your head off."

"Hey, you didn't bolt out of the restaurant, so it could have been worse."

I sigh because I know he's right. I'm hopeless at conversations like this, especially when I know they're going to hurt.

"I fucking hate it when there's things unspoken between us, and I'm starting to think there are things we *both* need to say." Those beautiful blue eyes are sincere and fixed on my face as he waits for my response. My heart does a double backflip, and I glance up toward Liesel. She's looking at Marcus this time, and the lingering hurt in her gaze is palpable.

I look back to him, and the backflips in my chest stop. Instead, my heart is sinking as I whisper, "Yeah, okay. I know we need to talk."

THE WHOLE REASON I went to the gynecologist last month was because my periods are no longer predictable. Some cycles are so long, some are so short…but even so, when I get home from the restaurant and realize my period has arrived, I'm not prepared at all. Numbness settles over me. I'm not even disappointed or upset. Not yet.

I go back to my computer to let Marcus know but there's already a message waiting from him.

Marcus: Abby?

I sit my hands on the keyboard and draw in a deep breath, then burst into tears. I knew becoming pregnant in the first month was a long shot, but hope sucked me in. I've been floating along on a cloud of happiness over the last few weeks and I let myself get carried away.

It didn't work. What if it never works? What if it's too late?

The disappointment starts to rise, and my dignified tears become something altogether different. I'm heaving sobs and I can't even see the screen anymore. All I want is for Marcus to take me into his arms and tell me it's going to be okay.

I want my friend Marcus to come home.
I want my *lover* Marcus to come home.

Marcus: Abby? You there?

Abby: Hi, yes, sorry. Distracted.

Marcus: I'll let you get back to work. Will you be home tonight? Can we talk? Please?

I reach for a Kleenex and blow my nose, then take another deep breath and give him the news.

Abby: No luck this month. Sorry.

Marcus: You got your period?

Abby: Yep. I'm really sorry.

Marcus: Stop saying sorry. Are you okay?

Abby: I've had my period a few times before so I'm pretty used to it :)

I'm impressed with my ability to make a joke about it even while I'm sitting here at the keyboard weeping. The sobs are hitting me so hard I can barely breathe. I'm upset and I'm disappointed and I'm scared and I'm confused and I'm just not at all sure why I have to feel every single one of those things at the same time just because my stupid period showed up today and I wasn't expecting it.

Marcus: You know what I mean, Abs.

Abby: I'm fine. Disappointed, of course, but I'm fine. We knew it was a long shot the first month. Mostly shocked because I didn't expect it yet.

Marcus: Do you need anything? Want me to come home?

Oh, I want him to come home so much I cry even harder at the thought of it.

I can't ask that of him.

I won't.

I need space. I need to sort the tangled mess of confusion in my mind, and my emotions are too loud right now to even begin that process. He can't come home and see me like this.

Abby: And do what exactly?

Marcus: Hot water bottle? Chocolate?

Abby: Ha. No, but if you want to come home and write this article for me, I wouldn't say no.

Marcus: Sure. What's it about?

Abby: That beta I've been playing around with.

Marcus: I do think they'd probably notice if I wrote it since it would be a cut-and-paste from Wikipedia.

Abby: Good point, but in that case, I'd better get back to it. Catch you later.

Marcus: You know I care about you, right?

I stare at the IM box, and a shiver runs down my spine. I *do* know he cares about me…deeply, the way close friends do. Surely that's the way he means it.

Why do I have to swallow the lump in my throat as I write it back? Why do I type the right words, then delete them several times? Why do I agonize about how I can make the phrase more casual? My mouth is bone-dry by the time I can finally bring myself to send a simple:

Abby: I care about you, too.

Seeing that exchange on the screen makes my heart race. I feel the kind of nervousness that only comes from being completely out of your depth or backed into a corner, and I battle the urge to shut the chat window and turn the computer off as if it might electrocute me.

I'm oversensitive today, that's all—that incident at the restaurant was awful, and now my period… God, no wonder I'm a little off-balance. I add a smiley, as if that will remind me that words have only as much power as I give them.

I'm being ridiculous. I need to get my shit together and refocus on work. I stare at the screen and take a deep breath and tell myself that's more than enough sulking for one day.

THE LAST THING in the world I expect at 6:15 p.m. is for Marcus to walk through the door carrying several paper bags and a bottle of wine. He's as surprised to see me as I am to see him, no doubt because he's expecting me to be at the gym where I *always* am at 6:00 p.m.

"What are you doing here?" he asks.

"I think that's fairly self-evident." I am lying on the couch in my yoga pants and my well-worn Comic-Con 2011 T-shirt. The heat is blasting, and so is the television. I'm binge-rewatching *Star Trek Voyager*—my favorite version of the franchise; I've always had a soft spot for the Borg. There's a bowl of corn chips on my lap, a half-eaten chocolate bar on the table and a banana skin resting on the carpet beside me.

This is my version of sulking, and I am well and truly into the groove of it given I closed my laptop *immediately* after I decided it was high time I got back to work, and I've been sitting here ever since.

Marcus gives me a helpless look as he starts to unpack the food. But when I notice *what* he's pulling out of the bags on the countertop, I freeze.

"What's that?"

Marcus glances at the bags, then at me, and his expression is blank as he states the obvious.

"Alfino's," he says.

"Why?" I whisper thickly.

I remember thinking he was smart bringing pasta to his flings when he planned to break up with them. I remember thinking the delicious pasta would soothe the ache of it all.

Turns out, I was wrong.

I cross my arms over my chest because my hands are shaking. I try to imagine exactly how it's going to go down so I can put on my brave face as it unfolds.

Sorry, Abby. I can see you're starting to feel things

for me you shouldn't and we need to knock this off before it gets too messy. I just want to be friends again.

Who am I kidding? There's no chance of a brave face. Not tonight, not ever. When The Talk comes, it's going to shatter me.

"Why did I bring home Alfino's?" Marcus repeats blankly. "I thought you might need cheering up, and I know you love their food."

"That's *not* why," I whisper the accusation, but it's hard to force myself to speak because my throat feels tight.

"That's *exactly* why." He leaves the bags to approach me on the couch. I watch him warily—as if he's a physical threat, which is beyond ridiculous because I trust him more than anyone else on earth.

With my body, anyway.

My heart is a whole other matter, and apparently he's holding that right there in his reckless hands.

"What's going on?" Marcus reaches for my hand, and when I reluctantly let him take it, he pulls me all the way across until I am half sitting on his lap. He wraps his arms around me and kisses me gently on the hair, and I start to cry.

"Well, today was a shit day, then, wasn't it?" he whispers into my hair. I breathe him in and let the tears come. "I'm so sorry we didn't fall pregnant this month, Abs," he adds softly. The sincerity in his tone is heartfelt, and I close my eyes as a fresh wave of tears surges.

"Me, too," I whisper.

I'm needy enough that I sit hard up alongside him while we eat, and cuddle close on the couch as we settle in for a movie. He suggests a latest release rom-com, but when I roll my eyes at him, he grins and hands *me* the remote.

"You never let me drive the TV," I gasp.

"These are exceptional circumstances," he says softly.

Much later, when it's time for bed, I reach for his hand—an unspoken invitation that I don't let myself question too much. But Marcus stares at me as if he doesn't understand what I want.

"Will you sleep with me?" I ask him, and we part to brush our teeth in our bathrooms before he comes to my bedroom. I'm already in bed by then, and he strips completely without a hint of self-consciousness. I see him naked but unaroused for the first time since our skinny-dipping escapades in our late teens, and it doesn't feel weird at all, because I know his body like I know my own now. He climbs in and pulls me into his arms, and I rest my head against his chest. We lay in the silence and the darkness for a while, and then I ask, "You'll stay tonight in here?"

"If that's what you want me to do," he says softly.

"Do you want to?"

"I want to be here for you, Abby. Whatever that means."

He's stroking my hair as I drift toward sleep, and it feels right, and I feel safe and loved. I promise myself I'll sort everything out tomorrow, but for tonight, I let myself be comforted by his nearness and his care.

CHAPTER TWENTY-TWO

Marcus

I WAKE IN Abby's bed just before dawn, and even in her sleep, she's clinging to me like a barnacle. I kiss her gently before detangling our limbs, but I can't wipe the smile off my face as I retrieve my workout clothes from across the apartment. I think about the innocent night we've shared and wonder what she'll make of it in the cold light of day. She was upset last night—almost as upset as I've ever seen her.

Then again, it was a pretty intense day all around.

That run-in with Liesel yesterday was hardly my finest hour, but I'm actually glad it happened, because it unsettled Abby so much that she let her defenses slip. I stepped into the restaurant unsure of whether or not I'm the only one *feeling* so much these days, and I left an hour later walking on air. She might have fooled me in the cab, but yesterday in that restaurant, Abby left no doubt in my mind that she is starting to feel something for me, too. She would never have been upset like that by the run-in with Liesel if she wasn't, and we *both* knew it.

I'm disappointed right along with her in discovering that she's not pregnant yet, and I *hated* seeing her so upset last night. But we've only just begun this journey together, and most likely this won't be the last disappointment or challenge. One thing I'm sure of is that we handled our shared pain last night the *right* way— we drew comfort from each other. We can get through anything if we have each other, and after last night, I hope Abby realizes that, too. That's *exactly* why I'm going to sit her down today, and try to convince her to give this thing between us a real shot.

I am so buoyed that after my workout a subtle celebration is in order. I return with coffees and takeout, and I'm conscious of the spring in my step as I return to our building. It doesn't last long, because when I step into the apartment, I find it cold and silent.

"Abby?"

I dump breakfast on the bench and sprint to her room, but the bed is empty. Only then do I think to check my phone, and as I read the message on my lock screen, my heart sinks all the way to my toes.

I had to go out. Let's talk tonight.

WHEN I OPEN the front door to our apartment at 5:30 p.m., Abby is sitting on the sofa in front of the blank TV. She faces me slowly, face pale and gaze hollow.

"Hey," I say softly. "I missed you today."

She takes a deep breath, then releases it in a rush. "We need to have that talk."

If her absence this morning wasn't clear enough, her radio silence today was a message in itself. She didn't even log into the instant-message program, and she didn't reply to my text asking how she was. And

now, her tone is a mess of things I don't want to hear—
confusion, frustration and ice. I've never really been
at the receiving end of Abby's cold voice. *That* tone is
reserved for rude people and companies who pay her
freelance invoices late. She hardly ever uses it, either,
because she hates confrontation so much that she tends
to retreat rather than stand up for herself.

I set my laptop case carefully on the kitchen bench
and slip off my suit jacket, then hook it on the coatrack. My movements are deliberately slow; I'm trying
to buy some time to collect my thoughts, because I
know I'm not going to like what she has to say. When
I run out of procrastination tactics, I cross the room
and sit beside her.

"I've been thinking." She draws in a deep breath
and stares at the blank television screen. "We need to
stop this. We need to go back to normal."

"Stop?" I repeat quietly. She glances at me impatiently.

"Sex. Sleeping in the same bed. Holding hands.
Kissing in restaurants. All of the things that have
started since we decided we were going to have a baby
together. I need everything to be just as it always was.
And…" She draws in a deep breath, and then she completely blindsides me. "This weekend, I'm going to
move out. Just for a while. I've asked Izzy if I can use
her spare room."

I'm prepared for most of what she says. Disappointed, but prepared. She's given me plenty of warning signs today that this chat wasn't going to be easy.

That last bit is so unexpected that there's no tem-
pering my reaction.

"What the *fuck*?"

I can barely drag air into my lungs. She's *leaving*? Just like that? She's giving up on us altogether? She's giving up on *our baby* altogether? Because I know immediately that is what she's really proposing here: if she walks out that door, Abby isn't just leaving the apartment. She's not just leaving the sex. She's leaving thirty years of friendship. And never in a million years will she battle the awkwardness to come back to it.

"We can have a reset if I move out. We can get things back to normal and stay friends. It's the smart move," Abby says defensively.

I stare at her, trying to figure out how to say everything boiling inside of me without making even more chaos, but adrenaline and hurt and fear muddle my thoughts and I can't form the right sentence. When I finally speak, the words are laced with frustration.

"You're scared so you're running away."

"I'm *not* running away, Marcus, I just need…"

She trails off as if the fight has gone out of her. She looks miserable. I listen to the sounds of our breaths—mine tight, hers uneven.

"You have feelings for me, and it's freaking you out," I say softly, and Abby gives an indignant gasp and turns to glare at me.

"It should be freaking *you* out, too! You *know* me. You know I'm not like you. I can't just turn my feelings on and off when it suits me."

"That's not fair, Abby. I'm not like that."

"You *are* like that. Just ask Liesel."

Maybe I deserve that; it was definitely a dick move to forget Liesel's name, and the brutal truth is that I did use Liesel. I thought we were using each *other*, and when I realized she was starting to take our hookups seriously, I told myself that breaking things off was the kind thing to do.

I know that doesn't make me a saint. In fact, I'm starting to understand that what I did to Liesel wasn't kind at all. It turns out that being rejected by someone you care about hurts like fuck, regardless of their intentions.

Abby's barb hits its mark, and I can't mask the surprise and the pain of it. She looks a bit like she might want to suck those words back in—the nastiness isn't natural for her. She's backing away from me, and just to be doubly sure I don't chase her, she's trying to push me away.

"You're a wonderful man and a fantastic friend," she says. "But I *can't* let things go on this way if we're going to have a baby together. I need to put some distance between us, just for a while. If things can go back to normal and we can go back to just being friends, then maybe we can try again at some point once things settle down. But no more sex. I can't...*we* can't keep doing this."

"Abby," I say as calmly as I can. She's staring stiffly at the blank television again, so I gently take her hand, and she turns to face me with visible reluctance. "I don't know if we can go back."

She seems shocked by this declaration, as if she actually expected me to take this lying down.

"We *have to* go back," she insists.

"Listen..." I start, then stop and clear my throat before I start the process of ripping my heart out of my chest to offer it to her on a tray. I'm scared again. It's striking to me how these new feelings for her come tangled up with so much fear, and I have another sudden pang of regret and sympathy for the women I've dated. I just didn't *know* a person could feel like this.

I'm also not used to feeling unsure, which is why I've been uncharacteristically hesitant with Abby until now. But every time I let the fear hold me back, she slips away, and this time she might slip all the way out of my life. I take a deep breath. "Abby, I really feel like there's something special between us. Do you feel that, too?"

"It's confusing," she admits, but her gaze narrows immediately after and she shakes her head at me. "We're already close, and now there's sex. It's messy. I was scared of this all along. We start fucking and the next thing I know we're boyfriend and girlfriend and I can't be your girlfriend, Marcus. I just can't."

"You're not my girlfriend," I correct her automatically.

"Good." After a pause, she nods, as if satisfied. "I mean, I know I'm not."

"You're so much more than that. You're my best friend, and I…" Her gaze grows wary, but I take a deep breath and force myself to press on. "I have feelings for you, too, Abby." She frowns even as I wince in disgust at the inadequacy of those words, because it's got to be the understatement of the century. I just don't know how else to explain, and in trying to, I wind up babbling like a fool. "I feel… I mean, *such* intense feelings… I feel so much for you and I've never felt anything like this before and… I didn't know that…uh…"

Oh God. This is a disaster. I can't believe that jumbled mess of words came out of *my* mouth—me: the man voted Most Likely to Charm His Way Through Life in my senior year. And it's ridiculous because all I have to say to her are three little words and she'll know *exactly* what I'm trying to tell her.

If only I was sure.

But I'm not sure, and although saying *I love you* would absolutely get her attention right now, it would also imply a promise of a future together. I can't say *I love you* and then qualify it with *For now, so be with me and we'll see what happens.* I'm trying to convince her to stay, not to scare her out the door even faster. I fumble again for words, and my inadequacy is as frustrating as it is bewildering.

"I feel… I want…"

Abby is staring at me in horror. I try to regroup.

"I'm fucking this up again. But you just have to know one thing—I'm going to fight for you this time, and I won't let you pretend this isn't happening. We could have it all, Abby. Maybe we already *do* have it all. More than anything else in the world right now, I want you." I clear my throat, and dare to meet her gaze again as I whisper, "I want *us*, Abby."

Well, at least I managed to get that last bit right. For a split second, I think this is it. I've told her how I feel, and maybe she feels the same, and maybe this is the start of a new period of honesty between us.

That is not what happens.

Abby shakes my hand off hers and stands abruptly, eyes filling with tears. Even her shoulders slump forward, as if she's suddenly carrying a great weight.

"Tell me you don't want to be with me, too," I chal-

lenge her. Maybe it makes me an arrogant, overconfi-
dent prick, but I was so sure this was the time to tell
her. But Abby is crying—really crying, and these are
not happy tears.

I thought I was scared before. What I'm feeling right
now is so far past that I'm not even sure what words to
use to understand it. Jess comes to mind, and the way
she described how love felt to her.

*Like stripping myself bare and stepping out onto
a battlefield.*

That's exactly what I feel right now, and I'm hating
every terrifying second of it.

"Talk to me," I say, voice breaking. I don't want this
to escalate in case she retreats before we have a chance
to thrash this out, so I stay seated, but reach up for her
hand. Abby gives me a frantic look and takes a step
backward—out of my reach.

"But, Marcus—you—"

"You don't have to tell me that I'm a shit boyfriend,
Abs. I *know*. But with you, it's different. I *promise*
you. I'm so fucking crazy about you I can barely think
straight."

"You're confused," she exclaims, throwing her
hands in the air. "You're as confused as I am. Because
we're already so close, and now we've been having sex,
and we don't know what's *what* anymore!"

"That's because best friends who have fantastic sex
aren't just best friends anymore, Abby," I say as pa-
tiently as I can.

Abby immediately jabs a finger in my direction and
hisses at me. "This is *exactly* why I have to move out.
I want things to go back exactly as they were—I *need*

them to. And the only way we're going to clear all of this confusion out of the air is if we get some distance."

I'm not getting through to her, and desperation is setting in. I try to temper my voice, but it rises, anyway.

"Distance is not going to do a fucking thing to the way I feel about you."

I rise to my feet, unable to handle the nervous energy coursing through me any longer, and Abby stares up at me, brown eyes still swimming in tears. Her face contorts as if I've said something cruel. She tries to muffle the sob but it escapes as a fairly undignified snort, and I gently pull her into the circle of my arms. I'm shaking with the force of everything I'm feeling and I know she can feel the intensity of the storm. "I know this scares you, Abby. I know you're freaked out by all this change. But I can't hide it anymore. I can't pretend anymore."

She pulls away, face red with frustration. "You're going to destroy me. Can't you see that?"

"I won't—"

"You *saw* what happened with Roger!"

I don't think I've ever heard Abby *shout* before. She's backing away again, too.

"I did see," I whisper. It hurts just to remember her like that—but I know her depression after Roger had much more to do with her general well-being than the breakup itself. She found her way back from that period of her life, and she learned from the experience. Besides which, I am *nothing* like that asshole.

"You think that was bad, Marcus? You think I was in a hole then? You'd *bury* me in that fucking hole.

You'd get bored of this and I'd be left with nothing—no best friend, no baby, nothing."

She's not sad anymore—now she's furious, as if I've already hurt her. Apparently, she's so certain of that outcome she's already livid about it.

"I won't hurt you," I say. My voice breaks, and I'm pleading, but I don't even care anymore. How do I explain to her how sure I am of that? This is my last-ditch attempt to keep her here, so I'll throw it all on the line. Maybe I should be embarrassed at the desperation in my voice, but I'm not anymore. Pride and dignity are luxuries for people who aren't a heartbeat away from losing everything. "I don't know exactly what the future holds, but I know that much for sure. Just give me a chance to prove that things would be different for us."

"No!" she exclaims. She's pulling away—I can see it in her eyes and in her stance, and especially in the way she's shuffling toward the door, even though she's still facing me. "I just want to be friends. I need for us just to be friends. I'll go to Isabel's for a while and we can revaluate in a few weeks…"

"So if this move is temporary," I ask her unevenly, "are you planning on taking your things?"

She winces, and I can't tell if that's from the roughness in my tone or the question. Then she clears her throat and nods. We stand in ragged silence for a moment, then I whisper, "You're not fooling me, Abby. You know as well as I do that if you walk out that door, it's over. Everything. Our friendship, the baby, everything." It's not a threat—it's a statement of fact.

"I don't know what else to do!"

"Stay," I plead. "That's what you need to do. Stay and let's see where this takes us."

"I have to go out now," she says, and her eyes are on the door. "I'll be late for Pilates."

"Abby…" I groan. I can't very well block the doorway, but I'm running out of ways to plead with her to stay and it's frustrating as fuck. "For once in your life, try facing something head-on. Please."

"I'm not running away," she says stiffly, but I recognize all too well the set of her shoulders and the stubborn lift in her chin. She averts her gaze as she scoops her bag up off the floor and moves to brush past me. I catch her elbow as she does, and gently turn her back to face me. She tilts her face up toward mine, eyes closed, as two heavy tears roll silently down toward her neck. I wipe them away with my thumbs, and then I kiss her cheek. With our faces close together, I close my eyes, and I breathe her in—in case this really is the last time I get to do it.

"I want to be with you," I whisper. Everything is falling to pieces, but it feels so good to say those words to her so I say them again, firmer this time. "I *want* you, Abby Herbert, more than anything I've ever wanted in my life. I know you're scared of getting hurt. I know you think if you hide from this, you'll be safe—but you're safe *with* me, I promise you."

She shakes her head as she pulls away.

The apartment has never felt as empty as it does when the door slams behind her.

CHAPTER TWENTY-THREE

Abby

JESS AND ISABEL are waiting at the door when I get to the gym. I'm astounded I made it here without stepping in front of a car or someone dragging me off for an involuntary medical checkup.

The conversation with Marcus was bound to hurt and it was always going to be difficult. But even yesterday, when I realized I was starting to have real feelings for him, it didn't even occur to me to hope he'd feel the same way about *me*.

"What's going on? *Moving out? Are you serious?*" Isabel gasps when I near them. She squeezes me into a tight hug.

"Everything is so messed up," I choke, and Jess sighs and steps toward the road to hail a passing cab. "Class starts soon. Izzy, aren't you instructing?"

"I swapped shifts with Aria and called Jess when I got your text about the spare room," Isabel informs me. "Is there a chance you're pregnant?"

I shake my head, and Jess mutters, "Well, just for tonight, that's a good thing. Because we're all going to get very drunk."

At first, I think they're whisking me away for an

emergency girls' support meeting—but by the time we get to Jess's place, I've reassessed the mood of my friends. Both Jess and Isabel are unusually somber, and as we make our way into Jess's plush apartment, I'm feeling defensive. Isabel sits beside me on the white leather couch, and Jess takes the multicolored wing chair opposite. We're each nursing a full glass of wine, and Jess has materialized an elaborate platter of cheese and crackers onto the coffee table.

"Talk," Jess says.

"He said he has feelings for me," I say. Jess and Isabel look at me blankly.

"All of this drama is because Marcus stated the fucking obvious?" Jess says, and I groan impatiently.

"No, Jess. He said he has *feelings* for me." I know I'm making no sense, so I try to clarify with, "Not friendship feelings. Romantic feelings."

"Are you already drunk?" Jess asks. "Of course he has feelings for you, Abby. The man is hopelessly in love with you and it's as plain as the boobs on your chest."

"But he *isn't* in love with me," I snap. "That's not what he said. He said he has *feelings* for me."

"What kind of feelings did you think he was referring to? Indigestion? A headache?" Jess laughs. I scowl at her, and she gives me a pointed look. "Want to know how I'm so sure about this, Abby?"

"Because you're arrogant?" I mutter, and she grins at me.

"Well, that *and* he *told* me."

I guzzle down the entire glass of wine I'm nursing. Isabel gets an immediate promotion to my first-best friend when she refills the glass without comment, but then I think about Marcus again, and I slump. I glance at Jess warily.

"What did he say exactly?"

"He said…" She pauses, then she frowns. "Well, he said a lot of things about love, in the context of his relationship with you."

"But did he say, 'I am in love with Abby'?" I demand. "Specifically? Because he *did not* say those words to me."

"Okay," she says impatiently. "He didn't *say* it specifically. But he implied it, besides which—did you hear the bit about me having eyes in my head? Because trust me, chick. It's fucking obvious that he's in love with you. I suspected it all year, but these last few weeks, he's been positively giddy."

"Marcus doesn't get giddy over women," I whisper.

"Correction," Jess says pointedly. "Marcus *didn't* get giddy over women. Then the last few weeks happened."

"Abby," Isabel says softly. "I think what Jess is trying to say is that for a while now it's been pretty obvious to the rest of us that Marcus was kind of crazy about you. And honestly, honey? I think you're pretty crazy about him, too."

I raise my chin.

"I'm not. It's been great, but we can't let it go any further."

Jess shrugs.

"Okay, well, that's sorted, then. What's your plan? You run away to Izzy's place and abandon your lifelong best friend?"

"I'm not abandoning him, Jess," I exclaim. "I'm just

trying to reset things. I really do just want everything to go back to normal. For *him*, too—he's clearly as confused by all of this as I am. Leaving is the smart thing to do. I should never have let it get this far."

"Let me understand," Isabel asks. "*Why* are you so determined to go back to just being friends?"

"He'll assume he can make it work because his ego is the size of Texas and he's never failed at anything. But it's just not worth the risk—not to me. There's too much at stake—the baby, and our friendship, and *everything* is on the line if we don't stop now."

"Abby," Isabel says gently. "Maybe it was on the line all along. I really don't think Marcus fell in love with you in just a few weeks, honey. Maybe this last little while has *shown* him the depth of his feelings, but I really think things changed between you guys a while ago. It's just something you can't ignore anymore."

"Even if it *was* true, that doesn't change who he is. Love isn't some magic panacea that makes people compatible." I raise my chin. "Marcus is *nothing* like the man I thought I'd end up with."

"Agreed. It's possibly his best feature." Jess snorts.

I scowl at her. "What's that supposed to mean? He doesn't have long-term relationships because he doesn't want them. I don't have long-term relationships because I *can't* make them work!"

"That's not even what I meant, Abby. It's just that after ten years of watching you date needy losers—" Jess starts to say, but Isabel interrupts her.

"Abby, I think what Jess is *trying* to say is that maybe part of what works with you and Marcus is that you're both strong and independent. You're both successful. You're both responsible. So maybe you don't have gaming or your nerdy stuff in common, but what you *do* have in common is probably even more important."

"That's exactly what I was trying to say," Jess says, then she adds, "I was also going to say that Marcus isn't a scared man-baby who wants you to carry him through life, and that's a nice change from *everyone else* I've ever seen you date. So—" she shrugs "—there's *that*."

My jaw drops. "Not all of my ex-boyfriends were like that." I look to Isabel, expecting her to agree with me, but she gnaws her lip and looks away. "They weren't! I mean, maybe Roger was, but—"

"Abby, you're a nurturing, caring woman." Jess has never sounded so gentle, and it makes me wary. "You clearly *want* someone to nurture. But you've always been attracted to the kind of guy who doesn't reciprocate, and you deserve better. I'm not just being a bitch when I say that the best thing about you and Marcus being together is that he's nothing like your previous boyfriends. The reason your relationship with him is so beautiful is that you care for *each other*. It's balanced and it's healthy."

"But my other boyfriends—"

"Were generally bloodsucking parasites, hoping to catch a free ride through life. Via you, in case you missed that part."

"Jess," Isabel sighs. "Come on. She's had a rough day, go easy on her."

"Maybe it looked that way," I concede hesitantly. "But it's more complicated than that. Part of the reason I can't let anything more happen with Marcus is that

I couldn't even make those guys happy, you know? I spend too much time alone, and my gaming and my work is too important, and—"

"Oh, for fuck's sake, Abby," Jess says impatiently. "Plenty of people work long hours and enjoy their own company. You didn't make those guys happy because it was never your job to *make* them happy. They wanted a mommy, and you wanted a partner. The definition of insanity is doing the same fucking thing over and over again, so maybe it's time for you to try something different."

We fall into a strained silence. Izzy tops up my glass again, then slides her arm around my shoulders for a hug.

"Is she right?" I whisper, my throat tight.

"Well, she's not *wrong*," Izzy whispers back apologetically.

"But…what if I try with Marcus and one or both of us gets hurt?" I whisper back.

"There really is such a thing as playing it too safe," Jess says. "You can't live your entire life without taking any risks at all."

"I support myself playing *video games*. Do you think that's playing it too safe?" I say stiffly. "I'm fine with taking chances. I just do it in a controlled way."

"Babe, I was around when you were starting your business," she says wryly. "You won't convince me that was risky. You didn't commit to it until you had no choice. You were laid off a year *after* you should have resigned from that magazine job, anyway." She cocks an eyebrow at me. "You play things so safe that, next to you, the rest of us look like adrenaline junkies."

"We're talking about gambling what's left of my relationship with the most important person in my world here."

"There's a reason people gamble, Abby." Jess shrugs. "They do it because sometimes it pays off."

"Even if I do go home and we stay together like this, things will end, anyway, and it will be messy—*that* would be the end of us. There's no possible payoff that's worth that risk."

"What about happily-ever-after?" Isabel asks quietly, and now I'm stricken.

"People don't live happily-ever-after," I whisper, and we share a sad glance. I know she's thinking about Paul, and I squeeze her hand. "Life isn't a fairy tale, is it?"

"Things didn't work out for Paul and me, but I'm still glad we tried."

Jess sips at her wine thoughtfully. "In the business world, the high-risk investments have the potential for the greatest reward. But then at the other end of the scale, one thing is always true—one hundred percent of the time. No risk, no reward."

"This is like betting the house on red at Vegas. The odds are insurmountable."

"You have thirty fucking years of successful friendship behind you." Jess sighs impatiently. "If that doesn't show you're compatible, I don't know what will."

"That's the point," I say, and I raise my chin. "Thirty years of friendship is not something you put on the line just for some good sex. It was stupid for us to go there in the first place."

"You're seriously going to try to tell us you're not already in love with him?" Jess says, and I shake my head.

"We're good friends—very good friends. The sex confused things, that's all, and I found it hard to keep my feelings out of it. But that doesn't mean I'm in love with him, and it doesn't mean it's wise for us to continue down this path. I just want to be friends again."

"And what about Marcus?" she asks me pointedly. "Have you thought about what he wants? How much he must be hurting right now?"

"He's as confused as I am, that's all," I say miserably. "The best thing for us both is to move on now, before we get any more tangled up in it. It's the only safe way forward." I glance at Izzy, and my gaze grows pleading. "Please let me take your spare room. Just for a while."

"It's hardly a 'spare room.'" She sighs. "It's a study nook without a door, and it's still full of moving boxes. I think we can fit a stretcher bed in there but it's going to be tight."

"That's fine," I assure her. I don't care about the details. All I care about is retreating.

"You're not even going to ask me?" Jess scowls. "You've been here thousands of times. I'm sure you noticed the two unoccupied, fully furnished bedrooms."

I sigh.

"Can I stay here, Jess?"

"No fucking way. Stop running away from your problems." She snorts, then she flashes me a grin. "But thanks for letting me say it—that was magnanimous of you on this night of great drama and heartbreak."

"Can we talk about something else now?"

We waste the next few hours skirting around the elephant in the room, because every time the conversation circles back to Marcus, I forcibly change it. Eventually, Isabel heads home because she has a class at 6:00 a.m., but Jess and I decide to press on. Once we're alone, Jess tops up my wine, and sinks back into the wing chair.

"Let me bring it up one last time," Jess says. I'm more than a little tipsy by now, and the wine has done exactly what I needed it to—it's dulled the throbbing regret and pain in my chest. I look at Jess, assess the determination in her gaze, then sigh.

"Fine."

"I always thought that heartbreak was the worst thing, you know?" she says thoughtfully. "Not that I make a habit of falling in love, but…the *one* time I did, I discovered that heartbreak is a bit like a wound. Give it some air and some time, and it'll heal, even if it leaves a scar. What'll *really* fuck you up is regret, especially regret over missed chances. That's like a festering infection that never goes away, because you find yourself waking up every day of your damned life wondering, *What if?*"

"Jessica Cohen," I say blankly. "Was that *vulnerability* in your voice?" I can't even imagine who she might be referring to. She's had plenty of boyfriends over the years, but not one of them was serious. She sighs and looks away.

"I don't know why I bother since you're clearly too stubborn to listen to me, anyway," she mutters. "So one last time—are you still absolutely sure you aren't in love with Marcus?"

"Absolutely sure."

"And you definitely just want to be friends?"

I nod stiffly.

"Well," she says, then pauses. She flicks me a hesitant glance. "The timing might be a bit off, but there's something I've been meaning to talk to you about for a while. There's this woman in the development department, her name is Helena."

I narrow my gaze at her.

"Jess, if you're trying to make me jealous, you're going to need to try harder than that."

"No, Abby," Jess says softly, then she shrugs. "I'm not playing games. I'm just trying to make the most of what's obviously a bad situation. I know you're trying to convince yourself he's not *really* in love with you, but I happen to think Marcus is going to be very upset about you leaving. He and Helena have always had a good rapport, and she recently broke up with her long-term partner… Maybe with a little nudge, they could console each other. I wouldn't normally encourage these things at work but they don't really work together directly and I think… I don't know. I've always just thought there might be something there. A distraction like that might actually help you, too, since you want him to move on and just go back to being your friend."

The *right* answer here is to give my blessing. Jess knows it. I know it. I sip at my wine, and I will myself to say the words. Then I gulp at my wine, and I force myself to do it.

"Go ahead," I say. My voice sounds pretty normal and I'm proud of myself. Jess nods and flashes me a brilliant smile. She picks up her phone and starts texting, and the panic hits me all at once. "You're doing it now? You're setting them up *now*?"

She shrugs again.

"No time like the present."

"I just need to go to the bathroom," I blurt out. I spill the wine as I push it back onto the coffee table and sprint toward her bathroom. The instant I close the door, the tears erupt, and once they start, there's no stopping them.

I'm sobbing, but trying desperately to keep the noise down so Jess doesn't hear. The tears just keep coming and coming. I sit on the floor behind the door so she can't walk in and catch me, and I nurse a box of Kleenex and I let it all pour out. Because I can't bear it—I just can't stand the thought of him with someone else, especially not this *Helena*, who in my mind is a magnificent, extroverted blonde woman in a business suit. She'll be so perfect for him.

But he's mine.

The muddle of my thoughts consumes me. I tell myself this is all normal and a part of the process of getting back to just being his friend. I tell myself the jealousy will pass. But it doesn't feel like it's going to pass—it feels like it's going to crush me, and I don't know what that means. I *genuinely* never cared when he had lovers before. How can I make myself stop caring now? It seems impossible, like I've undergone a permanent change.

It feels like I've only been in the bathroom for a few minutes, but when I go for a fresh Kleenex and discover I've reached the bottom of the box, I know it's been a lot longer. I hear movement at the door, then a hesitant knock.

"Abby," Marcus says softly. "Can I come in?"

I look around myself—there's a soggy mess of tissues strewn across the tiles, and my face is hot. When I look down, even my hoodie is tearstained all along the neckline.

"What are you doing here?" I mutter as I frantically try to scoop the tissues up.

"Jess called me. Please let me in."

"I don't think that's a good idea."

"Well, I'm either coming in, or I'm waiting in the hallway until you come out, so make your decision." He sighs. He sounds so tired, and now I feel jealous *and* guilty. I groan and pull myself to my feet, then dump the tissues into the trash and force myself to look in the mirror.

I look like shit. My eyes are swollen, my face is blotchy, even my nose is red. How long have I been *in* here? I run the tap, and splash my face, then dry it on the hot-pink hand towel. This does literally nothing to improve the ghastly sight reflecting at me in the mirror. The door opens, hesitantly, and then I see Marcus and the tears start all over again. I was so brave earlier, but there's such exposed pain on his face now. I hate that he's hurting, too, and that I did that to him.

"Abby," he says. "Come home."

"This isn't about you and Helena," I insist, and he looks at me blankly.

"Who's Helena?"

"Helena from the development team. Jess is going to set you two up but that's not why I'm crying." My voice breaks as an unexpected sob catches me, and I clear my throat. Marcus raises an eyebrow at me, then leans back into the hallway.

"Helena?" he calls to Jess. His irritation is palpable. "Really?"

"I had a point to prove," Jess yells from somewhere deep in the apartment. Marcus sighs.

"Isn't Helena retiring next year? How old is she, anyway?"

"Sixty-four, I think. But Paul assures me she's still one of his sharpest coders. Actually, now that I think about it, Helena is probably too smart for you, anyway," Jess says wryly, and I hear the click of her heels on the floor so I know she's coming closer. "Anyway, Abby has been in the bathroom crying for forty-five minutes, so I'd say my point is successfully proven." She pushes Marcus out of the way, then leans into the bathroom. "Sorry, chick. I had to do something. You were being an idiot."

I growl at her, and she winces and disappears from the doorway again. Marcus's gaze returns to me.

"Abby. I don't want *anyone* except you."

"Well," I say unevenly, "I don't even care if you do."

But then I start to cry again, and he steps into the bathroom and closes the door gently behind himself. He comes to me, and he wraps his arms around me, and he kisses the side of my hair, the way he has when I was upset for as long as I can remember.

If I had to condense our whole relationship down into one single gesture, it would be those kisses. They are innocent and gentle, and they speak of affection and concern and the connection that's always transcended our differences. And now, those kisses send delicious shivers down my spine, and leave me wanting more, just like our relationship does. Just like our relationship always will, if I give in and go home with him. And that's what it all boils down to.

"I know you're scared, Abby. I know this is new, and it's pushed you *way* outside of your comfort zone. I know there's a lot at stake. I know you can't control what's happening here, and that makes you so stressed. You know *how* I know those things?" I'm crying again, pressing my face into the strength of his chest as I do. I shake my head, and he leans down to whisper in my ear. "Because I see you and I know you. You're the most important person in my world, Abby Herbert, and no matter what happens between us now and in the future, that's never going to change. There's no path back to where we were, and I'm actually *glad* of that. Because the minute you kissed me on that rooftop, you owned me, and I'm tired of trying to force our relationship to be what it was before. The only way forward is to give this a shot."

"What if we both want different things out of life, Marcus?"

We both know *exactly* what I'm talking about. He only hesitates for a second, but it's long enough to confirm my fears. Maybe he is really crazy about me—head over heels in love for the first time in his life—but even if that's the case, it still isn't enough to make him want a long-term commitment.

I can't pretend anymore. I *do* want so much to be with him, but I know if I let him talk me into coming home, I'm going to fall in love with him. And where can it possibly lead, when we both have such different visions for our future? How do we have a baby together now if he's completely okay with the idea of an end-date on any romance between us?

"I think the important thing is that we both want the same thing right now, Abs—and that's each other," he says. He pulls away to look down at me, and our eyes lock. "Everything else, we can figure out along the way."

I inhale sharply, and I hold his gaze as I ask flatly, "Are you in love with me, Marcus?"

His eyes widen in surprise at my directness, and fair enough, since this is probably the first time in my entire existence I've voluntarily confronted something potentially painful and embarrassing. He hesitates for just a second, then he swallows and murmurs, "I don't know. I think so? I just don't know what that means yet. That's why I want time—*with you*—to figure all of this out."

I shake my head fiercely.

"This is my point. This is why I left. You're asking me to blindly trust that you'll find some way to smooth things over if we get to a point that I need more and *you* don't want it. I'm always going to want the stability of a commitment, Marcus. That's who I am. And who *you* are is someone who has explicitly, purposefully, stated that you *do not want that* for at least two decades. That's why I think we're better off just going our separate ways now, taking some space and coming back together as friends once the air clears."

"Abby." He exhales in frustration, then he runs his

hands through his hair. "I don't know what you want from me right now. Are *you* in love with *me*?"

I raise my chin.

"I don't want to be."

"You've made that abundantly clear, Abs," he says wryly, then he sobers, and now there's no denying the guarded hope I see in his gaze as he asks, "But *are* you?"

"I don't know, either," I whisper. Marcus gives me a wry look.

"That's what I figured. But you feel something, right?" I nod reluctantly, and he shrugs. "So here's what we know for sure—we both feel something. That's all we know. And with that *very limited* dataset, you're asking me to predict a long-term future between us and to give you some kind of guarantee. Can't you see how unfair that is to me?"

I'm blushing, because when he puts it like that, I feel ridiculous. Marcus gently pulls me back into his embrace, and when he speaks again, I hear the rumble of his voice through the wall of his chest.

"Abs, all I'm asking you for is a chance, okay? We might not be sure what our end goal is here, but let's start the journey, anyway, and see where it leads us. I know we might not have a lot of time, but let's put the baby off just for a bit…let's just focus on *us* until after Christmas. We don't even have to be intimate. We'll hang out. Hold hands. Kiss sometimes. Go out for dates. Let's just be together."

"We don't have to be 'intimate'?" I repeat, and then I can't help it—I laugh at him. "Marcus, you sound like my grandmother."

He laughs, too, but then he sobers. He lifts a strand of my hair into his hand, and he twirls it around his fingers as he whispers, "I fucking hated it when you called it 'just sex' before. It wasn't just sex to me—I've had plenty of *that* and when I'm with you it's something altogether different. I'm so into you I can't even think straight."

"I thought you'd freak out if I caught feelings for you," I say, and he shakes his head almost violently.

"I told you, sweetheart. Things are different with you."

"I don't want to put the baby off, Marcus," I admit. "But I don't think we have a choice."

I'd accepted today that there was going to be a pause on any attempt to get pregnant—I just thought it would be while we readjusted to life as friends. Maybe that's why I'm still reasonably calm now about the idea of waiting.

Everything he's proposing is a gamble. A gamble on our friendship, a gamble on our relationship and a gamble on my chance of becoming a mom. *Everything* is up in the air, and there's nothing I can do to control where any of it lands when the dust settles.

Just the thought of that makes me feel so anxious I want to run away again. But maybe Jess is right. Maybe it's time to stop hiding. Maybe it's time to take a risk.

"We need to figure *us* out first, Abby," he murmurs. "Things are different now. But I know we can figure this out, and I know it'll be worth the wait when we do."

Marcus steps to pull the door open before he turns back and extends his hand toward me. I look at his hand, and then I reach for it and let him entwine our fingers.

"Let's go home," he says. There's no pretending otherwise; home is where I want to be, and home is wherever Marcus is.

"Let's go home."

I WAKE UP with Marcus in my bed. Early-morning light is coming through my window, and Marcus still holds me close. His arms are around me just as they were when we fell asleep, as if he didn't even dare let me go once through the night. His breath is stirring the hair at my ear.

It's Friday morning and we have nowhere to be. All we did last night when we got home was to arrange a spontaneous long weekend, then we tumbled into bed where we just held one another. But now, a loud grumble sounds from Marcus's stomach, and I giggle.

"Forgot to have dinner," he mumbles. I roll over and brush the curls back from his forehead, and survey his sleep-rumpled face. He's so beautiful to me. I could stare at him all day, and now I really can. I feel oddly relieved this morning. It takes me a minute to realize that feeling comes from the simple knowledge that I don't have to fight my attraction to him anymore.

"Morning," I whisper.

He opens his eyes just a crack, and surveys me cautiously.

"How are you feeling today?"

"Okay," I whisper back, and the smile that breaks over his face is transformative.

He brushes his lips against mine and whispers back, "Thank fuck for that."

He gets up to go for breakfast, and I lie in bed and doze lightly until it occurs to me that I really need to ring Isabel.

"What time are you coming around, roomie?" she greets me.

"I'm not," I say apologetically. "I'm really sorry to mess you around, Izzy."

"Oh, Abby," she says softly. "Don't apologize. Things are better?"

"I'm home, and we're going to have a trial period. Date for a little while and see what happens."

"Good," she says, and I hear the smile in her voice.

"I still don't know where this can lead," I admit.

"Forgive me if I'm a little skeptical about your judgment here, honey," Izzy says softly. "Since you were so determined *it* couldn't happen in the first place. But I'm really glad you decided to take a chance."

"Me, too," I admit, and then a smile catches me by surprise. The underlying fear is still there, but it's quieted by a sense that I'm right where I need to be. If I was at Izzy's place right now like I'd planned, I'd be a mess and I'd be wondering about what might have been.

Despite the obvious flaws in her delivery, Jess was right about at least one thing. Sometimes, the potential reward really is worth taking a risk.

I hang up just as Marcus steps back through the doorway, carrying a tray of coffees and a paper bag. I'm still in bed, wearing only a T-shirt and pair of sweatpants. I toss the phone onto the bedside table and glance up at Marcus, who's staring at me thoughtfully.

"What?" I prompt, impatiently waving for my coffee. He shakes his head, then goes right back to staring.

"Let me finish what I'm doing."

"And what exactly *are* you doing?"

"I'm enjoying the view."

I roll my eyes and lift my hands again.

"Stop messing around and give me my coffee!"

"Have I ever told you that you're sexy as fuck?"

I giggle and shake my head at him.

"That would have been a pretty weird thing for you to say until recently. And you can flatter me all weekend if you want. But coffee first!"

Given I've been talking to Marcus since I *learned* to talk, it feels remarkable that we still somehow find new topics of conversation—but we do. We resettle in the bed with our breakfast and the newspapers, but the papers remain untouched because we're feeding each other and cuddling. By early afternoon, we find our way to the couch where we huddle under a blanket and Marcus suggests we watch some TV. Without our usual fake-negotiation, he loads an episode of *Dr. Who*.

"See?" he teases me. "See how committed I am to this? I watch *sci-fi* with you. Voluntarily. I've never gone to such extreme lengths for *any* other woman."

I laugh like a tipsy teenage girl, and I burrow against him, wanting to cuddle him ever closer.

"This started for you at New Year's?" I ask him.

"I really thought I'd moved on but…there was no pretending otherwise once we made love that first time."

We take a nap together when we've watched enough mindless TV, and when he stirs and murmurs something about dinner, I turn to face him and I stare into his eyes. I feel so close to him—like I can see every part of him, and he can see every part of me. It's pure, unadulterated bliss.

"Hey," he whispers. "You okay?"

I kiss him gently, and I let myself *love* the way he cares for me.

"I couldn't be better."

BY TUESDAY, WE'RE well and truly back into a routine of being together. That's as long as it takes for this new version of us to become habit. Everything is just as it always was—our great life together, now enhanced by a new degree of honesty and vulnerability, *and* limbs entangled while we sleep.

As Marcus leaves for the office after our impromptu long weekend, he's whistling softly, and I grin to myself as I putter around the apartment getting dressed. When I sit at the keyboard in my cave, I'm suddenly back in my groove. I have achieved so little in the last few weeks that I have a backlog of work to deal with, let alone the two new livestreams I need to plan out. I plow straight into it all, and I'm making amazing progress when a chat window pops up late in the morning.

Marcus: Hey there.

Abby: Hey, you.

Marcus: How's your day going so far?

Abby: Great. Yours?

Marcus: Every day is good for me when you're in it.

My heart skips a beat at the simple message, and then another as I reply.

Abby: Same for me actually :)

Marcus: Busy tonight?

Abby: I really hope so.

The intercom rings, and I step away from the computer and answer it.
"Ms. Herbert?"
"Yes?"
"Flower delivery."
"Ah...okay."
When I open the door, there are two men pushing trollies loaded with a random assortment of flowers. There are lilies and roses and orchids and daisies, in vases and boxes and baskets. The deliverymen unload them all to fill the kitchen counter, accept my signature and finally pass me a note as they leave.

I know how much you hate clichéd romantic gestures but suck it up, princess—sometimes a man is allowed to express what's in his heart and bunches of Dungeons and Dragons figurines just weren't going to cut it this time. You are beautiful, and I am so grateful that you're in my life— my best friend, in every way.

I brush my fingertips across the petals of a rose and clear my throat as tears start to rise. I battle them— because this is *nonsense*. It's a ridiculous, over-the-top gesture and he's right—I fucking *hate* this kind of thing.

But not today. I'm awed by him and by the way we are together, and this gesture feels fitting somehow. I breathe in deeply; the apartment smells like Marcus's aftershave, but that's rapidly being overtaken by the scent of the flowers, and it's all delicious and it's *all* good. I carry a vase with me back to my study and sit it on my desk beside the monitor.

Abby: Marcus?

Marcus: Hmm?

Abby: Thank you.

Marcus: For?

Abby: I think you know what for.

Marcus: No tirade of abuse for the cliché?

Abby: Not this time. But pull that shit again and you'll hear about it.

Marcus: You don't scare me, Abigail Herbert. And I intend to "pull this shit" again, often.

At lunchtime, I greet him at the door against the backdrop of flowers. I'm wearing my lacy red lingerie and a smile.

"Ah," he says, eyes wide. "Aren't we…waiting…"

"We can wait if you want to," I say innocently, and

I slip a finger under one of my bra straps and knock it off my shoulder. "Oops."

Marcus growls at me, and I laugh as I stride toward him. I drop to my knees and reach for his belt buckle, drag his suit trousers and boxers down to his ankles, then plant a gentle kiss *right* at the top of his thighs. He leans back into the door and groans.

"So, what I'm hearing is, you've had all the time you need and you're ready for us to be intimate again already?"

"Enough with the grandma talk," I mutter, and he chuckles, but the laughter quickly fades as I get right to work—working with my mouth and tongue until his knees are buckling and he starts to slide down the door. Marcus catches me in his arms as he reaches the carpet, and he kisses me—hot and hard and hungry.

"I want to make love to you," he whispers against my mouth.

"Oh, thank God," I groan, and I kiss him again. "You spent all of those weeks getting me addicted to this, and then we just *stopped*. A girl has needs, you know."

He grins, and we kiss again for a moment, until he tears his mouth from mine and he checks, "Is now a good time?"

"Now is the best time *ever*," I confirm, and I toss my underwear across the room, press him down into the carpet and straddle him.

"It's been too long," I say, and he laughs.

"Abby, it's been…what? Five days?"

"*Too* fucking long," I mutter, and I'm ready to sink down onto him, but I pause. I love it like this with Marcus. When I'm on top, *I'm* in control and I can stare right into his eyes.

This time, our gazes lock and my chest tightens until I can't even breathe. His cheeks are flushed and his hair is mussed and his eyes are shiny and he's excited and aroused and into me and into us and I am the happiest woman on the face of the planet...right up until the moment when I realize that I've forgotten something very important.

"We're not going to try to make a baby right now, right?" I ask hesitantly.

"Is that still okay?"

"Yeah. Except that I meant to get a condom but I heard you at the door so I ran out here to meet you and I forgot."

He looks at me blankly, then he groans and reaches up to my shoulders.

"I'll get one from my room."

"One more time with nothing between us?" I whisper, and when he nods, I start to shuffle closer again. "It's too early, anyway. It's safe."

"Okay," he whispers back, and his hands slide down to my hips, and he guides me down onto him. When he's *home*, buried within my body, he holds me still for just a second as he murmurs, "I missed you, Abby. I missed this."

"Me, too," I promise him, and then we both fall silent, because sometimes there are better ways to communicate than with words.

Later, Marcus pulls me onto his chest and tucks my head under his chin. I try to subtly wipe the tears from my eyes before he can see them, but then I hear his whisper. "You cry sometimes."

"I told myself I was imagining it. I don't think I'll ever get used to it…how beautiful it is with you. How good it is. It always catches me by surprise."

"I know what you mean," he murmurs.

"All that time we wasted," I say lightly. "We spent thousands of hours talking when we could have been naked."

"Those hours weren't wasted," Marcus says. "I kind of think those hours are what brought us to where we are today. Like we just couldn't see each other this way until we were really ready."

"I like that idea," I say. "Maybe all of those years of friendship are the foundation for what we have now."

"I think that's why it's so intense between us."

I twist a little, so that I can look into his eyes. He offers me a gentle smile.

"I really like being with you, Marcus," I say.

His smile broadens to a grin as he whispers back, "I really like being with you, too, Abs."

Now I just need to make sure I don't fuck things up.

I'VE BEEN DOING a lot of thinking about some of the things Jess and Isabel said about my ex-boyfriends last week. I'm still not sure I agree with everything they had to say—but maybe there's *some* truth in the accusation that my past relationships tended to be unbalanced.

I always tried so hard to make things work, *especially* with Roger. He seemed like an exact fit for the man I'd been waiting for, and I really threw myself into that relationship with abandon. It wasn't long before he started complaining that I spent too much time gaming, so I tried to limit my time at the computer to the bare necessity while we were together. I loved him, but although I never wanted to admit it even to myself, I felt suffocated by him sometimes. He didn't respect my need for routine, and in trying to please him, I sacrificed that—which made me feel uneasy, but then he got *so* offended when I tried to retreat for some alone time to rebalance myself.

Roger never understood that my need for space wasn't about rejecting him. I'm introverted by nature, and now my job involves me effectively performing for a large audience several times a week. Time to myself was never an indulgence. It's always been a necessity for me.

And he really didn't like Jess and Izzy, but I let him gradually manipulate my schedule until I saw my best girlfriends so much less than I wanted to. And God, Roger was *super*jealous of my relationship with Marcus. I used to let him tag along whenever we hung out, and he'd sit there in stony silence half the time. If we were at a function, Roger clung to me like a barnacle. He only did chores around the house that I nagged him to do. He was forever forgetting to pay his share of the bills and he never had any savings…so I had to put in extra there, too.

At long last, I recognize that my connection to Roger stopped being love at some point and became codependency. I just couldn't see it until now. I gave up too much of myself with Roger. I sacrificed the things that I love about my life to try to make him happy. I want things to work with Marcus—but I *won't* do that again. I can't.

The problem is, I don't think I've ever had a romantic relationship that *didn't* operate that way to some extent. But I want things with Marcus to stay exactly as they've always been. I want to share my life with him, and for him to share his with me. I just don't want to *lose* myself in a relationship with him, and I don't want to lose my independence.

But on the flip side, I really don't want to let him down, and I don't want him to feel neglected. I want to be sure that if I am taking too much time on my own and he's lonely or he's disappointed, he knows he can talk to me about it without me getting defensive.

In fact, maybe I *need* him to promise me he'll tell me, so I don't have to ruminate on this.

As I ponder this, it occurs to me that the only way to make sure that we're both happy with the balance of our lives together and our time apart is for me to work my worst possible skill: open, honest communication. I have to get out in front of the potential problem, face the awkwardness head-on…and have a brutally honest conversation about our expectations here.

We're cuddled up on the sofa after dinner on Thursday night, and I'm due to head into my room for a livestream in half an hour. I sit up and draw in a deep breath.

"I have some things I want to say to you," I say.

Marcus sits up and takes my hand. He scans my face, and then he nods.

"Go," he says quietly.

I glance at him. He's watching me closely, his expression a little guarded, but he's listening. I draw in a deep breath.

"This is hard for me to say. You know I don't like confrontation."

"I am well aware of that," he says, but he's read the mood and he's not making a joke. "Abby, have I done something to upset you?"

"No, not at all. But…" I suck in a deep breath, and I make myself press on. "I want this to work. A lot."

"Me, too. More than anything."

"Well, I'm not *good* at relationships. You know what I'm like—I spend so much time in my cave. I *like* having time to myself. Roger said that I didn't meet his needs and that's why he cheated on me, but—"

"Having your own interests and needing alone time aren't fucking mistakes. It's not your fault that he cheated on you," Marcus says, aghast.

"He was wrong obviously," I say hastily. Marcus looks like he's going to throw something, so I squeeze his hand. "The thing is, I actually tried *really* hard to meet his needs. Maybe I actually tried too hard."

The anger in Marcus's expression clears instantly.

"Yeah," he says softly. "I can see that."

"And I just want to tell you that I'm not going to do that with you. I want to care for you, but I don't want to do it at the expense of looking after myself and doing the things I love."

"Good."

"After Roger and I broke up, I told myself I'd only date guys who were into gaming. It seemed like the only way I could keep the hobby I loved, *and* have a relationship. But it's kind of occurred to me that there is another way I can be a good girlfriend and still enjoy my own life."

"Yeah...like dating someone who actually wants you to be your own person?" Marcus suggests softly. I nod, and he smiles. "He needed you so much more than you needed him, and at a guess I'd say he was pissing himself that you'd realize it and dump his sorry ass."

"Maybe," I sigh.

"Definitely," he corrects me. "I can't believe that weasel didn't even have the balls to take responsibility when he cheated on you."

"I *know* you're not like that," I say quietly.

"You're fucking right about that." Marcus snorts. "I'm strong enough to be completely secure in who I am. I don't need you to carry me, Abby, and I sure as fuck don't need or want you to feel stifled by this relationship."

"Do you think it's weird that I like so much time on my own? I don't want you to think I'm not into you because I still want time alone sometimes, too."

"That's just who you are," he says softly. "I know you better than anyone. And in case you haven't noticed, I happen to like who you are very much. This thing between us is going to work because we care about each other and we already have the perfect balance of time together and time apart doing our own thing. You're your own person with interests and routines that matter to you. Don't sacrifice that for me. Hell, don't sacrifice that for anyone."

"It just means that I need you to tell me if this isn't working for you, okay?" I say. "I want you to promise me that if you need more from me, you'll tell me. If I'm playing games too much or working too much or even just spending too much time alone…" I trail off, then I whisper uncertainly, "I need to be true to myself, but I'm also scared that I'll let you down."

"Abby, I know your routine by heart. I *know* how much alone time you need, and it doesn't scare me one fucking bit. But I do promise that as a grown, fully evolved *man*, in the event that I'm not happy about some aspect of our life together, I will use actual words to explain to you what my needs are and to negotiate a way with you that we might both feel satisfied," he says, then he hooks his finger under my chin and lifts my face so that I meet his gaze. "And you'll do the same when I get things out of balance or fuck up, which I guarantee you, I *will*. We'll resolve our problems by talking honestly like this, and by taking responsibility for our own shit. How does that sound?"

"It sounds wonderful," I say, and I kiss him gently, then grin. "You see what I did just now?"

"I do see. You initiated a slightly awkward but very adult conversation." He tugs me across the sofa and kisses me. "And I'm proud of you for it."

"Me, too." I grin. He kisses me again, then playfully pushes me away toward my "cave."

"Go be a nerd. It's what you were born to do."

WE AGREED TO focus just on *us* until after Christmas, which gave us about six weeks to test the waters. It felt like a decent chunk of time when Marcus suggested it, but now, it's slipping past me all too fast. I'm trying to be sensible and reserved, but the truth is, I'm bumbling through my days with a stupid smile on my face.

It's good. It's easy. The shift in our relationship feels effortless.

"Hey, you," I say, surprised by a phone call from him in the middle of the workday. I glance at my monitor, and see he's active on chat, so I wonder why he didn't just message me. "What's up?"

"Absolutely nothing," he says softly. "Just wanted to see how you're doing."

"Since when do you *call* me during the day to 'see how I'm doing'?" I laugh.

"Since I can't stop thinking about you, and I just needed to hear your voice."

That surprises me even more than the phone call.

"Wow," I say, then I blink a bit, because my eyes are feeling suspiciously misty. "You know, I was just thinking about you, too."

"Yeah? What were you thinking?"

"I was just thinking how happy I've been lately actually. How happy I am with you."

When we hang up, I burst into tears. They are happy tears, overwhelmed tears.

A few days later, Marcus adds a ritual to our schedule at home. He waltzes in from his workout with Paul just like he usually does, only now he's carrying takeout coffee, and he brings it to me in bed. When I reach for it, he shakes his head and puts it up on a bookshelf near my bed, just out of my reach.

"No way, missy. You haven't paid for it yet."

"Paid for it?" I repeat blankly.

He grins at me and bends to kiss me tenderly, then he stands again and retrieves the coffee.

"The price of your morning coffee, m'lady, shall heretofore be one loving kiss."

I hide my delighted grin behind the coffee cup, then add solemnly, "Very well. I concede that is a fair trade, m'lord."

He starts to leave stupid Post-it notes around the house—I find a sticker on my mirror one day that says, *You're looking at the most beautiful woman I know,* then a few days later, one on the fridge that says, *There's an Alfino's tiramisu in here with your name on it.* One night, he's out with Paul at a hockey game, and I find one on the A/C panel that says, *The reason you need the place so warm is because you're HAWT.* When Marcus gets home, I laugh at him and tell him he's an idiot, but secretly I love it.

I love a lot of things about this new dimension to our relationship actually. I love how he cares for me. I love how he understands me.

I love…*him.*

The realization doesn't come in a moment; it comes by degrees, until a light suspicion becomes a deep-seated, soul-deep knowing. I've always loved Marcus as a friend, but that love has changed and grown.

Being in love with him—*knowing* I'm in love with him—is every bit the terrifying event I thought it would be, because I have so much to lose here. I'm in love with my best friend but I'm flying blind—he seems happy enough, but I still have no idea where his head is at. He told me he needed time to figure out his emotions, too, so the fact that he's yet to update me on that suggests he's still working on it.

I've thought about saying it first, but I just can't.

I don't want to find myself crushed if he tells me he doesn't feel the same. I don't want to spook him.

Besides, Marcus has a *lot* going on right now. The reunion with Warwick is just a few days away, and I can see it weighing on Marcus's mind. He doesn't say as much, but I come home one evening to find him sitting on the sofa staring at his iPad with Warwick's messages on the screen. I glance at the front door and see his shoes dumped on top of the messy pile of my own. My gaze slips to the kitchen and I see that he's eaten the dinner I prepared for him, but he's left the dirty dishes on the bench.

It probably doesn't sound like much, but for Marcus, this is a full-blown meltdown.

"Hey," I say, and he looks up from the iPad and visibly shakes himself. A smile transforms his features as he pushes the iPad away so he can reach for me. I slide onto his lap and nuzzle his neck. "Let's cuddle and watch a movie tonight."

"Are you sure?" he asks softly. "You're not gaming tonight?"

I shake my head and plant a kiss against his cheek. It's funny how, knowing instinctively that he needs me tonight, I don't even *want* to hide in my cave.

"Nah," I say quietly. "I just feel like hanging out tonight."

I'm sure he sees right through my attempts to support him, but he doesn't draw attention to them. Instead, we snuggle under a blanket on the sofa while we watch a mindless comedy, and then when we go to bed, I hold him as close as I can.

CHAPTER TWENTY-FOUR

Marcus

IT'S FRIDAY AFTERNOON and tomorrow morning Austin and Luca are going to meet us so we can all drive to the Catskills to meet with Warwick.

I put off thinking about this meeting for weeks after I agreed to it, but this week the looming reunion finally caught up with me. It's playing on my mind all the time, and I keep trying to tell myself that it's *just one day*, and then I can get back to enjoying my life with Abby.

This afternoon, she rang me at the office and suggested that I take off early and go for a walk with her. A good half foot of snow fell over the city last night, and after a gloomy, freezing morning, the sun has emerged, and the city looks like a winter wonderland.

"Are you seriously suggesting we go *outside*? In this weather?" I gasped.

"I'd only ever do something so drastic for you, Marcus Ross." She laughed.

We took the subway uptown and now we're walking through Central Park, our gloved hands entwined, enjoying the way the carpet of snow has muted the harsh sounds of the city. Instead, the air is filled with musical sounds: people laughing and chatting, and children squealing with happiness as they play in the snow. There's something magical about a sunny afternoon like this after a fresh blanket of snow falls. The park is teaming with joy this afternoon, and no one seems alone. Couples like me and Abby are strolling hand in hand. Families are sledding, the children dressed in their bright winter coats, the colors so much bolder against the blinding white backdrop of the snow. Hell, even the pigeons are busy in their flocks, even if they are just huddling together for warmth.

"This is nice," I say, but the words are woefully inadequate. After a tense, anxious week, I'm looking around at the life that's bustling here in the park today, and my heart feels so full it could burst.

"It is nice," Abby agrees through chattering teeth. I laugh.

"Did you suggest this to distract me from tomorrow?" I know that's what her little "let's watch a comedy" routine was about last night, and the gesture meant the world. *This* one is even more extreme, and maybe I actually love her for it.

"Is it working?"

I glance at her, and she's breathtaking—the tip of her nose is a little pink from the cold, but she's beaming despite her protests. I lean over and kiss her gently, then go right back to walking.

"It really is," I say softly. She squeezes my hand, hard.

"You're going to buy me the biggest hot chocolate in the city after this, right?" she asks a few minutes later.

I laugh. "Yes, I will."

"Good. Because I think I'm getting hypothermia and I'm going to need to defrost."

Looming meeting with Warwick aside, I've never been as happy as I am right now. I'm not entirely sure I'll ever be able to admit this to my mother, but being with Abby feels like a missing piece of my life has finally fallen into place. We've been *officially* together now for a few weeks, and somehow, every day with her feels better than the one before.

No one told me it would be like this. Then again, I probably wouldn't have believed them if they did.

Maybe the intensity of my feelings will change with time. The infatuation will wane, we'll even argue— God knows we've done that in the past and it's only a matter of time before it happens again. But I'm starting to realize that no matter what she throws at me, one important thing is never going to change.

Everything I want in life now can be summed up in a single word… *Abby*. I want it all with her—I want to build a home with her, and to make a baby, and I want to raise that kid with her. I want to suffer through sci-fi movies for however many decades life gives us together. I want the highs and the lows. I want the arguments and the makeup sex. I want to live it all, and I want to share it with her and only her.

I need to tell Abby that I love her. If I'm the luckiest guy in the fucking universe, she'll tell me she loves me, too. And then I'll promise her I'm in this for the long haul, that the word *forever* doesn't scare me anymore—in fact, *forever* now sounds too damn short for what we share.

It's just that every time I try to say those words,

something kind of sticks in my brain. Resisting commitment is a habit, even now that I'm with someone I desperately want to keep by my side. I'm not sure what to do about that. Things are still new with Abby. Maybe once I settle into it some more, I'll get over this bewildering hesitance.

We finish our walk and I make good on my promise of hot cocoa. Now we're cuddled up together on the single free chair in this crowded café in Columbus Circle. I all but inhaled the chocolate bouchon I ordered, but Abby took the time to savor her assortment of tiny macaroons. She's perched on my lap and, in typical Abby fashion, she's sipping her hot cocoa while she stares around the room, her big brown eyes taking it all in.

"Recovering?" I ask her wryly. She laughs, then kisses me quickly. I taste the chocolate on her lips, then catch her and kiss her deeper, harder. The woman beside us makes a sound of disgust and stands, then walks briskly away. Abby breaks her mouth apart from mine, shoots an apologetic glance at the retreating back of the woman we have offended, then settles happily into her chair while I laugh.

My phone buzzes and I reach into my pocket to read the message.

Luca: Not that I'm doubting you, bro, but you didn't forget about tomorrow, right?

I sigh.

Marcus: I wish I could have forgotten about tomorrow. But no, I'm still coming. Abby's coming, too.

Luca: Good. By the way, if we get there and he's an asshole, I call dibs on being the one to tell him to fuck off.

Marcus: Deal.

"Hey," Abby says. I glance up at her, and she smiles. "Whatever happens tomorrow, it'll be closure, and then you can get on with the rest of your life."

I reach for her hand and bring it to my mouth, gently kissing my way along her knuckles. I really hope she's right, because it's not just the rest of *my* life I'm wanting to get on with. It's the rest of *ours*.

CHAPTER TWENTY-FIVE

Abby

ON SATURDAY MORNING, the four of us climb into Marcus's car and we set off for the bed-and-breakfast Warwick now owns in the Catskills. We drive in near-silence, the atmosphere in the car too heavy for the small talk Austin and I try to start up. Marcus parks in the sole remaining space in Warwick's parking lot, but even once he hits the ignition off, no one moves.

There are half a dozen cars in the lot, and through the large windows at the front of the building I can see patrons sitting at tables eating, and the flickering light from an open fireplace. It's a large bluestone house, with a huge yard that's been cultivated into an elaborate and immaculate garden. Snow is falling again today, and that gives the entire place a dreamy, romantic feel. Warwick's B & B is a stunning property in an incredible setting, and I can't help but think I might have liked to visit this place on an ordinary weekend away.

"He loved to garden at home," Luca says suddenly.

"The garden fell to shit when he left," Marcus replies, almost absentmindedly. "Until Mom met Jack and he fixed it up. She hates gardening."

They fall silent again. I reach across and take Marcus's hand.

"Let's do this," Luca announces, and he opens the door abruptly and climbs out. Austin follows and closes the door behind him.

Marcus reaches for the door handle. At the last second, he pauses and turns back to me. "Thanks for being here, Abs."

"I would always have come with you."

We walk up the path to the house, and the door to the café opens. There's no mistaking Warwick Chester—he looks exactly as I imagine Marcus will in twenty years' time. Warwick is tall and broad, too, but that oh-so-familiar curly brown hair is sprinkled with gray. Warwick's eyes are surrounded by lines and shining with tears, but the shape of them is so familiar.

"You really came," he says unevenly as we all crowd onto the little porch at the front door.

"Warwick," Marcus says smoothly and evenly. It's his business voice—the one I hear when he's on the phone with his staff and VIP customers. He releases my hand just for a moment, then extends it toward his biological father. The two shake hands briskly, but Warwick brings his other hand to clamp it around Marcus's wrist.

"Marcus," the older man breathes. As calm as Marcus's greeting was, Warwick's is drenched in emotion. Marcus stiffens and withdraws his hand, then glances back at me as he begins an introduction. "Maybe you remember—"

"Abby!" Warwick interrupts him, and then he grins at me. "Of course I remember you. Welcome."

As soon as I release Warwick's hand, Marcus slides his arm around my shoulders and gently pulls me against him. We shift to the side a little to let Luca and Austin greet Warwick, but the awkwardness lingers even after introductions are done. It doesn't help that Warwick is staring at his sons as if he can't quite believe what he's seeing, leaving long, uncomfortable pauses between pockets of small talk. It's *freezing* out here, and I'm impatient to move inside, hoping I can position myself close to that open fire. When one silence stretches to a particularly uncomfortable length, Marcus clears his throat. Warwick seems to snap out of his reverie and he turns toward the doors. "Come inside," he says. "Let's sit down and have that chat."

He's reserved a table for us, and there's an array of sandwiches and cakes laid out on it. We settle around, and a woman with an apron approaches us, notepad in hand.

"I'm Rita," she greets us warmly. "So nice to finally meet you all."

"Rita is my wife," Warwick tells us, and Rita drops a gentle kiss on his cheek before she turns back to us. I watch Warwick as he watches Rita, and I'm struck again by that odd familiarity. Then it hits me—I *know* the intense affection he feels for Rita because I see it all the time when Marcus looks at me. Something about that recognition makes me like Warwick Chester, despite the fact that I've loathed the man for most of my lifetime.

"Can I get you all some coffee? Something else? Whatever you want, it's on us today, of course," Rita says. We order some coffees and then she leaves, and all at once, we all turn to Warwick.

"I thought a lot about what I'd say to you boys

today," he says heavily. He watches as Rita retreats, but then his gaze sinks to the neutral objects in the middle of the table as his shoulders slump. "I figure the best way to get this done is to get on with it, without dancing around the issue."

"We know you left," Luca says stiffly. "We know you didn't come back. That's about all we know."

Warwick nods, then clears his throat and says softly, "I guess you boys also knew your mom and I were having some rough times before I left."

I glance at Marcus, in time to see his neutral expression shift into a frown. "No. We don't know that at all."

"Well, we tried to protect you from our troubles but...we talked about separating quite a few times," Warwick says. "I thought two happy houses would be easier on you than one bitter one, but we kept convincing ourselves we could do better if we just tried a bit harder. But, boys—we married too young, and we really didn't know ourselves yet, let alone how to raise two kids *and* care for each other. And then..."

He clears his throat, then pauses. With every second that passes, the guilt in his face intensifies, until he's slumped toward the table.

"Then," Warwick admits weakly. "Then I met Rita."

This particular pause is more "shocked" than "awkward."

"*This* Rita?" Marcus says, altogether failing to hide his disbelief. "You're still with the woman you left us for?"

"I *never* left you boys," Warwick says fiercely. He straightens his spine and he meets Marcus's gaze. "Never."

"It sure fucking felt like you did," Luca says, and his tone is a perfect blend of wry humor and intense bitterness. Warwick glances toward Luca, then he slumps again.

"At least…" Warwick swallows. "I never *meant* to."

"Wait a second," Marcus says impatiently. "You were unfaithful to her for years. You left because she was going to throw you out if you didn't."

"Who told you *that*?"

"Grandpa Don," Marcus says abruptly.

Warwick frowns as he shakes his head. He looks genuinely bewildered.

"I stuck it out with Lindy for years after we realized we'd made a mistake. I only left her when I met Rita at work and I realized how unfair it would be to stay in that miserable marriage when I was in love with another woman."

"Okay, fine," Luca says. "But it doesn't explain why you never came back for us. One minute you were there, the next you were gone. How the fuck can you excuse that?"

For the first time, I feel like an intruder here, and I glance at Austin and he grimaces at me, so I know he's feeling the same way. We're surrounded by men who look exactly like Marcus—Luca a scruffy version of him, Warwick an aged one—and it's eerie and uncomfortable, and if not for the fact that Marcus needs me, I'd find an excuse to leave.

But I can *feel* how much he needs me—in the way his gaze constantly floats back to me, and in the tightness of the grip of his hand against mine.

There's very little I hate more than awkwardness.

There's *nothing* I love more than Marcus. I can deal with these difficult moments in our lives because *he needs me to*. Running away doesn't even register as an option anymore.

The café is bustling around us, staff and other patrons carrying on their mornings as if a broken family isn't thrashing it out by the window over an untouched tray of gourmet cakes.

Warwick raises his chin now, and pushes his hair back from his forehead, then he clears his throat and he says carefully, "I won't say a word against your mother—I know she raised you mostly on her own and she's a fiercely proud, brilliant woman. But I had to juggle her needs with mine, and there was no escaping the fact that she was devastated and furious when I left. I called every night for a few weeks but…usually we'd both end up shouting, and I'd hear you boys in the background getting worked up because she was upset, and mostly she'd just hang up on me. Eventually I thought—I'll give it a few days, you know? Let her cool off."

Rita returns, carrying a pot of coffee. She silently starts to pour it into the cups, and Warwick's gaze lifts to her face. They share another glance—she offers him a very gentle smile, and he just stares at her, as if he's drawing comfort from her return.

"The problem was, when I left a gap between my calls, Lindy was angry about that, too, and I just didn't know what to do. So I got Don to liaise with her so I didn't have to upset her more. Or maybe, because I was a coward and I needed to hide from how I'd hurt her, and how I was hurting you boys."

"Baby, maybe you made some mistakes right at the beginning, but you figured that out pretty quick," Rita scolds him very gently. "And we tried *everything* to fix it."

"For a while, I just kept trying but…eventually Don insisted I should give it a break. Give her some space to calm down. He said she was a mess and you boys were suffering for it."

Marcus is staring at the other side of the cake tray now, his gaze distant.

"Why are we only hearing from you now, twenty-five years later?" Luca suddenly demands. Warwick sighs heavily.

"From there, everything snowballed. Every time I tried to get in contact again, Lindy was Don's priority—of course she was—and he never thought the timing was right. But then she met Jack, and he said you seemed to have settled into a new family and I should leave it be…"

"But we kept asking," Rita interrupts. "Boys, Warrie kept asking—every few weeks for years. Don always had some reason, some excuse, why we shouldn't come for you—and we were scared to upset him because he was the only link we had to you. At least while Don was keeping an eye on you boys, we knew you were okay, you know?"

"And then by the time you were adults," Warwick whispers unevenly, "I knew I could try to track you down directly but…I was scared if I did you'd tell me you didn't want me in your lives *and* Don would be furious and he'd stop giving me updates. I couldn't bear… I just couldn't bear *not knowing* if you two were okay."

Warwick keeps talking—more and more detail, until he's giving us all far too *much* detail in a blatant attempt to prove he's telling the truth. His regrets pile upon regrets until he's openly sobbing and Rita leaves the café duties to their young staff so she can sit beside him and hold his hand. Luca softens a little over the course of the conversation. The hardness and the anger in his eyes gradually fade. Soon, he just looks sad.

I keep waiting for that same softening to happen in Marcus, but *his* gaze remains guarded, and his hand stays so tightly wrapped through mine that I gradually lose the feeling in my fingers. When Warwick runs out of words and the gap between his apologies grows, Rita starts talking for him.

"You didn't try my cakes…you must still be hungry. Can I fetch you some proper lunch, or maybe you could—"

"Actually, it's a long drive back so we'd better get going soon," Marcus interrupts her quietly, and I glance to Luca and Austin, who both stiffen. "Thanks for your hospitality."

And then Marcus stands abruptly. I stand, too—well, he's still holding my hand so it's not like I have much choice. Luca and Austin join us with visible reluctance.

"It was nice to see you again," Marcus says stiffly to Warwick, who's looking a little worse for wear as he stands and walks around the table toward his sons. Luca offers him a brief hug. When he steps back, Warwick shakes Austin's hand, and then he turns to Marcus, who extends his hand for a very stiff shake and then takes a few steps toward the door without further preamble.

"I…" I'm tempted to apologize, although I'm not really sure Marcus has done anything *wrong*, and to do so feels disloyal. So instead, I pull Warwick close for a hug, and whisper into his ear, "Give him some time to get his head around all this, okay?"

He nods curtly, then embraces me again.

"I'm so glad you two are together, Abby. Your father and I used to joke about who was going to pay for the wedding," he whispers back, and I flush and laugh softly as I shake my head.

"There won't be a wedding," I say, but I do so absentmindedly, because my gaze is already on Marcus. His back is stiff, his jaw is set and to anyone else he'd seem almost expressionless, but I can see the turmoil he's trying to hide. I step quickly toward him and wrap my arm around his waist. He glances down at me, and he offers me a half smile.

"Let's go home," he murmurs. Rita is hovering around as we make our way to the door, and just as Marcus pulls it open, she blurts, "You know, if you're tired, I kept two rooms free for tonight just in case you wanted to stop awhile."

The offer hangs heavily in the air for just a second, before Marcus shakes his head.

"Thank you, Rita. Very kind of you, but we really need to get back."

We offer a final round of farewells at the car, and then Marcus starts it and without pausing pulls out onto the road.

"Do you think any of that was true?" Luca says as

Marcus quickly accelerates to the speed limit and focuses hard on the road. He activates the voice controls on his phone and says curtly, "Call Mom."

Lindy answers a few seconds later, her voice bright and cheery. "Marcus! Darling, how are you? So—"

"Mom," he says abruptly. "After Warwick left us, did he ever call?"

I can almost hear Lindy's smile deflating over the line. After a pause, she says stiffly, "At first, yes. Don't you remember? When he stopped calling you started sneaking out of bed and I'd find you sleeping on the floor in the foyer by the phone."

I glance at Marcus. He's white as a ghost.

"I thought…but I thought I was waiting for him to come through the door?"

"Well, maybe that was part of it. But you'd always put your pillow under the table in the hall where the phone was, so if he rung, the noise would wake you up. You boys spent half your life beside that phone in the months after he left. If you weren't talking to him you were waiting for the next time you could, which is what made it all the more cruel that he stopped calling so suddenly." Lindy's sad tone soon gives way to a slightly defensive "Why are you asking me this?"

"Did he keep in touch with Grandpa?" Luca asks from the back seat.

"Luca? Are you boys together today? What's going on?"

"*Did* he?" Luca asks insistently, and Lindy sighs heavily.

"I guess he must have. Grandpa never told me the details. He just passed the checks on when they came."

There's a moment of awful silence before Marcus says incredulously, "Checks? What *checks*?"

"The child support, Marcus," Lindy says impatiently.

"He paid you child support?"

"Of course he did. How do you think I fed you boys? The man has his flaws but he always provided for you two financially. I had to get Grandpa to tell him to stop once you'd both finished your studies, because the checks kept on coming long after me and Jack stopped cashing them."

"And you didn't think to mention this to us at some point?" Luca snaps.

"Honestly, Luca Joel, when I was raising twin boys *on my own* it wasn't high on my list of priorities to make sure you fully understood the *one thing* your rotten father had done right by you," Lindy says. I can hear her defensiveness rising, and the tension in the car is winding tighter with every second that passes.

"Did he ever ask to see us?" Marcus asks suddenly. I hear Lindy's sharp intake of breath, and I find myself holding my own as we wait for her reply.

"Well, in the first few weeks he did, sure, all the time…but… I was just so angry when he left, and when he called we kept quarreling. I *never* intended to keep you boys away from him forever. We all just needed some time for the dust to settle. Honestly, I couldn't believe it when he just disappeared altogether. I even asked Grandpa to see when he would come for a visit, but he said he had tried and Warwick wasn't interested." She pauses, then she demands, "Now you tell me right this instant why you're dredging up the past like this!"

"We *saw* him," Marcus says stiffly.

"I know," Lindy says carefully. "I saw him at the funeral, too. I didn't realize you talked to him. He seemed to stay way back."

"He did," Luca says quietly. "He stayed all the way out of our way, like he wanted to pay his respects without upsetting anyone."

"So, what's with all the questions?"

"He looked us up on Facebook," Marcus murmurs. "We met with him today." Lindy doesn't say anything at first, until he prompts, "Mom? Are you okay?"

"I'm fine," she says stiffly. "I…I'm just surprised, that's all. All this time…"

"Maybe Grandpa didn't tell us the whole truth, Mom," Luca says cautiously. "Maybe Warwick still wanted to see us, but Grandpa never passed the messages on. Do you think…"

"Grandpa hated Warwick from the moment we told him I was pregnant," Lindy admits, then she sniffs. "But I don't know about all that. He left us. He left me, and he left you two, and he never came back. That's all I *needed* to know."

By the time Marcus and Luca have said goodbye to their mother and hung up the phone, the atmosphere in the car is so tense it's almost stifling.

"I'm confused about who I should hate most right now," Luca says with a frustrated growl. "How could Mom let Don manipulate us all like this?"

"You said it yourself, weeks ago in the bar," Marcus murmurs almost absentmindedly. "Don never said any of that shit about Warwick when Mom was around. Sure, she made mistakes along the way, too, but if you're trying to figure out who to hate here, you're wasting your energy because the bastard who played us all is dead."

He falls silent, his jaw set hard.

"You okay?" I ask him under my breath. He nods curtly, reaches down to his thigh to rest his hand over mine, but his eyes are locked on the road ahead of us, as if he just can't bring himself to look back for even a second.

CHAPTER TWENTY-SIX

Marcus

THE SILENCE IN the car is so loud my ears ring. Austin is staring at Luca, and Luca is staring out the window.

Something doesn't feel right, but my mind is racing too fast for me to identify what the issue is. All I know is that the farther away from that B & B we get, the tighter my chest feels.

"Marcus," Abby says suddenly.

"Yeah?"

"I need some air," she says. I glance at her, and she squeezes my hand. "It was so stuffy in that café…"

"Yeah," Austin agrees hastily. "Stuffy. I could do with some air, too, a walk, maybe…"

"Me, too," Luca agrees. I'm about to protest that there's nowhere to pull over on this windy mountain road—but just like that, there's a picnic area ahead, so I sigh and pull into it.

"We're going to take a walk," Austin says. As the car slows to a stop, he and Luca scramble out, entwine their hands and start walking away. I turn to Abby.

"I don't get it. It *wasn't* stuffy in there, and it's fucking freezing out here."

"Marcus," she says softly, gently. "Are you sure you want to head home already?"

"We said we'd just have a coffee with him today—"

She rests her palm against my cheek. I lean my face into her hand and close my eyes.

"I think you wanted to stay, and I *know* Luca and Austin did," she whispers. "You're not going to fix this in a single day or even a weekend, but there's a lot of catching up to do. It's okay to let yourself want to start that."

"He gave up on us," I say.

"Yes. He made some god-awful mistakes. But I think he knows that, and I'm pretty sure he's sorry for it."

"But if even half of what he said is true," I say uneasily. "The way I've understood him for my whole life was wrong."

And the way I've understood myself.

I've always feared that I was just like him—a man so fickle he could up and leave a woman at any second. A man who shouldn't be trusted with a relationship. A man who couldn't commit. A man who would always crave freedom.

Maybe that wasn't the voice at the front of my mind, but it was sure as fuck the voice in the back of it, buried under layers of bravado and ego.

You're just like your father, Marcus. Such a ladies' man. What goddamned charmers you pair turned out to be.

I can hear Don's voice echoing in my ears even now. I don't know what to make of any of that now.

"It's not too late to understand him a different way.

It's not too late to give him a chance to *be* someone different," Abby says gently, and for a second I'm not sure if she's read my mind and she's talking about *me*, or she's talking about Warwick...because surely that statement applies to us both.

I've let myself think that I had to keep living to the beat of the script in my mind—that if I was "just like my father," I was doomed to inherit his flaws along with his strengths. The foolishness of that is undeniable now, because Warwick is nothing like the man I loathed for so long, and *I'm* nothing like that man, either. In this moment, Abby's patient, loving gaze becomes a mirror I can see myself in.

She sees a man she can trust to stand by her.

She sees a man *I* can trust to stand by her, because there isn't a force on this earth that could tear me away from her side.

"Abby," I say suddenly. "I couldn't have done this without you."

"Please," she says wryly, and she rolls her eyes. "That statement applies to every significant thing you've done in your life since you were two years old. It almost goes without saying by now." Her laughter fades, and she glances at me as she sobers. "And it goes both ways, you know."

"How did you know?" I say, and she raises her eyebrow at me. "How did you know I needed to do this? I don't think I'd have come with Luca today if you didn't encourage me to. I'd have put this off forever."

"Oh, I know *all* about putting things off." She laughs, and I smile at her. She shrugs. "I didn't know it would go like *this*. Truthfully, I thought it would be a disaster—I thought he'd be the bastard we've all assumed he was, but… I could just tell it was something you needed to do. When I saw you letting that situation with the messages linger, I realized that even if you weren't ready to admit it to yourself, you kind of wanted to give him a chance."

"You know me better than I know myself."

"I see you and I know you," she whispers, and it takes me a minute to realize she's echoing my own words back to me from that moment we shared in Jess's bathroom, all those weeks ago.

"And I love what I see, and I love what I know," I say. The words come easily, without fear or hesitation. Abby's eyes widen and I cup her face in my hands. "I love you so much. I've *always* loved you so much, but now I'm *in* love with you, too, and it's the best thing that ever happened to me."

"I love you, too," she breathes.

"You do?" My voice breaks as I say the words. I pull her close and breath her in, then rain kisses all over her face as she laughs weakly.

"I do. I just didn't want to say it first. I know we still have so much to figure out but the way I *feel* about you—"

My idiot brother chooses that exact moment to fling the back seat door open and announce, "We want to go back to the B & B—*holy shit*, you two. I don't care what you do behind closed doors, but you don't have to rub it in my face."

Abby breaks away from me and dissolves into a fit of giggles, and I sigh and twist to roll my eyes at him.

"Get in," I say. "Let's go back and spend the night."

THERE ARE TENSE moments over the weekend. Cracks in a relationship take time to heal, especially when they've had twenty-five years to gather dust. Every now and again something awkward comes up, but we all work hard to press past it, because we have to.

Life can rarely be boiled down to villains and heroes, and with every minute I spend speaking with Warwick, I can see that he is both. He's a man who made mistakes, and who failed to have courage when his kids needed him to. But he's also a man who has been crushed by regret for half of his lifetime, and a man determined to make amends now.

"Will you see us again?" he asks when we're saying a much warmer round of goodbyes at the front of the café on Sunday afternoon.

"We'll come back after Christmas," Luca tells him, sharing the decision we came to privately earlier this morning. "And you keep on sending us those Facebook messages. We'll reply quicker now."

Warwick pulls him close for a hug, then he turns to me and extends his hand to shake mine. I brush it out of the way and embrace him.

"We'll talk," I say quietly. "Let's catch up on the phone, too. There's a lot of lost time to make up for."

His arms contract around me, and there's nothing about this moment that would have satisfied my childhood fantasies of reunion or my adolescent fantasies of revenge, but to the adult me? This is pretty much as good as it's going to get, and I feel okay with how things have turned out. As we pull away from the B & B for the second time this weekend, Abby winds her hand through mine and rests it on my thigh, and I glance over at her.

I love you, I mouth at her, and she beams at me and mouths it back.

"Get a room, you two." Luca sighs.

"I hope you know," Austin adds, "Lindy is going to lose her *mind* when she finds out about—" he waves his hands between us "—whatever *this* is."

Abby winces, but the comment only gives me pause. Mom *is* going to lose her mind when she realizes I'm in love with Abby. And she's going to start pressuring us to make all of her overbearing mother-in-law dreams come true right away: engagement, wedding, babies…

And for the very first time in my life, the thought of all that doesn't scare me one little bit.

"MARCUS? WHAT THE hell are you doing here?"

I step out of my car into my parents' front yard. Their home in Syracuse is five hours' drive from the apartment Abby and I share in Tribeca. Abby will be pleased when we come together for the holidays next week—there's only a few inches of snow on the ground.

I lied to her this morning for the first time ever. I told her I'd had a client emergency and I had to take an overnight trip to sort it out. She'll be pissed when she finds out, but I hope the surprise will be worth the subterfuge.

I breathe in the icy air as I survey the landscape of my best memories. I can almost see young Abby running from the side door of the Herberts' house, into the tree house our dads built us in the park between our houses. Our bedroom windows face each other, because Abby bribed Luca into swapping rooms with me, just so she could teach me Morse code via flashlight and we could "talk" long into the night when our parents thought we were asleep.

She's the key player in all of my best memories, and now, she's the star of all of my dreams for the rest of my life.

"Hey, guys," I say, and Mom throws her arms around me, muffling an excited exclamation.

"I told Jack he was seeing things when he said your car was in the drive. Why aren't you at work?"

At 4:00 a.m. this morning, I emailed Jess, Paul and my team and told them I needed two personal days urgently and to please not mention it to Abby, that's why.

"I have important business to attend to up here today," I say vaguely.

"Are you here to talk more about Warwick?" Mom asks me hesitantly.

"You, me and Luca do need to sit down and talk about that some more," I say quietly. I'm not relishing the idea of explaining to Mom just how much her father messed us all up over the years, but Luca and I have discussed it a little since we got back from the Catskills, and we agree it needs to be done. "But there's something more pressing we need to talk about first. Can I stay tonight?"

"Of course you can! Are you sure everything's okay?"

Jack gives me his customary fist bump, and then he hugs me, too.

"Welcome home, son. This was a wonderful surprise."

The surprises aren't over, Jack.

I glance toward the park, and Abby's parents' house beyond. Sudden anxiety prickles at me, and I clear my throat.

"Do you know if the Herberts are home?" I ask as mildly as I can manage.

"Pete and I walk to the mall on Thursday mornings. We got back a few hours ago. He said he and Edie were going to head to the library this afternoon, but I haven't seen their car leave." Jack and Mom exchange a glance.

"Is Abby okay?" Mom asks cautiously.

"Don't panic, guys. She's fine. Let me chat with Peter and Eden and I'll be right back."

I've walked across the park a million times, but never like this. I'm shocked by the churning in my stomach, and the tightness in my throat—I clear it a dozen times between my parents' and Abby's front door. Then I ring the doorbell, and when Eden sees me, her eyebrows shoot upward and her gaze grows concerned.

"Oh, no. Something is wrong, isn't it? I heard it in her voice on the phone. Is she sick? Is she—"

"Can I come in? Everything is okay. I just need to talk to you and Peter."

"Of course," Eden murmurs, and I step into the sauna-like blast of the Herbert heating system. No tolerance for cold, these Herberts. Must be genetic. Hopefully our kid inherits my more weather-tolerant genes. Eden leads the way straight into the family room, where Peter is watching the television.

Star Trek.

Shit. Maybe the sci-fi thing is also genetic. Am I *sure* I want to breed with this woman?

Fuck yes. I've never been more sure of anything in my entire life.

"Marcus! Son, what are you doing here?" Abby's father frowns, and Eden answers for me.

"He needs to *talk to us*," she says carefully, then she glances at me. "I'll offer you a drink, *after* you tell us what this is about."

"I'm not here to ask your permission," I blurt, and Eden's and Peter's eyes widen. I cringe and wipe my sweaty palms on my pants. "That came out wrong. I just mean, Abby would have my balls if I tried to suggest anyone other than *she* had the right to give her permission to do anything with her life. But I'm going to ask her to marry me, probably when we're back home for Christmas. And I didn't want to spring it on you. I just wanted to let you know and give you a chance to express your concerns if you thought it was a bad idea. But I have to warn you, it would be pretty impossible to talk me out of it at this point. I love her, and she loves me, too."

Eden and Peter stare at me for a moment, and I scan their expressions, desperately looking for an indication of horror or pleasure or *anything*, but for the longest time, neither one reacts.

Peter finally says, "You'll forgive me for asking this question, Marcus, but…are you and Abby actually romantically involved? Because we all knew you were in love with her, but she's always seemed to think of you just as a friend…"

"Wait. How *long* have you known that I was in love with her?"

"Hmm…" Eden pauses thoughtfully. "Well, we

could see that things had changed when you came up for Lindy's birthday in January." She chuckles quietly. "You couldn't keep your eyes off her, Marcus. It was just like you were seeing her for the very first time."

"I kind of was, I guess," I say ruefully.

"Abby was adamant that nothing was going on," Peter remarks.

"It took us a while to figure it out…but things *have* changed between us." I can't help it… I grin at them. "And she was worth the wait."

"I'm glad for both of you," Eden says, then she gives a little squeal and launches herself at me. I laugh as I embrace her, and she kisses me on the cheek.

"Have you told your parents?" Peter asks.

"No, I wanted to talk to you two first."

"I hope you know," he says as he pulls me in for an embrace, "your mother is going to lose her mind."

MOM AND JACK are both waiting right at the door when I return to their house. Jack seems nervous. Mom's gaze is simmering between desperate and hopeful.

"So," I say teasingly. "How are you guys? What's been happening?"

"Marcus Ross," Mom says flatly. "Tell me what's going on. Right this instant. Is Abby okay?"

"Abby? Abby Herbert?" I say innocently. "Yeah, she's fine. Got anything to eat?"

I ignore their incredulous looks, walking past them into the kitchen, then I go to the refrigerator and pull it open to survey the contents. I hear Mom's impatient huff as they follow me, and I smother a smile.

Well, I figure she's tortured me enough over the

years, and this is probably my last chance for revenge before I make her dreams come true, so I might as well toy with her for a bit.

"Stop messing around and tell me why you're here," Mom demands.

I withdraw a carton of milk and take a few steps toward the pantry, where I know she'll have cookies—Mom always has cookies on hand. They'll be in a Tupperware container with the date she baked them marked carefully on the lid. She steps in front of me and crosses her arms over her chest. I'd intended on dragging this out some more, but there's thunder in her gaze. I laugh and pull her close for a hug.

"Sorry, Mom," I say, then while she's still close against me, I add softly, "Everything is fine, and I'm here because I'm going to propose to Abby and I wanted to give you all some warning."

Mom stiffens in my arms, then she steps back to stare up at me suspiciously.

"If you're joking, you better tell me right now."

"I'm not joking."

"This is not the kind of thing you joke about, Marcus Ross. If you're doing this to try to be funny, it's *not* funny, and you need to stop."

"Mom," I laugh. "I'm serious."

"You're really going to get married?" She's pale, and her eyes are wide. "To *Abby*? Our Abby?"

"If she'll have me, yeah. And that's okay, right?"

Mom twists and looks at Jack. Jack stares back at her. Then he stares at me.

"Son," he says carefully. "If this *is* a joke…probably better tell us before it goes any further."

"I'm dead serious," I assure him. Mom turns back toward me. Her eyes fill with tears and she starts to shake. This isn't dignified trembling—Mom's entire body is twitching.

"Mom," I say, and I help her take a seat at the breakfast bar so she doesn't injure herself, but she immediately slides off the chair, walks stiffly to a cupboard and withdraws a bottle of brandy. Jack reaches to comfort her, but she brushes his hand away and returns to the chair. Now, she unscrews the lid and takes a hearty swig straight from the bottle. I carefully remove it from her hands and ask, "Mom...are you okay?"

She pins me in place with a glare.

"Are you toying with me, Marcus Ross?" she says flatly. "You can't toy with me. Not about *this*."

"I promise you, Mom. I'm not kidding. It's not a joke—this is really happening."

She reaches up, snatches the bottle from my hands, takes another gulp, then turns to Jack and bursts into tears.

"I *told* you he was in love with her, Jack," she sobs.

"Yes, Lindy." Jack laughs softly, and he embraces her. "You were right, as usual."

"I'm going to propose to her on Christmas morning," I tell them. "I wanted to pick up Grandma's ring and have it resized while I'm here."

Mom chokes on a sob, then fans her face, struggling to breathe.

"I was so scared" *sob* "n-no one would" *sob* "ever use that ring" *sob* "after Luca came out." *Sob. Sob. Sob.* "This is really happening?"

"Yes, Mom."

"But you said you were never going to get married!" Mom is outright wailing now.

"And then I fell in love with Abby and I changed my mind."

She leaves Jack's embrace and throws herself against me.

"I'm so happy, Marcus." She sobs into my chest. "I'm so happy for you. And for her. And for me. I'm just so happy for everyone."

"Okay, Lindy, take some deep breaths before you hyperventilate." Jack laughs, then he glances at me. "When are you headed back into the city?"

"Eden and Abby are the same ring size, so I'll get her to try the ring on and if it needs resizing she's going to come with me to the jeweler at the mall. I'll stay overnight and hope they can have it ready to pick up so I can head back tomorrow."

"Let's go out for dinner with the Herberts," Mom weeps. "We should celebrate. We need champagne. And lobster. And more champagne. Then some cake. We need to start thinking about the wedding cake. We should talk about options tonight."

"Don't you think we should see if she says yes first?" Jack asks, amused. Mom slaps him on the forearm.

"Jack! Don't even joke about it. Of *course* she'll say yes."

CHAPTER TWENTY-SEVEN

Abby

"CHRISTMAS?"

Once upon a time, if Marcus went away for work, I'd barely have noticed. It's amazing how quickly things have changed. He was gone less than forty-eight hours this time, but I felt his absence so keenly it was as if he'd moved to another planet.

"Earth to Abby," Marcus teases me, and I blink and shake myself. We're cuddled together in bed—in *my* bed, where we always sleep these days. Last night I slept curled around his pillow just so I could smell him. Right now, I'm lying naked over his bare chest and he's playing absentmindedly with my hair.

"Sorry, what did you say?" I ask him.

He shifts me gently off his chest and onto a pillow, so that he can look at me as we speak. I try to tuck myself back into the crook of his neck, and he holds me off with a pointed frown.

"What's up with you tonight, Abs? I said, I know you were hoping to go home early, and I'm sorry I can't take any extra time off. Did you tell your mom yet?"

"I rang her tonight."

"Was she upset?"

"Strangely, no," I say, and then I frown. "Actually, now that you mention it, she was really odd on the phone. She was giggling and carrying on. I thought she might have been drunk or something, but you know Mom—she rarely drinks."

"Christmas spirit, probably," Marcus says lightly, and he brushes my hair back from my face as he asks, "Did she say anything else?"

"Just that she was looking forward to seeing us. Actually, Marcus." I look past him. I can't meet his gaze while I say this. "I wanted to talk to you about that. I don't want to tell them."

"Tell who what?" he says softly.

"Our parents. Families. I don't want to tell them about…" I wave a hand between us vaguely. "About this."

Marcus's eyes widen ever so slightly.

"Uh, why not?"

"Lots of reasons."

"Such as?"

"Did *you* want to tell them?" I frown at him. Marcus shrugs.

"They'll probably notice when we're fawning all over each other."

"Then we *won't*," I suggest, and Marcus gasps.

"Oh, now you're going too far," he says, shaking his head. "I can't keep my hands off you for four whole days. That's a completely unreasonable request—I'm only human."

"I'll meet you in the tree house, then," I mutter. "For fawning-all-over-one-another top-ups as required. But I don't want…" I don't know how to explain myself, and Marcus's playful smirk gives way to a frown.

"Abs," he says cautiously. "What's going on?"

I draw in a deep breath.

"I don't want to tell them. I don't want the scrutiny, or the pressure or the expectations. Okay?"

I glance at him hesitantly, but his eyes have narrowed.

"You're not having second thoughts about this, are you, Abby?" Marcus asks me. The intensity in his voice surprises me.

"I just think it would be easier if they didn't know yet."

"But you're still into this? Into me? You're sure you love me?" he asks me, and I blink at him.

"Are you *kidding* me?"

Marcus cups my cheek in his hand, and he stares right into my eyes as he whispers, "I need to know where your head is at. If you're having second thoughts, you need to tell me. Because I'm not having second thoughts, Abs. I'm *all in*."

"I'm into this, Marcus," I say wryly. "You were gone for one day and I was beside myself. I'm not sure how much more 'into this' I could be."

He flashes me a relieved smile, then kisses me sweetly before he asks, "So what are you worried about, sweetheart?"

"We're only going to be there for four days. Can't we just keep this between us until after Christmas?"

He stares at me, and the silence stretches. He's not going to drop it. I fumble for the right words and start to fluster under the growing concern in his gaze. I gnaw at my lip, and then finally blurt, "Your *mother*, Marcus. Lindy is going to be all *blah blah blah get*

married and even *blah blah blah give me a grand-
baby.* I *love* you and I would shout it from the roof-
tops…except for Lindy. But only because she's going
to lose her mind, and I just *know* that you're going to
hate it. Can you imagine how you'd feel if she knew
things had changed between us and she was nagging
at you to propose? God, she'd be talking wedding cake
before you even finished telling her we were together.
It would be *awful* for you."

Marcus opens his mouth, and then he starts to laugh.
I frown at him, but the laughter bubbles up and he
can't seem to stop. He laughs so hard that tears well
in his eyes and he rolls away from me, his whole body
shaking.

"What?" I frown at him, then thump him in the shoulder. "What!"

"No, no." He holds up his hand, then wipes his eyes
as he turns back to me, the chuckles fading. "You're
completely right, that's *exactly* what she would do. God,
how awkward—what a nightmare. Yeah—good idea,
let's keep it between us. I'll text Luca and Austin tomorrow and tell them to keep their big traps shut, too."

He's saying the right words, but he's still chuckling. I'm scowling at him now, and he grins and takes
me into his arms, flipping me onto my back. "You're
so cute when you try to make my life easier for me."

"This is funny to you?"

"You're funny to me." He grins, then he brushes his
lips over mine. "Less talk, more kissing."

WE'RE IN THE car on the way to Syracuse on Christmas Eve. I'm resting my hand on Marcus's thigh as he

drives. He's put some irritatingly jazzy Christmas carols on and he's drumming against the steering wheel. Every now and again, he glances at me and he grins, and it makes my heart dance. I focus on the light in Marcus's eyes and the smile that seems permanently fixed on his lips today.

"What's gotten into you?" I ask him. Marcus grins again.

"Christmas spirit. What's gotten into *you*? You're freakishly quiet."

I shrug and go back to looking out the window. I'm a bit nervous about our charade—whether or not it will somehow be blindingly obvious to every member of our families that things between us have changed. I mean, if Luca could see it, surely our mothers will. But I'm also feeling a bit off, and I ponder this for a while as we sit in holiday traffic. I can't quite put my finger on it, but then a dull thud starts in my lower abdomen.

I haven't paid any attention to my cycle lately, and I forgot to note down the date of my last period because things with Marcus went crazy around the same time and I was distracted. But I think that was five weeks ago—or was it six? For sure, my period is due but... period pain? I don't *get* period pain. It must be something else.

"I think I'm getting sick," I say after a while, and Marcus frowns.

"You're kidding."

I shake my head and grimace at him, motioning toward my stomach with my hand.

"I just feel really strange."

"Do we need a bathroom, honey?"

I ignore the fact that we're sitting in a ten-mile-long traffic jam discussing emergency toilet trips and let myself enjoy the way he says the word *honey*. He uses endearments all of the time now, casually, like they just trickle off his tongue when he talks to me. I thought I'd be getting used to that by now, but I'm not, and the word sends pleasant shivers down my spine—momentarily distracting me from the thud in my abdomen.

"No, no… I'm just warning you. We might."

"Well, that's bad luck. I really hope you're not sick for Christmas."

"I know." It's Lindy's turn to host Christmas. That means Mom and Dad will host breakfast, Lindy will be making lunch and Austin apparently arrived last night and has prepared a meal for tonight, plus he'll rework tomorrow's leftovers into a magical second-chance feast. There's twenty-four full hours of delicious food ahead of me. I slump a little at the thought that I might not feel up to eating it.

"Just let me know if you need to stop. Or a drink or something, okay? Anything you need, honey, just say the word."

I thank him and go back to watching the traffic and listening to the carols. The traffic is heavy most of the way, and it's just before 5:00 p.m. when we finally arrive. Marcus parks in his parents' driveway, and then we glance at each other.

"How are you feeling?"

"Still off," I say, but I'm understating the severity of it. The pain has only intensified over the drive, taking my breath away at times. I'm starting to think I might need painkillers, and more than that, I'm worried that something else might be going on. Still, I'm so glad to be home, and I don't want to concern Marcus too much, so I smile as convincingly as I can manage as I add, "I'm okay."

"You ready for this?"

"Yeah."

"One last kiss?" he whispers, and he leans toward me, just as the driver's side door flies open behind him and Luca flashes a knowing grin at us as he whispers, "Happy Christmas, *lovebirds*."

"Hi, Luca," I say, a flush creeping over my cheeks as I hastily sit away from Marcus. "Come to carry the bags for us?"

Marcus laughs softly and slides out of the car to hug his brother.

"Great to see you, little bro," Luca says, leading Marcus toward the house. "Austin and Mom have been cooking all day. Come get some food."

WE SETTLE INTO Marcus's family home after the bags are unpacked. Everyone is in a buoyant, jovial mood—they're all almost hysterically excited for some reason this year, and I can't help but get swept up in it. Lindy insists I take a glass of champagne. I nurse it and watch the bubbles rise, but I can't bring myself to drink it—instead, I'm wondering if I need to bite the bullet and find some painkillers. I decide to look for a subtle moment to disappear into the kitchen to find some, but Jack has had a few beers already and keeps hugging me, and Mom and Dad are holding hands and singing terrible, off-key duets of Christmas carols and they keep trying to drag me into song with them.

"I think you two are embarrassing the family enough without my help," I assure them, but then Austin shows me some of the amazing food he's created, and while we're talking, Luca winks at me and I flush, thinking about the awkward request I made to him just two months earlier. At some point, Luca is going to tease me about that in front of our parents. I wonder how long it will take, and I make a mental note to beg him *not* to do it just yet, at least until I have a chance to talk to Mom.

Despite the revelry, the pain in my abdomen doesn't let up and it starts to spread to my back. I excuse myself, duck into the bathroom, then sneak into Lindy and Jack's kitchen to help myself to some painkillers. Mom finds me there, and she gives me a surprisingly tight hug. I can smell wine on her breath, and my eyebrows rise as I remember that giggly phone call a few weeks ago.

"Since when do you drink, Mom?" I ask her cautiously, and she laughs.

"Lindy bought this fancy champagne—she said it cost a fortune, but it all tastes the same to me. We started celebrating a few hours before you got here, so I guess I'm probably tipsy by now. Don't try waking me up at 5:00 a.m. like you used to when you were a kid."

"What was the hug for?" I ask her, giving her an uncertain smile.

"You just seem…" She hesitates, then smiles softly. "You just seem so happy, Abby."

"I am," I say, confused. "But I'm surprised you noticed. I'm not feeling great."

I reach up into the cupboard for the painkillers,

which are just where they always were—in a labeled box marked Medicines–General, beside two smaller boxes labeled for each of Marcus's parents. I pop two painkillers out of a packet as Mom asks, "Headache?"

"Period pain, I think," I mutter. I'm sure that's what it is, although why I'm suddenly getting it for the first time in my life today of all days, I have no idea.

"You get pain these days, love?"

"No." I reach for a glass of water and down the tablets, then add, "Not generally."

"I was the same." Mom rubs my shoulders slowly. "You got my lucky genes, I guess."

I think about the early decline to my fertility and smile sadly.

"Yeah, I guess I did."

"The only time I can ever remember having pain at all was the month I fell pregnant with you. I thought something was drastically wrong, but it passed within a day or so," Mom says vaguely, and she turns back toward the door. "Well, if you need to head off to bed, I'm sure Marcus would walk you back to our place."

I laugh softly.

"Mom, I've crossed that park a million times on my own at night. I don't need an escort."

Mom gives me a funny smile as she leaves the kitchen, and then I'm alone, and her words sink into my brain.

The only time I can ever remember having pain at all was the month I fell pregnant with you.

I walk stiffly to the bathroom, close the toilet lid and sit. I pull the phone from my pocket and check the dates. *Why the fuck didn't I note down my last period?*

Then I scroll *all* the way back through my IM messages to Marcus and find the one where I told him we hadn't made a baby.

November 15.

Huh.

I slip the phone back into my bag and stare at myself in the mirror. I'm pale, and I look exhausted and kind of scared. But I can't think about this now; it's Christmas Eve. Surely I can wait a few days and see if my period turns up. I splash my face with water and return to the party, but when I step through the doorway, all I can see is Marcus.

He's chatting quietly with Luca, and he looks so happy and content. I stare at him silently—watching as he nods and the chocolate curl flops forward onto his forehead. He pushes it back in that gesture I'm so familiar with—one that I find inexplicably endearing these days.

He catches me staring and winks. But suddenly, I *can't* wait to find out if my suspicions are correct about my mysteriously delayed period. I need to know right now if everything is about to change between us *again*. He rises and approaches me, and he asks me softly, "How are you feeling?"

"I'm okay. Can I take the car?" I ask him, and he frowns.

"Of course," he says. "But I'll come. Where are we going?"

"Ah, no." I give an uneasy laugh. "I forgot part of your present—just need to run down to the grocery store."

As soon as I hit the ignition button on the car, his

jazzy Christmas carols fill the air and I curse and flick the stereo off. At the department stores, I jog through the crowd of last-minute shoppers to the medicines aisle and I pick up a variety of tests. There's a huge line of people waiting at the checkouts, so I have plenty of time to read the backs of the boxes while I'm waiting to pay. The instructions say the tests are more accurate if taken first thing in the morning, so I tell myself I'll wait and do it after I sleep.

But I've bought a bunch of different tests just in case, and the moment I leave the checkout I make a beeline for the bathroom. I'm nervous, which I guess is normal. Maybe what's *not* quite as normal is that I'm shaking so hard I can barely manage the whole "pee on a stick" process.

As the three agonizing minutes tick down before the results are ready, I live out a thousand scenarios in my mind…and every single one of them is terrifying for one reason or another.

I've dreamed of being a mom for so long, but now that the possibility is *right* in front of me, am I actually ready for the dream to come true?

CHAPTER TWENTY-EIGHT

Marcus

"OH MY GOD, MARCUS!" Eden cries, the second Abby leaves the driveway. "This is fishing killing me! Why aren't we allowed to tell her we *know*?"

"*Fishing* killing you?" Austin repeats blankly.

"Eden doesn't curse, remember?" Luca reminds him. "She means 'fucking.'"

"Luca!" Eden gasps. "Language!"

I wince and open my palms. After the awkward chat with Abby in bed last week about our holiday plans, I had to text them all, and while everyone agreed to keep my confidence, *no one* was pleased about it.

"She wanted to keep it a secret. She was worried *some* people here might start pressuring us to get married." I look at Mom, then wink. Everyone laughs as she flushes. "It's only one night, you guys. I'll ask her in the morning and put you all out of your misery."

I can't wait any longer than that. The ring is wrapped up in Abby's Christmas gift, ready to go. I nearly proposed a hundred times over the last few weeks.

I'll pack the dishwasher. Also, will you marry me? What do you feel like for dinner? Marry me.

Let me just finish this email and I'll be done. Oh, by the way: marry me?

Did you have a good day? Marry me.

Yeah, just like that. That's so good. Marry me. Marry me. Marry me!

I can barely believe it myself, but I'm not just ready to commit to her—I'm so fucking excited about proposing I could barely contain myself to make it as special as she deserves.

Tomorrow morning can't come soon enough.

It's almost an hour later that I hear the car pull back into the drive, and I wait for the door to open and for Abby to return. Instead, my phone buzzes.

Abby: Sorry. Need to go to bed. See you in the morning?

Marcus: Abs, are you okay? Are you sick?

Abby: I'll be fine in the morning.

Marcus: Are you sure? Let me come and nurse you.

Abby: Uh, I think that might look a little odd.

Marcus: Innocent nursing! Get your mind out of the gutter, just for this one night. You can put it right back tomorrow ;)

Abby: No, seriously. I'm okay. Enjoy the time with your family and don't let my mom get too drunk. Xoxo

A few hours later, the festivities have wound up—or are at least paused until tomorrow morning. I climb into the double bed I convinced my parents I *had to have* when I was fifteen, and stare at the roof. I'm excited, but I'm nervous, and sleep feels a long way off.

I sit up when I see the flashing light, and I laugh softly and walk to the window to watch the light flash on and off in Abby's window. I pick up my phone and text her.

Marcus: I can't remember Morse code.

Abby: Ten-year-old Abby would disown you.

Marcus: Will thirty-year-old Abby forgive me? What were you trying to say, anyway?

Abby: Tree house. Now?

I try to find the perfect balance between running toward the tree house as I want to, and *not* alerting my entire family that I'm doing so. It's snowing heavily now and so cold that even I would rather be in the heat.

"I can't believe you're out here voluntarily," I mutter as I climb up the ladder. Abby doesn't answer me, but as I reach the top and my eyes adjust to the darkness, I see that she's seated in the corner, her knees tucked up near her chin. I crawl closer as I say, "I might fall through the floor of this rickety old thing."

"The neighborhood kids use it. I'm pretty sure the dads maintain it pretty well," she whispers back, but her voice is hoarse. She's been crying. I pull her into my arms.

"Oh, no…are you sick?"

"Not yet."

"You're still feeling off?"

"Kind of."

"Can I do anything?"

"You can try not to freak out."

I glance at her, bewildered. I wish I had a flashlight, so I could see her properly. "I'm not freaking out. What's up?"

"You might freak out."

"What are you talking about?"

"I thought it was period pain. But I don't get period pain."

"Is something wrong? Is this about your ovarian thing, do you think?"

I still can't see her face, but I feel her scowl regardless. "All of that reading you did and you think sudden onset period pain is because my eggs are shriveling up and dying?"

I have absolutely no idea what she's getting at, and I can feel the rising tension in her body—she's frustrated by my inability to read her mind. "I'm just not following you, sweetheart." She bursts into tears, and I pull her closer in alarm. "Abby, baby—what's wrong?"

"I took a test at the store," she sobs, turning into my chest. "Dr. Google said false positives aren't actually a thing."

I suddenly realize what she's saying, and I gasp.

"Abby—not—we're—"

It's so quiet tonight. All I can hear are her little sobs, and the thundering beat of my own heart. I, Marcus Ross, once determined bachelor, am hopefully about to become both a father and a husband, and turns out that makes me the happiest guy on the planet. Gratitude and happiness and joy overwhelm me and I have to set my jaw hard just to hold my own tears back.

"Abby," I whisper thickly. "That is the best fucking news I've ever had. My God."

"But we said we wouldn't try again yet." She weeps softly, and I shift until we're sitting opposite one another. I don't want the distance between us, but I need to see her face. I *need* to kiss her tears away. "We said it was too complicated now."

"I don't care. Do you care? I don't give a fuck about all of that. A *baby*, Abby. How could this be anything but incredible? It's a *miracle*."

"Are you sure? I feel so guilty." Her voice is so rough, and now that I'm adjusting to the darkness I can see how swollen her eyes are. I cup her face in my hands and stare at her, assessing her with my gaze. She's *too* upset. Is this hormones? I just don't know what's happening here. "It must have been that time at the front door. I told you it was too early but obviously I have no idea. I'm *so* sorry."

"Never apologize for that time at the front door. *Never*. That was the best moment of my life, until this one," I whisper fiercely. She gives me a weak smile, but it disappears too quickly.

"It's really early. Anything could still happen. I have cramps…they're pretty intense and I don't know what that means. Mom had the same thing when she was pregnant with me, but it might not be the same for me—maybe it's a bad sign. I don't even know." She's crying again now, her sobs building all over again.

"Can we be excited for tonight?" I ask her hesitantly. "Just a little?"

"I *am* excited. I'm just…" She pulls away from me and covers her face with her hands, then starts to sob all over again. "Marcus, what if this is a mistake? What if I can't handle it?"

"Can't handle *what*?"

"Motherhood," she whimpers. I take both of her hands in mine and I squeeze gently, reassuring her. She glances at me, then looks away again. "I want this, but I'm just so scared. How am I going to handle having a little person hanging off me twenty-four hours a day? How will I ever get time to myself? How will I work? How will I *breathe*? What if I can't make the baby happy—what if I can't even care for it? I don't know nearly enough about babies! What if I pick the wrong kindergarten or I forget to buy diapers or…"

"It's going to be a huge change for us, but a change for the better. We'll study that binder again together, and everything else we need to figure out, we'll figure out *together*. We're partners, remember? We always have been, but even more so now."

"But what if I get depressed again?" I can *see* her terror now—it's written all over her face. I grip her hands a little tighter, but wait for her to explain before I jump in. "Having a baby means so much chaos. You know I don't deal well with chaos. What if I fall back into the hole?"

"You *were* in a hole once upon a time," I say softly. "And you know who got you out?"

"You?" she whispers back, and I shake my head.

"I tried to fix things for you, and I couldn't. Abby, you didn't even need me to."

"You tried so hard to help me," she protests.

"I did. I always would." I squeeze her hand again and give her a sad smile. "But as much as I wanted to be your hero, you didn't need me to be. You went to your doctor. You found a therapist. You took the medication while you needed it. *You* changed your lifestyle. *Trust* your own resilience, Abby. I sure as fuck do. Yes, you have a vulnerability—but you overcame it once, and if it happened again, you know what to do to get help. That's not weakness, honey. That's *strength*."

Abby falls silent, and for long minutes, we sit like that. But she's freezing—her hands are so icy—so eventually I shift until I can take her in my arms again. I wrap my body around hers, keeping her warm while I wait for her to think this through and work it all out in her mind. After a few minutes, she rests her cheek against my chest. As she relaxes into me I feel the tension draining from her body.

"You supported me, but I saved my*self* from the darkness," she whispers eventually.

"Exactly."

"I'm just like Princess Leia, you know." There's a slight wryness to her voice now, and I relax, too, because I can hear that she's made peace with her fears, at least for now.

"Awesome hair?"

"That, too."

"You look amazing in a gold bikini?"

"Maybe I should invest in one so we can see."

"I like the sounds of that."

"I'm a self-rescuing princess," she says, and I smile and contract my arms around her.

"*That* is exactly who you are. And whatever comes at you, that's who you will always be. You're going to be a wonderful mother—because of *who you are.*

And when it's good and when it's easy and when it's bad and when it's hard, I'll be there as your backup."

"This might be our last Christmas before we have a baby, Marcus," she says, and she turns her face toward me. The fear in her eyes has faded, and now she looks peaceful and happy and just a tiny bit exhausted. I brush a soft kiss against her lips.

"In that case, we really should sleep in tomorrow," I say, and we share a smile. "I wish you could sleep with me."

"God, imagine that."

"Fuck it, Abby. Come and sleep in my bed."

"No, no…" She shakes her head, and she sighs. "Mom would freak out if she found my room empty tomorrow."

"I just want to hold you while you're asleep. I could rub your back."

"That does sound good…" she says, then she gives me a cheeky grin. "We could sleep on the couch in my parents' living room. Mom was kinda tipsy—I'd say they'll sleep in late. And if they do catch us we can say we just stayed up talking and fell asleep."

"Yeah," I say, and I kiss her. "And if they ask why we're naked, we can just say our clothes fell off." She giggles, and I add hastily, "I'm kidding. I know you're not feeling great, it's no pressure—"

She's already shuffling toward the stairs, laughing softly.

"Shut up, Marcus."

CHAPTER TWENTY-NINE

Abby

I WAKE UP in the warm circle of Marcus's arms. His hands rest over my belly, and I immediately remember the beautiful words on that test last night.

Seven to eight weeks pregnant.

I slip off of the couch and climb up the stairs to my own room, where I retrieve and then take a second test from my handbag. It's positive, too, the same result. The cramps have eased off this morning, and there's still no sign of my period. I run my hands over my breasts and wonder how I missed the strange sensitivity, then I stand and stare at my belly in the mirror. It's curved—but that's nothing new, it's always been curved. I don't feel any different yet—but maybe all of that is going to change.

Marcus's baby. It's a huge complication given the state of our relationship right now, but I could never regret it. It's magnificent to think that a part of him has joined with a part of me, and one day, hopefully, we'll get to hold that miracle in our arms.

I hide the pregnancy test in my handbag with the other one from last night, and walk down the stairs to Marcus. He's awake now, reclining on Mom's couch with a sleepy grin on his face. It's just after 10:00 a.m., which means the rest of the Ross family will barge through the door in about half an hour for breakfast. Mom and Dad are just starting to stir in their room, so I imagine that any minute now she's going to fly down the stairs in a panic and start cooking like a maniac.

"You should go back and see your family," I murmur.

"I can see *my family* right now," he murmurs back, and his gaze dips meaningfully to my belly, then back to my face as his smile broadens.

I feel a flush of pleasure and excitement, but push him out the door to go home and change, anyway. I take a quick shower and dress, and by the time I come back downstairs, they're all there, eating the slightly burned ham and eggs Mom has made. She's not eating, though—she's too busy clutching her head and groaning as she sips a black coffee. Dad is unsuccessfully trying to hide his amusement.

I make myself a hot cocoa, then settle in an armrest beside Marcus.

"Hey," he says softly. The affection in his gaze is obvious, and I give him a pointed look and a half nod toward our families. The Ross family are all sitting around Mom's elaborately designed tree—Aus and Luca are on the floor sharing a plate of food, and Jack and Lindy are on chairs side by side. In a tradition that's lingered since childhood, no one is eating at the table. We open the presents while we eat, because Luca and Marcus and I could never wait.

Marcus rolls his eyes a little as I shuffle away from him, and Dad's big booming voice announces, "Merry Christmas, everyone."

"Merry Christmas, Dad," I echo back with the rest of our motley tribe. He starts to hand out the gifts, and over the next half hour, I watch as everyone celebrates. Marcus loves the wallet I got him. Mom says she likes the Kindle I bought her, but she's not really sure how to use such a thing, can I show her? Dad nods approvingly at the Bluetooth speaker Mom told me to buy him for his workshop. And then when it's all done, I realize everyone is staring at me.

"What?" I say blankly, and I wipe at my cheek awkwardly. "Do I have food on my face?"

"Marcus hasn't given you his gift yet," Lindy says. Her voice is wobbly, and I frown. I glance at him, and find he's staring at me intently, too.

"You guys," I say uncertainly. "You're starting to freak me out."

Marcus reaches down beside him, and he lifts a package from the floor. It's the shape and size of a book, and I grin and start to tear the package open.

"Careful!" Lindy blurts. I glance at her quizzically, then take a little more care with the wrap.

It's a hardcover copy of *Harry Potter and the Philosopher's Stone*, and when I peek inside the front cover, I see J.K. Rowling's signature. I squeal and almost reach down to kiss Marcus, then catch myself.

"Thank you," I say, and I'm genuinely delighted. "I love it! How did you get this?"

"eBay." He laughs softly, then he nods toward the book. "There's a special bookmark, too."

I've already closed the book and rested it on my lap, but glancing down at it now, I can see the pages don't quite sit right. I flick the book open to the bump in the pages and my heart skips a beat.

Holy shit. No wonder Lindy warned me to be careful, because sitting there loose between the pages is her mother's engagement ring.

Marcus slides off the chair, onto one knee, and he stares up at me. Everything stops. The audience of family members dissolve from my vision. All I can see is him, and panic and pleasure crash together.

"Abby Herbert," Marcus whispers. His voice is strained, and there are tears in his eyes. "I love you. I have always loved you. I *will* always love you." His voice breaks, and he pauses, taking a moment to collect himself. "Can we please make this thing official?"

I look from his glistening eyes to the ring. My stomach is churning.

"Marcus, you don't have to do *this*," I say uncertainly, and his eyebrows knit.

"*Have* to?"

"I mean…is this just because of the baby?" I whisper, and the audience swims back into my sharp focus because everyone else in the room gasps.

He glances behind him, then gives me a wry smile.

"So, we're telling them about that, too, huh?"

"Oops," I say.

"*Baby?*" my mother gasps. "Did she say 'baby'?"

"Baby!" Lindy squeals. "She said *baby*!"

I look back at Marcus, who's still staring up at me from his position kneeling on the floor.

"The baby has nothing to do with this, Abs. It's icing on the cake, that's all. I came and got the ring resized last week. There was no work emergency."

"Oh," I say, then laugh softly. "You sneaky thing."

He grins, but then clears his throat. "So, are you going to put me out of my misery and give me an answer? Because I'd really like to put some tiny hand-cuffs on you before you run away again."

"You *really* want to marry me?" I whisper.

"Only about as much as I want to take my next breath," he whispers back.

I want to freeze time in this moment, when every-thing between us is perfect, and all of the dreams I had are coming true in a way I could never have imagined. Then it occurs to me—I don't even have to freeze time, because this is really my future, and now I get to *live* it.

"Yes," I choke. "Of course. *Yes.*"

He slides the ring onto my finger. As soon as he does, I lift my hand to survey it, and I burst into tears.

"This must be pregnancy hormones," I say unevenly. Marcus rises to kneel on the chair beside me, and he wipes the tears from the corners of my eyes with the pad of his thumb. I meet his gaze and I whisper, "I just love you so much."

"I know," he breathes, then kisses me gently. "And I love you, too."

"We're really going to do this?"

"Please," he says, and there's no doubting the sin-cerity in his gaze. "Please, can we do this? I'm ready, Abby. I'm so ready I can barely wait."

There's a round of applause from around the room, and I laugh tearfully as Marcus lifts my hand to display the ring to them. I'm engulfed by congratulations and hugs from Luca and Austin and our dads.

"You guys don't seem very surprised," I say uncer-tainly, and Marcus gives me a sheepish grin.

"I told them last week. Before you asked me not to."

"I'll bet *that* was a surprise."

"Not really. They could all tell I was smitten with you last January."

"Well, you could have told me."

"If you'll *let* me," he says softly, "I'll *tell* you every day for the rest of our lives."

"That sounds pretty good."

"Where did the moms go?" Luca asks suddenly, just as my mom comes flying back into the room, carrying a dusty box marked Baby Clothes, and Lindy is hot on her heels, carrying my mom's wedding album.

They're both speaking at a million miles an hour, talking over the top of each other in their haste and excitement.

"…I kept the outfit we brought Abby home in for the first time and maybe they can use it to bring their baby…"

"…the chapel on Fourth Street. Do you think? Or maybe if they get married back in New York we could have a *second* reception back here and—"

I squeak in panic and try to hide behind Marcus, but he catches me gently by the arm and settles me on his lap, then slides his hand over my belly. I relax into his embrace, then reach down and rest my hand over his. For several terrifying moments, we watch in silence as our mothers brainstorm a flurry of wedding ideas that we'll have to untangle later.

"How on earth are we ever going to manage *that* level of enthusiasm?" I sigh. Marcus chuckles.

"The same way we've always dealt with those two. The same way we'll deal with every *other* challenging situation that crops up in our lives over the next fifty years or so."

"Together?" I whisper.

"Together," he promises. "Always."

EPILOGUE

Abby

MARCUS IS SQUEEZING my hand so hard it's almost pain-ful. I squeeze back, and he releases a little and gives me a sheepish grin.

"Sorry," he mutters. "I'm nervous."

"Really?" I laugh wryly. "I can't tell."

We hear yet another buzz from his phone, and he sighs. "We shouldn't have told anyone the scan is today. It's been pinging all morning."

With his spare hand, he withdraws the phone from his pocket, then turns the screen toward me. His lock screen is full of notifications.

Mom: Any news?

Mom: Just text me when she's out and let me know if everything is okay.

Mom: Not that I think anything is wrong. I'm sure everything is fine. Oh, and send me a photo if you get one.

Isabel: Thinking of you two today.

Eden: Has she had the scan yet? Is she okay? Is there a photo?

Peter: Good luck today, guys.

Jess: Did you finish with that budget? Also, let me know how it goes! Bring pics back!

Warwick: Thanks for letting us stay with you two on the weekend. We had such a great time. I'm thinking of you today. Hope the scan goes okay.

Rita: Marcus sweetie, Warwick is a nervous wreck waiting for news about your baby. If you get a chance to text him once you know everything is okay, I'd really appreciate it.

Jack: I'm taking your mother out for a coffee so she doesn't pace a hole in the floor, so if you call after the scan, ring her cell.

Paul: Do you think the blue on the new menu bar is too blue? Is "too blue" a thing?

Paul: I forgot you're out this morning. Best of luck with the baby thing.

Mom: Why is it taking so long?

Mom: I just talked to Eden and we want to come to the next scan. Can you ask Abby?

Luca: Before I left for work this morning Aus said I

should text you "good luck for today." I forgot to ask him what for, so...good luck, whatever you're doing.

"Are you two ready?"

We look up to where the sonographer is adjusting a computer monitor. I hold my breath as she brings the wand down on my bare stomach, then squeal at the cold gel. Marcus strokes the hair back from my face, and then we hold our breath.

I've had an easy pregnancy so far, except for the fact that I'm already busting out of my clothes. Marcus says my curves are "sexy as fuck."

"Okay, and here we go," the sonographer says softly. On the screen is the flickering of a heartbeat. Relief and joy bring a wave of tears to my eyes. I look to Marcus, and he's blinking rapidly. This is my family. I can't believe how lucky I am.

He tried to convince me to marry him before the baby comes, but I told him he's just going to have to wait. I'm in no rush—there's no way I could doubt how committed he is. The man is so crazy about me he can barely think straight, and I'm every bit as smitten. We can get married next year, when I can fit into a dress that wouldn't also double as a tent.

There's a second good reason for waiting—we've been spending a lot of time with Warwick and Rita, and although Lindy was nervous about it at first, she's gradually becoming more supportive of Marcus and Luca reconnecting with their biological father. I think with just a little more time, we'll be able to share our wedding day with *all* of Marcus's parents.

"Everything looks good?" Marcus asks the sonographer urgently, and the woman nods.

"At a glance, sir, yes. I'll do some proper measurements now, and—*oh*."

"Oh? What's 'oh'?" I blurt. The sonographer is concentrating fiercely as she stares at the screen, and Marcus's death grip is once again cutting off the blood flow to my fingers.

"Just give me a moment," she says carefully, then she sits back in her chair. "Well, heck. Can you two see what I see?"

My vision is blurry. I can't make sense of the blob on the screen—it's moving too much to even see the flickering heartbeat anymore. Where did the heartbeat go? I turn to Marcus. The color has drained from his face.

"What's wrong? Something is wrong, isn't it?"

"Abby," Marcus says cautiously. "Just calm down and look at the screen."

"It just looks like blobs to me."

"Exactly," he whispers, then he grins. *"Blobs."*

It's my turn to pale as I drag my gaze back to the screen. Now there's no mistaking it—I can see not one but *two* flickering heartbeats, safely tucked inside not one but *two* little humans.

"Wait," I say urgently, and the sonographer smiles at me. "But are you sure? That's what's in there? That's definitely *my* stomach?"

"Yes, ma'am..."

"Are twins genetic?" Marcus asks.

"Mostly luck," the sonographer tells us, then she laughs. "Good or bad luck, depending on your perspective."

"Good luck," Marcus says, then he clears his throat and he squeezes my hand again. "It's good luck. This is the best luck."

"Holy shit," I say through lips that are suddenly numb with shock. "They said I might never have a baby, and we *accidentally* made *two*?"

"Sometimes," the sonographer says softly, "some things are just meant to be."

I look at Marcus. There are tears on his cheeks, and he brings our entwined hands to his face and leans into them. Our eyes meet, and I start to cry, too, as I whisper, "I know *exactly* what you mean."

* * * * *

Dear Reader,

In my earlier novels, I wrote about issues and history and family drama and love stories that don't necessarily have a happy outcome. When Marcus and Abby popped into my brain, I knew these characters had a different kind of tale to tell. Their story was always going to be a little softer, a little sexier, a little sweeter…and, it turns out, a whole lot of fun to write.

Abby reflects many women I know and admire in real life. She's flawed, and she's faced challenges, but she's kind and loyal. She's afraid, but she's moving forward anyway, and her independence matters to her—this isn't a woman who wants or needs to be rescued.

I tried to write Marcus as the kind of hero I'd be happy to see any of my real-life friends fall in love with. He's passionate and determined, but he's loyal, respectful and supportive, too. And just like Abby, he's made mistakes, but he's growing and actively trying to be a better person.

Isabel and Paul's story will be published in November 2019. Brace yourself, because they have tangled themselves up in quite a mess…and there'll be fireworks as they untangle it!

I *loved* writing this story, and I so hope you enjoy reading it. If you do, I'd be grateful if you could take the time to write a review online. Your review really does make a difference—it helps other readers to find my books.

I love hearing from readers, too—if you'd like to get in touch with me, you can find all of my contact details on my website, kellyrimmer.com.

Kelly

*Turn the page for a special preview of the next book
in Kelly Rimmer's Start Up in the City series*

Unspoken

Coming soon from HQN Books

CHAPTER ONE

Paul

I'VE BEEN DEVELOPING a single software application since I was seventeen years old. The sum of my life's work is 74 million lines of code which, to put it in layman's terms, enables people to use the Internet in a safe and efficient manner. I don't know all of that code off by heart of course, but if you were to give me any portion of it, I could tell you what it does, and why, and how.

Code is knowable. Understandable. Infallibly rational. Opening my compiler is like wrapping myself in a warm blanket on a cold day. Code is safe and familiar, and I am completely at home and completely in control in that sphere, which is pretty much the polar opposite to my feelings on my relationships with other humans. People are unfortunately illogical creatures, and today, people are ruining my day.

Well, one person specifically.

"Hello, Isabel," I say to my almost-ex-wife. Her sudden appearance is as unfortunate as it is unexpected. Whenever we find ourselves in the same room these days the tension is untenable, but it's certain to be even worse today, because this room happens to be in the very vacation home we spent most of the last year squabbling over as we negotiated the separation of our assets.

"You said that I could keep this house—" Isabel starts to say now, but I really don't like to be reminded that if the divorce was a cruel game, there's a clear winner, and it's not me. That's why I cut her off with a curt, "My name is still on the title for four more days."

Her nostrils flare. She makes a furious sound in the back of her throat, then closes her eyes and exhales shakily. Isabel is trying to keep her temper in check.

I lived with Isabel Rose Winton for four years, one month and eleven days. I know she likes almond milk in her coffee because she thinks it's healthier, but that she masks the taste with so much sugar, she may as well drink a soda. I know she sleeps curled up in a little ball, as if she's afraid to take up space in her own bed. I know she resents her mother and adores her father and brothers. I know she loves New York with a passion, and that she has an astounding ability to pluck threads from a city of 8.5 million people to weave them into a close-knit village around herself. Isabel makes friends everywhere she goes. She never forgets a name and people always remember her, too, even after meeting her just once. Everyone adores her.

Well, almost everyone. I can't say I'm particularly fond of the woman these days.

"You're supposed to be on retreat with your team this weekend," Isabel mutters now. She flashes me a look, but it passes too quickly. I don't have time to interpret it.

"How do you even know about my retreat?" I ask

stiffly, but then I sigh and we both say at the exact same time, "Jess."

Jessica Cohen is my friend and my business partner. Isabel and Jess are still friends, and they still see each other all the time. But Jess popping up in this conversation makes me uneasy, because she's the reason I'm at Greenport today. And Jess does so love to meddle...